# The Last Judgement

# THE LAST JUDGEMENT

R. D. SHAH

First published in the United Kingdom in 2018 by Canelo

This edition published in the United Kingdom in 2020 by

Canelo Digital Publishing Limited
Third Floor, 20 Mortimer Street
London W1T 3JW
United Kingdom



A CIP catalogue record for this book is available from the British Library.

Print ISBN 978 1 78863 739 8
Ebook ISBN 978 1 911591 69 6



Printed and bound in Great Britain by Clays Ltd, Elcograf S.p.A.

*To Olivia, Lincoln and Edan. Nephews new and nieces old.*
*Your journey is only just beginning*

# *Chapter 1*

James Titus enjoyed feeling the cool refreshing breeze against his neck one final time before closing his study window and sitting down at the grand oak work table. His soft leather slippers squeaked against the wooden floorboards as he reached across the green fabric-covered surface to retrieve a sealed brown Jiffy bag from the table's far edge. He held the package tightly to his chest and lovingly embraced it as one might do a lover or a child, while a single tear rolled down his leathery cheek.

'How many years has it been?' he asked himself. 'Thirty? Forty?'

Titus revelled in this moment and his mind wandered back through the decades of searching that had led up to this remarkable day. How lucky, fortuitous – no, how honoured he was to be gifted with such an item, and he yearned to know of the sights it must have witnessed since its creation. As to these he could only imagine, but for it to end up in his hands after such a long journey was a miracle in itself, and he took tremendous comfort in that knowledge. It still numbed his mind with a sense of awe to think that something so small and seemingly insignificant was the answer to all the questions that he and his kind had chased for so many years. Yet here it was, all neatly wrapped up and safely in his arms.

Titus caressed the brown package and lovingly ran his index finger along its corners as he contemplated the possibilities of the new world to come. For any other person on the planet, what was to follow and what he was soon to experience would be unfathomable – that is, if one did not know the truth.

'It's time, James,' a voice whispered, and Titus glanced across to see a shadowy figure standing in the study's open doorway.

The flickering log fire set far back into the stone hearth was the only source of light, but even though he could not make out any features, he knew who it was. 'I am ready,' he replied calmly, and placed the package back down on the desk before rising slowly to his feet and making his way over to the fireplace. He then reached down and grasped the handle of a brass poker which nestled between the burning logs, and lifted its bright red tip up towards himself, illuminating his face in an orange glow.

He didn't feel any fear about what would come next, yet nervousness was getting the better of him and his skin began to tingle and his throat tightened uncomfortably.

'Will it hurt?' Titus asked, still without any trace of fear in his voice as the figure glided past him and scooped up the brown paper bag from the table.

'Yes,' the figure whispered, now moving to join Titus at the fireplace. 'But pain has its own rewards, does it not?'

Titus managed a slight nod of his head, and his upper body began to tremble as the mysterious figure plucked the poker from his now sweating hands and then held the red tip of it between them.

'Do not fear what I bring you,' the figure rasped, and he moved the blazing-hot implement to within centimetres of Titus's eyes. 'I now offer you what you have searched for all these long years, and all I ask for in return is your obedience.'

'I understand, and I will serve you,' Titus managed, regaining some of his faltering courage as he clenched his fists.

'Good,' the figure hissed, glancing down at Titus's hands. 'Now conserve your energy...you'll need it.'

## *Chapter 2*

'Have you ever heard of the Codex Gigas?' the man asked, as he scratched his brow with trembling fingers which hinted at a nervousness not apparent in his voice. 'No, don't answer that,' he then said with a wave of his finger. 'The least I can do is answer it myself, seeing how gracious you have been in allowing me an audience. The Codex is a book, written about eight hundred years ago by a Benedictine monk in a monastery located in what is now the Czech Republic. As legend tells it, the monk, after breaking his monastic vows, was sentenced to be sealed up within the monastery walls and left to die. In a desperate last-minute bid to redeem himself, and thus save his own skin, the young monk vowed to compose a book in just one day that would contain the entire history of humanity and thus glorify his monastery until the end of time.'

There he paused for a moment, and his eyes began to bulge as if comprehending the true hopelessness of such an impossible task.

'With no time to spare, the monk set about the said task with all the enthusiasm and energy he possessed. But, as midnight approached, he began to accept the inescapable conclusion that, no matter how much he wished it, this incredible feat of extreme speed writing would never achieve fruition. With the consequences of failure at the forefront of his mind, and with the deadline approaching, the young monk then began to pray. But this was not a prayer to his Lord and Saviour, but rather to an angel. A fallen angel who could be relied upon to offer service to the truly desperate…for a price. That angel was Lucifer, and the price was to be the monk's soul. For it is said that the soul of any human being is a sweet meal for the Devil, but the soul of a devout man is the sweetest of them all. With such a prize on offer, the Dark Lord spared no time in revealing himself and completing the book before the stroke of midnight. With his life now assured, the monk added a picture of the Devil therein, as a show of gratitude, and it is this image that is believed by some to be the only true representation of Satan himself.'

The shadowy man pushed back into his chair and continued to gaze at his audience through wide, unblinking, hazel-coloured eyes. 'It's quite a story...if you choose to believe it.'

Professor Alex Harker sat motionless on a wooden lecture chair directly opposite and offered a dry smile. 'Not sure I'm in a position to choose anything at the moment,' he said, glancing down at the black muzzle of a 12-gauge sawn-off shotgun being pointed directly at him. 'Wouldn't you agree?'

Just twenty minutes earlier, Harker had been wrapping up his lecture to a group of Cambridge graduates about the benefits of using a professional trowel compared to unearthing finds with cheap, non-branded ones. It was a short, one-off class concerning archaeological equipment, and its boring and mundane content meant that all the other professors involved would do anything to avoid it. In fact, the mind-numbing lecture was so reviled by staff that an annual lottery had been set up and, unfortunately for Harker, this year he had drawn the wrong ticket.

An hour and a half later, and aware of numerous heavy eyelids in the front row, Harker had wrapped up with a bad joke that not a soul had laughed at and, to the deafening sound of silence, he'd hastily made a speedy retreat towards the exit. He had almost reached it, too, before being cornered by someone he initially assumed to be an older mature student seeking further information on the dull subject discussed – and this was when all things educational had come to an abrupt halt.

Without warning, the man had pulled out a sawn-off shotgun from underneath his long dark-brown overcoat and, as the now wide-eyed and alert students energetically ran screaming from the hall, the maniac had gestured to Harker, with a flick of his gun barrel, to take a nearby seat.

The first few minutes had been a calm, although nerve-racking, interrogation by the armed man to confirm his hostage was indeed the same Harker who had been mentioned in all the newspapers during a series of natural disasters which occurred some six months earlier.

At the time Harker had kept his mouth firmly shut, as he'd promised, and remarkably the media had finally settled on the idea of global warming and a solar flash that had knocked many of the globe's satellites offline. He had found the solar story the most persuasive because, although it was complete rubbish, it did go a long way to explaining many of the phenomena experienced. In fact there was only one thing that truly irked Harker, but it was a big one: the existence of HAARP, and its ability to control weather, had been shrouded in secrecy by various governments and specifically their intelligence agencies. Despite some interest by the press the story had eventually disappeared and, along with it, mention of the technology that was HAARP. With a number of G8 governments involved in the cover-up, it was doubtful that anything would be revealed to the public anytime soon, and so Harker had learnt to accept that.

All that aside, the past six months had proved an adventure in itself. Just a few weeks after the funeral of Sebastian Brulet, Harker had been offered a position on the Board of Scrutiny at Cambridge University which oversaw governance of the famous institution, and to top it off he had begun to receive a number of invitations to participate in radio and TV shows. He wasn't yet famous but his face had appeared enough in the media that some people did recognize him and stop him in the street, even if it was only with a vague awareness of who he was exactly. '*Hey, I know you. Aren't you the guy that did that thing…you know, a few months back, at that place?*'

The best thing to come out of it all had been in the form of Dr Chloe Stanton. In the months following their discovery of HAARP, they had really hit it off, to the point that she was moving in with him. Officially later that same week, although pretty much everything she owned had already been dumped unceremoniously in assorted heaps throughout Harker's house. He could not have felt happier about it, even if he was somewhat perplexed that a person of her drive and organizational skills could also turn out to be so bloody messy. Of course all that was of secondary importance as, with ever increasing anxiety, he now focused on the gunman in front of him and his now trembling trigger finger.

'Sorry, but I didn't catch your name.'

'My name is not important,' the gunman replied with a rasp, 'but for the sake of this conversation you can call me Lucas.'

'Nice to meet you, Lucas,' Harker replied as calmly as is possible with a shotgun pointed directly at one's groin. 'And, yes, I do know something about the Codex Gigas. It's a well-known work with a fairly chequered history.'

'Go on,' the gunman urged, obviously eager to know how much Harker actually knew on the subject.

'Well, it's said that the book always brings bad luck to those who get near to it. For example, after being looted as booty by the Swedish army at the end of the Thirty Years' War, it was housed in Stockholm's royal library. It stayed there for forty-odd years until the building burned down. The book itself was saved by being thrown out of a window by someone unknown, but it then landed on a passer-by who was badly injured. With respect, Lucas, it's not exactly the equivalent of the Hope Diamond.'

The barrel of Lucas's shotgun began to quiver as he gripped it even tighter, while his nostrils flared a little.

'But yes, you're right,' Harker backtracked respectfully, sensing his captor's annoyance at his apparently flippant answer, 'misfortune does appear to follow it.'

Lucas seemed appeased by this and the wavering barrel began to settle. 'Anything else?' he demanded flatly.

Harker immediately grasped this olive branch and began to rack his mind for any other titbit of information he could offer. 'Well, there was some argument over it but I think that the book originally consisted of three hundred and thirteen pages, whereas now there are only three hundred and ten. No one knows how or when the rest went missing, though.'

Lucas slowly nodded and a knowing smile formed across his dry, cracked lips. 'In truth there was originally three hundred and fourteen pages, although not many know that important little morsel of truth,' he declared. 'Four missing pages that, as legend tells, contained secrets divulged by the Devil himself.'

Harker attempted, and managed, to display the most serious and agreeable expression possible. Personally he had never heard this part of the story, and to his mind the missing pages had most likely held private information regarding the Benedictine monastery's way of life, which they would not have wanted ordinary folk outside its walls to know. Maybe the monks were not as pious as they wished people to believe, or perhaps they threw drinking parties on Friday nights where they all got totally hammered. Either way it had always seemed to him a reasonable explanation…but, as a rule of thumb, when a man is pointing the barrel of a shotgun at your groin, and is of a clearly nervous disposition, it's best to just agree with them and go with the flow, regardless.

'I had heard that, yes…but the Codex is not something I've ever studied in detail, although I do have some acquaintances who have.' He said this while trying to look as nonchalant as possible. 'I would be happy to introduce you to them.'

Harker's last remark came off as being a bit sarcastic and he immediately regretted it, but Lucas, thankfully, didn't seem to take offence.

'I would have liked that but' – Lucas nodded over Harker's shoulder towards the two armed policemen in blue Kevlar breastplates and holding Glock handguns aimed in his direction – 'I don't think it's really an option now, is it?'

The armed response team had arrived within minutes of the hostage situation beginning, thanks to the stream of screaming students running from the building and highlighting the one and only positive aspect of a country being on high terrorist alert – a lightning-fast response. At first they were highly, and understandably, aggressive towards Lucas, until Harker had negotiated for them all to hear Lucas out, for fear of getting himself caught in a firefight. The policemen had shown remarkable calm and had dutifully pulled back towards the doorway, where the pair of them had taken up position, allowing the two men's conversation to continue.

'No,' said Lucas with a shake of his head, 'it's you who needs to hear this.'

'Me? Why?'

'Because I know who you are, Professor Harker,' Lucas continued cryptically. 'Who you *really* are, and I know how you can find things.'

This remark was clearly designed to make Harker feel uncomfortable, and it did the job. A torrent of thoughts began to swirl around within Harker's mind. Did this person know about his affiliation with the Knights Templar, and the benefits it brought? Was it because Harker had gained a reputation for finding lost treasures, again with the help of the Templars? There was no way to be sure and, in any event, Harker certainly was not about to reveal anything.

'I don't know what you've heard, but I can assure you that with me what you see is what you get.'

The mysterious Lucas rolled his head from left to right in an unsettlingly playful manner. 'We both know that's not true, Professor Harker. However, now I want you to use your connections and track down those missing seven pages for me.'

Harker already had his mouth open to explain that it would be like searching for a needle in a haystack when Lucas raised his free hand towards his own mouth and extended a finger to his lips. 'This isn't up for discussion. You will find those pages and, when the time comes, one of my kind will find you and relieve you of the burden of them.' He then leant forward and spoke in little more than a whisper. 'That is, if you ever want to see your girlfriend again…at least in one piece.'

The insidious nature of the threat took Harker aback for a moment, and he pulled away from the now grinning Lucas and shook his head in confusion. 'What?'

'Your *girlfriend*,' Lucas repeated in a hushed tone so as not to draw unwanted attention from the policemen still poised by the doorway, 'Dr Chloe Stanton. She's quite lovely, by the way.'

Harker did all he could to quell the anger now swelling in his chest, and he felt his jaw tighten painfully.

'Now, now,' Lucas hissed. 'She's safe and sound…for now. Consider her a down payment for your help in this matter.'

Harker was already struggling against the urge to hurl himself towards his captor when the sound of the armed police behind him shifting position brought renewed clarity to his thoughts. 'Where is she?' he murmured through gritted teeth.

'Like I said, she's fine, and should you help me in this matter, then your reunion is assured.'

An uncomfortable calm settled between the two men, and Lucas now appeared to take this as confirmation of Harker's willingness to help.

'Hand me your phone, and be subtle about it,' Lucas demanded, glancing over at the two policemen. 'I don't want to attract any undue attention.'

*Attract any undue attention!* What could be more attention-grabbing than taking someone hostage at gunpoint? If the current situation had not been so serious, Harker would have laughed out loud, but instead he furtively pulled out his phone and passed it over. Lucas began to tap at the keypad with one hand as the other held tightly to the shotgun.

'Go to this address,' he ordered as he discreetly passed it back to Harker. 'You'll find everything necessary to get you started.'

As the man's grin morphed into nothing short of a grimace, Harker suddenly felt light-headed, his mind a blur with confusion and rage at the blackmail being inflicted upon him. He swallowed deeply and composed himself as best he could.

'Tell me why I shouldn't tell the police everything you've just spouted,' he spat.

'Because doing so would not be conducive to Dr Stanton's well-being,' Lucas replied, waving a finger lightly, 'and I will be keeping an eye on you every step of the way.'

The confidence in the man's voice sounded assured, but in Harker's mind it was obviously misplaced.

'Is that a fact?' he replied, glancing back at the two armed policemen behind him, 'because, from where I'm sitting, you're not going anywhere.'

That only two of the officers so far had made their arrival known did not mean that a whole armed response unit was not waiting in the wings ready for the order to resolve the situation by force. In Harker's mind it was actually likely but, as he watched his kidnapper, he could not help but recognize how calm and unworried the man looked. Whatever the plan was, Lucas was without a doubt supremely convinced of being able to execute it. But how exactly does someone remove themselves from such a dangerous situation without getting taken down by the authorities? It was a question that was about to be answered.

Lucas settled back snugly into his chair and offered a nod of his head. 'Now, you might be absolutely correct in that assumption, but it really is time for me to go.'

In one swift movement, Lucas raised the barrel of the shotgun to just underneath his chin and, with his finger wrapped tightly around the trigger, he gave an emotionless wink of his eye. 'See you around.'

The man's head exploded into a brilliant burst of red mist as the blast from the 12-gauge sent a thick spattering of dark-red blood across the ceiling, and as larger portions of skull and brain matter slapped against the opposite wall of the lecture hall.

Harker instinctively lurched backwards, his chair toppling over to send him crashing onto his back, with his head slamming hard against the carpet-tiled floor. The brightness of the flash had dulled his vision and the deafening bang momentarily rendered his hearing useless. In fact he was in such a state of shock that it barely registered as the two armed police rushed over and pulled him to his feet.

As he was being dragged forcefully back towards the doorway, his eyes remained fixed on the globules of blood dripping from the ceiling and back down onto the headless corpse of what had recently been Lucas. With each second that passed, his mind began to stir from its slumber, but it was not the image of Lucas's still twitching body slumped on the chair opposite that preoccupied his thoughts, but someone else altogether…

Chloe.

# *Chapter 3*

'I demand to see immediately a member of my staff. I am responsible for this man and, more importantly, I am a dean of this college!'

Harker raised his head to see archaeology dean Thomas Lercher – or Doggie to his friends – arrive looking like a man possessed. The dean had a murderous look in his eye as he verbally tussled with the unamused-looking policeman wearing a high-visibility jacket. To the officer's credit he refused to bite back at the howling dean and, without further delay, allowed him through without even so much as a sigh of frustration.

'Thank heavens, Alex. Are you hurt?' Dean Lercher fumed, pausing to assess Harker for any injuries.

'I'm fine except from some ringing in my ears,' Harker replied, while batting away the dean's probing hands.

'Are you free to go yet?'

'I've given a statement,' Harker replied with a nod, 'and I've even had the offer of a counsellor, although I think I'll give that a miss. I don't feel like reliving this experience anytime soon.'

'Christ, you could have been shot dead,' the dean continued. 'What on earth is the world coming to?'

'Doggie, I told you I'm OK.'

'Yes, I can see you're fine,' the man acknowledged, his indignation only increasing. 'And I told you not to call me Doggie…you know I hate it!'

It was about this time that Harker realized there was something else his old friend and boss was far more annoyed about than the lapse in his colleague's safety, and it didn't take any wild guesses to figure it out. 'I'm afraid the lecture hall will need to be redecorated.'

Doggie stood now with his back to Harker and dismissed the comment with a flick of his wrist.

'It's not that,' he moaned, his tone now more relaxed. 'I'm not that bad, Alex.'

'Really?' Harker replied, with more than just a hint of sarcasm.

Doggie's shoulders began to twitch and then escalated to a quivering, until finally he spun around and allowed his temper to boil over. 'Your safety is the most important thing but...do you know how much it will cost to refurbish that bloody room? The interior newly sound-proofed...the cladding alone will cost a small fortune!'

Immediately after the shooting, Harker had phoned Blackwater asylum for the criminally insane, where Chloe had resumed her post as section head. Reception had assured him she was on site and they would get her to call him at the earliest possible convenience. Mercifully, it seemed that, whatever Lucas's true identity, he was clearly a troubled man and prone to lying. In fact it had already occurred to Harker that perhaps he may have been an ex-patient of Blackwater himself.

The shooting incident had left Harker shaken. Seeing anything so nasty up close might have an impact on the strongest of psyches, but the simple fact that Chloe was safe had now done much to soften the whole ordeal. Of course, Doggie here was clueless as to the whole Chloe aspect and, as Harker watched his friend gripe away about the cost of a refurbishment, he thought back to a telling incident in which the dean had been involved. A few years back someone had committed suicide by throwing himself onto the tracks of the Northern Tube Line, causing huge delays. While most passengers on the platform were quietly discussing the tragedy, Doggie was loudly throwing a wobbler and complaining that the fellow must have been a selfish bastard and that if he wanted to top himself then why not do it in his own home.

To many people who knew the dean casually, these characteristic displays were questionable, but to anyone who knew him well, as Harker did, they were nothing more than eccentricities from a man who deep down had a heart of gold, and who Harker could trust with his life. Even so, the dean was very much an acquired taste.

'I mean, who the hell kills himself in a lecture hall, for Christ's... Why not do it somewhere outside? The weather is beautiful at this time of year.'

Harker was still enjoying the dean's bravado when his mobile began to ring. He pulled it from his pocket and tapped the accept button.

'Hi, Mr Harker?'

'Yes.'

'It's Jared from Blackwater. We spoke earlier.'

'Yes,' Harker replied. 'Thanks for getting back to me so soon. Did you pass my message on to Chloe?' He was eager to regale her with every bizarre and gory detail of the day's events, until what he heard made his stomach curdle.

'I'm afraid I made a mistake earlier. Dr Stanton hasn't been seen here all day. One of the receptionists called your house but there was no reply, and I called her mobile after speaking with you but no one is answering.'

A cold sweat moistened Harker's forehead as Jared continued. 'Mr Harker, do you happen to know if she's coming in tomorrow? She has numerous appointments lined up and...'

The sound of the orderly's voice faded into the background as Harker retreated into himself, allowing his worst fears to take hold. It seemed no one had the slightest clue where she was...with the exception perhaps of Lucas!

'Mr Harker, can you hear me?'

'Yes. Thank you, Jared. I'll be in touch.'

Harker let the mobile slip from his hand into his jacket pocket, and he began to rub at his temples as grim possibilities began to clutter his mind.

'Is everything OK, Alex?'

Harker looked up to see his old friend, who had now ceased his tirade and was looking concerned.

'It's Chloe,' Harker murmured. 'She's missing.'

The next few minutes were a blur as Harker stumbled through an account of the threats Lucas had made, and by the end of it Doggie was looking even more worried than he did.

'Jesus, Alex, you need to tell the police everything.'

'He warned me not to tell anyone or there would be consequences…that he would be watching.'

'Watching! The man's dead. Believe me, the only thing that nutter's watching is an angel with a harp…or a guy with a pitchfork.'

Doggie's raised voice drew a brief stare from one of the policemen standing nearby and Harker immediately stood up and gently guided the dean further down the corridor and out of earshot.

'This isn't funny, Doggie,' Harker scolded.

'I don't mean it to be, but this Lucas character is *dead*.'

'I know, but seeing as Chloe's missing, then clearly others are involved.'

Both men then stood staring at each other in silence, their expressions continuing the conversation without the need for words. It was Doggie who spoke up first. 'It's your call, Alex. What do you want to do?'

Harker expelled a deep breath as if he was considering his answer, but in truth he already knew. 'I'm going to the address Lucas gave me. To see what's there.'

'Fine. I'll come with you,' Doggie quickly replied, nodding enthusiastically. 'There's nothing useful I can do here anyway.'

Harker gave him an appreciative tap on his forearm and, without another word, they both headed for the stairs leading to the front entrance.

'What are we expecting to find?' Doggie asked eventually, with rising apprehension in his voice.

'I honestly have no idea, but considering the dead man that gave me the address?' Harker replied, pausing as they reached the main door. 'I'll bet it's nothing good.'

## *Chapter 4*

The cool night air was a welcome respite from the evening's traumatic events as Harker briskly headed down Grove Avenue, in the suburbs of Cambridge, with Doggie close on his heels. Their taxi drive over had not taken long and, apart from a call to Chloe's mobile which went straight to answerphone, it had been accomplished in silence. Much to Harker's relief, his old friend had remained uncharacteristically quiet throughout the journey. Even the taxi driver had refrained from idle talk, probably sensing the tense atmosphere his two passengers were exuding. Just as a precaution, Harker had requested they be dropped off about a hundred metres from their intended destination. If someone was watching his every move, then he was determined to make things as difficult as possible for them.

The small apartment block was located just off the main road and facing an open stretch of grass common. The building itself looked fairly modern but had that grubby tell-tale black grime smudging the brickwork, so typical of houses situated near a busy main road.

Upon reaching the paint-cracked, green door, Harker immediately began scanning the area around him for any sign of unwanted observers. The common nearby seemed quiet for this time of day and, with the exception of a man walking anxiously behind his black French bulldog with a pooper scooper, nothing seemed out of place. Not that Harker could see, at any rate.

'How do we get in?'

'Well, knocking's a good start,' Harker replied, and he rapped on the door with a clenched fist.

After a few seconds the familiar sound of a latch being released could be heard, and the door swung open to reveal an elderly lady wearing an old-style pink floral apron, above wrinkled stockings and a pair of fluffy slippers. She reminded Harker of the archetypal dinner lady from his schooldays, with her silver hair tied up in a bob to complete the look.

'Sorry to disturb you, but Lucas asked me to stop by.'

He'd barely finished the sentence before the old woman began ushering them both inside. 'You took your time. Come on, then, chop-chop.'

With mutual glances of cautious surprise they made their way inside and into a small communal hallway covered in light-brown flock wallpaper.

'Lucas said you'd be here earlier and I'm already late for the bingo,' the pensioner complained as she closed the door.

'The traffic was a nightmare,' Harker offered, not wanting to shock the old lady with details of the man's suicide. Witnessing one death was enough without giving this old girl a heart attack. 'My apologies.'

'Fine, fine,' she mumbled grouchily, 'but you can tell him I'm not his personal doorman.'

'I can assure you, madam,' Doggie interrupted and smiling kindly, 'you'll not have any further trouble from Lucas. I guarantee it.'

She growled grudgingly and then passed over to Harker a bronze-coloured apartment key. 'It's number 2a – up the stairs and to the right.'

Key in hand and with a pleasant smile from Doggie, they headed up the narrow wooden staircase to the first-floor landing.

'This place could pass for an Indian restaurant,' Doggie quipped, grimacing at the walls with their tasty brown flock wallpaper.

'God, Doggie, when were you last in an Indian restaurant?'

'I don't know. It's been a while.'

'You're not kidding,' Harker replied, starting to wish he had not brought the dean along. 'Flock wallpaper died out in the nineties.'

Apartment 2a was at the far end of the landing. As Harker approached it he felt his stomach begin to tighten in apprehension. Who knew what they were going to find: an empty room or perhaps a couple of Lucas's friends? Harker was hoping for the former, because in a tussle Doggie became more of a liability than an asset. Place the dean in a room of socialites and the man shone, but when confronted with physical aggression he was not one to rise to the occasion with unrestrained vigour.

'This is it,' Harker said and placed his ear against the door. Apart from the sound of a washing machine rumbling away in the apartment opposite, all was quiet, and so he slowly slid the key into the lock. With a glance back at Doggie, and a nod to confirm that he was going in, Harker turned the key, keeping his palm placed squarely against the door to minimise any creaking, and then headed inside.

The apartment had an open-plan layout, with the entrance leading directly into one spacious room split into a kitchen and lounge with only a chest-high partition acting as a divider. The single door at the opposite end of the room was closed and a single thick tan-coloured curtain covered the only window, making for a gloomy if not menacing atmosphere.

Harker gingerly made his way further inside with Doggie closely in tow and, once satisfied they were alone for the moment, he tiptoed over to the connecting door and once again listened for any sounds coming from beyond.

Still nothing.

He turned the handle and allowed the door to swing back under its own weight, revealing a small bedroom with an open shower room off to the right. Once reassured there was no one lurking in the shadows, he flicked the light switch on the wall next to him.

The room lit up to reveal nothing out of the ordinary, just a bed with its white sheets neatly folded and a cheap single-file plywood chest of drawers next to it. A small darkly lacquered writing desk occupied the far corner, with a chair neatly under it and an empty plastic paper bin sitting next to it.

'The place is empty,' Harker observed after taking a moment to poke his head into the bathroom which, clean and tidy, was devoid of any lurking would-be attackers. Back in the main room, Doggie was drawing back the curtains and, even though he already knew the answer, Harker couldn't help himself from calling out: 'Chloe, are you in here?'

His cry was met with silence and, after checking under the bed and finding nothing, he moved back into the main room to see Doggie standing there aimlessly.

'If she *was* here, she's not now,' Doggie confirmed, and bit his bottom lip in frustration as Harker scanned the room carefully. The whole place was immaculate, with no trace of dust anywhere. Clean coffee mugs lined the kitchen shelf and the cooking utensils looked shiny, almost as if they had never been used. In fact, the whole interior of the apartment was so clean it could have served as a show room. That is, except for just one thing. Poking out from behind the still open door to the flat was a thin strip of dark-brown wood running from floor to ceiling. With the door wide open it was barely visible, but the contrasting colour stood out like a sore thumb in such a colour-coordinated interior.

'What's that?' Harker muttered, before making his way over to the door of the apartment and pulling it back only to reveal another entrance. It wasn't exactly well hidden but it had been cleverly placed so that when the front door was wide open, it disguised the opening behind it.

'Interesting,' Doggie remarked with raised eyebrows. 'I doubt that was part of the original design.'

Harker said nothing and instead took a step inside.

There was a tight, ninety-degree turn to the left, which meant that light from the main room was unable to penetrate the pitch darkness ahead. Wherever this narrow corridor led to, it was sure to be windowless, and Harker edged forward cautiously, sliding his palm along one wall until after a few metres it fell away. A faint draught of air swept across his face, suggesting a larger open space just ahead, and it was enough to convince him to stop dead in his tracks. He began to fumble around in the blackness for a few moments until he came across a light switch. Squinting in preparation, he flicked it and above him a single bulb lit up, bathing him in light. After a few seconds under this bright yellow hue his eyes refocused; what he saw now was as creepy as it was confusing.

The room itself was only a few metres across, with just enough room for a cheap folding wooden chair and not much else. The walls, though, were another matter altogether. To the left were fixed a jumble of colour pictures taken of what he knew to be the pages of the Codex Gigas, displaying the various texts it contained; the nearest one was the infamous image of the Devil himself. It was not unlike the usual representations of the Devil in that some of the classic details had been included like the horns and a forked tongue, but that is where any similarities ended. The face itself was green and covered with scales, yet with very human characteristics such as ears, eyes, a nose – and a row of teeth that appeared to have been filed down to points. Large red spiky talons protruded from the hands and feet as the creature sat on its haunches with arms held high above its head intimidatingly.

'Ugly little fellow,' Doggie remarked, having now ventured into the hidden room himself. 'It looks like a circus midget with haemorrhoids.'

'It's from the Codex, and goes to confirm how obsessed Lucas was with it.'

'I'm afraid that's not the only thing he was obsessed with, Alex,' Doggie replied soberly, gesturing towards the opposite wall which was covered with numerous photos of Chloe Stanton and himself. 'Looks like he had you both under his magnifying glass for some time.'

Harker leant closer to inspect the photos and what he saw only served to fuel his fears, because it was clear that Lucas had been following them both everywhere for months. There was even a picture of Harker on the doorstep of his house, paying the pizza delivery man. It wasn't the work of some crazy operating on the spur of the moment. This was organized and methodical. 'Jesus, who was this guy…? And where the hell is Chloe?'

Still preoccupied with that thought, Harker turned his attention to the final wall straight ahead, and it was here that he encountered the most disturbing aspect of the entire room. A world map had been Sellotaped to its surface, on which eight pins had been placed at various locations. From each pin hung a tag with several pieces of information scrawled upon it, and tiny pictures had been attached to the individual tags.

Harker moved in closer to inspect this hodgepodge of images, trailed by Doggie, who was looking just as mystified.

'What the hell is that?'

'I'm not sure,' Harker replied before pointing to a number of pins, 'but they all have names, dates and' – he paused to focus in on one of the attached photos – 'dead people.'

Seven of the pins had either photos or sketches of dead people – men and women – and all with something in common. In each case the victim's throat had been slit from ear to ear, and then the tongue had been pulled through the gap and left to hang like a glistening, crimson neck tie. In addition the bodies had been posed spread-eagled, clearly in an attempt to remove the last vestiges of dignity from the victim. In a final act of grotesquery their eyes had been burnt out, leaving nothing but blackened sockets.

'That's brutal,' Doggie murmured, his nose wrinkling in disgust as he now examined all of these vile mementos. 'Why do you suppose some are photos while the others are drawings?'

Harker quickly pointed out the details on each pin. 'Look at the dates of their murders. Photography wasn't invented until

1827, so these deaths go back long before that. Out of the seven pins only four have photos. Take another look.'

He gestured to each one in turn, beginning with one dated 1737 and running all the way up until 1977. Whether it was a photo or pencil sketch, each of the victims had been arranged in the same pose along with a few words detailing the location of the murder.

'What we have here are seven murders, committed in exactly the same fashion, and taking place every forty years dating back to 1737!'

The notion already had Doggie shaking his head. 'But that's obviously not possible. The killer would have to be almost three hundred years old!'

It was now Harker's turn to look at his friend in disbelief. 'I agree it makes no sense. More important still, what the hell has this got to do with the Codex? Christ, for all I know the bastard Lucas murdered Chloe and then committed suicide as an act of atonement.'

'Don't ever think that, Alex,' Doggie replied sharply. 'Now pull yourself together, young man. Chloe needs you, so stop feeling sorry for yourself and let's figure this out.'

Doggie's berating was just what Harker needed, and he now stood up straight and sucked in a deep lungful of musty, if oddly refreshing, air.

'OK, let's say Lucas was on the level and there are others in his "gang", and they're the ones who have Chloe. Now, they want the seven missing pages of the Codex. Why, I have no idea, but it doesn't matter because, whatever their reasons, the reality is I need to find them.'

Harker crossed his arms and focused his attention again on the world map. 'There are seven murders indicated on this board, and I'm looking for seven lost Codex pages… Coincidence or design?'

'Could be either,' Doggie replied, attempting to keep his thoughts relevant to the task at hand even though none of this was making any sense to him.

'Could be,' Harker replied firmly, now finding his stride. 'But Lucas said this address would be the starting point, and the only thing that stands out on that map is the eighth pin, which is missing the details of any murder.'

'OK...and that means?'

'C'mon, Doggie, use your head.' Harker was sounding more confident with every second. 'These murders have been taking place every forty years, to the day, which means the next murder will take place tomorrow night at *this* location.' He pointed to the eighth solitary pin and the handwritten time and date scrawled there in red biro. 'Lucas may have been crazy, but he got one thing right...the timing.'

This idea definitely resonated with Doggie, but he was still looking doubtful about something. 'Are you absolutely sure we shouldn't inform the police?'

Harker was already shaking his head. 'And do what? Wait twenty-four hours before I can finally fill out a missing person's report? No. The police can't help me...but I do have some friends who can.'

'You mean the Templars?' Doggie replied, suddenly looking extremely excited at the prospect. With all their wealth and connections, the Templars were seen by Doggie as the ultimate in social hierarchy and power. As a result, of course, he had been pushing to meet them since learning of their existence.

'That's exactly who I mean and, before you ask, no, you still can't meet them or mention them to anybody. Not unless you want to end up dead.' Of course, the Templars would never actually kill Doggie, but this served its purpose in keeping the dean from blabbing about things that were not his to share.

'Yes, I know,' Doggie growled. 'And thank you for the umpteenth time for reminding me of that fact.'

'Hey,' Harker responded with upturned hands, 'just trying to keep you alive, my friend, which is I why I need you to stay here in the UK.'

'What...why?' Doggie complained, not happy at the suggestion.

'Because I have no idea what I'm getting myself into, and if it does all go pear-shaped, then I need to know I've someone I can trust to help me. And anyway, with Chloe's life on the line, I'm going to need all the help I can get.'

'Well, you would perish without me so that part is true,' Doggie said, and then he thought about it for a moment before offering a grudging nod. 'Fine, I'll be waiting for your call.'

'Thanks, Doggie… Sorry, Tom.'

The correction received an appreciative smile from the dean, who then pulled out his mobile. 'I'll call a cab. Where exactly are you going anyway?'

Harker leant over to extract the eighth pin while noting its exact location on the map. 'Berlin. I'm going to Berlin to stop a murder… And I have absolutely no idea how or why!'

## *Chapter 5*

The sun was just beginning to rise as Bishop Esposito traversed the narrow side street and headed back towards his parish. It was a strange thing but, for the life of him, he had no idea where he had just been or how he had got here, but he felt no panic despite the fact that his recent memory seemed patchy at best. His mind felt numb as if it were wrapped in cotton wool, and this same sensation was now spreading into his chest and throughout his entire body. The feeling was surreal, like being in a dream even though he knew that he was still awake.

Off to his left, a local tradesman was in the process of rolling up the metal security shutters of his small coffee shop, and Esposito raised his arm and politely waved to him but the gesture was met with a grimace and the shutters fell back to the floor.

*How rude*, the bishop thought, and then he noticed his hand was filthy black and the tips of his fingers covered in small, bloody cuts.

*Had he been involved in an accident? Is this why he couldn't remember anything?*

Despite the damage to his hands, he continued on along the picturesque winding streets of a village whose name he should have known but which now escaped him. He was definitely in Italy, somewhere near Rome, that much he was certain of... Or was he? For some reason it didn't seem to be that important.

Esposito continued until he reached the small town square and then, as if on autopilot, he crossed over to the other side and came to a stop outside a small stone church. The modest building was splendid in its rustic beauty and, since it was so early and the streets were deserted, he found himself revelling in the sounds of birds cooing in the distance.

*So peaceful*, Esposito thought, turning his attention back to the church entrance. He was glad to have now reached his destination, although why it was his destination he couldn't really say. Because he was a bishop? Or was he really a bishop?

These questions seemed insignificant and they melted away with a soothing numbness as he pushed open the small wooden door and then headed inside with a real sense of peace and tranquillity in his heart. What a wonderful day to be alive.

The church was dark but not gloomy and the sun's first offering of light shone through the stained-glass windows above the altar, casting a wondrous multitude of colours onto the red stone tiling of the knave. The colours had a particular glow to them this morning, an almost golden tint to their edges, and Esposito stood in awe, enjoying them – until, at the other end of the building, he spotted a young man kneeling in prayer. The familiar black and white vestments of a priest were unmistakable; the cleric was surely offering his morning thanks. Esposito raised his arm and called out to him, but no words came out. He tried once more but still nothing… Strange.

Unconcerned as yet, Esposito glided down the aisle with the unique sensation of walking on air, enjoying this so much that he stopped, turned around and did another tour up and down the nave before joining the still-kneeling priest.

He then reached down to place his hand lightly on the young man's shoulder, and the contact made the priest jerk backwards. He jumped to his feet and spun around quickly, clearly caught off guard by the interruption to his prayers.

Esposito attempted to offer him a friendly greeting, but again nothing came out. However it was not this that concerned him; it was the wide-eyed expression of abject terror on the priest's face as he raised a hand to his mouth and stumbled backwards before collapsing on the floor at the base of the altar.

Esposito looked on in confusion as the priest stood up and headed back to the vestry doorway until he was out of sight.

*What the devil?* he thought, and was just about to pursue the grief-stricken man when he caught a reflection in one of the shiny silver plates displayed upon the altar. The face he saw there made him jerk back in utter terror as he took in the disgusting image of a man – and, when he realized this was his own reflection, he almost threw up. The top portion of the face was entirely devoid of skin, revealing the dark-red lines of muscle beneath, and one of his eyes was completely missing, leaving nothing but a gaping black socket. What skin there was left hung from the skull like an ill-fitting jumper, and it drooped from his cheek so as to warp the shape of his single remaining eye on the other side of his face. Such gory features paled into insignificance, though, compared to the lower half of his face, and it became clear now why the priest had not heard him call out upon first entering the church. The entire lower jawbone was missing, exposing the back of his throat and the white bone of his larynx, while an oversized tongue hung downwards where the muscles had stretched apart.

Esposito prodded tentatively at each of the blood-filled clots that had formed into dark black nodules where the skin had been tugged away, and he began to feel faint. He toppled forward and collapsed before the altar, tears flowing from his one remaining eye stinging his exposed facial muscles, and his whole body began to spasm. The previous numbness was now replaced with complete and unmitigated pain, which surged over him like a burning flame and singed every one of his nerve endings with crippling agony.

Esposito clawed his way up the side of the stone altar and then threw himself on top of it as the pain intensified. He stared up at the crucifix and into the eyes of the sculpted image of Jesus.

'My Lord, why have you forsaken me?'

# Chapter 6

Through the pitch darkness the lights of central Berlin glowed in the distance as Harker made his way cautiously through the dense undergrowth of the Spreepark amusement park. The park itself had been abandoned for years, and any amusement these days was surely only had by the animals who might be prowling the abandoned rides.

On the plane trip over, Harker had googled everything he could find regarding this once famous entertainment park, and everything he had learnt about it was pretty depressing. Built in what was then Soviet-controlled East Germany, during the cold war the park had served as the only one of its kind in the entire GDR and had drawn over a million visitors a year. When the Berlin Wall had come down the park had reopened with a new and more Westernized look, but by 2002, and with declining visitor numbers, the place had finally been abandoned.

To make things even worse, an act of arson had destroyed many of the buildings, only adding to the park's woes. Recently a bid had been made to rejuvenate the site to its former glory but, except for some clearing of the trees, it was unquestionably still a work in progress.

With the front entrance securely gated and the grounds regularly patrolled by a security guard with the biggest Alsatian dog Harker had ever seen, he had opted to find another way in and a gap in one of the chain fences had provided this.

The pin in Lucas's map had provided a rough location but, without truly knowing what he was looking for, Harker's task was proving difficult. Before departing the UK he had left a voicemail for his Templar contact, John Shroder, in the hope of getting some assistance, but so far he had heard nothing in response. The message he'd left had been deliberately short, stating only that he was attempting to gain access to the park, but said nothing concerning Lucas's suicide or Chloe's disappearance. The Templars, understandably, had a strict code of practice regarding communications, one that every associate of the order, and Harker was no exception, was required to follow rigorously. Still, it was strange that Shroder had not yet returned his call. Since the events involving HAARP, Harker had maintained a close relationship with the Templar and MI6 agent, and no doubt his delay in responding had been unavoidable. 'If you ever need me, I'll be there,' Shroder had once assured him and, as Harker approached a clearing and the eerie sight of abandoned and burnt-out buildings came into view, he found himself murmuring, 'Well, you're not here now, are you, John?'

Harker cleared the last thicket of undergrowth and entered a sparsely wooded clearing containing what must have been, at one time, an open-water ride, the abandoned white plastic swan boats being a dead giveaway. Long-stemmed reeds stuck up through what little water was left, and most of the swan boats were still tied to a rotting wooden dock that in its day must have seen many an excited child waiting to catch the next ride. Sadly, and judging by the number of used condoms floating upon the pond's surface, the only thing anyone was likely to catch here these days was hepatitis B. Still, at least the park was continuing to bring joy to the teenagers who ventured here looking for a safe place to fool around.

Not having received a tetanus shot in years, Harker warily made his way around this 'lake of love' and on through the soggy grass towards the only landmark that had been visible from the park's outskirts. The large rusty Ferris wheel soared about one hundred metres into the air, and even though it was a dark night the full moon provided excellent illumination.

Not surprisingly, there was no sign of anyone anywhere, but with dense woodland beyond the clearing, if there were anyone lurking nearby he would be the last to know it. Harker was genuinely considering, maybe foolishly, climbing up onto the Ferris wheel in the hope of getting a better look over his surroundings. He was still mulling over whether to traverse this huge metal deathtrap when a series of dim lights began to flicker in the distance.

Whether car lights or torches it was impossible to tell, but Harker eagerly began making his way towards them. He moved swiftly at first but a painful collision with a fallen signpost convinced him to slow down. It was not until he was passing through the treeline that he found a small dirt track hidden within. It was then that he began to pick up the pace with a jog towards the only visible lights in the area.

The route took a few minutes, and by the time Harker reached his destination the lights had disappeared, but by then he no longer needed them. Set off the muddy dirt track, and buried in the forest skirting the park, he came across a large red-brick building.

The house covered two floors and was large enough to support a small clock tower with broken windows on all its visible sides. This rose up from the centre of the roof, and Harker was at first certain the dilapidated building must be deserted. That was until he got nearer still and, from the right angle, he could see the glow of light shining through the cracks of the boarded-up windows, confirming there were visitors.

Harker ventured further around the side of the building and, as he passed the next corner, he came upon a group of cars, seven in total, parked tightly together outside the front entrance or along a connecting road leading off in the opposite direction from which he had approached. Three Mercedes-Benzes, three BMWs and a one white Range Rover made up this expensive collection; he doubted these belonged to teenagers frequenting the park to indulge in some nocturnal mischief.

Harker crouched down between the tightly parked cars, taking great care not to touch the sides of them for fear of setting off any alarms, then moved on until he reached the only doorway he could see. There was graffiti written in yellow that simply read 'BIG COCK' in German, which he attributed to some previous and youthful visitor who obviously thought a great deal of himself and not the house's current visitors, whoever they might be. Harker grasped hold of the worn black metal doorknob, turned it gently and entered.

The interior of the place was filthy, in line with the rest of the amusement park's appearance, with the wall plaster broken and desiccated in places, leaving dusty piles beneath the areas of damage. There was no lighting except for a single lit candle perched upon a metre-high candelabra, but he could make out that he was in a hallway. To his left was a bare, spacious room with ripped-up carpet tiles strewn throughout, and to his right was a similar-sized room bearing the same type of damage except for a broken metal-grate fireplace covered in ash. Further on, two open doorways led off on either side of the hallway, and at the end rose a wide wooden staircase leading to the upper floor, with most of its steps either cracked or missing.

Harker ventured along the hallway tentatively, taking care not to scuff his feet on the debris scattered about the floor, and he had almost reached the first open doorway when he heard a voice. It was muffled, but the tone was deep and resonating, and seemed to come from somewhere beneath him. He peered in through the first doorway to find nothing but a dark empty room, with all the same detritus of dirt and rubble, but the second doorway proved much more interesting. Another lit candle sat on what must have once been a kitchen unit because an AGA cooker, with its door hanging from the hinges, was positioned immediately next to it.

The voice now sounded louder and, as he approached the centre of the room, the floor began to creak.

Harker froze and stared down at the wooden trapdoor directly beneath him, but just then the muffled voice suddenly went quiet.

The next few seconds had a swarm of butterflies doing the tango in his stomach, and as he stared at the entrance below he began to let fear get the better of him.

Almost every member of humanity can feel fear, even the ones that society labels as fearless. Firefighters, policemen, soldiers, boxers – they all feel fear. The trick is how one manages that fear. If a person can push the sensation of fear from their mind and maintain focus then what they are able to achieve can be remarkable. But give in to the urge and it can produce a roller-coaster effect. Once it starts it isn't stopping, and mindless panic often ensues.

Harker now stood motionless, his eyes widening and the growing fear gnawing at his insides as his mind began to fill with doubts. What the hell was he doing in this place on his own? He didn't even have a weapon to defend himself. Up against who, or God knows what, and all within the rotting walls of this creepy building that might have given even Freddy Krueger nightmares.

The single image of Chloe suddenly popped into his mind and, like a mental Valium, the thought of her began to calm him. It was at that same moment the voice below started up again, and Harker realized that everything was still good.

With a rising sense of resolve, he carefully stepped off the trapdoor and then reached down, gently grasped the ringlet handle, and slowly pulled it open.

Much to his relief and probably, if he was honest, for the sake of a change of underwear, he didn't come face to face with any pairs of eyes staring back at him, but instead he found a short wooden ladder leading down to a basement passageway about a metre below. After checking the immediate area below was clear, he laid the hinged door flat on the floor and then proceeded to lower himself down onto the concrete floor, opting not to use the ladder in case it decided to make a noise by groaning under his weight.

The passage was lit by the same type of candles as used above, and they ran its full length as far as another room at the end.

Harker couldn't see what lay beyond but the voice was now clearly audible so he quietly made his way towards it and, just before the bend, with his face pressed up against the wall, he peered gingerly around the corner.

The room beyond had been carved directly into the earth and so it looked more like a cave than a constructed dwelling, with thick brown tree roots protruding from the walls, their tips dangling limply towards the soil-covered floor. Stubby red candles sat in black metal holders attached directly to the uneven dirt walls, and high enough up that their flames illuminated the ceiling more brightly than the rest of the room.

On the wall opposite there was fixed a wooden frame around double doors, both now closed, while the air was heavy with a mixture of aftershave and various expensive perfumes. This aroma was unquestionably exuded by the group of well-dressed men and women congregated in the centre of the room, whose attention was focused on a man wearing a shiny tuxedo, who stood upon a sturdy-looking wooden platform about two metres wide.

The stark contrast between their smart clothing and the shabby surroundings made for an unsettling atmosphere, while two of the women were even wearing flowing ballgowns and shiny high heels that dug into the grubby dirt beneath.

But it was the man in the black tuxedo who particularly caught Harker's attention. His shiny bald head, gaunt cheeks and dull unemotional eyes gave him a formidably intimidating look, and his deep commanding voice only added to this forbidding aura as he addressed the small crowd in front of him.

'And so here we are again, not just in flesh but in spirit, as our journey continues. In the centuries that have passed I wonder how many of us have occasionally questioned, if not doubted, the destiny that is owed to us?'

Many of the group began to shake their heads and glance at one another in defiance, which drew a thin smile from the speaker.

'Friends, do not be ashamed. The path has been long and therefore it would only be natural to question such things from time to time,' he continued amicably, exchanging glances with each of his audience in turn. 'But that you are all here tonight on this most hallowed of days proves the strength of your convictions, and because of that I commend your resilience and strength of character.'

Light applause broke out as the speaker's smile became wider, revealing a perfect set of glistening white teeth.

'It is our colleagues, our friends, our brethren who have all contributed so much in reaching this final step but I say it is now you, the best of us, that must ascend to it alone and embrace the legacy that has been destined for us by he who has guided over us for so many years.' He then clasped his hands together and waited for the applause to die down. But now his expression hardened, and he swayed slowly from side to side as if gearing up for some confrontation.

'As you all know, it is that same step that I have already taken in a display of my faith to you all, and although you could not be there to share it with me, it is now time that you joined me in experiencing that same truth.' The speaker raised his arm and pointed towards the double doors at the far end of the room.

'Enter,' he boomed, as a hush descended on the group.

The two doors slowly opened wide to reveal a man wearing nothing but a grey loincloth, flanked by two other men wearing white tuxedos. There was no alarm evident in the half-naked man's eyes, but rather a passive gaze, as he was paraded across the room, up onto the small wooden stage and into the waiting arms of the speaker.

'Welcome, friend,' the speaker declared, and he received a courteous nod from the newcomer before turning to face the assembled group. The man still said nothing but offered them only an appreciative smile as the speaker, who was standing immediately behind him, slipped his hands around the man's neck.

'But pay heed to this truth,' the speaker boomed, looking over the fellow's shoulder. 'That which is given may also be taken away.'

Crouching back by the entrance, Harker watched in astonishment as the speaker then began to tighten his grip, squeezing tighter and tighter until his victim's complexion began turning a light shade of blue. His eyes began bulging in their sockets as the speaker exerted his full force on the victim's throat.

Harker's natural instinct to do something was now gnawing at him, but he resisted. Firstly the half-naked man seemed more than willing, and secondly what consequences would any interference have on Chloe? Was it reasonable to allow the loss of one life to save another? He was here simply to secure pages of the Codex, which there was no sign of as yet and, despite the depraved act being committed in front of him, shouldn't that remain his priority?

As the seconds rolled by Harker decided that had the man been an unwilling participant, then he would have fought against being led in here, but seeing the degree of complicity on display and with Chloe's life at stake, he decided to stay where he was and merely watch, no matter how difficult it may prove.

This, as it turned out, took a surprisingly long time.

In the movies when a bad guy strangles someone, it is all over in seconds, but the reality is far different. After thirty seconds the man's legs began to buckle and finally he sank to the floor. A further thirty seconds and the victim was turning from blue to deep scarlet, and spit and froth began to ooze from his open mouth and his tongue extruded as the pressure from the grip around his throat pushed it upwards and outwards. It was at this point that Harker chose to look away as a sickly feeling overcame him, and he tried to focus on anything else he could. His childhood dog Mr D...the Rolling Stones song 'You Can't Always Get What You Want'...how much of an annoying tool Doggie could be at times...anything but the man being slowly suffocated nearby.

The whole procedure, at a guess, took about three minutes in all, and it wasn't until the sounds of scuffling and gasping had ceased that Harker allowed himself to take another look.

The victim lay sprawled and motionless on the stage as the speaker finally released his grip and stood back up, his chest heaving as he strove to recover his breath. He took another few moments to compose himself and then, with a commanding wave of his hand, he beckoned the group towards him.

'Come,' he said, still struggling for breath, 'see for yourselves.'

The group crowded excitedly around the dead body and began prodding and poking it, one woman even leaning close to the corpse's mouth and checking for any sign of breathing, as another drove a hairpin deep into its thigh, watching for a reaction.

There was none.

Once all seven were satisfied that the man was dead, they began whispering in each other's ears, and for the first time Harker got a good look at their faces. There was nothing that stood out except maybe their age – all were in their late thirties or forties – and that they were smiling and clearly happy about what they had witnessed. They looked normal...clearly mentally sick, of course, but normal.

Harker pulled out his iPhone and began snapping off a few pictures with his camera; despite the dim lighting he was able to get a couple of good shots before the speaker reached into his side pocket and pulled out a thick wad of discoloured material. He lovingly unfolded it and, because of its size, Harker was now sure it had to come from the Codex Gigas. Almost a metre in length and half a metre wide, the page was massive, and Harker watched motionless as the speaker began to read aloud from it.

Words flowed from the man's lips in little more than an inaudible mutter and his audience dipped their heads in prayer as, with linked hands, they stood in a semicircle around the corpse.

After no more than a minute the quiet murmurings from the speaker subsided and, while the small group of people continued to stare at the dirt floor, he folded up the page and laid it down on the dead man's chest.

'And now,' said the speaker, before inhaling a deep and satisfying breath, 'let us eat.'

In the room beyond, lights sparked into life revealing a substantial dining room containing one long table covered in white linen, on which sat an impressive array of food: roast suckling pig, pheasant and other dishes impossible to see from Harker's crouching position. The room itself was a far cry from the rest of the house, enclosed with beautifully crafted wooden panelling adorned with paintings, and he could feel the heat from two fan heaters as the hot air flowed into the room.

Harker watched the group make their way inside to take their seats and, as the doors began to close, he saw two of the men in white tuxedos begin lighting the silver candlesticks set upon the long dining table.

The doors had barely closed before Harker was reaching for his iPhone. He began dialling furiously before pressing it to his ear, and noticed for the first time that his hand was shaking.

'I need to report a murder,' Harker explained in German. 'The old Spreepark amusement park… I don't know the exact address but it's a red-brick building at the northern edge of the grounds, set into the trees. The windows are boarded up and… The kitchen leads to the basement, which is where the murder took place… Because I witnessed it and the killer is still here… Thank you.'

Harker hung up the phone, ignoring the policewoman's request for his name. He couldn't afford to get dragged into all this, especially not now, and besides, there were other witnesses who could do that job, even if they'd have to be forced into it.

Harker made his way over to the stage and hovered above the corpse, briefly listening for any signs of life, but this told him what he already knew, that the man was dead. He picked up the folded, weathered document and examined it. The material was actually vellum, finely treated goat's skin which had been widely used for writing on during the Middle Ages. It crackled under his touch, showing its age.

*Could it be one of the pages Lucas had mentioned?*

He was just about to unfold it when, to his right, one door leading to the banquet room began to open. With nowhere to go, he flung himself around one side of the stage and out of sight, which was easier said than done given its small size. Over the laughter and chatter from the banquet hall beyond, he listened to the sound of footsteps scuffling over the dirt floor, making their way closer to the stage. There was a pause and Harker held his breath as a few moments passed, then the scuffling continued, this time heading in his direction. Closer and closer.

A dark shadow loomed over him and Harker looked up to see the speaker, wide-eyed and staring at him menacingly.

'Who the hell are you?'

Without a pause Harker leapt forward, driving his shoulder hard into the bald-headed man's chest, sending him flying backwards onto the dirt floor with a hefty thump. In the banquet room one of the men wearing a white tuxedo, who was in the process of serving a ladleful of soup, had noticed the commotion and was already shouting a warning to his counterparts.

Harker flew out of the room, down the candlelit corridor, knocking a couple of them to the floor as he went. He jumped the first two steps of the ladder before heaving himself up through the opening. With no time to stand up, he reached over to the trapdoor, but before he could grasp the edges of it a hand clothed in a white sleeve grabbed his ankle. Using all his strength to not get pulled back down through the opening, Harker watched in terror as the scowling face of a man appeared and then, grasping at Harker's clothing, he began to pull himself upwards. Harker was landing every blow he could against the man's head and shoulders, but unable to get a decent swing it had little effect and within moments the man had clambered up his body until they were face-to-face. Finally in range, his pursuer then clasped his hands around Harker's throat and with all his weight pressed down and began to squeeze, tighter and tighter.

The smell of body odour masked by Old Spice was nauseating and Harker reacted instinctively to this rather than the increasing pressure around his neck, slamming his knee into the man's groin, who instantly released his grip and toppled off to one side.

As his attacker groaned and cupped himself in pain, Harker jumped to his feet just as another hand appeared from the opening in the floor. He immediately reached down and grabbed the trapdoor, swinging it down to slam against the person's fingers.

The painful sound of breaking bones was accompanied by a high-pitched yelp from below as the man who had been attending to his injured testicles began to stagger to his feet. With nothing nearby to use as a weapon Harker did the only thing he could and, with full force, he once again kicked the man in the groin, sending the poor fellow to the floor in a heap. With the sound of pained sobbing ringing in his ears, Harker winced in empathy and then took off, running like a maniac.

The short dash to the front entrance took him no time at all and it wasn't until he reached it that he heard the thud of the trapdoor reopening behind him, echoing throughout the empty house. He wanted to glance back but resisted the impulse and, without pause, wrenched open the front door and sprinted outside into the cool night air. He was running so wildly that he came close to tumbling down the stone steps at the entrance, but he managed to regain his balance quickly and then shimmy past the parked cars, colliding with a wing mirror which dug painfully into his ribs as he passed it.

Harker continued to race along the dirt path and located the way he had come by using the shadowy outline of the Ferris wheel looming above the trees as his guide. It wasn't until he got within twenty metres of it that he slowed and skidded to a stop in order to catch his breath. His lungs were burning from the exertion and in the distance he could hear the hum of car engines starting up and it suddenly occurred to him that the occupants were either making a quick exit before any police arrived, or preparing to hunt him down. The latter notion ensured that he immediately took off again, although this time in a fast jog, past the 'lake of love' and back towards the undergrowth from which he had first emerged. How he didn't catch himself on any sharp debris from the remnants of the abandoned rides was nothing short of miraculous, but he just focused on one mantra, mumbling it over and over again:

*Get me the hell out of here.*

The exhausting escape took him almost ten minutes, and by the time he reached the break in the fencing he was dripping in sweat. He slipped past the green tarpaulin fence cover and shot through the gap onto the pavement outside with such speed that he almost slammed face first into the door of a blue Toyota Prius with the letters 'Polizei' printed on the side.

'Stop right there,' a voice ordered in German, and Harker looked up to see an officer in a dark-blue patrol uniform, who reached down and pulled him to his feet. 'You're trespassing on private land, sir,' the young officer berated him. 'You'll get a hefty fine for this, so I hope for your sake it was worth it.'

Harker steadied himself and then groped the top side of his inside jacket pocket, fingering the thick section of folded vellum he had stolen. 'Yeah, me too.'

# *Chapter 7*

'Well, you will be glad to know, Mr Harker, that the trespassing charge has been dropped, but consider this an official warning. If you attempt to go back there while you're our guest in Berlin, I promise you next time the law will not be so forgiving.'

Detective Jerome Krause laid a Titanium Apple laptop carefully on the desk in front of him and dropped into his seat with a frustrated groan. 'Why a man of your age feels the need to go traipsing around an abandoned amusement park in the middle of the night is beyond me.'

After being arrested on the spot, Harker had been brought directly back to the Landespolizeiverwaltungsamt station house to be processed, before then being placed in a holding cell. Of course, he had meanwhile informed the duty officer about the grisly happenings back in Spreepark, and to the man's credit, he was taken seriously. Yet for the last couple of hours he had been left in the cell on his own, before eventually being pulled out and frogmarched up to the second floor and into this plain, blue-painted interview room.

'Pardon me, Detective, but did no one tell you what happened out there earlier tonight?' Harker enquired, frankly shocked by Krause's seeming lack of concern over the reported murder.

'Ah yes,' Krause replied sarcastically, placing both elbows on the table before resting his chin upon his clasped hands, 'the *supposed* murder.'

'Supposed! I saw it with my own eyes. I even took photos.'

Detective Krause stared at him with disbelief before leaning back in his chair and folding his arms. 'I am sure you did, Mr Harker—'

'It's Professor,' Harker interrupted, hoping the title would afford him a degree of credibility that was evidently lacking thus far.

'Oh, I know who you are, Professor. You have something of a reputation.'

'Reputation!' Harker spluttered, only just managing to contain his anger. 'And what reputation would that be?'

Krause bit his bottom lip and then sucked in a deep breath. 'You are the same Professor Alex Harker that was involved in the Vatican shootings last year, are you not? And who was also involved in events surrounding the complete destruction of many national landmarks, including a large portion of the Vatican itself. That is, if one believes some of the outlandish stories that appeared in the British tabloids.'

Harker stared blankly at him for a few awkward moments and, for some reason, he suddenly felt a tinge of embarrassment. 'Oh, *that* reputation.'

'Yes, that one,' Krause replied with a derisive smile. 'Not to forget your highly dubious archaeological discoveries.'

'Highly dubious!'

'I will admit,' Krause continued with a smirk, 'I found that particular nugget through a Google search. God bless the Internet, eh?'

Outside the interview room, a butch-looking officer sporting a thick black moustache glanced in through the window and gave Harker the once-over before shaking his head condescendingly, and continuing on his way.

'Forgive me, but your point is?'

'The point is, Professor, that you have a habit of implanting yourself into events, whether they be Vatican scandals or natural disasters, and given your most recent tale of ritualistic murder, forgive me when I say that I don't believe you.'

The scorn now being heaped upon Harker's declaration of a murder had him at a momentary loss for words, and his bottom jaw hung open in disbelief. 'Did anyone even check out that house in the Spreepark?'

'Oh, we checked it out. Quite a few officers responded to your call.'

'And?'

'And we found an empty basement but with, just as you described, a wonderfully decorated dining room. The food was still warm and the victim you described, still wearing his loincloth, was dutifully taken to the Berlin morgue.'

Harker was completely dumbfounded. 'So there was a body – exactly as I said.'

Any amusement in the detective's expression now vanished as he reached over to open up the Apple laptop, then swivelled it around so the screen was facing Harker.

The display contained the image of a corridor with covered fluorescent strips reflecting shiny patches on the plastic-tiled floor below, and the twenty-four-hour clock in the lower left corner suggested surveillance footage.

'Just press play,' Krause directed, motioning to the laptop with a flick of his finger.

Harker did as he was told and tapped the play symbol in the centre of the screen, letting the footage roll.

At first it showed nothing except the corridor itself, but after ten seconds things began to get interesting. A double glass door on the left-hand side slowly opened and the figure of a man in an oversized white lab coat shuffled out. The individual's back was turned to the camera and all Harker could make out was his black hair and that he was barefoot. The figure staggered about halfway along the corridor, before leaning against the wall as his feet buckled under him. After a few moments he stood up straight again, and it was what happened next that sent Harker reeling backwards. The figure looked backwards, allowing a good view of his face for the first time.

'That's impossible,' Harker murmured, dumbfounded at what he saw. 'I watched him die.'

The face of the same half-naked man Harker had seen being strangled to death in that house in Spreepark stared back at him, before turning away and heading off along the corridor until he was out of sight. The image quality was not great but it was definitely him.

'That was taken from one of the morgue's security cameras less than an hour ago,' Krause declared in an angry tone. 'Well...' He paused until Harker raised his head from viewing the screen, now looking like a rabbit caught in the headlights. 'It's quite a stunt, I'll give you, but whatever drug you gave that man to facilitate the appearance of death, it was extremely dangerous. He could have died for real.'

'What...?' Harker stuttered, still stunned by what he had just seen.

'I said it was quite a stunt. Would have made a great story for the papers and put you squarely back in the news, and we know how you love that. What were you going for this time, the whole resurrection thing?' Krause gave an annoyed sigh. 'So what are you coming out with next, a book? Or is it to do with your latest archaeological find?'

Harker shook off the feeling of sheer bewilderment, not only at the sight of a dead man walking but also the notion this was just part of some audacious marketing stunt to draw attention to him. 'You really think this business is all down to me?'

Krause was already nodding before Harker had even finished speaking. 'Given your past history with the press, I absolutely do – and I'll tell you something else. You're not going to get a single column inch of press coverage out of this, or drag the Berlin police into it either, which is why I am now throwing you out of my station.'

Detective Krause stood up, slapped the laptop shut and hauled Harker to his feet and out of the interview room.

'This is ridiculous,' Harker pleaded as he was escorted downstairs to the main entrance. 'I'm telling you I saw that man strangled lethally right in front of me.'

'The only person who's going to get strangled here, *Professor*, is you if I catch you anywhere near the Spreepark again. Understood?'

Krause then roughly pushed Harker out of the main door and onto the pavement outside, while offering one last word of warning. 'And if we find that idiot of a partner of yours dead from a heart attack, brought on by whatever drugs you gave him, I promise I will have you pulled in on murder charges. Do you understand?'

The question was obviously rhetorical and, taking took it as such, Harker remained silent.

'Enjoy the rest of your stay in Berlin, Professor Harker,' Krause spat before slamming the door closed behind him and leaving Harker standing outside alone in a state of stunned confusion. The street was empty, it being the early hours of the morning, and he stood there for a moment contemplating what to do next.

Without any real understanding of what he had been drawn into, and even less about the resurrection trick and its creepy witnesses back at Spreepark, Harker was feeling the need for some serious help. From someone who had an interest in cults and societies. Someone who could shed light on the night's bizarre events. Someone he could rely on for sage counsel. Unfortunately he only had one acquaintance in Berlin, and although secret societies were right up his alley everything else about the man was a complete disaster. Add to this the fact that they had not spoken in years and it made for a pretty desperate choice.

*Beggars can't be choosers*, he thought.

Harker pulled out his phone and auto-dialled from one of his contact numbers. By the seventh ring he was considering hanging up, when the line connected and a grizzly-sounding voice answered.

'What?'

'David, it's Alex. Alex Harker.'

The line went quiet for a few seconds, then the voice came back on.

'Alex! What time is it?'

'It's both late and early,' Harker offered, aware the man sounded thoroughly pissed off. 'Depends on your perspective really.'

'What the hell do you want?' the voice demanded grouchily.

'I need to see you… I wouldn't be calling if it wasn't important.'

'Where are you?'

'I'm in Berlin.'

'Oh, for Christ's sake,' the voice moaned. 'Fine, come on over, but don't expect a pleasant welcome. I've got a bitch of a hangover.'

'Fair enough,' Harker replied, lowering his voice and not wishing to antagonise him any further. 'Are you still at the same address?'

A deep grunt confirmed it, and Harker was already searching his pocket for the taxi card he had picked up earlier.

'Oh, and bring some coffee. There's a twenty-four-hour shop opposite me. Espresso, full fat, four sugars…and a pastry,' the voice gruffly demanded. 'Maybe Black Forest cake or something with buttercream icing.'

Harker shuddered at the idea of such an early-morning pick-me-up. 'Leave it with me. I'll see you soon.'

'Sure, whatever,' came the indifferent reply. And with that the line promptly cut out.

The old acquaintance he was about to visit was awkward enough to deal with when sober, let alone when suffering from a hangover. Besides that, he knew few other people who considered such rich desserts a breakfast snack. Their dialogue had not been exactly encouraging but, with few friends in Berlin, Harker had limited options. Besides which, the short trip would cost him nothing but a bit of time and the expense of some artery-clogging confectionery.

As Harker dialled in the taxi contact number and began to amble his way along the pavement, he remained unaware that he was not the only one making a call. Across the street, a man wearing a flat cap and a dark-brown raincoat stood and watched him while raising a mobile phone up to his ear.

He watched intently as Harker continued up the street, then whispered into his mobile, 'It's me... He's out.'

# *Chapter 8*

The old man pushed the two pills between his lips and, with a shaky hand, raised the glinting crystal tumbler to his mouth. Two sips were all he could manage, but it was enough to wash the medication down his throat. Then he placed the glass down upon the crescent-shaped, walnut side desk next to him. The tremors in his hands were worse than usual and he prayed the drugs would calm them, because writing was proving nearly impossible. These days he even struggled to pick up the TV remote without dropping it, so constantly had to rely on someone else to retrieve it for him.

*How the hell had it come to this?*

There was a time when his energy knew no bounds, and then, in what seemed like no time at all, it had been taken away from him, reducing him to little more than a cripple who needed help to simply take a piss.

Time was a cruel mistress.

The room was large, with a finely woven red carpet and an ornate crystal chandelier hanging from the ceiling, bathing the antique furniture below in a dim glow of crimson light. His eyes were far too sensitive now for a regular bulb, and forget about sunlight. Even a thin ray of natural light stung his corneas and felt like red-hot tongs being jabbed into his pupils.

The old man gazed around at his luxurious surroundings with a heavy heart. Here he was with his own personal library, filled with books so rare, and yet his eyes were so far gone he could barely read a word – with or without spectacles.

He was still wallowing in self-pity when there was a knock at the door.

'Come,' he managed, with a croak that made his chest ache.

The door slowly opened, the lights outside it emitting the same crimson light, and a neatly dressed man wearing a black suit and tie entered and made his way over to the old man's wheelchair. He then knelt beside him on one knee and whispered quietly into his ear.

'Harker made it out of Spreepark.'

This information drew raised eyebrows from the old man. 'How did he look?'

'Shaken up, as you'd expect.'

'Quite. Did he secure the pages?'

'We don't know yet. The police picked him up afterwards and he was just released.'

The old man looked content with that answer and he forced a smile through his discoloured lips, revealing blackened teeth behind them. 'Very well. Have our man initiate contact.'

The neatly dressed man offered a nod and began to stand back up, but he stopped halfway and returned to his original stance. 'Would it not be best just to kill him?'

The question received a dismissive grunt form the old man and he waggled one of his bent fingers without moving his hand which was resting on the chequered blanket draped across his lap. 'No, Harker deserves more than that.'

'Very well, sir. But I do suggest we keep things moving along.'

The old man thought for a moment, and then smiled. 'All in good time, my friend. All in good time.'

The neatly dressed man said nothing but rose to his feet and headed back through the open door, closing it behind him.

Alone once more, the man in the wheelchair reached under his blanket and pulled out a small colour photograph of Alex Harker delivering a lecture to his students. He gently ran his feeble index finger across the image.

'All good things come to those who wait.'

# *Chapter 9*

Harker pressed the dirty white buzzer for a second time with his little finger, allowing the brown-paper pastry bag to slap against the door as he did so. The small house was located on the outskirts of Berlin and the place seemed hardly changed during the years since his last visit, despite the neighbourhood gentrifying.

The upstairs curtains were drawn closed and, with no signs of life, Harker was preparing to give the buzzer another go when a small porch light above him switched on, and he could now hear the sound of heavy footsteps approaching inside.

Quite why the light had been necessary wasn't clear because the sun was now up, but considering his friend's mention of having a crashing hangover and therefore probably not knowing what time it actually was, it seemed fitting.

With a clattering of locks being undone, the door swung open, whereupon Harker took a step backwards and held up the pastry bag in front of him like a protective crucifix warding off the unsavoury advances of a vampire.

The short, pudgy frame of David Carter was revealed in the narrow hallway, wearing white trainers, a ripped pair of dark-blue tracksuit bottoms and a grey jumper with the Nike logo '*Just do it*' printed in red across the middle. 'Alex bloody Harker. What the hell are you doing here, anyway?'

Although he was in his mid-forties, one could be forgiven for thinking David Carter was close to sixty, with his unkempt white hair and deep crow's feet a testimony to a life of reckless living. In fairness to the man, he had not always been this way, and it was not until the death of his wife ten years earlier that he had fallen into a spiral of alcoholism and deep depression. Happily married to a German girl, the British-born expat had at one time been a respected lecturer at Cambridge University when Harker had first been offered his place at the archaeology department there. With degrees in theology, philosophy and religion, Carter had garnered much praise from the academic community and students alike, and therefore a lifetime career within the walls of Cambridge had seemed guaranteed. Sadly that was not to be after an articulated lorry jackknifed on the southbound section of the M6, just outside Birmingham, and the unfortunate Mrs Carter's white Ford Sierra had taken the brunt of the impact, killing her instantly. What followed was a sad fall from grace as Carter became consumed with grief, and when his excessive drinking began affecting his professional life, his position was terminated and he eventually ended up taking a lower-paid teaching job at a small college here in Berlin. But why Berlin? Who could tell, but Harker had always suspected that his deceased wife's German origin had played a part in the decision. Maybe the culture and language allowed him to feel still connected to her in some way, a kinship of sorts. Whatever the reason, it was clear now that the move had not done him any favours and, as he looked at the shell of the man Carter had become, Harker struggled to hide the sympathy he felt for this ex-don.

'Good to see you, David, and thanks for seeing me at such short notice. Can I come in?'

Carter turned his gaze to the brown-paper pastry bag and large coffee that were being extended towards him.

'Beware of Greeks bearing gifts,' Carter grumbled loudly through bloodshot eyes.

'I was born in Belfast,' Harker replied with an amused smile, remembering Carter's offbeat sense of humour.

'Well that means you can come in, then, can't you?' Carter reached over and snatched the offerings from Harker's outstretched hand and, with a beckoning nod, he headed back inside.

The house looked in a cleaner state than Harker remembered, which wasn't saying much, and the living room he was led into, although not spacious, was large enough to act as a leisure area and study, with a green felt sofa and TV set alongside a wooden desk piled high with philosophy and history books related to everything from Nietzsche to the medieval feudal system.

'It's the cleaner's day off,' Carter quipped as he placed Harker's consumable offerings on the table, before grabbing a half-empty bottle of Glenfiddich whisky from the sideboard. 'Although it's possible she's buried somewhere underneath all this shit.'

With a chuckle Harker sat down as Carter unscrewed the bottle cap before administering a generous dose of Scotch to his steaming espresso.

'Nothing better than an Irish coffee and a slice of cake to wake you up,' Carter said after taking a sip from the cardboard coffee cup and joining him on the sofa. 'So, to what do I owe this visit at such a pain-in-the-arse time of day?'

Before Harker could respond, Carter picked up the whisky bottle again and waved it in front of him. 'Fancy a nip before we get started?'

'Considering the night I've had, I'm tempted, but no thanks.'

'Oh, go on,' Carter pressed him. 'Allow me the small indulgence of feeling that for once my rampant alcoholism is normal.'

Carter's candour made Harker laugh out loud. 'Yeah, go on, then.'

Harker's assent garnered a contented smile from his host, who jumped up, plucked a small tumbler from the desk top, and then poured a quarter measure before passing it to Harker, who took a sip. He forced down the brown liquid and stifled the urge to choke. He had never been much of a whisky drinker.

'You don't have any vodka, do you?'

'Please, Alex, I'm a respectable man,' Carter growled, placing the whisky bottle back on the coffee table. 'Right, we can get started now. So, once again, what the hell are you doing here?'

'I need your help,' Harker explained, pausing to force another sip from his whisky glass, 'and when it comes to my problem you're the most knowledgeable person I know.'

Carter stared at him blankly for a few moments, then a smirk creased his lips. 'Bollocks, Alex, you know me. Why *really*?'

Harker had forgotten how blunt Carter liked things, and now he himself was smirking. 'Fine, because you're the only person I know here in Berlin – besides which, I think you could help. This problem I have is right up your alley.'

'Now that's more like it. You know how I feel about pleasantries and bullshit. Give me raw honesty any day of the week.'

'OK,' Harker conceded, pulling the thick, folded piece of vellum from his inner jacket pocket and unfolding it on the table top. The size of it was impressive, at almost a metre in length and half a metre wide, and it was filled with intricate text inscribed in black ink that had faded with age.

'As you can see, most of it's in Latin,' Harker continued, having taken some time to read through it while he was locked up earlier at the police station, 'but these sections here are not in any language I recognize.'

He pointed to the relevant paragraphs as Carter slipped on a pair of black-rimmed glasses and began to study the text for himself.

'These parts you mention look like they've been written by a different person,' he offered eventually, pointing to the same paragraphs.

'That was my conclusion too.'

Harker sat back and watched as Carter now pored over the massive document with fascination. After a few minutes of muttering to himself as he attempted to decipher some of the text, he then turned to Harker with an intrigued expression.

'Is this what I think it is?'

'What *do* you think it is?'

'Well, if I didn't know better... I mean, the size especially, but the style, even the material it's written on, I would say it comes from the Codex Gigas, but I know all the pages inside out and this is definitely not one of them.' Carter tapped the parchment lightly with his finger. 'Where the hell did you find this?'

Harker polished off his drink in one gulp and placed the glass on the table next to the document. 'It's not where I got it but from whom.'

Carter was instantly curious. 'Go on.'

The majority of people who knew David Carter were aware of his academic achievements and his impressive degrees and teaching prowess, but few knew that the ex-Cambridge don had an absolute obsession with all things occult: cults, secret societies, legends...and anything else that the mainstream today would label under the category of 'conspiracies'. He loved it all, and to say it was his private passion was an understatement. Of course he tended to keep quiet about his personal hobby for fear of eliciting ridicule from his peers because, to his mind anyway, such ideas tended to cast a person in an unfavourable light. But that was going back ten years ago, and whether Carter still had any interests these days outside of the bottle remained to be seen.

Harker decided to lay down everything, including the suicide and Chloe's disappearance that had prompted – no, forced – him to make this trip to Berlin in the first place. And as he described the ritualistic murder and the apparent 'resurrection' of the victim, Carter became noticeably enthralled.

'Christ alive,' he spluttered, completely absorbed by the story. 'This is the most bizarre thing I've heard in a long time...and the most fascinating.'

'Bizarre is right,' Harker agreed.

Carter stroked his chin, suddenly looking lost. 'Are you sure this man was really dead? I mean *dead* dead?'

'David, he was dead as a dodo, no ifs or buts.'

Carter continued stare at him with a vagueness that made Harker feel uneasy, and he immediately sought to keep the conversation going.

'Look, I'm not even sure what it is I need from you, and there's not a lot to go on but…can you help? I mean does any of this ritual I described and this group's interest in the Codex ring any bells at all?' There was desperation in Harker's tone and Carter sensed it right away. He sat back up straight thoughtfully.

'Well, you're right about there being not much to go on, but there are groups – not just in Germany but around the world – who practise these sorts of things…minus the bringing a guy back to life.' Carter raised his eyebrows then. 'But most of those groups have Satanic or pagan elements embedded into their beliefs, and I've never previously heard of any connection to the Codex.'

Carter took a moment to unscrew and take a swig directly from his whisky bottle before continuing with a renewed enthusiasm, as if the alcohol provided him with some clarity of mind. 'Let's put aside the more outlandish parts of your story and focus on the more down-to-earth aspects, shall we?'

The use of the word 'outlandish' left Harker feeling somewhat foolish, and Carter recognized this and raised his hands submissively.

'For the record, I believe what you say. You may be many things, Alex, but a bullshitter is not one of them.'

Harker was slightly irked by the 'many things' part, but he kept his mouth shut and offered only a grateful nod.

Carter continued, 'The Codex Gigas has always been surrounded by legends and mystery but, as you know, it primarily focuses on the pact made between the Devil and the monk and not on any significance these missing pages may have, as this Lucas character suggested.' He paused and a deep frown spread across his brow. 'He really blew his head off right in front of you?'

'As close as I am to you right now,' Harker replied, gesturing towards Carter at the other end of the sofa.

'God, that must have been horrific. I'm not sure I would cope with seeing something like that.'

'It's not something I want to experience again, that's for sure,' Harker replied coldly before pushing the bloody, partially headless image of Lucas from his mind. 'Please, David, go on.'

'Of course,' Carter said apologetically, 'best not to think about it.' And then his eyes began to squint. 'You're still thinking about it, aren't you?'

'I'm trying not to,' Harker replied in a raised tone of voice, provoked by his host's morbid probing of the grisly event.

Once again Carter bowed his head apologetically. 'Sorry, Alex…where was I? Oh yes, Lucas and his willingness to commit suicide.'

Harker let out a small sigh. David Carter had a way of winding people up, and to the uninitiated it could appear deliberate. But Harker knew better, because the ex-don had a habit of going around in circles during conversations, and the constant drinking certainly wasn't helping.

'Well, no one takes their own life willingly unless they are either mentally ill, doing it for the greater good, or are getting something out of it spiritually. Discount the first two and you're left with the spiritual aspect. And, judging by what you told me concerning the dead man seemingly coming back to life, then who knows…maybe there is some truth in all this.'

Carter turned to the oversized page of the Codex and ran his fingers down that same illegible section of the text. 'Can you imagine if what we are looking at here truly was written by the Devil's own hand?'

The thought had Harker shaking his head and he rubbed his cheek in frustration. 'Come on, David, I can't accept that.'

Carter looked surprised at this. 'Why not? You were a priest once, weren't you, a man of the cloth? If you believe in God, then you have to believe in the Devil. Not just as an idea but as a tangible and real entity.'

Harker let out a weary groan as Carter continued, apparently unfazed by Harker's reaction.

'It never ceases to amaze me how human beings clasp onto the idea that everything we see can be catalogued and rationalized according to our own realm of understanding, despite the wider reality we find ourselves in. We live on a planet hanging in space that encompasses billions of other planets, and surrounded by billions of galaxies – and with absolutely no idea how the hell we got here in the first place.'

This remark got merely a sharp look of surprise from Harker.

'Yes, we can follow the timeline back to the Big Bang, but we have no idea how it all started, or why, and' – Carter was clearly gaining traction with the idea – 'mathematicians and scientists now think we could be part of a multiverse, with each "verse" potentially conforming to different laws of physics from our own, and inhabiting the same time and space!'

'And your point here is?'

'My point is that if that's how crazy our own reality is, then is it such a leap to think that there may be forces at work that we can barely comprehend, let alone understand. Sure, maybe we just call it the Devil for our own reference, but who knows what such an entity really is? It could be anything.'

Carter turned his attention back to the Codex page. 'Could these words form part of some ancient wisdom passed down to us from God-knows-who that has been lost to history?'

'OK, that's enough,' Harker said sternly as he proceeded to lift up the Codex page and carefully refold it. 'This is getting altogether a bit too weird. To think that you can overcome death by just saying a few words is laughable.'

Carter was almost bouncing in his seat as Harker slipped the thick wodge of vellum back into his inside pocket.

'Alex, those words are like nothing I have ever seen before, and I couldn't even begin to guess at a translation. Besides which, you said you witnessed a man die and then come back from the dead! I mean, Christ, that's a miracle in itself. This is an adventure, my friend. A real goddam supernatural adventure!'

The mention of an *adventure* was getting Harker annoyed and, although he could see his old acquaintance was genuinely buying into his own sales pitch, it seemed time to call it quits. He raised his hand directly in front of Carter's face. 'Enough, David,' he fumed. 'This isn't a bloody adventure. This is about trying to get back the woman I love, and that's the only thing I care about at the moment.'

This outburst stopped Carter in his tracks and he leant back in his seat as Harker lowered his arm back to his side.

'You love her? I thought she was just a girlfriend.'

'So did I until just now,' Harker grunted, shocked by his own personal realization. He fell back onto the sofa with a thump and took a deep breath. 'Chloe's life is on the line and I'm scrambling to figure out everything...anything. The what, why, how. Maybe it's time I went to the police and reported her being kidnapped.'

The words had just left Harker's mouth when the iPhone in his trouser pocket began to ring, causing both men to freeze. Why they did so, they had no idea – perhaps it was the timing.

Harker retrieved the mobile and pressed the answer icon. 'Hello.'

'Mr Harker, so good to finally speak to you. I believe you've already met my friend Lucas.'

The man's voice was husky and unsteady as if the caller had very little strength in his lungs.

'Where's Chloe?' Harker demanded, Carter immediately perking up at the mention of her name.

'She is fine, of that I can assure you, but her future well-being lies solely in your hands.'

'Let me talk to her.'

'We're not there yet, Mr Harker,' the wheezy voice rasped, 'but you will get a chance to do so as we progress further.'

'Progress!' The word implied some long-drawn-out association with this feeble-sounding old man, and Harker felt totally vexed at the idea.

'As Lucas informed you, Mr Harker, there are another two pages required, along with the one you already have on your person.'

'How do you know I have the first one?' Harker growled, not wanting to feel like he was on the back foot.

'Because I know,' the voice croaked. 'We told you we would be watching.'

'Lucas did say that...just before he blew his head off. Just remind me never to work for you.'

A dry cackle reverberated through the speaker. 'How very quaint of you, Mr Harker, but a life given is a life saved, and I wonder how jovial you will be when your girlfriend is lying cold on a mortuary slab?'

Harker remained silent. After all, what could he do but start hurling insults down the line? Although extremely tempting, it would do little to help.

'Good, I like a person who knows when to shut up,' the voice continued. 'Now go to the front door and open it, and I warn you, Mr Harker, not to do anything stupid that we will both regret.'

Harker didn't answer and, under the watchful eye of Carter, he headed into the entrance hallway and opened the door to find a tall man in a red duffel coat who was wearing sunglasses and a baseball cap. He stood in the porch with one of his gloved hands extended.

'Give the man in front of you the page, please,' came the request and, even though Harker was tempted to grab the courier by the throat and beat any information he might possess out of him, he instead did as he was told.

The courier palmed the folded Codex page and put it into a black satchel with two brass-coloured metal straps. Once it was secured, he did an about turn and, without a word, headed off down the road.

'Good,' the old man said. 'Now go back into the lounge and put me on speakerphone.'

Harker headed back and pressed the speaker icon, before placing it on the table. Whatever the mystery man wanted to say, he wanted it to be over as soon as possible.

'Mr Carter,' the voice puffed, 'you don't need to talk. You only need to listen.'

Carter was suddenly looking nauseous. He rubbed his hands together nervously at having his name mentioned.

'I am afraid that you are now caught up in all this, whether you wish it or not. And should you have any gripes about it, then I suggest you direct them towards Mr Harker, who should never have involved you in the first place.'

Carter shot Harker a look not born out of anger but of alarm, and the two men now sat quietly, waiting for the voice to recommence.

'I am afraid it does not pay to be a friend of Mr Harker's, but there you have it. Anyway, it's a case of join him now or I have you killed, and none of us want such an unnecessary and messy complication, wouldn't you agree?'

'Oh, I agree,' Carter stammered fretfully, noticeably unsettled at the suggestion of his murder being an option.

'Shut up,' the voice hissed, 'I was being rhetorical. You will both travel to the cathedral at the Piazza dei Miracoli and meet there a person who will be waiting for you. I trust the location is well known to you, Mr Harker.'

'I know where it is,' Harker replied, while ignoring a questioning look from Carter.

'Good. The person I mention is in possession of another Codex page, and I want you to retrieve it. The individual in question will be seated in the front pew, and is expecting to have the item picked up by someone unknown to him but using the password "The watcher watches us all, but you are free to do as you will" as identification. Follow his instructions to the letter, and be aware that it took a lot of effort to acquire that password, so don't screw this up. Then, maybe, I will allow you to speak to Dr Stanton.'

Sensing the end of the conversation, Harker leapt in on the back of the final sentence. 'What do I call you?'

There was a short pause and then the voice came back on the line. 'God,' he rasped with a snigger. 'You may address me as God.'

Before either of them could reply the line went dead, and Harker found himself staring into the glazed expression of David Carter, whose cheeks now appeared to sag.

'I'm sorry for getting you dragged into all this, David. Are you OK?'

They sat in silence for a few moments and Harker wasn't sure if his host was going to offer him anther drink or lunge off the sofa and attempt to throttle him. But when Carter eventually spoke up, he sounded remarkably calm and collected.

'Well, that's the first time anyone has ever made a threat against my life, and I must say' – Carter's lips were beginning to tremble – 'I am extremely excited.'

'What?' Harker replied, feeling totally shocked by his response. 'Why?'

'Why?' Carter shouted enthusiastically. 'Forget about the threat for a minute.'

'Oh yeah, let's,' Harker said sarcastically as Carter jumped to his feet with all the energy of a tomcat. A severely overweight tomcat.

'Alex, I have spent my entire life reading about conspiracies and secret societies, and suddenly I am dropped right into the middle of one. A bit nerve-racking, yes, but bloody exciting nonetheless.'

'That's what everyone says…at first,' Harker muttered, shaking his head.

'Everyone?' Carter replied, his face full of curiosity.

'Just an inside joke.' Harker waved a hand dismissively.

'Oh, OK. Well, then, let's go… Where are we heading anyway?'

'You should know this one, David. The Battistero di San Giovanni is in Pisa, Italy. You know, right next to the famous Leaning Tower.'

'Of course, how stupid of me. Any idea why?'

The question had Harker shaking his head. As well as being known for having one of the architectural wonders of the world, Pisa, and its surrounding areas, was steeped in a history that made Spreepark look like nothing more than a rubbish dump. Yet this was his next port of call for reasons he couldn't yet fathom. Whatever 'God' had in store for them would clearly only be revealed by following the path being laid down before him, and that uncertainty was extremely unnerving to Harker. 'I honestly don't know, David. This is "God's" game we're playing, but I'm guessing it'll be nothing pleasant. All we can do is meet with the contact and go from there; besides, it's my only lead to Chloe.'

Carter's look of excitement remained solid and he slowly nodded his head. 'Then let's go and save your true love, my friend,' Carter bellowed, totally caught up in his own personal delight at being involved in such an adventure – as he saw it. 'Worry not, we will get her back.'

'Look, David, I'm glad you're with me on this, but just take a minute to calm down.' Harker felt unsettled by the ex-don's somewhat childlike enthusiasm. 'This could prove very dangerous.'

'Of course.' Carter nodded understandingly and his shoulders heaved as he sucked in a stabilizing breath. 'Now let me get my passport.' He slowly picked up the whisky bottle from the table and placed it back onto the sideboard. 'I won't be needing this.'

*Hope springs eternal*, Harker mused, though uplifted by the thought that his friend might have found a reason to stop drinking…for the time being. 'Good for you, David.'

Carter glanced at the nearly empty bottle, and then back at Harker with a twinkle in his eye. 'Bollocks to that,' he replied stoutly, 'I'm picking up a fresh bottle at the airport.'

## *Chapter 10*

'Beautiful, isn't it?' Harker said as he ran his eyes across the impressive stone masonry of the Torre di Pisa or, as it was more commonly known, the Leaning Tower of Pisa.

Built within a walled eight-hectare area called the city's Cathedral Square or Piazza del Duomo, the Tower was only one of the many striking religious edifices to be found herein. Next to the Tower, the massive cathedral itself offered a similarly impressive sight alongside the open-sided cemetery, the Camposanto Monumentale, which was said to contain soil taken from Golgotha, the site of Christ's crucifixion. Shipped back to Pisa during the fourth Crusade, any interred bodies were said to rot fully within twenty-four hours when placed in this hallowed earth, only adding to the mystique of such a beautiful and unique religious site. Last and, certainly not least, there was the Baptistery, whose construction had begun in 1152 and was not finished until 1363, making its appearance all the more distinctive. Essentially it consisted of one huge dome, but the lower half was made up of Romanesque arches whereas the upper half had windows with pointed steeple arches reflecting the cultural transition to the more popular Gothic style towards the end of its lengthy period of construction.

For the thousands of tourists who came every year to see the better-known Leaning Tower, their expectations were usually overwhelmed by the magnificence of the holy site in its entirety. And that same feeling was not lost on Harker.

'It really is something, hey, David?' he said with admiration, and he turned only to find Carter lovingly caressing the label of a whisky bottle.

'I know,' he said, still shaking his head in disbelief. 'Only forty quid for a bottle of Macallan! What a surprise bargain.'

'I meant the Tower,' Harker replied, nevertheless with an amused sigh. Carter was proving to be far more fun to travel with than he would have ever expected. Problem was that fun was not a prerequisite on a quest like this.

'Oh, the Tower! Yes, beautiful. Took hundreds of years to build, you know,' Carter declared knowledgeably. 'I've visited here many times, oh yes, and always enjoyed the mesmerizing and hearty banquet of historical beauty on display.'

'Really,' Harker remarked, and Carter gave him a droopy-eyed double take.

'Well, I've been here a few times. Well, once...for an hour.'

The ease at which Carter sometimes tended to contradict himself was extremely amusing to Harker, and he found himself smirking widely as his friend continued to chisel away at his own credibility on the subject.

'I was with the wife, on holiday – must be ten, fifteen years ago now. Don't remember much about it, if I'm honest. I spent most of my time with the picnic hamper. Anyway' – Carter gave a shrug of his shoulders – 'shall we get this over and done with?'

Harker nodded and they began walking back towards the cathedral entrance, some two hundred metres away, with the Leaning Tower looming behind them. The cathedral itself was a classic example of Romanesque architecture with four levels of sculptured arches, each set on top of each other, and rising up to a triangular roof. In the middle stood a sculpture of the Madonna with Child, and as they reached the heavy bronze doors of the entrance, Harker took a moment to gaze up at this image which so symbolized the Christian faith.

'You know this almost got wiped out during the Second World War,' he explained while still looking at the statue. 'The

Germans were using the nearby Tower as an observation post, so the advancing American forces came close to flattening the whole area with artillery.'

'Why didn't they?' Carter said, obviously not as impressed as Harker was with the architecture.

'Why do you think?' Harker replied, turning away from the awesome sight to face his friend. 'The American officer in charge did some recon the day before the attack, and he was so taken by its beauty he decided that they couldn't destroy it.'

'I'm sure the Nazis would have pulverized it to dust if they had felt inclined to,' Carter remarked with a disconcerting snort.

'That's the point, isn't it?' Harker said, slightly riled by Carter's naivety. 'It's that same attitude that lost them the war. Winning people's hearts and minds with empathy is greatly underestimated during wartime. Putting a gun to a nation's head rarely beats the power of allowing them hope.'

'No, I agree, but there's something about churches and cathedrals that I find...well, a bit creepy!'

'Creepy!' Harker scoffed.

'Yes. They're just so cold and...well, old.'

Carter's comment had Harker shaking his head, and he gently nudged his friend across the threshold of the cathedral's entrance. 'Do you really find this creepy?'

The interior was beautiful, but not as imposing as others to be found throughout the Catholic world, with a long central aisle leading from the doorway to the altar lined by sturdy white pillars stretching up into arches, with a smaller row of arches set above, reaching up to the roof. The ceiling was composed of a wondrous number of gold squares criss-crossing, and at the far end a double arch funnelled into a concave altar top alcove adorned with a mosaic of Jesus flanked by angels.

'How about that?' Harker said with admiration, gesturing with an arm raised upwards.

Carter took a moment to take in the sight, then began to nod his head appreciatively. 'Beautiful, yes...but still a bit creepy.'

'You're an odd one, David Carter.'

Carter smiled widely, pushing his glasses back onto the bridge of his nose. 'Now, on that we can both agree.'

They made their way along the lengthy nave until they were within a few metres of the sole occupant of the front pew, who was hunched over and seemingly deep in prayer. Harker motioned for Carter to hang back, then took a seat next to their supposed contact, before quietly repeating the words 'God' had told him: 'The watcher watches us all, but you are free to do as you will.'

Even as he said it, he felt a tad foolish, but the balding man glanced up immediately and with such a sour expression that it dispelled any such feelings in an instant.

'You're early,' he declared in a thick French accent. Then, noting Carter hovering a short distance behind them and suddenly looking decidedly shifty he added, 'I was told there would only be one of you.'

'It couldn't be helped,' Harker replied softly, now growing into his role, 'but that is not really your concern, is it?'

The bald man thought about it for a moment, then with a nod he reached into his tweed jacket pocket and produced a bulky brown package that was, without doubt, large enough to hold another page from the Codex. 'You are to take this for the ceremony,' he instructed before dropping a separate piece of paper into Harker's breast pocket. 'I trust there will be no delay.'

He placed the bulky package into Harker's waiting hands and then, without another word, began to make his way up the nave towards the front entrance.

'Is that it?' Carter asked, obviously surprised by the brevity of the encounter.

'Looks like it,' Harker replied, likewise wasting no time in heading for the door.

'That was easy.'

'I know,' Harker agreed, also surprised by such a hasty exchange.

'So what now?'

'Well, "God" told us to follow the instructions, so I guess we follow the instructions.'

They emerged through the bronze doors into a cascade of beautiful warm sunlight and stepped onto the small white piazza bustling with sightseers.

'I'll call a taxi,' Carter said, retrieving his Samsung mobile. 'Can I have the address?'

Harker pulled the slip of paper he had been handed from his top pocket, and it was promptly snatched from him by Carter, who sauntered away, busily tapping at his phone.

*This seems far too easy*, Harker thought to himself, but after all, what should he have been expecting. He was here to pick up a package and that's exactly what he had done. In fact he should be thankful for the ease with which this secretive rendezvous had occurred.

Taking a moment to enjoy the sun on his face, he closed his eyes as his thoughts turned to Chloe. She must have felt terrified at being kidnapped and, even though he knew she was a natural toughie, an experience like that was likely to rattle the strongest of personalities. The idea of Chloe fearing for her life left him with a bitter taste in his mouth, and he gritted his teeth in anger. He wasn't sure how or when but, when the time came, he would get her back regardless of the cost, and leave her captors with a serious boot up the arse with the help of every and any law-enforcement body he could get hold of. Maybe even the Templars could give him a hand...that is, if they ever got back in touch with him.

It was with these thoughts swirling around in his head that he heard a voice with a distinctly German accent whisper into his ear.

'Enjoying the sights?'

Harker jolted back in shock to find a slim man in his thirties beside him, wearing a black suit and tie and with neatly cut blond hair hanging to one side of his face.

'My apologies,' he said with a peculiarly over-friendly grin, 'I didn't mean to startle you.'

'Not a problem,' Harker replied, shaking off his surprise. 'I'm sorry, but do we know each other?'

'No, no,' the stranger said with eyes wide. 'It is just that I saw you standing there and all I could think of was here is a man with a lot on his mind.' He leant towards Harker and once again offered the same inane grin. 'Everything OK?'

'Fine, yes, thank you,' Harker uttered, starting to feel uncomfortable at the stranger's pushy behaviour.

'Well that's good to hear, because when one visits such a wonderful place, it is a crime not to enjoy its splendour and instead become wrapped up in more personal concerns, is it not?'

There was something about the fellow that gave Harker the chills; not just his words but the way he held himself, and that grin that not only seemed entirely false but appeared to be offered in an attempt to add credibility to his sentiments. And then something occurred to him. 'Do you work for "God"?'

The stranger's grin melted away and his bushy eyebrows tensed into a frown. 'Well, I suppose you could say that every person on this planet works for God, but I myself am not on first-name terms with him...if that's what you're implying?'

Before Harker could answer, Carter bounded up next to them with his mobile phone in his hand.

'I got the taxi and it should arrive in fifteen minutes, give or take,' he stated, before eyeing the stranger warily. 'Is there a problem here?'

'Not at all,' the man offered politely, taking a step backwards. 'We were just, how do you say, shooting the breeze.'

This reply did little to quell the tension now rising between the men and Carter immediately linked arms with Harker and pulled him off to one side.

'Well, nice to meet you, but we have to go now.' Carter gave a wave of his hand and strengthened his hold on Harker's arm, who seemed transfixed by the stranger's unwavering stare.

'Yes, nice to meet you also,' the odd fellow called out after them as Carter and Harker now rapidly put some distance between them.

'Who the hell was that?' Carter asked, glancing back to see the stranger still watching them as they walked away.

'I don't know but…'

'But what?' Carter growled. 'He's obviously some kind of lonely weirdo. Bloody solo sightseer desperate to make a new friend. Come on, we've got a taxi to catch.'

Back in front of the cathedral, the stranger continued to watch his two new acquaintances as they headed back towards the piazza's exit and the busy road beyond. He waited until they were just out of sight and then, with a double clicking of his tongue, he rubbed his hands together, licked his lips…and followed them.

# *Chapter 11*

Dark storm clouds covered the night sky as Harker brought the red Fiat Uno to a stop outside the Cervete cemetery on the outskirts of Rome, its headlights lighting up the rundown entrance building. He had decided to swap their taxi for a rental car after discovering that the address was almost a four-hour drive away, despite complaints from the driver, who understandably coveted such a lucrative fare. Of course, had he known the only car available on such short notice would be this clapped-out 1.1 diesel Fiat Uno, he might have reconsidered staying with the taxi ride.

'This place looks deserted,' Carter observed and, based upon the decrepit and cracked stone walls surrounding it, Harker had to agree.

'It certainly does,' he replied, taking in the unwelcoming sight. The entrance building was an eerie wreck, with its two facing windows boarded up and a battered, sorry-looking wooden door in between them, which had a single splintered plank of wood nailed across its front. It was impossible to determine how far back the cemetery actually ran because of the thick pine trees surrounding the site, but a small visible section of spiked railing starting at the building itself, and disappearing off in between the trees, suggested much further.

Harker switched off the ignition, leaving the headlights on, then retrieved two black Maglite torches they had bought on the journey from the back seat. The instructions had stated they were to drop off the package at four a.m. for the supposed ceremony and, although the exact role they would be playing in it all was still a mystery, he didn't have much choice in the matter. With all this in mind, Harker had decided to arrive early so as to at least scope out the area. Despite the lengthy drive, they had still needed to kill a lot of time along the way. Carter had proposed a late-night bar but was then persuaded, amidst grumbling, to wait in one of the all-night roadside diners they had encountered. Not to be denied, the ex-don had taken to nursing his bottle of Macallan, and it was not until Harker threatened to empty it down the toilet that he had slowed his pace and settled instead for sandwiches and multiple coffees – which of course he 'Irished' up.

'That's yours,' Harker said, dropping one of the Maglites into Carter's lap. 'Let's take a look, shall we?'

His suggestion was met with a disapproving glare from Carter. 'You want me to go inside that rat-infested shack?' He sat, unbudging. 'Not a chance.'

'Fine,' Harker replied before exiting the Fiat, 'but just remember how in the movies it's usually the one left on his own in the car that's the first to get it.'

The comment didn't really make much sense but just the suggestion had Carter glancing in the Fiat's side mirror, and Harker had only taken a few steps towards the decrepit building when Carter called out after him.

'Wait up,' he shouted and, stepping out of the car, he paused and began rummaging through his pocket. It took a moment to retrieve the steel drinking flask he had purchased in the same hunting shop where they had acquired the torches.

Carter flipped back the cap and took a swig before shoving the flask back into his trouser pocket. 'Adequate supplies are essential on any expedition, Alex.'

'So is clarity of mind and good judgement,' Harker retorted with a hint of playful sarcasm that had Carter looking offended.

'That's a bit below the belt,' he muttered under his breath, then made his way over to the boarded-up entrance of the building that Harker had already reached and was now carefully examining.

'Most of the nails have rusted away,' Harker decided, and he roughly jammed his torch between the board and the door, then used his weight to lever it from the few remaining nails.

The board popped off its supports, and Harker caught and then gently laid the section of worn plywood on the ground. Next, with torch in hand, he turned his attention to the door itself, and its rusted lever handle. To his surprise the latch undid with a disagreeable squeak and, after shooting Carter a warning glance, he slowly pushed at the door which swung open with a lengthy creak.

Harker shone his torch around the room beyond, which was empty bar a couple of dusty deckchairs and a three-legged display table in the centre of the room.

The air in here was stale and earthy, with a distinctly spicy aroma that most likely emanated from the dead Campsis plants hanging from thin cracks in the ceiling, which only added to the place's dilapidated atmosphere.

After a quick check behind the door, due to a rising sense of unease, Harker made his way across the room to another door set in a rounded arch directly opposite. Without pausing this time he turned the handle, letting it creak open as with the entrance door and, after a few cautious sweeps of his torch, he continued through it with Carter close behind him.

The cemetery was narrow and, from what Harker could see, about the same rectangular shape and length as an Olympic-sized swimming pool, with imposing four-metre-high stone walls lining its perimeter. The front section where they now stood, about a fifth of the open area, was nothing more than a small earth lawn with two lone gravestones in the middle, and peppered with small clusters of dead brown grass, yet another visual reminder that the place had not seen maintenance for some time.

The cemetery became a lot more impressive at the far end of the lawn, where it met three rows of cobbled paths with a vast assortment of small personal mausoleums or single grave sites bordering them.

'Now that's creepy,' Harker remarked, glancing back at Carter, who merely gave a slow shake of his head.

'Oh, I don't know. I find cemeteries very peaceful places.'

It was hard to tell if he was being genuine or just liked saying the opposite to anything Harker said. Whatever his intention, it was annoying, and Harker simply did not reply. Instead he headed straight for the only thing that drew his attention: two freshly dug graves.

'So what exactly are we looking for?' Carter asked, plodding after him.

'Your guess is as good as mine but these look a good place to start.' Harker had by now reached the two lone gravestones. Both were made of expensive cracked white marble, and he knelt down beside the first one to read out the inscription, which was in Latin. 'Alfonso Bianchi, 1978–2017 and' – Harker shone his torch onto the second stone – 'Daniele Russo, 1980–2017.'

He stood back up and considered these names. 'Don't ring any bells with me. How about you?'

'Never heard of them,' Carter replied with a shake of his head. 'But definitely Italian.'

They stood there in silence, with Harker racking his brain for any kind of lead. He was even running through a list of anagrams for the pair of names when Carter abruptly nudged him on the arm.

'Alex,' he asked, in little more than a whisper, 'when did that "God" fellow say this ceremony would start?'

Harker glanced at his watch and then towards Carter. 'It's only three a.m. now and it's meant to start at four. Why?'

'Well, if that's the case,' Carter said, looking extremely uneasy, 'then who are *they*?'

Harker turned to see the dark silhouette of a man standing no further than seven metres from him. He swung his torchlight towards the figure, and what he saw made him take a few steps back.

The man was wearing a black jumper underneath a dark-brown cloak which descended from his shoulders to barely a few centimetres from the ground. Under that a pair of shiny black combat boots, with shiny metal trims lining the soles, glinted in the beam of Harker's torch. If that wasn't bizarre enough, this attire was topped off with a chilling matt-black face mask with eye holes and a protruding beak, not unlike Gonzo's from *The Muppet Show*.

Most people would not have understood the significance of such get-up but Harker knew. For this was the attire of a plague doctor. Such outfits were worn by medical practitioners in Europe's plague-ridden era and although meant to identify the bringers of life and health, they were often seen as a sign of imminent death and therefore dreaded by most people. It was this same dread that Harker now felt in the pit of his stomach and, as he backed away, he became aware of other figures approaching out of the shadows and beginning to circle them both.

He spun his torch, as did Carter, catching each of the darkened silhouettes in turn and revealing them all to be wearing the same ominous plague-doctor attire as the first.

The small group moved closer, at equal pace, until they formed a circle around the two men, whereupon they halted and stood there silently with their arms crossed.

The feeling of being hemmed in made Harker retreat until he was standing back to back with Carter, whose breathing sounded shallower with each passing moment.

'Who are you?' Harker demanded.

The ensuing silence only added to the rising tension, at least on Harker's part, before one of the mysterious figures took a step forward. He raised his hands in the air and then clapped them together with a sound that echoed throughout the enclosed cemetery. Up above, torches ignited into flame around them in unison, revealing the other dark figures holding them, who were standing all along the sides of the walls and now pointing the fingers of their other hands directly at the intruders.

From the inner circle, one of the masked doctors took a step forward, also pointing an accusing finger, as a deep voice bellowed out from underneath his mask. 'It is we who should ask who you are,' the voice growled, before the pointed finger clenched into a fist. 'You people should not be here.'

The sheer sense of intimidation had Harker at a sudden loss for words and, without revealing anything, he found himself thinking up truly stupid excuses. 'It's a public place' or 'My mother's buried here' were sadly some of the better ones, and he was still in the process of forming a verbal response when the same figure moved a few steps closer, then slowly took hold of the top of his mask and slid it off to reveal a familiar face.

'You,' Harker gasped as he recognized the man who had engaged him in idle talk back at Pisa cathedral.

The blond-haired man revealed the same conceited smile, his lips parting to reveal a set of glinting and unnaturally white teeth. 'Still sightseeing?' he asked coldly.

'Yes, as it happens,' Harker replied politely, already taking a step sideways in the direction of the way out, 'but maybe we should just come back another day.' He had hardly moved when the blond man slapped the back of his hand across Harker's face. It happened so quickly that Harker had no time to react and the impact tipped him off balance, pushing him into Carter's back, who managed to steady them both.

'There's no need for that,' Carter huffed with a genuine air of defiance. 'We will be leaving immediately.'

The click of a gun cocking ended any further debate on that matter, as Harker found himself staring into the barrel of a 9mm Colt automatic held firmly in the blond fellow's fist.

'You're not going anywhere,' he declared, before turning his attention to the nearest masked 'doctor'. 'Take them.'

Starting a fight to resist at this point would have been futile, so Harker allowed himself to be restrained by two of the faux medics. Then, along with Carter, he was marched back inside the entrance building.

The interior was, of course, still bare but with one notable difference in that a part of the side wall had been pulled back to allow access to a further area beyond. Harker couldn't see any hinges and figured the partition must have been on a weighted pulley of some sort. It was a clever yet simple feat of engineering.

Harker was shoved through the opening and found himself being brusquely hauled up two short flights of stairs leading onto the flat roof of the entrance building, which allowed a broad view over the entire cemetery and its surrounding woodland and the fields behind.

The countryside beyond was blanketed by overcast skies and the only available light came from the eight people lining the walls and holding up torches which flickered in the light breeze, illuminating the costumes they wore.

To call them costumes was a stretch, because to Harker they looked more like grey leather butchers' aprons which hung down to their shins, and the simple, yet intimidating, outfit was finished off with a pair of thick black gloves.

Even if these costumes were extremely disturbing, it was the masks that offered the *coup de grâce* and set each of the torch bearers apart. Whereas their body outfits were identical, offering uniformity to the henchmen, the individual masks could not have been more personalized – each with unique symbols, colours and ornate carvings cut into their surfaces.

The only mask Harker could assess in any proper detail belonged to the nearest torch bearer standing up on the wall just a few metres from the rooftop. And although Harker did not recognize all the symbols and letters it bore, he did recognize a few. They were decidedly similar to the text he had seen on the Gigas page from Spreepark. The small parcel they had picked up back in Pisa presumably contained another one of the Gigas pages. 'Presumably' because, despite Carter's pleading for him to open it and take a peek, Harker had resisted, not wanting to tamper with the packaging. It was a precaution that now seemed to have been wholly unnecessary as he was bustled over to one side of the roof, together with Carter, and it irked him not to have found a better hiding place than the inside pocket of his jacket.

'Now,' the blond man continued, approaching Harker, whose arms were still restrained by a couple of personal chaperones, 'perhaps it is time for you to tell me your names?'

Harker eyed the man warily, before reeling off the first name that came to mind. 'Tom Whittington.'

'Tom Whittington!' This answer drew a disbelieving raised eyebrow from the blond man, who immediately turned his attention to Carter, who was doing his best and failing miserably to look calm and relaxed despite his predicament. 'And you, little fat man.'

'William Scratchworth,' came Carter's reply, sounding more like a question than an answer.

'Tom Whittington and Billy Scratchworth? How very Dickensian,' the man announced with a frustrated smile, then he landed a hard slap across Carter's cheek. 'OK, let's forgo your names and start with something a bit closer to my own heart. Why did you pick up a package earlier that was specifically meant for me?'

Clearly the fellow knew they had picked up that item, but Harker was not about to reveal a thing. He raised his chin defiantly and calmly shook his head. 'I'm afraid I have no idea what you're talking about.'

'Mmmm,' their interrogator murmured, and without warning he delivered a hard punch to Carter's ribs, causing the ex-don to bend over in pain before being pulled back up straight by the two 'plague doctors' at his side.

'Well, then,' the interrogator snarled, as Carter whimpered in pain. 'It appears we're in for a long night, doesn't it?'

'Looks that way, because I don't know anything,' Harker said with a defiance that had Carter groaning in anticipation of receiving the next blow.

'Give me a break, Alex,' Carter muttered – and the name was immediately picked up on.

'So it's Alex, is it? Well, that's a start.'

Before Harker could respond, a man in one of the now familiar outfits appeared at the top of the stairs, waving a brown package in the air. 'I've checked their car, Vlad,' he announced in a Slavic accent, 'and it's not there.' The blond man immediately shot the new arrival a look of reproach and it was this awkward slip of the tongue which Harker was quick to seize upon.

'Nice to meet you too, Vlad,' Harker said, and Carter was already bracing himself. But Vlad only offered a smile before turning his attention to the small bulge in Harker's jacket, and with his forefinger he reached over and lightly tapped on his chest, directly upon the Codex page that was nestled in his inside pocket.

'And what do we have here?' Vlad continued, ignoring the gaffe made by his own man, and he reached over and calmly retrieved the package and gently opened it to reveal a folded piece of vellum – undoubtedly another page of the Codex Gigas. 'So I'm guessing you were the one at Spreepark, then? Seems you have been a busy boy.'

Harker said nothing as Vlad passed the section of vellum to one of the men dressed as a plague doctor, who with a respectful nod stood off to one side with the valuable page grasped protectively in his hands as Vlad returned his attention back to his two visitors.

'The whos and whys can wait for now. As you said, it will be a long night for the both of you, and your diligence in pushing your way into our business should be rewarded.' Vlad leant over to whisper in Harker's ear. 'But if you make another sound, I will have your tongue cut out, understand?'

The way he curled his lips when speaking each word was chilling, and Harker offered a stone-faced nod. Vlad then approached the centre of the rooftop and began to address the motionless torch bearers, who still waiting silently along the perimeter.

'Welcome, brothers and sisters, on this most hallowed of nights, to bear witness to the truth that we and our kind have sought since mankind came of age. Your very presence here tonight attests to the resilience and spirit of our beliefs.'

Harker found it an interesting start to the ceremony because it was so close to what he had heard in Spreepark. You didn't have to be a brain surgeon to deduce that these people were all part of the same group, but to have it confirmed was an additional piece of the jigsaw in an otherwise confusing series of events, and Harker was grateful of it.

A hushed murmur of approval now arose from the torch bearers as Vlad continued, his voice gaining in volume.

'Many sacrifices have been made to reach this milestone, and we should never forget that. Even though we are on the precipice of such monumental change, there are still those who would seek to destroy everything we have built so far. But, as you have seen tonight, they will fail as they always do.'

Vlad turned and pointed towards Harker with a scowl before returning his attention to the torch bearers, who were all nodding in agreement.

'For far too long we have been branded outcasts and traitors by the Church, which has seen fit to hijack individual thought and enslave humanity in the process. Well, no more. Tonight sees the birth of a brighter light and a breaking dawn, where the old ways – our ways – lay claim to a world that has not only been promised but bequeathed to us by the true Holy Spirit. I refer to the fallen angel, and the one who was persecuted for embodying everything that it is to be human.'

With a look of fanatical fervour, Vlad raised his hand to the sky even as the torch bearers lifted their flames high. 'Satanael,

Prince of Grigori, we call out to you, Lucifer, to guide our hands and reshape the world in your own image – not His.'

Harker watched uneasily as the nearest plague doctor passed Vlad the now unfolded Codex page, and without hesitation he began to read aloud from the text. The words were like nothing Harker had ever heard before, although he recognized a couple of them as possibly being Aramaic in origin. For the most part, though, it was totally incomprehensible and he shot a wide-eyed glance of astonishment at Carter, who was looking equally perplexed.

The recitation took about two minutes, during which the masked torch bearers, their flames still held high, murmured something unintelligible to themselves. Then, as it came to a close, Vlad refolded the Codex page, dropped to one knee and began to speak in English.

'The two men buried here before us were heretics and judges of the masses.' Vlad pointed down to the two freshly dug graves in the cemetery below. 'Now let those who have judged be among the first to be judged themselves.'

The entire place went silent and then every person went down on one knee, with even Harker and Carter being forced to kneel by their chaperones. Meanwhile Vlad placed his head in his hands, as if he were crying, and began mumbling what sounded like a prayer.

Harker shot Carter another look and, with eyebrows raised, the ex-don mouthed the word 'Awkward'. Although amused, Harker did not smile but it did give him a small sense of relief, like a faint breeze of normality blowing over him while being surrounded by such unpleasantness.

The hushed silence persisted for a couple of minutes, during which time Harker was formulating an escape plan. He was contemplating rushing at Carter, knocking them both off the edge of the roof, with the hope that they might land down below without breaking any bones. The drop could not be more than five metres and he was already tensing his thigh muscles in readiness when something shifted down in the cemetery itself. It was difficult to be sure because the only light came from the flickering flames of the torch bearers ranged along the walls, and he was about to dismiss it as dancing shadows when this time he definitely did see something move.

Harker watched as soil from one of the freshly dug graves began to swell upwards until something thin poked through the surface like the stalk of some plant.

All around the walls, gasps of excitement could now be heard as everyone focused on the fresh grave and as the object continued to rise, it suddenly became clear that it wasn't a stalk...but a hand.

Harker slowly pulled away and, unrestrained by the plague doctors at his side, he stood up to get a better look. In fact they were now doing likewise as the hand below extended further upwards. With the exception of Vlad, who was still praying, everyone was now enthralled by the bizarre spectacle.

The hand rose a few more centimetres and then, like during the formation of a sinkhole, the earth on either side fell away and a man's head emerged, then the upper torso, sitting up and scattering soil all around. The shadowy figure then bent over, placing the palms of his hands on either side of the grave, and hoisted itself upwards until standing upright, sending clouds of dust in all directions. It bent over, sucking in a deep breath before, with head held high, it emitted a blood-curdling, high-pitched scream...as the soil above the other grave also began to tremble.

The figure then stumbled forward and, for the first time, Harker could make out its features in the torchlight. What he saw made him want to throw up as he felt saliva fill his mouth. The creature's face was swollen and a bluish green, where decomposition had begun to set in, and its eyes looked dull and grey. No doubt due to the onset of putrification, the swollen fingertips gave an even more inhuman appearance, and splotches of blood peppered the white shroud it was wearing.

Harker stared in revulsion as the apparition once again screamed loudly, before it stared up towards the flaming torches and swung its arms from left to right as if wishing to grasp them.

'Jesus Christ,' Harker gasped loudly, and his exclamation caught the attention of Vlad, who now finished praying and looked over in his direction.

'No,' he said with a victorious smile. 'You won't find *him* in this place.'

# *Chapter 12*

Another ghastly wail cut through the cool night air as Harker watched the second corpse rise up from the grave and steady itself on its two blackened and seemingly charred feet. It was unquestionably a man but, like its counterpart, the features had been distorted through decay. As it gazed into its own bluish and rotting hands, it released a deeply horrified yelp.

'You see, the judgement is complete,' Vlad declared, gesturing down at these two abominations. 'They were not worthy of the rebirth that we ourselves shall enjoy, but that is not surprising given their choice of faith.'

A low, eerie chanting began to fill the cemetery and, as it grew in volume, Harker watched the two wretched figures now do something that displaced any of the disgust he had felt due to their appearance. The pair stared for a long time at one another and then, falling down on their knees, they embraced with their heads hung low, and it suddenly occurred to him that these two creatures were…terrified.

'They are right to be fearful,' Vlad yelled, before fetching a shiny black rock no bigger than a golf ball from his trouser pocket. 'For *they* shall be the ones to be cast into the lake of fire for all eternity, and we must now show them the disdain they deserve.'

He raised his arm and hurled the stone down into the courtyard, clipping the nearer man on the side of his skull with a painful-sounding thud.

Without need for further incitement, all the torch bearers now produced their own black rocks and, one by one, hurled them down upon their still-cowering victims.

The first couple of blows prompted little reaction, but by the third both men had got to their feet and, with their arms held in front of them for protection, they began to scream wildly, clearly enraged.

To Harker this stone casting was evidently symbolic, but it served its purpose and, by the time the last one had been thrown, the decaying men had reached a fit of rage and began slamming themselves against the nearest wall in a futile attempt to reach their attackers above.

Above their furious screaming, Vlad, with his arms raised skywards, called out to his followers. 'And so here it is – the beginning of our journey. And now let us feast and celebrate the new path that is laid down before us.'

One by one the torch bearers hurled their flaming torches into the courtyard, then descended some ladders on the opposite side of the wall as the screaming pair below them continued to scrape and claw frantically against the cemetery wall.

'Awesome, isn't it?' Vlad announced triumphantly, turning his attention back to Harker. 'To see the power of divine intervention.'

'I don't know what I've just watched but it sure as hell wasn't divine,' Harker replied with a sickened expression.

The comment instantly had Vlad grinning his now familiar inane grin. 'Divinity is in the eye of the beholder, Alex, and you should feel blessed to have witnessed such a sight.'

'Blessed is the right word,' Harker replied, gazing down at the two partly decomposed men still scratching at the stone wall till they left bloody finger marks trailing down its surface.

'Well, how about you?' Vlad turned to Carter, who looked as white as a sheet. He was sweating profusely, with his eyes darting back and forth manically.

'What on earth just happened there?' he stuttered, looking like he was about to throw up.

'So many questions and so little time, hey?' Vlad stated ominously before chewing his bottom lip. 'The power of the Codex is something to behold.'

Both Harker and Carter stayed silent as if encouraging Vlad to explain further, and the man took great pleasure in obliging them.

'What if I told you that the Codex was indeed written by a hand not of this earth?'

In truth Harker was still reeling from the grotesque display he had just witnessed, and to say that he felt baffled was an understatement of huge proportions.

'I know the story,' he said, struggling to maintain his composure. 'About the monk who called upon the Devil to complete the Codex Gigas for him. It's quite a legend.'

'Legend!' Vlad almost spat the word and pointed down at the two men below, still thrashing ineffectually against the wall. 'Does that look like *legend* to you? The Codex was written by the Prince, indeed, but it wasn't the only thing he wrote.'

'The missing pages,' Harker guessed, as Vlad drummed his fingers against his own chest in delight.

'These missing pages contain far more than you could possibly imagine, and tonight revealed but a small part of the power contained within them. There are only a few who can translate the text, and I am one of them.'

Vlad almost managed to sound magnanimous as he continued with an unabated excitement. 'Lucifer knew all too well the hypocritical power of the so-called Lord Almighty, and he saw fit to pass on his knowledge to those who would seek it...within the pages of the Codex.'

Harker already had a dozen questions he wanted answered but decided to focus on just one, which in his mind was the most important. 'If what you're saying is true then what knowledge could be so important that the Devil felt the need to impart it?'

Still grinning, Vlad took a step closer to Harker, his lips opening as if he were preparing an answer. But then he paused and slowly closed his mouth again, as if pondering his reply. It did not take long. 'Do you really not know, Alex? Weren't you the one who stole the page from us in the first place? Perhaps it's high time you explained to me your involvement in all this?'

As Vlad stood back with folded arms and waited for an answer, Harker mulled over his options. If he told this smiling psycho the truth, then Chloe was certainly dead, and if he remained quiet, then both he and Carter were destined for a night of torture and most likely death. With neither option particularly appealing, he remained silent, still trying to figure out what the hell to say. Finally, Vlad flicked his hand dismissively and turned his attention to the still nervous-looking Carter.

'How about you then, porky?' Vlad sneered. 'Want to live through the night?'

With the desperate look of a man willing to sell his soul for a doughnut, Carter offered a sharp nod. 'Of course. We both do.'

Vlad clasped his hands briefly and then grabbed Carter's left cheek and squeezed it between his thumb and forefinger, like a teacher chastising a cheeky schoolboy. 'Good man,' he said, turning his attention back to Harker. 'So we won't be needing you.'

He grabbed Harker by both lapels and, with surprising strength given his slight build, hurled him off the edge into the courtyard below. The landing was hard but fortunately Harker fell on his side on a soft piece of earth, though within centimetres of a jagged piece of masonry sticking up from the soil that would have killed him instantly had he connected with it. The impact knocked the wind out of him but he instinctively jumped to his feet and waited to recover his breath as the nauseous feeling of asphyxiation clouded his senses.

A few unpleasant seconds followed until Harker felt his lungs released from the grip of paralysis, whereupon he sucked in a deep breath and glared up towards the rooftop, where Vlad was waving down at him.

'Don't you even think about hurting my friend,' Harker gasped, concerned less for himself now and more for Carter.

Such concern received a deep bellow of laughter from Vlad, who dropped down on one knee and craned his head over the edge. 'Seriously, he's not the one you should be worried about right now.'

It was just then that Harker realized the screaming and yelling that had been going on in the background had ceased. With a nervous chill gathering in the pit of his stomach, he turned around.

Two sets of dull, grey eyes watched him intently and Harker froze as those two rotting corpses looked him up and down. He couldn't be sure if his imagination was playing tricks, but he could have sworn that one of them licked his swollen black lips.

Up on the roof, Carter began protesting in a most English manner, bawling words such as 'outrageous' and 'despicable' as he was bundled down the steps until out of earshot, with the only noises Harker could hear now coming from inside the courtyard.

A deep wheezing emanated from both of the corpses, their chests heaving, as Harker now found himself in his own personal Mexican standoff.

The two corpses appeared to mimic everything he did. If he swayed to the right, then they did likewise; if he turned his head, then so did they in unison, and a surreal kind of amateur ballet now began to take place upon the dusty ground of the cemetery.

The whole performance could have looked comical, but in Harker's mind there was one thought that kept repeating itself: *Keep them as far away as possible.*

With only this in mind, and after a further rolling of his head which was copied immediately by the gruesome duo, Harker took a single step backwards and, to his relief, they did the same. It was as if they were both looking for guidance on how to behave, happy to be shown how to act, and Harker found himself becoming morbidly fascinated...so long as they kept their distance.

'Hello, lovely evening isn't it?' he called out, pointing up towards the gloomy, overcast night sky. He felt foolish saying it, but if there was a handbook on verbal etiquette for conversing with the undead, then he hadn't read it. As the two corpses opposite him took a moment to gaze upwards, Harker realized he was indeed communicating – on some level at least. While the duo continued to stare at the dark clouds overhead, Harker found himself searching around for a point of escape. The perimeter walls were no more than four metres high but therefore frustratingly out of reach without any kind of step up, and worse still the only possible opportunity to do so appeared to be from the mausoleums scattered over on the far side of the cemetery.

Harker was considering making his way slowly back towards the entrance behind him, with the duo inevitably in tow, when a dark object whistled past him and smacked one of the pair right in the forehead with a loud crack. The corpse barely had time to react before his friend was similarly clipped, but this time on his chest.

Harker looked up to see Vlad retrieving another stone from his pocket. Then, with a delighted grin, he pelted it at the nearest corpse with such force that it embedded itself into the creature's bloated and rotting black thigh with a squelch.

'This isn't meant to be a friendly reunion, Alex,' Vlad shouted out, and Harker winced at this odd use of the word 'reunion'. If he had ever met these two things before he would have remembered for sure, and he pushed the comment from his mind as, nearby, some high-pitched screaming and yelling started up again.

'I would wish you good luck but it would be completely insincere,' Vlad said coldly, and with a wave he disappeared down the rooftop stairwell, leaving Harker alone with his two companions, who were becoming increasingly agitated.

He stretched one arm out in a placating gesture but it was received like a red rag to a bull. The duo immediately began to run towards him, yelling their maddening screams and bringing with them the stench of decay.

Without any need for further encouragement, Harker took off at a sprint through the ruins of the cemetery and towards maze of paths and mausoleums beyond. Leaping onto the nearest path, he caught his shoulder against a sculpture of the Virgin Mary jutting out from the corner of one of the smaller mausoleums. He yelped in pain but continued pushing onwards through a thick and flowerless rose bush whose thorns cut into his face and hands, but thankfully missed his eyes. Harker ignored the burning pain as the sounds of desperate screams echoed around him. Although visually terrifying, the corpses were slow on their feet, which Harker put down to the rotten state of their flesh, but he never looked back and it wasn't until their groans began to fade behind him that he slowed up.

This area of the cemetery was more like a labyrinth and, with only the emerging moonlight to guide him, Harker struggled to navigate it. This was made far worse by not knowing where he was actually trying to get to, and by the time he reached the cemetery's rear wall he was in full panic mode. There was no way out so far as he could see, and he slammed his fist against the stones in frustration before turning to face back down the dark passages running through the cemetery, as the distant groans suddenly petered out into silence.

The sound of a strong breeze whistling between the numerous crypts was all Harker could hear now as he quietly and cautiously made his way over to the nearest mausoleum wall and crouched down against it. The only way out of this place was through the entrance building, which Vlad would have surely secured, and the thought of having to make his way back past those creatures was a frankly terrifying prospect, which left just one option open to him.

Harker stared over to the nearest mausoleum and tried to estimate how far it might be from the cemetery walls. In daylight it would have proved an easy task but, given it was nearly impossible from his location to see the wall's edges, he had to make the best guess he could. Certainly the mausoleum he was next to was too close to the centre of the cemetery to be of any use, but on his frantic dash over here he had passed a couple of smaller tombs with roofs that might prove close enough.

Harker was still figuring out exactly how to get back to them through this maze of monuments when a foul odour began to assault his nose, so he retreated in the opposite direction and around the far side of the mausoleum. He couldn't hear anything but he knew it was close, maybe only metres away, and he did his best to breathe as quietly as possible.

The idea of finding himself suddenly locked in the arms of either of those monstrosities was too horrifying to contemplate but it was through this numbing fear that he eventually found his nerve and a clarity of purpose. There was no way he was going to end up being ripped to shreds by those creatures, not a chance, and he steadied his shaking hands. Staying at a crouch, Harker began to stealthily make his way back along the darkened pathways.

Much to his relief, the further he went the weaker the foul stench of rotting flesh became, and he felt a tremendous sense of relief that every step he was taking served to put a greater distance between him and those walking corpses.

The mental image of their faces and bodies was disgusting, and every time it popped into his mind he immediately extinguished it with thoughts of more salubrious things. If he entertained for one moment the gruesome reality of his situation, that two hideous and disintegrating corpses were at that very moment nearby and looking to get their blackened fingers into him, he might come close to cracking up. So it was with an assortment of wondrous architecture and famous art that Harker filled his mind as he continued silently along the cobbled path until he finally reached a mausoleum within jumping distance of the enclosing wall.

The small private burial vault was plain, decorated with little more than a sculptured angel with wings spread outwards above the sealed entrance, but which provided the means for someone to pull himself up onto its flat roof.

Harker grasped hold of the angel's body and, after a firm tug to confirm it would hold his weight, he prepared to haul himself upwards. But something caused him to pause and he found himself frozen, as the unmistakable odour of death suddenly suffused the air all around him.

Off to his right a pair of eyes glistened dully in the moonlight, and Harker turned to see the disfigured and bloated corpse staring towards him only metres away, just before the apparition unleashed a deafening scream and lunged towards him.

Instinctively Harker kicked one leg up to catch the corpse squarely in the centre of the chest and send it flying backwards before it tumbled to the ground in a heap. As it began to drag itself back to its feet, Harker was already heaving himself up onto the mausoleum rooftop. He had only just managed to get one of his knees safely up there before a hearty force tugged at the other leg that was still dangling. Not wanting to glance downwards, he began to kick out wildly. The first two attempts had little effect against the hands clawing at his trouser leg, but the third finally connected with something that gave way under the impact, and felt like stepping into a bowl of jelly. The thud of a body dropping to the ground motivated Harker to pull himself up fully, and he then glanced back down to see the thing lying on its back while clasping its face with both hands in obvious pain.

Harker scrambled to his feet and steadied himself on the short and narrow rooftop, before taking up position directly facing the main perimeter wall. The jump involved was no more than two metres in distance but the edge of the wall stood higher, and about half a metre above Harker's head, which meant that he not only needed to assess distance but height as well. It would have proved an awkward feat in broad daylight let alone in the almost pitch dark with only shadows as references, but it is remarkable how having a rotting dead guy chasing after you can make one attempt the impossible. It was with this thought that Harker tensed up, took one long stride, and hurled himself towards the outer wall.

His left hand landed too low and slammed painfully against stone, but two fingers of his right hand managed to grip onto the edge and, feeling them beginning to give way under his weight, he lurched upwards and grasped quickly on with his left hand. The weight displacement had without doubt twisted some muscles in his two right-hand fingers but, given the circumstances, it was a price he was happy to pay as he began to pull himself higher up.

As Harker stood upright on the thick stone wall, the clouds overhead dispersed slightly and again the welcome light of the nearly full moon shone through, bathing the cemetery in a silvery glow. 'About bloody time,' Harker hissed as he began making his way along the wall towards the entrance building, leaving the groans and stench of the gruesome twosome behind him.

It took no time at all to reach the end point where the wall met the entrance, now giving him a clear view of the access area beyond, where the interior light of a four-wheel-drive BMW X6 M50d revealed a man tied up inside being shouted at by one of the guards wearing a plague doctor's outfit.

'I want you to sit there and think very carefully, tubby, because we're taking you somewhere very special tonight, and if you haven't told us everything by the time we arrive, then don't expect to ever leave. Understand?'

David Carter stared up at the beaked mask and, with flared nostrils and eyes wide with fear, replied, 'I've told you everything I know—'

At that point the guard landed an almighty slap across Carter's face, before he slammed the rear passenger door shut. 'We'll see,' he muttered audibly to himself and then disappeared out of sight into the main entrance building.

Harker quickly lowered himself from the wall onto the ground, needing to drop the last couple of metres and landing with a light thud. He then manoeuvred his way around to the BMW's driver side and carefully opened the door before sliding inside, keeping his head low.

'Hello?' Carter called out nervously as Harker poked his head around one side of the front seat.

'This is quite a mess were in.'

The look of relief on Carter's face was priceless, and Harker genuinely thought his friend was about to burst into tears.

'Oh, thank God,' he exclaimed, his initial relief now evaporating 'And where the hell have you been?'

'Oh, you know, David, being hunted by two killer ghouls around an eerie old cemetery in the pitch black…and you?'

Such sarcasm was totally lost on Carter, who was already shaking his head defiantly. 'They threatened to torture and kill me, Alex. That man said he was going to ram a cattle prod up my bottom, until I either became "fully charged" or my rectum prolapsed!' Carter was now visibly shaking in anger. 'I mean what kind of sickos are these people anyway?'

Harker didn't reply but instead reached over and was relieved to find the ignition key still in place. Even better, the Codex Gigas page that Vlad had taken back was sitting squarely on the front passenger seat and he almost yelled out loud in relief. 'We're leaving,' he whispered, his voice quivering excitedly, then reached over and turned the key. With a purr, the engine rolled over and, despite requests from Carter to untie him, Harker pressed down on the clutch and was already reaching for the gearstick when the entrance building's door swung open. A long shadow fell across the ground between them followed by the figure of Vlad, whose attention was now fixed firmly upon the BMW.

Harker jammed the gearstick into first and released the clutch so quickly that, when the reviving engine connected, the wheels spun fast and hard against the loose soil and pebbles underneath, sending gusts of dust in Vlad's direction. The road was dry but it felt like steering through thick mud until Harker noticed the red handbrake light glowing. A rookie's mistake to be sure but, given the circumstances, he forgave himself and released it, much to the benefit of the car's engine as it lurched forward and began to pick up speed.

The BMW had already reached 60 mph and Harker was only just managing to keep the car stable on the narrow dirt road when a bullet hit the wing mirror, which shattered, sending pieces flying everywhere. It had to have been of a large calibre to do so much damage and, considering the distance they had already driven from the cemetery, the gunman was a demon of a shot.

A second bullet slammed through the rear windscreen and turned the passenger headrest into a puffball of shredded nylon and leather. It almost caused Harker to careen off the road and into the thick bushes alongside it.

Mercifully there was no third shot and, with no one appearing in pursuit, Harker headed off the back roads and towards the autostrada SS3 leading into Rome. But it was not until they were securely surrounded by other cars all heading into the city that either one of them finally spoke.

'Thank you,' Carter said, having obviously calmed down after the idea of being on the receiving end of a rectal probe.

'I'm just glad we got out,' Harker admitted.

'What the hell did we just witness back there? I don't know whether to believe what I saw or put it down to something like a weird dream.'

'A nightmare is more like it,' Harker replied, still shaking off the thought of those two festering dead men walking. 'We're going straight to Vatican City,' he continued, pausing as he swerved to avoid some idiot in a silver Audi A5, who was jumping lanes without looking. 'There's someone I need to speak with. Someone who might be able to help us.'

There was a moment of silence as both men came to terms with the unholy nature of the events back at Cervete, but it was

Carter who spoke first as he tugged at his bound hands. 'I would appreciate it if you could untie me first, Alex,' he suggested, as the rope began to chafe.

'Of course,' Harker replied, having entirely forgotten about his friend's restraints. 'We'll stop at the next service station, OK? Anything else you need?'

'Yes,' Carter replied, with a look of renewed determination in his eyes. 'A stonking big drink!'

## *Chapter 13*

'Welcome, Mr Davies. It's good to see you again, and looking so well I might add.'

Davies pulled down on the lapels of his Savile Row pinstriped suit and made his way further into the red-lit room and over to the wheelchair and the old man slumped on it.

'Thank you, Mr Winters. You look well yourself.'

'Rubbish. Still, I appreciate the thought.' Jacob Winters smiled through cracked lips and pulled the thin tartan blanket closer to his chest. 'So to what do I owe this welcome, if not unexpected, visit? I trust everything is proceeding to your satisfaction?'

Davies looked troubled as he sat down in the cushioned armchair placed next to the old man and squinted due to the lack of lighting. 'The plan is bearing fruit but the group has some issues with regard to outside interference.'

'Ah yes,' Winters replied with an understanding nod. 'This Harker individual and his friend?'

'Exactly,' Davies agreed with a frown. 'Many of us are feeling rather exposed at having these rogue elements interfering in our business.'

Winters reached over and placed his shaky and crusty hand on Davies's forearm. 'I assure you they are nothing more than a couple of flies in the ointment, and we will get them swatted soon enough.'

Winters's answer did little to alleviate his guest's concern. 'That may be so, but secrecy and anonymity is our greatest protection and, considering Harker's uncanny ability to know where we are meeting on two separate occasions now, we assume he is getting information from someone on the inside.'

Winters didn't look concerned at the possibility but his cheeks flared, creating thick wrinkles around his eyes. 'The thought had occurred to me but I can state unequivocally that it did not come from my side of the fence. The only men involved are but a chosen few and above reproach, which can only mean one thing.'

Winters pulled back his hand and placed it on his lap, with his index finger tapping upon the blanket.

'And that is?' Davies replied awkwardly and already suspecting what the answer was.

'That there is an informer somewhere on your side.'

Davies glared at the old man, looking deeply offended. 'Impossible. That would make no sense whatsoever.'

'Really, and with what reasoning do you reach such a conclusion?'

'Because every one of our families has been chasing this knowledge for generations, and to think that with it finally in our grasp any of us would sabotage it...well, it's unthinkable.'

Winters was already wavering his quivering hand in a dismissive manner. 'Calm yourself, Mr Davies, I am certainly not accusing you. Far from it – your family has been at the spear tip of this endeavour, but don't forget it was we who approached you with the offer of this gift, and not the other way around.'

'For a price,' Davies stated coldly.

'Yes, for a price – which is the very reason that I know it is not from my end that these problems stem.'

Winters took a pause to sip from his water glass as Davies considered the point just being made and then, with a cough, he wiped his lips and with a pained grunt shifted closer. 'You said yourself that your group has been searching for the answer we offer you for generations – with what it would be fair to call an obsession. With that in mind, is it so hard to entertain the possibility that one of them has decided they now want it just for themselves?'

The idea of betrayal appeared to gain some traction in Davies's thoughts, and he sat back in his seat thoughtfully and mulled over the prospect.

'Is there anyone you can think of that might have had the audacity to seize upon such an endeavour?'

Davies remained quiet until finally he crossed his arms and then pursed his lips tightly. 'Maybe.'

It was the answer Winters had been wanting to hear and he rubbed his hands together menacingly. 'Then it appears we now have a place to start. In the meantime I think it would be prudent to have a meeting of all of us to allay any fears this meddling may have caused. How long would it take to gather everyone?'

'Our members from Spreepark are already back in the country, preparing, and the rest from Cervete cemetery can be with us within hours,' Davies replied, getting to his feet.

'Good. Then please arrange it all as quickly as possible,' Winters instructed politely. 'And if you could give me the name of the potential traitor you have in mind, I will have him or her looked into for any...irregularities.'

'Of course,' Davies replied. 'But we need to be sure before any accusations ae made.'

'I understand and, rest assured, I will settle for nothing less than concrete evidence before any accusations begin to fly.'

'Thank you. I will be in touch.'

With that Davies began to head for the door, then paused as Winters called after him with a quavering voice.

'Would you be so kind as to send Albert in, once you have spoken with him?'

'Of course,' Davies replied as he left the room.

After a few minutes a man with dark hair and a loose-fitting grey suit appeared and strode over to stand by Winters.

'Did you get all that?' the old man asked with a sneer, revealing brown-stained teeth.

'I heard everything and I will therefore begin the checks. I'm sure we can dig up something on the person Mr Davies mentioned,' Albert confirmed. He moved closer and bent down on one knee. 'This is a dangerous game you're playing, sir. If anyone discovers that you're the one informing Harker, then it will be all our heads on the chopping block.'

Albert's warning was met with a grimace and Winters patted the man on his chest. 'Dangerous games are the only ones worth playing and, besides, no one is ever going to find out. Not after the meeting that Mr Davies is about to arrange.'

Winters's response was of little comfort to the younger man and he sighed heavily. 'This cat-and-mouse game may seem fun, but wouldn't it just be better to have done with them all, including Dr Stanton? I could arrange that immediately.'

'No.' Winters waved a spindly finger. 'We may need her as leverage and, anyway, this isn't about fun; it's about atonement. Alex Harker will get what's coming to him, but not yet. His troubles are only just beginning.'

# *Chapter 14*

'No,' Cardinal Piero Baptista yelled as he slammed his palm down hard upon the sturdy oak conference table. 'We cannot allow this person to force his way into official Vatican business, especially given the consequences of his last visit.'

Cardinal Michael Boyle sat patiently as Baptista lowered himself back into his seat with nothing further to offer than a scowl. Of course some of the cardinal's reasoning was correct, but to heap all the blame on just one individual was completely unjustified, and Boyle couldn't help feeling much of this animosity was more personal in nature.

'Come on, Piero, that's not fair…the poor man was dragged into this like everyone else. And I might remind you that if he hadn't been, then who knows where it would have led us? Besides, he's a friend of ours.'

This last comment had Baptista seething once again. 'No, he is a friend of *yours*…there is a difference, you know?'

'You're right,' Boyle conceded, 'but, given what he told me over the phone, he may hold some of the answers that we've been searching for.'

Boyle stood up and rested both hands upon the table top, not in a threatening manner this time but rather as a gesture for them to meet halfway. 'Let's see what he has to say, then. What harm could it do?'

Baptista's scowl disappeared and was replaced with a serious look of concern. 'That is what everyone said last time and we all know how that turned out, don't we?'

Cardinal Boyle took this downbeat reply as a yes and, with a gracious nod of his head, he strode over to the double doors, pulled one ajar and muttered quietly to someone outside, 'Send him in.' Boyle then headed back to his seat but decided to stand behind it rather than sit down.

The two cardinals waited in silence and listened as the crisp sound of footsteps on marble flooring grew ever louder, until coming to an abrupt stop just outside. There followed a short knock at the door.

'Come in,' Boyle called out, as the doors swung open and two papal Swiss guards, each wearing traditional blue and yellow striped uniforms, trimmed with red and topped with a military-style black beret, marched inside with their visitor in tow.

'Alex,' Boyle called out with a welcoming smile, offering his hand. 'It's good to see you.'

Harker grasped the cardinal's outstretched hand and shook it firmly. 'Thank you for seeing me at such short notice, Michael. I appreciate it.'

Boyle offered a nod and turned his attention towards the other cardinal, who had already risen from his seat. 'This is Cardinal Piero Baptista.'

Harker reached over and shook the man's limp and obviously unenthusiastic hand. 'It's a pleasure, Cardinal,' he said politely, but his greeting was rewarded with little more than a sneer. So when Boyle motioned to the spare chair next to him, he was happy to take it.

In his late forties and with thick strawberry-blond hair, Michael Boyle had always been a straight talker, willing to give anyone a chance, but unforgiving to anyone who betrayed his trust or did not behave 'on the level', as he was so fond of putting it. Harker had met this Irishman at a charity event long after quitting the priesthood, and the two of them had rapidly clicked and become good friends. Although they rarely met up, Harker made a point of emailing the man several times a year, just to keep the bond alive. And when Boyle was made a cardinal earlier that year, Harker had been one of the first to congratulate him.

The grey-haired and much older Piero Baptista, on the other hand, was a complete unknown to Harker and, despite hearing the name over the years, the only thing he had to judge the cardinal by was the look of deep mistrust being aimed at him as he took his seat.

'I asked Cardinal Baptista to join us here because of the' – Boyle paused and rubbed his brow uncomfortably – 'unusual nature of your phone call. Something to do with...living corpses, I believe?'

The very mention of such a notion had Baptista wincing and, as Harker began to elaborate upon the telephone call he had made earlier, even Boyle developed a sceptical glint in his eye.

'Before we begin I want you to know that, no matter how strange this sounds, I'm only telling you the events I witnessed with my own eyes, and not making any assumptions that I myself may or may not have drawn.' This came out of Harker's mouth sounding more like a plea than an explanation, and although both of the cardinals remained silent, their expressions signalled deep misgivings.

'I'm not sure exactly how to say this, so I'll just say it,' Harker continued awkwardly. 'During the past twenty-four hours or so, I have seen three people – all of them dead – come back to life. The first I had seen strangled in front of my eyes only for him to wake up and walk out of a Berlin morgue several hours later. The other two had been dead for, I guess, several days or more, but managed to pull themselves out of their graves and begin walking around...as if alive.'

'How do you know they had been buried for days?' Baptista asked, stony-faced.

'Well, their rotting skin and bloated bodies were a dead giveaway. And if you smelt the stench coming off them, I think you'd have reached the same conclusion.'

The cardinals both stared at him in shocked silence.

'You say you saw a man actually strangled to death?' Boyle finally asked uneasily.

'Yes, I did,' Harker replied firmly. 'He was almost as close to me as you are now.'

'Was it reported to the police?'

'Yes, but after showing me security footage of the same man walking out of the morgue on his own two feet, they reckoned it was some kind of publicity stunt and didn't want to know any more.'

'Perish the thought,' Baptista muttered coldly, while rolling his eyes.

'What's that supposed to mean?' Harker queried blankly, not allowing his anger to get the better of him.

'It means, Mr Harker – or is it Professor?' Baptista subdued Boyle with a raised hand as he was on the verge of intervening. 'It means that since you showed up at the Vatican…what, over a year and a half ago, the Church has suffered more destruction than in the last two hundred years.'

'What?' Harker protested, feeling genuinely shocked by this accusation.

'Since your initial mysterious meeting with the last pope, John Wilcox, we have had that same pope go AWOL, then a shooting inside the Basilica, directly in front of the world's media, not to mention world leaders. And, on top of all the malicious and damaging gossip that I will not even go into now, out of respect for the unfortunate dead…there now comes this.'

Cardinal Baptista rose to his feet and made his way over to a drawn curtain on the opposite side of the room, flinging it open to reveal the crumbled ruins of what had once been St Peter's Square. 'Behold the aftermath of the atrocious event that not only led to the deaths of over fifty thousand innocents, but that of the recently elected pontiff himself, his holiness Salvatore Vincenzo.'

Harker, followed by Boyle, walked over to the window and gazed down upon the destruction. The media had been awash with images of the devastation which the HAARP weather machine had left in its tracks and, even though Harker had watched all the television coverage, this was the first time he had actually seen it with his own eyes. Emergency services had spent over a week sifting through the rubble, and the fifty-metre crater underneath it, before completely walling off the entire area from the public and banning any helicopters or planes from flying over Vatican City. The whole expanse had been kept from the prying eyes of the media by order of the new pontiff himself and, with so many people lost and the near impossible undertaking of identifying all of the dead, including Pope Vincenzo, there was talk of turning this pulverized holy site into one large ceremonial tribute to the dead.

Next to it, the entire facade of St Peter's Basilica had been ripped away, revealing the crumbling remains of individual rooms. And although covered with giant yellow tarpaulins, it now looked more like a crumbling classical ruin than the epicentre of the Catholic faith. Below its remnants, JCB diggers lined the crater's edges, along with two giant cranes erected at opposite ends of the square and, even as Harker took in the awful sight, workmen continued clearing rubble and laying new foundations for whatever restoration plan the Vatican had decided upon.

'Surely you can't blame me for all this?' Harker ventured, in barely more than a despondent whisper.

'Oh yes,' Baptista replied angrily, 'the weather machine. Reported by the media and then discounted soon after by the same journalists as pure fantasy. That was quite a story you concocted.'

Even though it seemed the blame for all those terrible events was now being dumped at Harker's feet, he remained silent for a moment as he surveyed this utter destruction that had cost so many lives. He had not been directly responsible, although used as pawn in the Magi's twisted plans, at every stage of the way under the guidance of Pope Adrian VII, better known to his acquaintances as John Wilcox. But, of course, the cardinals didn't know that important detail. That sinister and despicable group of zealots, which evolved out of two thousand years of hate and greed, and their vile attempts to take control of the Catholic Church and hijack the minds of its followers – no, he had not been party to it at all. And even though that same twisted organization had been obliterated, with help from the Knights Templar, Harker could do little to stem the feeling of guilt and responsibility that suddenly hovered over him now like a dark cloud. Could he have done more to prevent those disasters?

'What are you saying exactly?' he asked, suddenly feeling drained of energy.

'I am saying that even as the fortunes of the Catholic Church have declined,' Baptista rasped, 'your own fame – or should I say infamy – has risen. And, after all that has happened, you now turn up here with further tales of murder and resurrection which debase the memories of all those who lost their lives in events that, at every turn, you have been connected to.'

Harker felt his spirits sag as Baptista speedily swished the curtains shut. 'You, Professor Harker, are what sailors term a Jonah,' the cardinal continued, before taking his seat again at the conference table. 'You bring bad luck to all those around you.'

This damning attack left Harker speechless and, in a moment of weakness, he began to feel sorry for himself. It was true that, since establishing the existence of the Knights Templar and their ongoing war with the Magi, everyone he held dear had experienced some measure of bad luck – and Chloe was just the latest victim. Sure, the Magi were gone, defeated, but he still found himself embroiled in events that served only to hurt the ones he loved. Could Baptista somehow be right? Had something unseen rubbed off on him during his recent exploits? Something real? Was he genuinely a Jonah of sorts, destroying the lives of all those around him by just being alive?

As he asked himself these questions, and before his feeling of self-pity grew any stronger, he remembered something that Sebastien Brulet, the now deceased former Grand Master of the Knights Templar, had written in his goodbye letter.

> *I leave you therefore with one last piece of advice. Some secrets have the power to warp a person's sensibilities, and in doing so transform them into the very thing they most deplore. Be wary of this, my friend, and never allow yourself to veer aside from the path of what you know to be right.*

Those simple words of guidance immediately renewed a sense of purpose in Harker and suddenly he felt himself imbued with renewed determination. He couldn't control the extraordinary events that seemed to follow him, but he would damn well make sure he did everything in his power to bring them to a righteous conclusion.

'Please forgive him, Alex,' Boyle offered, placing a reassuring hand on Harker's shoulder. 'Piero lost many friends in the great destruction and I am afraid, you, unjustly, have become the focus of his anger.'

Harker looked over at the glaring cardinal and patted Boyle's arm reassuringly before returning to the conference table, now with renewed vigour.

'There are no words that can adequately describe the tragic loss of life or the damage done to the Church, but I will not let myself be blamed for things that were totally out of my hands,' Harker declared resolutely, standing there with a steely look in his eyes. 'My actions have always been in the interests of preserving life and if you can't accept that, then that is something for you to come to terms with...not me. And I hope in time you will come to realize this, but it is your decision to make, not mine.'

Harker's abrogation of responsibility appeared to only chip away slightly at Baptista's anger. But as he continued, the man's glare began to soften.

'Everything I have told you about these "resurrections" – or whatever you want to call them – is true. I have no cause to lie and the only reason I came to you is that, given the disturbing and ungodly nature of what I have witnessed, I felt that you could give me some guidance, because frankly... I am out of ideas. Now you can either help me to figure out what the hell is going on or not, but either way I am resolved to find out... It's your choice.'

The anger in Baptista's eyes had now diminished noticeably, but he still sat there motionless and without saying a word.

'Of course we'll help, Alex,' Boyle stated resolutely, smiling at Baptista. 'It's just such a lot to take in... Tell me, do you even know who these two "corpses" might have been?'

Boyle's conciliatory tone brought a lighter atmosphere into the room and Harker seized upon it, finally resuming his seat and planting both his elbows on the table.

'There were two names on the headstones: one was Alfonso Bianchi and the other Daniele Russo. I can't remember the birth dates but the dates of death were definitely this year.'

Harker had barely uttered the names when both cardinals exchanged a look of wide-eyed astonishment. Without pause, he pushed for further information. 'Do those names mean anything to you?'

It was clear that Boyle did know something, because he had begun to bite his bottom lip nervously. Then he turned back to face Harker, despite a warning shake of the head from Baptista.

'Eight days ago there was an accident—'

'Michael, this is not the time,' Baptista interrupted, visibly annoyed with his colleague's admission.

'If not now, then when?' Boyle replied and, still under the disapproving stare of Baptista, he continued. 'As I said, there was an accident just outside Rome eight days ago. A truck careered into a passing car, killing all three of its occupants.'

'Who were they?'

'Three local priests on their way to a regular meeting of the local clergy. Nothing out of the ordinary. They were taken to Rome's American Hospital but were sadly pronounced dead on arrival. Then four days ago each was interred in his own parish's cemetery.'

Boyle, now looking considerably perturbed, glanced over at Baptista, who also appeared increasingly uncomfortable.

'Please continue,' Harker prodded, sensing their uneasiness.

'That night two of the graves were desecrated, and in the morning both bodies had vanished.'

Harker already knew who they were talking about and ventured the names: 'Father Alfonso Bianchi and Father Daniele Russo?'

'Yes.' Boyle gave a sombre nod as Baptista looked on. 'We thought it was some kind of sick joke... You wouldn't believe the things some people do these days.'

*Oh I believe it all right*, Harker thought to himself, reflecting on the cemetery at Cervete. 'So what happened to the third body?'

Boyle's face began to pale as he contemplated what appeared, from his pained expression, to be the most difficult part for him to reveal. He first glanced over at Baptista, and this time received a grudging nod of the cardinal's head.

'I'll inform Dr Wheatley that we're on our way.' Boyle abruptly rose from his seat. 'Perhaps it's best you should see for yourself.'

## *Chapter 15*

The muffled rumbling began within moments of Harker entering the dimly lit corridor, like a warning to any and all that dared venture within the bowels of the Vatican's Governorate building basement. At first it sounded like the vibrational buzz of a clothes dryer but, as Cardinal Boyle led Harker ever deeper, followed by Cardinal Baptista, it became clear that what he was hearing was something entirely different.

'Don't worry,' Boyle reassured him in acknowledgement of the ever-increasing noise. 'It's secure.'

This mysterious response to a question no one had asked made Harker feel even edgier, but he wasn't sure which part of the statement he was more concerned about: the mention of an 'it' being secure or that anything needed securing in the first place. Despite the numerous questions brewing in his mind, starting with the reason for sneaking around in the lowest levels of the Vatican's administration building, he remained quiet, even as the noise escalated into a ferocious banging sound.

'Here we are,' Boyle announced loudly, and he waved first Harker and then Baptista through a doorway situated at the end of the corridor, before closing it behind them all with a hefty clank.

Inside, two heavy-set men in jeans and matching leather jackets sat at a desk facing nothing but a single metal door lined with double reinforced edges.

The two guards stood up and greeted the cardinals respectfully, and Harker could not help but notice the 9mm black steel Berettas holstered to their thighs.

'Is it normal to have armed guards here inside the Governorate building?' he asked, as one of the men moved over to the secured doorway and, unclipping a key from his belt, began to unlock it.

'No, it is not,' Boyle responded, 'but unfortunately necessary, given the circumstances.'

The cardinal's response only heightened the tension as the guard swung the door open, but Harker continued to stay tight-lipped as he followed Boyle and Baptista inside, both cardinals now taking the lead.

The secured entrance opened into a brightly lit and much larger room with grey concrete walls serving to complete the basement feel, and with a separate passage leading off to some other area at the far end. Neon strip lighting hung from the ceiling, while narrow steel benches lined the perimeter and looked in towards a central desk flanked by white metal filing cabinets. From behind a desktop PC monitor, a man in an olive-coloured wool jumper and dark-brown slacks rose to his feet and welcomed the new arrivals with a strained smile.

'There's been another change,' he explained in a Southern American accent, and then paused abruptly on noticing Harker.

'It's fine,' Boyle replied, 'he's a friend, so feel free to speak candidly. Professor Alex Harker, this is Dr Gavin Wheatley, who is kindly affording us his services.'

Harker reached in between the two cardinals and shook Wheatley's hand. 'Pleasure,' he said, which was received with a polite nod, and the man now turned his attention to the hellish thudding sound emanating from along the passageway at the end of the room.

'What is that noise?' Baptista asked, turning paler with every thud.

'We gave him a mild muscle relaxant and something to help him sleep but, as you can hear, it's not had much effect. He keeps pounding on the walls. It's been non-stop for the past half an hour.'

'I thought he was secured?' Boyle quizzed, glancing anxiously towards the source of the heavy thumping.

'We had him in a straightjacket earlier but he ripped through it, so we've now secured him with straps as best we can. But as you can hear, the restraints are having a limited effect.'

'He ripped a straightjacket?' Harker asked, amazed that such a thing was even possible.

'I know,' Dr Wheatley replied, 'but, given his current size, it's understandable.'

'Current size,' Harker repeated. 'Who is this man?'

While the other two stood silently, Cardinal Boyle headed over to the furthest filing cabinet, slid open the top drawer and pulled out a thin brown folder containing two A5-size photographs. 'This is Bishop Alfonse Esposito.' Boyle passed one of the photographs over to Harker. 'He was the third unfortunate to die in the traffic accident I mentioned earlier.'

The picture showed a thin black-haired man wearing a blue T-shirt and jeans, who was leaning against a wooden fence in an obvious pose. 'OK,' Harker said, turning his attention back to Boyle, who was now looking decidedly reticent. 'So what happened exactly?'

Boyle paused to clear his throat, then clutched the image side of the second photo to his chest, obviously not yet ready to show it. 'He was buried along with the others, on the same day, and as with the other two men his grave was desecrated overnight and the body removed.'

'Go on,' Harker coaxed, feeling like extracting an explanation was akin to pulling teeth.

'Well, unlike the other two, Bishop Esposito reappeared yesterday within his parish...' Boyle licked his lips with distaste. He then flipped over the photo to reveal the image of Esposito being forcibly restrained between a couple of suited men, his body contorting violently as he attempted to break free.

At first it looked to Harker as if the man's mouth was impossibly wide open and in the act of screaming but, as he moved closer he realized it wasn't that the man's mouth was open, but that there was no mouth at all. Esposito's entire bottom jaw was missing, revealing the bloodied opening of his throat, with a swollen black tongue that hung limply downwards.

'Oh my God,' Harker muttered as he plucked the photo from Boyle's fingers and began to study it in depth. The macabre appearance of Esposito's mouth was nauseating in itself, but the fact that the entire top portion of the man's face was skinless, and with only one clouded eye remaining, was enough to make Harker gag before thrusting it back into Boyle's hand. It wasn't only the photo that was now causing him to gag, for it bore some of the gruesome qualities of the poor devils he had seen back at Cervete cemetery, and he took a moment to compose himself as Boyle replaced the offensive photo in its folder.

'Is this how the two men you told us about looked?' Baptista asked.

Harker was quick to shake his head. 'There are similarities, like the swollen tongue, but the damage to the men I saw were the result of decomposition, whereas that...'

'Looks like it was inflicted with violence,' Dr Wheatley said, finishing Harker's sentence.

'Exactly,' Harker replied, as Wheatley went on to confirm.

'Well, it was. The removal of the jaw, skin and eye all happened sometime between the burial and his reappearance at his parish, because it was an open coffin and he certainly didn't look like that during the funeral service.'

'Why would someone do that?' Harker exclaimed, more as a statement than a question, but it was jumped on furiously by Baptista.

'Why! The only question pertinent at this time is how is he still alive? The man was dead!'

All three men looked over at Dr Wheatley, who was looking just as perplexed. 'Every test I've done shows that Bishop Esposito is indeed alive. His lungs, heart, blood transfer are all functioning well within the normal range, but apart from the obvious, there are some bizarre processes at work that I just can't account for.'

'Like what?' Harker asked.

'Like the fact that his body has visibly gone through the early stages of decomposition but it refuses to begin any form of healing itself, and yet it doesn't degrade any further.' Wheatley rubbed the palm of one hand across his lips in frustration. 'It's as if his body is suspended in a kind of biological limbo...or it was at least up until last night.'

It was now Wheatley who was looking shaken, and at this exact same moment the noisy thumping coming from along the corridor ceased.

'So what happened last night?' Harker demanded, ignoring the sudden silence.

His question was met with a blank stare from Wheatley, and Harker glanced over at Baptista, who offered a nod of approval.

'Last night Bishop Esposito began to...change.'

'Change!' Harker sputtered, and he leant in closer, as beside him Boyle began nervously playing with his fingers.

'Yes, his red and white blood-cell count almost doubled within an hour, along with increased brain activity so far as we can tell.' Wheatley motioned to the sparse-looking corridor behind him. 'We don't have all the necessary equipment for a comprehensive test but that's what appears to be happening and, given his shift in muscle mass and the increasing facial distortions—'

'Muscle mass?' Harker interrupted, not quite sure what the man was alluding to.

'Take a look for yourself.'

With a wave of his hand, Wheatley did an about-turn and made his way down the corridor. Harker was already following when he noticed that both Boyle and Baptista were not moving a centimetre. Warily, he stopped in his tracks.

'You're not coming?' he asked, surprised by their sudden unwillingness to continue.

'We've already seen him,' Boyle replied nervously. 'There's no need to do so again.'

Baptista said nothing and, seeing that the two cardinals clearly had no wish to discuss it further, Harker turned and hurried to catch up with Wheatley.

'Dr Wheatley?' Harker called out, and although the physician momentarily glanced back over his shoulder, he continued to walk at a brisk pace. 'Has anyone thought of getting some extra staff in here to deal with this? I mean you look pretty undermanned down here.'

His comment on the vacant corridor drew a wry smile from the doctor.

'Understaffed? The word you're looking for is non-existent,' Wheatley said disparagingly. 'I'm the only one here and, given what's been going on, it has to stay that way. The cardinals are only right to keep this business under the radar. I mean, can you imagine what would happen if word got out that a dead Catholic bishop suddenly decided to just jump out of his grave and start walking around again? Especially looking as he does: dead but yet alive.' Wheatley's shoulders shuddered at the idea. 'The media circus would be one thing but there's no telling how all the other cardinals would react.'

'Just a minute,' Harker said, grabbing the man by the arm and bringing him to a stop. 'Are you telling me that no one else knows about this? Not even the Pope?'

Wheatley appeared twitchy at the question and his jaw muscles tensed firmly. 'Apart from you, me, both cardinals and those two guards who were brought in privately, no one knows a thing.'

Harker was dumbfounded by this response and he was already opening his mouth to voice concerns when Wheatley raised his hand between them.

'The cardinals believe, as do I, that until we know what is happening here, this must all stay hidden. Look around you, Professor.' The doctor gestured towards the empty corridor.

'This part of the building was constructed for storage, not medical purposes. The whole thing happened so fast, we're only just managing to keep on top of it.'

Wheatley resumed his brisk pace, clearly agitated at the position he found himself in.

'I'm not saying you have to tell the Pope this very minute,' Harker continued, while keeping up with him, 'but didn't you even consider getting some other doctors involved? There must be others you can trust over this, if only for a short time?'

'Up until last night I might have agreed with you, but not now given the current state of Esposito.'

Wheatley's tone was final, and Harker now accepted it as such. It was clear that man was under tremendous pressure from Boyle and Baptista to remain shtum, and their stance was understandable, although in Harker's opinion slightly misguided.

The rest of their short walk was made in silence and, after passing several empty storage rooms with their doors all wide open, they finally reached the only one which was firmly shut.

'He's in here,' Wheatley said softly, resting his hand on the door. 'This room was designed to keep any valuables that the Vatican was storing temporarily, works of art and the like, so there's an inner barred door as well as this one.'

'That's handy,' Harker replied, and if the remark sounded sarcastic, the doctor didn't notice.

'It's why we chose it.' Wheatley exhaled deeply. 'He now reacts very badly to the light, as it sends him into a rage like you heard when you arrived, so after I open the door, we'll wait for him to acclimatise to the corridor lights, dim though they are.'

'And then?' Harker pressed, beginning to feel a tightening in the pit of his stomach.

'And then I'll turn on a few of the smaller side lights, as they don't seem to bother him so much.'

Harker gave a nod and then took a step back as Wheatley pulled a Yale key from his trouser pocket and tentatively inserted it into the lock.

'No loud noises,' he warned ominously, 'and no matter how irate he gets, stay calm.'

The doctor's last few words sent an unpleasant shiver down Harker's spine just as the lock released with a click, and Wheatley slowly swung open the door.

Harker's apprehensive stare was met by what seemed a wall of pitch black, as the corridor's strip lighting cast a single thin path of light beyond the interior barred door, creating a pattern of squares along the green linoleum-tiled flooring and up onto the concrete wall at the rear. From what he could see – which wasn't much – the room looked empty. But, as Harker ventured closer to the bars, something shuffled off to his left. What it was he couldn't tell but, as his vision began to adjust, he started to make out a hunched shape – over close to the floor in the far corner of the room.

'He's over there,' Wheatley whispered softly, pointing to the dark shadowy mass. 'He goes through these periods of violent rages followed by lengthy moments of unresponsiveness.'

Now knowing roughly where Dr Wheatley's patient was, Harker felt emboldened to move closer to the bars until just within centimetres of them. He called out in the most compassionate tone he could muster, 'Bishop Esposito.'

The sound of Harker's voice caused the shape to twitch slightly and then the momentary glint from an eye could be seen glancing over in his direction before becoming shrouded once again in the gloom of the cell. The shuffling started up again and began to get louder as the huddled shadow shifted slowly from one side to another, moving quicker with each repetition, and the now audible sound of heavy breathing quickly turned into a forced panting. The swaying continued with increasing speed, faster and faster as the panting morphed into a low-level growl, and then in an instant the movement stopped. The shadowy mass gradually began to stand up until its back was straight and taut, revealing bulky shoulders that jutted out on either side.

'Careful,' Wheatley warned. 'He's very unpredictable.'

Harker glanced over at the doctor and acknowledged him with a nod before turning back towards the cell just as something massive exploded from the darkness into the light and slammed hard against the metal bars with such a force that the whole frame shuddered. It was as Harker recoiled in alarm that he got his first proper look at the thing that was Bishop Esposito.

Both the man's shoulders protruded outwards like bony shoulder pads, while the arms bulged in places with lumpy fat deposits that almost enveloped the thick leather restraints strapped around each wrist. Every one of his fingers was missing its nail, and the denuded tips had become hardened and withered, resembling a claw more than a human digit. Worst of all though was the head, which looked painfully swollen around the forehead, and the orbital bones surrounding the eye sockets had increased in size to give a goggle-type appearance but without the lenses, and in just one of them, nestled deep, a single red eye whose capillaries had burst. The jaw itself was clearly missing but the tongue seemed more ridged than in the photo, and it flapped up and down with each foul-smelling breath expelled as the creature began to howl incessantly.

'What the fuck is that?' Harker gasped as he was steadied by Dr Wheatley, who was vastly more relaxed, having undoubtedly become used to the grotesque sight.

'That is Bishop Esposito…or what's left of him.'

Harker suddenly felt weak and held on to Wheatley's shoulder in a bid to remain upright. Even the disgusting sight of the two decomposing men back at the cemetery paled in comparison with this horrendously deformed creature now rattling violently against the bars of its prison.

'Close the door,' he begged, and Wheatley obligingly reached over and pushed the door shut, plunging the still screaming Bishop Esposito into complete darkness once again.

Harker collapsed back against the corridor wall and fought the instinct to throw up, but the urge was too strong and he hunched over and vomited. Wheatley placed a steadying hand on his back and then passed him a clean handkerchief.

'If it makes you feel any better, I'm a physician but I had exactly the same reaction.'

'No, it doesn't.' Harker coughed and wiped the spittle from his lips, then offered the soiled handkerchief back to its owner.

'You can keep it,' Wheatley said with a smile, whereupon Harker managed a thankful nod and placed it in his jacket pocket. He then stood up, his composure now returning to him.

'How long has he been like that?' Harker asked, aware of the beads of sweat forming on his brow.

'Like I told you, since last night. So the change from what you saw in the photo to that thing in there has happened in only hours.'

The thought of such a drastic transformation made Harker feel somewhat lightheaded. The concept of the dead returning to life was hard enough to swallow, but this approached the incomprehensible.

'I know this is a lot to take in,' Wheatley offered sympathetically as he guided Harker back along the corridor and away from those ear-piercing screams, 'but there's something else you should see.' He reached into his pocket and pulled out several scraps of paper with scrawled notes pencilled on them. 'When the bishop first arrived, I gave him paper and pens in an attempt to communicate, given his' – Wheatley motioned towards his own lower jaw – 'inability to talk. Take a look at what he wrote.'

Harker plucked the crumpled notes from Wheatley's hand and began to examine them carefully. The writing was no better than a child's but, given the poor fellow's condition, it was remarkable he had managed to write anything at all. He scanned the pages and saw that they consisted of – the same three words repeated over and over again.

'*Giorno del giudizio*,' Harker uttered and, with a rising sense of dread, he looked over at Wheatley, who was looking decidedly pale and gaunt.

'*Giorno del giudizio*,' the doctor repeated, for the first time looking truly afraid. 'Judgement day.'

# *Chapter 16*

'Where the hell have you been?' Carter thundered. 'I've been waiting here for almost three hours.'

'Not now, David,' Harker snapped as he made his way out through the Vatican's southern entrance and onto the scorching hot pavement. He had left the ex-don with strict instructions to sit on the bench nearby and wait for him but, judging from the somewhat glazed expression on his friend's face and the smell of whisky on his breath, those orders had been totally ignored. 'And I thought we agreed to no drinking.'

Carter's bloodshot eyes widened with incredulity and he shook his head, swaying from side to side with the posture of a drunken driver pleading his innocence to the officer arriving on scene. 'I have not been drinking,' he protested fervently. 'Not real drinking, anyway – only a few scoops from the local watering hole. And, anyway, what would you have me do while you take off and leave me for hours on end?'

It felt like the beginning of the nightly row between an old married couple, and Harker took a deep breath. He knew all too well about his friend's 'life choice', and arguing about it right now wasn't going to help one bit. 'Fair enough, David. It's just been a difficult couple of hours.'

'Are you all right?' Carter replied, now taking note of Harker's dishevelled appearance. 'You look like you've been to hell and back.'

In Harker's mind that wasn't too far from the truth, given the demonic appearance of Bishop Esposito, and he slumped onto the same bench that he had ordered Carter to stick to like glue before himself entering Vatican City. 'I think I just have,' he admitted in little more than a whisper as Carter sat down alongside.

'So what happened in there? Can they help?'

'No, I don't think so. In fact I'd safely say they have their hands full at the moment.'

Harker wasn't being deliberately evasive, but his vague response had Carter now insatiably curious.

'Well go on, then,' Carter slurred. 'Spill the beans.'

This distinctly British expression made Harker smile and, for some inexplicable reason, he began to relax. 'It turns out that those two corpses we saw rising from their graves weren't the only examples of such a miracle. There was another, too, who at this very moment is being confined in a storeroom underneath the Governorate building.'

If Carter was shocked, he certainly wasn't showing it but, considering how soused he was, there was probably no surprise there.

'If that wasn't crazy enough, as of last night the third dead man has transformed into a snarling creature the likes of which I could never even have dreamt of. And, to top it all, the three words he seems obsessed with are "*Giorno del giudizio*", which means Judgement Day in Italian. Oh, and did I mention that all three men were priests who died in the same car accident earlier this week?'

Carter finally appeared to be grasping the gravity of what he was hearing as it sank into his inebriated mind. Nevertheless he remained obligingly quiet as Harker despondently finished his tale.

'As of this moment I have absolutely no idea what the hell is going on. And therefore I'm no closer to finding Chloe, whose life, I don't need to remind you, is on the line.'

'Bloody hell, Alex,' Carter finally exclaimed, appearing to have sobered a bit. 'Do you really think there could be some truth in…you know, Judgement Day being at hand?'

Harker had already been mulling over that possibility on his way out of the Governorate. He had ultimately been unable to offer Boyle and Baptista anything that might help, but he had promised to say nothing to others beyond Carter.

The two cardinals had been unwilling to say what they themselves thought it all meant, but Harker could tell that the idea that Judgement Day could already be set in motion as of that moment was genuinely having an impact on them too. Christ, the newly transformed Esposito could even be described as looking like a traditional demon. Of course, reality had then kicked in and although, yes, what he had seen had undoubtedly appeared to defy the laws of nature, it was a far cry from thinking that Judgement Day was imminent. Just considering the whole concept gave him a headache.

'All I know is that during the past few days I've witnessed one suicide, one murder, two corpses risen from the dead – make it three if you count the strangled guy – also a creature resembling something out of a Stephen King novel. And, to top it off, my girlfriend's been taken hostage by a man I know nothing about, calling himself "God", who has had me running around all over Europe.' Harker rubbed his eyes and slumped even lower on the bench. 'I doubt things could get any worse now, do you?'

A bleary-eyed Carter was still attempting to find something positive to say when a black Mercedes limo pulled up alongside the pavement next to them. A blond-haired man wearing a snazzy silver-grey suit and aviator steel-rimmed sunglasses got out from the driver's side and, with the door still open, he rested both elbows on the car's rooftop.

'Professor Alex Harker?' the man began in a deep voice, pointing a gloved finger in Harker's direction. 'We've been looking for you.'

The timing could not have been more perfect and Harker rubbed his eyes once more, then turned to Carter. 'Great, now even the Mafia's after us!'

The driver slammed the door shut and walked around the vehicle until he stood within a metre of them. With a courteous bow he removed his sunglasses to reveal a pair of light-grey irises, and in that instant Harker felt heartened. This man was unquestionably a Templar.

'You have an invitation to meet with Tristan Brulet,' the Templar announced before he opened the Mercedes's passenger door. 'If it's convenient, that is?'

Harker was already on his feet, and pulling Carter to his, when the man raised an open palm towards them.

'The invitation is only for you, Professor.'

Harker looked over at Carter, who, perhaps influenced by the drink, was now gazing up at him with puppy-dog eyes that said 'Don't leave me, please.' So, with a woeful sigh he turned back to face the Templar. 'I am afraid it's both of us or neither of us.'

The Templar thought about that for a second, then gave a polite nod. 'Two it is, then.'

Without another thought, Harker bundled Carter into the back seat and slid in next to him before the Templar slammed the door shut and made his way over to the driver's side.

'Who's Trixy Brulet? She sounds like a go-go dancer,' Carter muttered groggily, clearly excited at the prospect. 'Are we going to a strip club?'

Harker shook his head in despair. His friend wasn't just tipsy; he was completely trashed. 'She is a he, and he's certainly not a go-go dancer.'

Harker now found himself preoccupied with the unpalatable notion of turning up to meet the legendary Grand Master of the Knights Templar along with a pissed, middle-aged man hoping to catch a lap dance.

'Should take about an hour and a half to get there,' the driver informed them on catching Carter's jovial grin in the rear-view mirror. 'Should give enough time for a little snooze, if anyone needs one.'

'Thank you,' Harker replied, shooting a dirty look at Carter, who was blissfully unaware of the reproachful jibe directed towards him and more preoccupied with a couple of short-skirted brunettes walking by.

'Let's get going, then.' The Templar started up the Mercedes and pulled out into the heavy traffic.

In the back seat, Harker settled down, allowing the day's accumulation of tension to drain away He had no idea where they were heading, which was standard practice when meeting Brulet, but he knew it would be a safe journey and he was cheered that they'd sent a Templar with those extremely rare – yet to him familiar – grey eyes. Of course not all Templars shared that trait, but sending one who did had surely been deliberate on Brulet's part, to help make Harker feel secure that the man was exactly who he said he was.

Closing his eyes to the peaceful hum of the Mercedes's engine, he began to slip into a deep sleep. He had not slept properly since the flight to Berlin over a day ago, and the only thing keeping him going right now was the buzz of adrenalin in his veins. Besides which, if events up to now were anything to go by, he was going to need all the energy his body could muster.

Of course, if he only knew what was about to come, he would have demanded not just a short rest but a full-blown holiday.

## *Chapter 17*

'Welcome, ladies and gentlemen,' Jacob Winters announced as he was wheeled into the grand marble-floored conference room, before being positioned in the last remaining space at the enormous circular conference table. Long red drapes hung from ceiling railings, covering the oversized windows, and overhead a glimmering crystal chandelier with gold trimmings cascaded sparkles of white light down onto the central table and the fourteen people seated around it. The wooden surface was split into fifteen equal sections by dividing lines that allocated each of the attendees, with their own individual zone, like triangular slices of a giant pie, and within each section was a heraldic emblem.

'Thank you for attending at such short notice,' Winters continued as Albert locked his wheelchair in place and then backed up against the closed door, his hands clasped, and his tuxedo making him look like a bouncer at the entrance to a VIP nightclub. 'I cannot tell you how honoured I feel to see you all gathered here together and sitting opposite your family crests.' Winters motioned with a limp hand towards the emblems engraved into each triangular section. 'This assembly is unsurpassed in terms of wealth, power and sheer determination.'

There were very few smiles from the fourteen attendees and their expressions remained stony, hard and unyielding, with an air of entitlement emanating from each and every one of them.

'I know there is much preparation to be done but I, along with Mr Davies' – Winters gestured to the man sitting directly opposite – 'have learnt of something extremely troubling that could entail ramifications for us all if not dealt with.'

His audience remained silent but attentive as Winters now began to reveal the 'conspiracy' that both he and Albert had concocted just hours earlier.

'I am aware of your concerns regarding this Harker fellow and his associate, who have been sticking their noses into our business, appearing at gatherings in Berlin and the like, and it is not something I take lightly. We cannot have these men attempting to thwart our plans, but' – Winters raised his finger skywards, though only managing to hold it there for a few seconds – 'I am far more interested in how these two were able to find us in the first place. Why it was these particular individuals were chosen is a moot point at present, because the real question is who recruited them.' Winters now beckoned over Albert, who immediately joined him at the table. 'And to that question we have an answer.'

Albert now bent over and picked up a shiny black document folder resting against the table leg beside Winters, unwound the string binding it then pulled out a photograph and held it up for all in the group to see.

'This man is known as Lucas,' Winters explained, 'and we have discovered that he met with Alex Harker shortly before this meddling began. What we also know is that, soon after their meeting, he was found with his head blown off.' Albert now held up the disturbing crime-scene photo showing the aftermath of Lucas's suicide. 'So far, there have been no leads to his murderer's identity.'

Of the fourteen attendees, there was only one who was beginning to look uncomfortable, and as Winters continued, she looked more and more worried.

'It would appear that he was silenced by whoever wanted the Codex pages for themselves. As for this Harker person... As I have said, we don't know why he has been involved but, whatever the reason, he has been successful in taking those pages from us.'

The entire group now erupted into a flurry of anger at the news but, before any one of them began shouting, it was Albert who slammed his fist down on the table, making them all fall silent as Winters continued to explain.

'There is nothing to be concerned about,' he declared confidently. 'Even as we speak, my men have pinpointed the three Codex pages and are retrieving them. They will be back in our hands within a matter of hours.'

This last piece of news had them all settling back into their seats and, although many were still visibly angered at the breach in security, they all looked mollified…except for one.

Winters's demeanour now became colder as he stared around the table with a grimace. 'This whole sequence of events does lead us, unfortunately, to the rather unpalatable conclusion that we have a traitor in our midst. A person – one of us – who decided they wanted the spoils of our endeavour all to themselves, and at any cost.'

A nervous-looking woman rose from her seat and jabbed her forefinger vigorously towards Winters. 'How dare you accuse me of such a thing?'

'I didn't accuse you of anything, Miss Rochet,' Winters replied, extremely happy to elicit the reaction he had been attempting to provoke. 'Not yet.'

The rest of the group were now looking towards the red-haired forty-year-old with suspicion, and the two sitting on either side of her even began to their push their chairs back slightly, leaving her standing apart as Winters now pursued his case.

'Ladies and gentlemen, it is no surprise that Miss Rochet has reacted in this way, because what I know, and you do not, is that Lucas was working for her directly. Isn't that right, my lady?'

Rochet was now struggling to keep calm and gave Winters a venomous scowl. 'He has worked for me, yes, but that means nothing. I didn't even know he was dead!'

'Oh, I doubt that,' Winters replied, and then sat back smugly in his wheelchair as Davies took over the role of accuser.

'Your family has always been the one weak link in our chain, and we know your ancestors had a habit of swapping sides from time to time, but your blatant betrayal is the bitterest pill to swallow. Let me ask you, did you intend to have us all killed once you partook in our success?'

'This is outlandish,' Miss Rochet yelled defiantly as the others began to glower at her. Winters now flicked a withered finger towards her, whereupon Albert dutifully moved to the other side of the table and roughly shoved her back down into her seat.

'We cannot allow anyone to compromise our cause,' Davies announced, now turning his attention back to the rest of his group. 'Let us vote.'

Without even a pause, the other thirteen raised their hands in unison. And, as Rochet continued to shrilly insist her innocence, Albert pulled a cotton handkerchief from his pocket and thrust it into her mouth like a gag. He then pulled her to her feet and forcibly held her hands behind her back before slapping on a pair of handcuffs retrieved from his pocket.

'You have chosen to treat the rest of us as nothing better than dogs,' Davies snarled, 'and now you yourself will die like one.'

Albert began dragging the screaming and kicking woman towards the nearest curtained section of wall, and two of the others pulled it aside to reveal a set of double doors. He pushed them open and thrust the woman outside onto a slabbed patio linked to a lush green lawn surrounded by tall conifers.

While the others began to reassemble outside, Winters stayed where he was and reached for a pair of dark sunglasses as the morning light seeped in through the open doorway, stinging his eyes.

'Your treachery disgusts me and all your assets shall be seized,' Davies hissed as the other thirteen silently urged him on with their expressions.

Rochet staggered to her feet and continued struggling against her restraints, still protesting her innocence. But then a deathly hush came over the angry crowd and she too fell silent as she noticed the two black Rottweilers growling at her from the far side of the patio.

'Please, no,' she begged as the dog handlers began to unclip their leashes.

'Now run,' Davies ordered, giving her a hard kick in the middle of the back. 'And hope, when the time comes, that the judgement you face is a favourable one.'

Back in the conference room, Albert had returned to join Winters, and he looked at his Samsung mobile before kneeling next to the old man. 'Harker is currently meeting with the Templars,' he announced, displaying the texted message as, from outside, the high-pitched screams of Rochet mingled with the barking of the dogs echoing through the room.

'Interesting,' Winters replied. 'We should give our boy a call.'

Albert was already releasing the old man's wheel locks when his hand was brushed away.

'But first,' Winters declared, as the sounds of screams outside began to turn into a gurgled yelping, 'I want to catch the show.'

## *Chapter 18*

Harker awoke to the sound of laughter coming from outside the Mercedes Benz. Jerking forward anxiously in those first few disorientating seconds between slumber and consciousness, he slammed his forehead against the back of the front passenger seat's headrest.

'Welcome to Civitavecchia,' the Templar offered warmly, eyeing him in the rear-view mirror. 'I trust you slept well?'

'Yes, thank you,' Harker replied, rubbing at his temple before glancing over at Carter, who was still out cold and emitting a long-drawn-out snore with each breath.

'I was tempted to wake you a few minutes ago,' the Templar explained, 'but you looked like you really needed the rest.'

'I did,' Harker replied before turning his attention to the yachts moored up on the twinkling blue waters. 'Civitavecchia? So we're on the west coast?'

'We certainly are,' the Templar confirmed as he brought the Mercedes to a halt at the impressive entrance to the town's main port. 'Superb vacation spot, if you ever find the time.'

'I wish,' Harker replied longingly. He had never been to this maritime town situated about eighty kilometres outside Rome, but had always wanted to visit it. The main harbour had been constructed by the Roman emperor Trajan in the early second century for defence and trade purposes, but in the modern era it had become a centre for cruise ships as well. The town had seen massive bombing raids during the Second World War, and much rebuilding had taken place in the aftermath. Thankfully the famed Maschio tower overlooking the port, which had been built in part by none other than Michelangelo himself, survived the bombings, and as Harker exited the Mercedes to stretch his legs he gazed upon the impressive stone fort with reverence. This building had been the reason for he'd wanted to visit Civitavecchia in the first place, although unfortunately that sightseeing trip would have to wait for another time.

'If you head down the main gangway, there's a boat already waiting for you,' the Templar directed after winding down the passenger door window. 'It's the *Excelsior*. You can't miss it.'

'You're not coming?'

The Templar gestured over his shoulder to Carter, still sprawled out on the back seat and continuing to snore loudly. 'I think your friend needed more sleep than you did. Don't worry, I'll find a parking spot and then bring him along to join you if and when he wakes up.'

Harker was grateful and nodded. 'Thank you,' he said as the Templar gave him a friendly salute and proceeded to drive off into a large parking area on the opposite side of the road.

The harbour's edge was in the shape of a semicircle, providing protection from the Adriatic waves, and gigantic cruise and container ships lined its inner wall, unloading their goods and passengers. But one vessel stood out immediately, not because of its size but rather the opposite. The name *Excelsior* gleamed in gold and, although striking, it paled in comparison to its much larger brothers and sisters. The 73-foot super-yacht contained three decks, with black-tinted windows wrapped around each level and graced with an open area at the bow. What this contained was impossible to tell from where Harker stood, but he guessed a small swimming pool in view of the private craft's lavish size.

'Wow,' Harker muttered as he approached the awesome vessel, and noticed a man in a white shirt, shorts and plimsolls waving at him from the foot of the gangplank.

'Professor Harker,' he called out, briskly making his way over. 'Pleasure to meet you. I'm Jeffrey Hawkins, the captain.'

'Nice to meet you, Captain. I have an invitation from Tri—'

Hawkins silenced him with a gesture and waved him towards the gangplank. 'No need to mention his name, sir. He's expecting you.'

This comment seemed a bit cloak-and-dagger but Harker obliged, and followed Captain Hawkins up the plank and onto the first level of the ship. If the exterior was impressive the interior was unbelievable. With an open bar and thick white carpet, it looked like the VIP room of a top-end nightclub, complete with a glossy wooden dance floor. The wall panelling was a combination of expensive rosewood and gilt, which gave the whole room a classical yet modern feel, and two darkened-glass double doors led out to a narrow seven-metre bathing pool beyond.

'Nice,' Harker commented, seriously impressed.

'She's one of a kind,' Captain Hawkins replied proudly before pointing to a compact spiral staircase over in the corner. 'Mr Brulet is waiting for you on the top floor. Please, go on up.'

Harker left the captain and made his way up the staircase, past the second floor and onwards to the top level. As he got closer, he could hear what sounded like a heated argument going on.

He paused at the top step and, instead of making his way directly inside, he hovered at the open doorway and saw a man sitting with his back to him being berated by a red-haired gentlemen smartly dressed in a dark-blue Armani suit and black tie.

'...that's not the point. We've been doing this for far too long to change now, and your brother would have agreed with me,' the speaker argued aggressively. He had a twitch in his eye that fluttered at the end of each of his sentences. 'We need to press our advantage and ensure our security as we have done so far! Not to do so would be a breach of our sworn oath, and I'm not the only one who thinks it...'

The red-haired man fell silent as he caught sight of Harker hovering in the stairwell. He glared at him challengingly as the other man, sensing a new presence, turned around.

'Alex Harker,' Tristan Brulet, wearing a pair of dark, thinly rimmed sunglasses, proclaimed with a smile. 'Please join us.' He gestured with his hand outstretched.

'It's good to see you, Tristan,' Harker said, making his way over to shake Brulet's hand and feeling glad to have been acknowledged rather than made to feel like an eavesdropper.

'My apologies, but we were just in the middle of discussing something.' The Grand Master shook Harker's hand firmly.

'Do you want me to wait downstairs?' Harker asked, already preparing to retreat towards the open doorway.

'No, not at all,' Brulet insisted, turning to introduce the red-haired man. 'This is William Havers, and don't let his disposition fool you. He's a good friend.'

The kind mention appeared to soothe some of Havers's hostility and he shook Harker's hand with only a grimace. 'I know who you are, Professor Harker.'

'Please, call me Alex,' Harker replied, wanting to at least try and break the ice.

'Very well…Alex.'

There was an awkward pause before Brulet placed his hand on Havers's shoulder. 'Let's discuss that matter another time, shall we?'

Havers emitted a growl of displeasure, then he forced his way past Harker, brushing shoulders with him lightly, and headed down the spiral steps to the second floor.

'Try not to judge him from this encounter alone,' Brulet requested. 'He is a good man but he has a lot on his mind at the moment.'

'I can see that.'

Harker's sharp observation had Brulet shaking his head. 'Take a seat and I will tell you all about it. You are a Templar and so you have a right to know.'

Brulet motioned to a green three-seater sofa pressed up against the wall, then waited for Harker to settle before taking a seat next to him. 'A lot has happened since we last met, and that discussion you may have overheard is just a part of it.'

'How so?' Harker asked, still struggling to find a comfortable spot on the extremely slippery shiny leather sofa.

'Now that the Magi are no longer a threat, there has been a difference of opinion within the Templar Council as to how we proceed,' Brulet explained, also taking a moment to steady himself on the awkward seat. 'Some – myself included – believe that the Templars need to create a new role for ourselves, focusing on our associated charitable and humanitarian organizations around the world. We may have begun as protectors of the Catholic Church but, as you know, over the years that role as guardian has evolved to encompass all religions. Our ranks are made up of people from every race and creed, and for centuries we have sought to serve humanity as a whole. In such a precarious and diverse modern world, I see that role as now being more important than ever. Unfortunately' – Brulet glanced towards the doorway – 'not everyone sees it that way, and many, Mr Havers included, feel that the Templars' role as a "protectorate" is needed now more than ever.'

'Sounds like the end of the cold war?'

'Something like that, yes,' Brulet sighed. 'You gear up your entire apparatus and all your assets to maintain and whittle away the power of your enemy and then, when you finally succeed, what is there left to do?'

'Find another enemy?'

'Exactly.' Brulet groaned. 'Human beings are by their very nature a tribal species, with the potential for both good and bad, but with the very concept of religion being eroded in a world increasingly dependent on science and technology, there are those who are already looking to draw up new battle lines.'

Brulet's answer was a curious one but Harker got the gist of it. 'You mean how religion instils in people who the good guys and the bad guys are?'

'Yes,' Brulet replied. 'There is now a mindset, especially in the Western world, that human beings are born with an instilled sense of morality, which is a misguided notion. It is the old "nature over nurture" argument: are we born as empty vessels who are taught to act a certain way, or do our genes dictate what we become?'

'It's a conundrum, yes,' Harker agreed, finding this philosophical discussion a bit much, considering he had only just woken up after the long car trip, 'but you could argue that culture and society can shape those young minds just as well as religion does.'

'True,' Brulet said, 'but you only need to look at the overused but accurate example of the Nazis to show how dangerous that can be. Teach young minds a particular ideology, no matter how despicable, and they will add to it and defend it with their dying breath, because we are all of us a product of external influence. And social norms will change far quicker without a basic set of morals in place. Every person on the planet is essentially brainwashed in some way, and we are all shaped by our experiences, but the only question that matters is are we brainwashed to be good or bad? Religion has always been the mechanism by which this was accomplished, and it has caused as much division as it has harmony. But still it's the best system we have. If you never teach a young child that murder is wrong, then how would that child ever know that the act of murder was wrong in the first place...and so a cycle begins. They pass it on then to their children, and so on and so on.'

'I see your problem,' Harker replied, noting how Brulet possessed the same open mind as his late brother and previous Grand Master of the Knights Templar with a view to the bigger picture.

'The Knights Templar have fought the Magi and all their terrible, narcissistic ideals for two thousand years, always debating whether our role was to defeat them utterly or merely contain them and thereby balance the scales, as it were. But our principles have always been guided by religious ideals, which I will admit were at first Catholic but over the years have broadened to encompass shared values from all religions

– meaning that the Templars now act as a protectorate for all devout people. Templars have passed on this duty of protection from one generation to the next but, with such protection from the Magi not required any more, a new debate now rages as to our purpose.'

'You're talking about changing the very nature of the Templars?' Harker suggested, fully understanding now what Brulet had been alluding to.

'Exactly. Do we remain a wholly bipartisan organization and stick to the religious guidelines that developed into what the Templars are today, or do we become one that seeks to actively hunt down and destroy those whom society deems unfit?'

Brulet frowned, shaking his head uneasily at the thought of such a choice. 'For that is something that could easily change well-intentioned idealism into dangerous fanaticism – and the line between those two concepts is remarkably thin.'

'What would it mean in practice?'

'The first path would mean putting every resource we have into our charitable organizations and assuming a new role, with our vast network of political and business contacts, in shaping a fairer world and thereby helping oppressed countries to become fair and free societies through peaceful means.'

'You mean pull the strings from the shadows?'

'Come now, Alex.' Brulet shrugged. 'On a planet filled with over seven billion people, no single person pulls the strings. There are some powerful players out there, of course, but no one could ever possess the kind of control that so many Internet conspiracy theorists would have you believe. But, yes, we would aim to do so from a distance.'

'And the second way?'

Brulet slumped back in his seat. 'The second way is to actively go after those who do not share the ideal of a fair and free world: terrorists on all sides of the religious spectrum as well as politicians and leaders who oppose it.'

Brulet's mentioning of such a path made Harker's blood run cold. 'That's a dangerous road to go down, Tristan,' he said, leaning forward attentively. 'The Templars would essentially become a group of assassins and death squads. Don't take me for being naive, though. I know that some measure of force will always be needed to create a truly peaceful world, but long-lasting peace is rarely created down the barrel of a gun. In the short term, yes, but not the kind of lasting world society you're talking about.'

'Wise words,' Brulet remarked. He now removed his glasses, wincing in the daylight as he stared at Harker with those uniquely cross-shaped pupils of his. 'But, as of now, the Knights Templar have a captain but no course to chart, and there are those who question their new leader's ability to create one.'

Up until that point Harker had assumed that Brulet's position was unassailable, but as the Grand Master continued it became apparent how transformed the secretive organization had become since the Magi's demise.

'There are many within the Council who believe, as I do, that the more measured and peaceful approach is not only better suited to the Templars, but also simply the right thing to do… However there are others, Mr Havers included, who believe we should take what they term a more *proactive* role.'

'Proactive!' Harker exploded, almost shouting the word. 'It's a bit more than proactive. It could be a route to selective murder on a vast scale.'

'I agree with you.' Brulet raised a calming hand. 'But if faced with a situation, let us say a man is about to kill someone with a knife right in front of you and let us also say that the victim is not a popular individual, even hated by some, do you allow it to happen or do you attempt to grab the knife and plunge it into the attacker, thus preventing the intended murder from ever happening?'

'I'd wrestle it from his hands and then put him in jail for the rest of his life.'

'It's a fair point, but what if that very act of imprisonment serves only to give the offender martyr status, and others then seek to go after the original victim as revenge? As a consequence of not killing the attacker right there and then, many further acts of violence might follow.'

There were obvious holes in Brulet's theory and it was clear to Harker that, among the similarities he and his late brother had shared, arguing effectively was not one of them. But he nevertheless remained quiet and allowed the Grand Master to finish.

'This is the lens through which many of the Templars and their Council view things, and their opposition to my more "peaceful" approach is, I am afraid to say, gaining in strength.'

Harker had always seen the Templars as a beacon of strength and purity, irreproachable in their thinking and their ability to discern the black and white in a world awash with grey. But he now detected, as was the case with every other mortal being, a chink in their armour, and it made him nervous. Brulet obviously was just a man trying to do the right thing – for himself and for those who followed him. The very thought that the Templars, who Harker had always seen as a rock of incorruptibility, could waver in their mandate made him feel uneasy, and suddenly he realized how crucial Sebastien Brulet's leadership had been. Tristan was undoubtedly a strong and worthy Grand Master, but did the man actually have what was needed during such a crucial moment in Templar history? Of that Harker was unsure, but only time would tell.

'Anyway,' Brulet said, putting his sunglasses back on and then energetically jumping to his feet and making his way over to the drinks cabinet. 'Enough of my problems. Drink?'

'Vodka and Red Bull, thank you,' Harker replied, 'and I wouldn't say no to a double.'

'Having a bad day, are you?' Brulet suggested, clearly happy to move on from his own issues, and with a smile he pulled a litre bottle of Russian standard vodka from its silver holder.

'I've had better,' Harker admitted despondently, 'and I've been trying to get hold of John Shroder for the past twenty-four hours.'

'That's odd, as I've not heard from him either, and we only found you thanks to one of the security men on the Vatican gate.' Brulet looked thoughtful as he began to mix their drinks. 'I wouldn't take it as a slight, though, given those recent terrorist attacks on British soil. I suspect both MI5 and MI6 are pretty busy at the moment.'

Harker didn't reply but instead settled himself deeper into the green sofa. As he watched Brulet pour a generous serving of vodka into each crystal glass he found himself thinking about this man's deceased brother Sebastian. The two men looked so similar with that shared condition of Waardenburg syndrome, which caused such a distinct, almost silvery-grey skin tone and strikingly white hair. The brothers even moved in the same way, with that fluid cat-like gait one usually only sees when a feline is on the prowl while hunting prey, but apart from the uniquely shaped irises, that is where the similarities stopped. It was difficult to pinpoint, but Tristan seemed far more like a free-spirited playboy, not in the traditional sense but rather in the way in which he seemed far more willing to take a gamble on the unknown – and, of course, his love of anything exquisite such as this impressive yacht. Sebastien had seemed far more conservative and – how could one put it? – more salt of the earth.

'This yacht is a far more lavish thing than anything my brother would ever have favoured, wouldn't you agree?' Brulet said out of the blue, surprising Harker from his thoughts. 'That is what you were thinking, wasn't it?'

Harker sat expressionless and silent until Brulet moved over to him and placed the double vodka with Red Bull in his hands. 'How did you know that?' he replied finally, as Tristan sat back down beside him and placed his own drink on the glass coffee table in front of them.

'The window to a man's soul is not just the eyes, Alex, but his facial expressions – or, to put it correctly, micro expressions.' Brulet smiled, revealing a set of perfect white teeth. 'Psychics and clairvoyants have been aware of that for centuries.'

Brulet's answer had Harker realizing another trait the two brothers shared...*instinct*. 'Well, this is indeed a remarkable yacht, Tristan,' he managed.

'It certainly is.' Brulet took a sip of his own drink. 'But unfortunately it's not mine.'

'Rented?'

'No, borrowed actually,' Brulet continued. 'Sebastien did so love aeroplanes. I would say he spent half his life in one, either in the air or parked up at an airport. It made him feel secure, I think, whereas I cannot stand them.'

'Not a fan, huh?'

'Anything but, I'm afraid. It's only trains or boats for me.'

Brulet leant forward and lowered his sunglasses to reveal those highly distinctive eyes. The condition of coloboma had left both brothers with malformed pupils, each one in the shape of a cross. It was a genetic abnormality that had been passed down from one generation to the next and, as Sebastian had told it, the reason his family line were long seen as such important figureheads within the Order of the Knights Templar. Whether there anything godly about such an inheritance was something Harker had never really considered, but one thing was for sure: they were fascinating to see.

'So I heard you ended up in a Berlin police station the other day?'

The question took Harker by surprise, though it should not have. The Templars always had an uncanny knack of knowing about one's comings and goings. 'Your information is impeccable, as always, Tristan... But did you hear why?'

Brulet was already shaking his head. 'The details we received were sketchy at best, but apparently you were involved in an attempted murder or something.'

Harker could feel himself flush as Tristan eyed him curiously. There was no easy way to explain the bizarre events that had occurred during the past few days, so he thought it best to start at the beginning. 'I was giving an archaeology lecture in Cambridge when this man who identified himself as Lucas—'

Suddenly Harker's iPhone began to vibrate and, with an understanding look from Brulet, he retrieved it from his pocket and answered it.

'Alex!' Chloe Stanton called out in a quivering voice and, before Harker could answer, hers was quickly replaced by the familiar crusty voice of 'God'.

'Say hi to her,' 'God' demanded, 'and remain calm. We don't want to alert anyone else to our private conversation, do we?'

'Hi,' Harker managed causally.

'Good. Now I don't want any outbursts from your end, because what I have to tell you might be a little upsetting,' 'God' continued with a tinge of enjoyment in his tone. 'There is a man standing before me with a knife held to Dr Stanton's throat, and if you do not do exactly as you are told, he will cut her from ear to ear.' 'God' emitted a sarcastic snigger. 'So just keep your mouth shut and listen.'

## *Chapter 19*

All Harker wanted to do was scream threats and obscenities down the line, but he remained calm regardless. 'I understand,' he replied, while shooting Brulet a relaxed smile.

'I know where you are and also who you are with.'

'OK.'

'You can tell him anything you want about your little adventure up till now, but you will omit the parts regarding any contact with myself. Nor should you make any reference to the fact that I have your pretty girlfriend in my possession. Understood?'

Harker's blood boiled at the word 'possession', and he was sure it was only being used to goad him.

'Got it,' Harker replied, glancing again over at Brulet, who was now looking increasingly concerned.

'Everything all right?' Brulet mouthed quietly.

'Sorry, Tristan,' Harker replied with a grimace. 'It's the university...problem with a student.'

Brulet raised his eyebrows sympathetically and sat back in his seat, sipping at his drink, as Harker returned his attention to 'God's' hoarse voice.

'Ahh yes, Tristan Brulet – one of the earth's viler creations,' the voice continued, sounding revolted at the very mention of the Grand Master's name. 'The Templars have in their possession another of the Codex pages, previously thought lost to that ragamuffin bunch of Satanic zealots you keep running into. I *want* it. I believe it is kept in one of their famed storage vaults, along with all the general garbage they see fit to hide away.'

The request to drag the Templars into this whole thing without being totally upfront was unacceptable to Harker, but at this point in time what choice did he have? More persuasive still was the fact that not only did 'God' know who he was sitting with, but that the Templars even possessed one of the pages. Of course he knew the Templar vaults held a wealth of antiquities and items collected throughout the ages, but what were the odds they would have a missing page from the Codex Gigas?

'That wasn't the deal,' Harker replied serenely and with no hint of irritation.

'No, the deal was that you would retrieve the second page before those lunatics had a chance to recite from it, and you failed miserably,' 'God' hissed. 'You do manage to get yourself into some scrapes, don't you, Professor. Enjoy your tango with the dead?'

That it was 'God' who had instructed him to follow their contact's instructions to visit the cemetery in the first place seemed irrelevant at that moment, and therefore Harker ignored it. 'I've had better experiences.'

'Right, then do your job this time, because your little blunder means this last page is now vital to stopping those charlatans.'

'Leave it with me,' Harker replied, and then the line went dead.

'You sure everything's all right?' Brulet asked with a tilt of his head.

Harker took another moment to take everything in. Chloe had sounded totally distraught and he now fought the urge to 'spill the beans' – as Carter would have put it – and tell Brulet everything. However, 'God' appeared to know everything he was doing…but how?

'No, nothing's all right. I mean *that's* all right,' Harker replied, indicating the mobile in his hand. 'It was a student of mine who keeps getting herself into trouble – but nothing that can't be sorted. It's everything else that's a nightmare.'

'Tell me all about it.'

Harker proceeded to recount everything that had happened, but left out those bits he had been ordered to. He covered the suicide of Lucas and the discovery of the dead man's secret study, Spreepark and the dead man walking, the insanely disturbing impossibility of Cervete cemetery...and finally ending up with the Vatican and the horror of the monster being confined in its basement. The whole crazy tale just spewed from his mouth, and every word was expelled with such venom that Brulet looked ever more shocked with each startling admission. Once he had finished, Harker fell back into the sofa limply, as Brulet stared at him blankly.

'I have seen and heard some crazy things during my life, but that has to rank top of the list,' Brulet finally admitted, rubbing at his cheek. 'And you witnessed all of this?'

'With my own eyes,' Harker declared firmly, but not sure if the Grand Master was taking him seriously. 'What do you think?'

'Think about what? The zombies that tried to kill you or the mutant they have housed under the Vatican Governorate?'

'About everything,' Harker replied, realizing the story he told would have seemed laughable to most.

Brulet pondered for a second, then sat back up and eyed Harker with those cross-shaped pupils now peeking over the rim of his sunglasses. 'Alex,' he said, before resting a hand on Harker's shoulder, 'I want you to be honest with me, and believe me when I say that I'm not judging you in any way, but...are you taking any medication at the moment?'

The question was asked sincerely, but it had Harker jumping to his feet and snarling angrily as Brulet continued. 'I mean you've seen and been involved in some remarkable events in recent years, and no one would blame you if you'd been taking something to maybe calm your nerves.'

Had his story not sounded so outlandish even to himself, he would have been highly insulted, but all Harker felt now was frustration and anger. Anger that Chloe had been kidnapped, anger that this 'God' person was using him as a pawn in something he didn't understand – but mostly because, ever since reading Bishop Esposito's note and its reference to Judgement Day, he had been having a damn hard time taking it all seriously himself. The whole thing was screwy, and he knew it. He reached into his jacket pocket and extracted the folded page of the Codex Gigas before throwing it down onto the sofa next to Brulet. 'Just take a look at that, would you? And for the record, I am not on any drugs and neither am I having a nervous breakdown – although that might be preferable right now because at least I could do something about it.'

Brulet silently unfolded the page and began to examine it carefully before he next spoke. 'I suppose you are aware of the legend surrounding the lost pages?' he said, trailing his finger across the mystery text. 'There was a time when even the Templars took such things seriously, but that was long before the modern world came into being. It was a time when monsters, ogres and witchcraft were very real presences in the minds of men.'

Finally, Harker thought, someone was at least willing to take him vaguely seriously. 'And what happened?'

Brulet rested the oversized piece of vellum on his knee and looked across at Harker solemnly. 'We are talking centuries ago, Alex, when people believed that demons lived in the woods and witches could steal your soul with just a look.'

'Medieval times?' Harker suggested, now retaking his seat next to Brulet.

'Yes. Back then the Templars had already gone underground, after the Church broke up their organization. The majority had taken refuge in Scotland, which was not under close papal scrutiny, so was a perfect place to hide. The Templars saw it as their sworn duty to protect people from any evils they encountered or heard about as they travelled about. Goblins, wraiths and a whole manner of beasties – I joke not. Back then it was a serious business, and the Templars took it as such.'

Brulet paused to scratch an itch on his neck, as if he found the reciting of such ridiculous Templar adventures irritating in some way. 'Anyway, getting back to the point, the Codex Gigas came to their attention – and with it the tale that the Devil had indeed written the book in return for the soul of a Benedictine monk. That part of the story you know, but what you may not know was the rumour of seven additional pages in which, apparently, the Devil not only placed intricate knowledge of himself but also the process by which his followers could open the very gates of Hell and bring about—'

'Judgement Day?' Harker guessed as he found himself becoming increasingly engrossed in the story.

'Not just Judgement Day, but one in which Satan himself or herself, depending on who you listen to' – Brulet gave a wink and now seemed to be enjoying retelling Templar lore – 'would sit in judgement, instead of Jesus Christ, and plunge the entire world into Hell.'

Brulet folded up the Codex page as he began to delve further into the legend. 'Well, as you can imagine, when the Templars heard about this they swore to locate the pages at any cost. Subsequently a group was tasked to scour the known world for these earth-threatening pages of "dark wisdom" as they called them, if memory serves me right. It took them almost forty years before they came upon a single page, protected by a clan of witches, in what is now modern-day Turkey and, as the story goes, a great battle ensued which lasted weeks. Finally, with the entire witch clan defeated and then burned at the stake, they retrieved the page itself and brought it back to Scotland, where they kept it hidden under their protection, hopefully for all time.'

Brulet dropped the Codex page unceremoniously into Harker's lap, then he slouched back into the sofa with an undignified creak of its leather upholstery.

'Where did it end up?' Harker asked, though he already knew the answer – that is if 'God' had been correct.

'It travelled with the Templars as they moved around and about to new locations, but for the past sixty years it has been residing in one of our oldest vaults. No doubt stuck in some dusty corner with little interest ever paid to it…until now, that is, Alex.'

Harker had to admit that Brulet's storytelling abilities were impressive, and he sat absorbed by the tale. There was something about those old times which intrigued him greatly; an age when the possibilities were endless and in people's minds the existence of creatures and monsters was only limited by the breadth of their imaginations. It was these same, practically romantic, notions that had originally led him into the world of archaeology, and why it continued to hold such a fascination. Of course, to be transported back to those ages would seem like hell for anyone born in the modern age. No sanitation or running water, rampant disease with no medicine that didn't require, by today's standards, torture of some kind, and none of the technology we all take for granted in the twenty-first century. Despite all this it was these very advances that had shattered the mystery of the world, and to look back at such a time and put oneself in the mindset of these fearful people was, to him, enthralling.

'How is it you know so much about the Codex pages?' Harker asked.

'Because of *our* codex, of course,' Brulet replied, smiling enigmatically. 'Not the Codex Gigas but the Templar Codex, or by its precise name the *Illuminismo*, which I have read many, many times.'

Harker had heard mention of the Templar Codex on numerous occasions but no one had ever explained its significance in the world of the Order. '*Illuminismo* – enlightenment,' Harker translated. 'What is it exactly?'

The question was met with a raised eyebrow from Brulet. 'That surprises me. I assumed someone would have mentioned it when you were first inducted into the Templars,' he replied, instinctively leaning in as if not wanting anyone else to hear. 'The *Illuminismo* is an historical record charting our history since the Templars' inception, and more. Every Grand Master adds to it, documenting everything significant that happens under his watch. It contains therefore not only every enterprise undertaken by the Order but also every individual member to grace its ranks...names, history, everything.' Brulet paused and pointed a long finger at Harker. 'You're mentioned in there as well...quite a bit in the most recent pages, I might add. But only a Grand Master ever gets to read it, so you will just have to take my word for that.'

Harker felt a sliver of pride at this acknowledgement but his real interest involved the vault, and he immediately sought to enquire as to its whereabouts, while appearing to be interested in the Gigas page alone. 'Amazing,' he remarked and, although not his top priority, he was genuinely fascinated by the idea of a book containing such a wealth of information covering almost a thousand years of history. 'It must be a huge.'

'It is comprised,' Brulet explained further, 'of many volumes but we refer to it as a single book.'

'And somewhere amongst them is one of the fabled missing pages of the Gigas?'

'Well, not in the book itself but, yes, it's in the same vault.'

Harker paused and mustered the nerve to ask if he could see this remaining page but, as usual, Brulet beat him to the punch.

'Would you like to take a look?' the Grand Master asked flatly.

'Very much so.'

Brulet polished off the remains of his drink, stood up and tapped thoughtfully at the glass with his forefinger. 'If you say you saw the things you have described, then for the record I believe you, no matter how surreal your story sounds. If this conversation was happening a few centuries ago, then I would already be organizing a Templar expeditionary unit to investigate it. But' – Brulet finally placed the empty glass down on the table and turned to face Harker with a look of deep misgiving – 'if I am to be completely honest, I find the concept of an actual Judgement Day extremely unlikely.'

It was the last thing Harker expected to hear from the Grand Master of the Knights Templar, and he let Brulet know it. 'But you're a believer in the Church and in God. Surely your faith compels you to believe?'

'It is true that the Templars and I myself believe implicitly in God and in those who serve him. But, as I have already said, we embrace all faiths and creeds and as such the mechanics of every religion are more of a human construct in my eyes. A way of understanding the incomprehensible.'

The look of surprise on Harker's face was obvious and Brulet continued to explain himself.

'We believe in the life and humanity that God has seen fit to bestow on all of us in this world. You cannot say that this few billion people are wrong in their beliefs whereas that few billion are right, when they all share the same ideals. The Templars have always sought to unite, not divide, and there is one single factor that binds every person of every faith.' Brulet spoke now with a comforting smile. 'It is that God exists and that he created every living creature.'

He began slowly pacing around the room. 'Vanquishing one's spiritual foes has gone on since humans began envisaging a creator and it always starts with good intentions but, as history has taught us, it invariably concludes with death, blood and retribution – before the whole cycle begins once again.'

As Harker watched Brulet outline his beliefs, he was struck by just how much the Templars had evolved. From being at the forefront of the Crusades to an ethos of liberty and harmony for all; he couldn't help but warm to the idea. It revealed a change in tone and belief that could only have occurred in the modern world, where the advent of nuclear weapons meant wars, or Crusades, would bring about the entire annihilation of the planet.

'So you're an agnostic, then?' Harker suggested, a little taken aback.

'I will always keep the Christian faith in my heart, for that I cannot and would not want to change,' Brulet declared firmly, 'but when it comes down to what you say...well, yes.'

In reality Harker shouldn't have been that surprised by this because, even during his induction into the Templars, the other witnessing members had all come from different religions. But just hearing Brulet say it was so unexpected that his mouth hung open slightly.

Brulet continued, 'As such I find it difficult to accept that Judgement Day, in any real or physical way, could be about to take place even as we speak, let alone be hijacked by the followers of the Devil!'

He stopped his pacing and stood over Harker with arms crossed. 'But I could be wrong. No one is all-knowing...with the exception of God.'

Even though what Brulet was saying resonated with Harker, he wasn't ready to shake off so easily the ghoulish and unnatural things he had witnessed and, despite which, his getting Chloe back safely hinged on retrieving the next Gigas page, no matter what the truth might be. 'And if you're wrong?' he asked, and the question drew a sober look from Brulet.

'If I am wrong and the Gigas pages truly have the power to thwart and twist such a monumentally important event, then we are all in for a lot of trouble.'

A subdued moment of silence passed between them until Brulet finally unfolded his arms and nodded. 'Very well, you're welcome to take a look. In the meantime I will delve deeper into your described cases of...necromancy,' Brulet said with revulsion, 'and see what I can unearth.'

Harker stood up and shook Brulet's hand eagerly. Perhaps too eagerly, as the Grand Master began to frown.

'You are telling me everything, aren't you, Alex?'

Brulet's instinct was clearly as acute as ever and, not wanting to raise any suspicion, Harker reached into his pocket and pulled out his iPhone. 'I did manage to take some pictures of those people back at the cemetery. It's the last couple of images,' he replied, offering him the device. Brulet plucked it from his hand, then reached down and pressed a round brass buzzer imbedded in one corner of the glass coffee table. 'I'll have these photos downloaded and checked for you,' he explained, then a devious smile crept across his lips. 'There's nothing too personal in here, is there? The kind of thing you may not want others to see.'

'No,' Harker replied, indignant at the insinuation of mobile-phone porn. 'Nothing like that.' Of course he now found himself scrambling to remember if he actually had left anything questionable on it. 'But if there is, then it'll be just something I'm working on.'

'No doubt,' Brulet chuckled, and he passed the phone over to a neatly dressed woman in a suit who had just entered the room. 'Could you please do an identity check on the last few photos, please?'

She nodded politely, then disappeared back the way she had come.

Brulet's expression turned more serious. 'Now I have a few questions for you, Alex.'

The way he said it had Harker suddenly feeling like a rabbit caught in the headlights. He simply nodded. 'What do you want to know?'

'Why did you go to Lucas's house in the first place?'

'Curiosity,' Harker replied, and apart from the matter of Chloe's kidnapping, it was the truth.

'But you could have told the police, and you didn't?'

There was more curiosity then accusation in Brulet's tone, and Harker proceeded to stretch the truth.

'Because he said he wanted me to go there and, given that the man subsequently blew his own head off in front of me, I needed to see for myself what could be so important for him to take his life like that. Besides, I very much doubt the police would have allowed me to tag along, if I had asked them.'

Brulet said nothing regarding this explanation, but immediately moved on to his next question.

'How did you know your contact would be waiting in Pisa, with the second page of the Gigas?'

It was a fair enough question and, without mentioning 'God's' tip-off, it was difficult to explain but not impossible. 'I overheard one of the cult members talking about it back at Spreepark,' Harker lied, and he would have been impressed with his own performance if he had not felt like a real turd for deceiving his friend.

'I see. Fair enough,' Brulet said, appearing to believe this answer, then he turned towards a large monitor set directly into the wall panelling next to the doorway, which Harker had not even noticed upon initially entering the room. 'Finally,' Brulet now asked, pointing towards the monitor. 'Who is that plump little man busy emptying my bar?'

Harker glanced at the colour screen to see David Carter sitting at the yacht's first-floor bar with a glass full of a dark-brown liquid in one hand and a bottle of Bell's whisky in the other. 'That's a friend of mine, David Carter. He's an ex-professor at Cambridge and the only other person, until now, who's been helping me with all of this.'

'Looks like he's happy helping himself,' Brulet commented as Carter took another generous swig. 'Considering what both of you have witnessed, I suppose I can't blame him, though.'

That Carter had been drinking furiously since their encounter at the cemetery, Harker had put down to the ex-don just doing what he normally did, and it had not occurred to him that his friend's excessive thirst might have been fuelled by the trauma of almost being tortured to death.

'I think you could be right,' he replied and, realizing that if Carter was due to take a trip to the Templar vault with him, then it was only proper that he at least gave Brulet a bit more information about the man.

'David used to have a highly respected academic career but, since losing his wife in a car accident, he's not been the same.'

'Poor fellow,' Brulet replied with a sympathetic wince.

'But he knows as much about the Gigas as anyone does, and has a personal obsession with secret societies, freemasons – anything conspiratorial, really.'

This revelation had Brulet raising his white eyebrows.

'Believe me, Tristan, when I tell you that if David realized I was talking right now with the Grand Master of the Knights Templar, he would probably wet himself in excitement.'

'Charming thought. In that case I would suggest it prudent that we don't ever meet.' Brulet was still looking troubled. 'Can you trust him?'

Since all that Brulet knew so far about David Carter was his tendency to drink heavily, Harker could understand the Grand Master's reservations, but 'God's' instructions had been clear: Carter went along wherever he did. 'He's a good guy at heart and, given what we've both been through, I can't just abandon him,' Harker said in defence of the dishevelled-looking figure still visible on the monitor.

Brulet nodded resignedly. 'OK it's your choice. But I want one of my men with you at all times until we get to the bottom of this. Agreed?'

'Agreed,' Harker replied, actually relieved at the prospect of having a bodyguard at his side.

'Good. So you leave for the vault once those pictures have been downloaded, and I would also like to have your Gigas page analysed.'

He motioned for Harker to pass it over and without pause he did so. After all, this page was now apparently worthless; 'God' had said so himself.

Brulet dropped it onto the coffee table. 'And, finally, I think I am going to have someone go and close the bar. Reckon your friend has had enough.'

Brulet was already heading out of the room when Harker called after him. The Grand Master dutifully stopped and turned around.

'Any chance you could have someone make our travel arrangements?'

'I can do better than that,' Brulet replied, beckoning him to follow as he made his way out of a side door and onto a shiny wooden deck at the rear of the yacht. This area took up around a third of the entire upper deck and, apart from the spotless gold-coloured railings running around the edge, it was completely empty.

'There you go.' Brulet gestured with a smile, and Harker glanced over the side of the yacht to see a modest-sized orange rubber raft with two black Yamaha outboard engines at its stern.

'I don't know exactly where we're going,' Harker croaked, 'but I'm fairly sure that raft's not going to get us there.'

'Not that.' Brulet almost laughed at the suggestion. He turned a red safety switch sticking out from underneath the railing, then pointed straight down to the deck itself. 'That.'

The sound of gears turning began to vibrate beneath them and a section of wood flooring slowly retracted, revealing a large holding space below. Then, with the familiar pneumatic noise of hydraulics pumping, the entire hold floor began to rise up and, with it, Harker's ride.

'Now, that is impressive,' Harker whistled as the silver AgustaWestland AW109 helicopter with two Pratt & Whitney engines rose upwards majestically, with its propellers lined up together, allowing for additional storage in the tight confines of the lower decks.

'I thought you told me you never flew?' Harker mused, as the lower floor extended and then locked itself into place.

'And I thought I already told you this wasn't my yacht,' Brulet replied with a smile, before patting the side of the helicopter lovingly. 'But if we began to sink somewhere out at sea, I can assure you I would take the risk.'

The sheer opulence of such a flying craft had Harker in awe, and he found himself drooling over the spectacle as he peered through the front window into the cockpit. 'So you're not coming with us, then?'

The very thought had Brulet grimacing. 'Not a chance, but I'm sure you and your intoxicated friend will have a whale of a time getting there.'

'Where is it we're actually going?' Harker enquired as two of the ship's crew, after a nod from Brulet, appeared and began unfolding the main propellers.

'Where would you hide a secret vault you wanted to keep hidden from prying eyes?' Brulet asked, as if it were a riddle.

'I don't know. Where?'

A crafty smile formed on Brulet's lips and he placed an arm around Harker's neck. 'In plain sight, of course, my dear friend…in plain sight.'

# Chapter 20

Dr Chloe Stanton remained quiet as the armed waiter retrieved the unfinished remnants of her lunch, then exited the room, allowing the solid steel door to lock shut behind him with a clink. The numerical keypad flickered from green to red, as it always did, leaving her alone in the small room measuring only three metres by six. The walls were totally bare, although a small writing table with several choice novels stacked on it had offered her a modicum of distraction during her visit. Of course, being kidnapped and then locked away here over the last few days did not, in her mind, constitute an agreeable visit but rather a sentence, and she lay on the basic metal-framed single bed and mulled over the same thing that had preoccupied her since arriving. *How to escape.*

The size of the building beyond the door was unknown to her because she had been blindfolded instantly on being snatched by two large men wearing suits in the car park of Blackwater asylum when she arrived for the morning shift. She had not even noticed them coming, though the darkness of the early hour before sunrise without doubt accounted for that. The next few hours had been terrifying, and at first she thought it might be a rape attack or worse, but when she was bundled into a plane, for a flight lasting hours, she had realized it was something worse still – if that was possible – and sex trafficking had come to mind. Finally, after the flight, followed by a short car ride, she had been dragged to this cell and her blindfold removed. Only after the guard had given her a brief set of instructions and the door was locked behind him did she burst into tears – not from fear but from frustration, and the additional worry that her boyfriend Alex Harker was most likely now in a similar predicament.

This was partly confirmed when she was dragged from her cell to a creepy red-lit room and told to announce her present predicament to Harker himself over the phone. The old man instructing her – one Jacob Winters, if that was his real name – appeared to be pulling all the strings, and he had allowed her to just say hello before she was rapidly frogmarched back to her cell. Since then her thoughts had consisted of a muddle of questions revolving around *why*, *where* and *what*; at the forefront was Alex, and the trouble they were both obviously in.

With a Ph.D. in psychology, Chloe Stanton had hoped to use her acquired skills to garner as much information as possible, and since her arrival she had put all her focus on the one person she saw regularly: namely the armed man who fetched her meals. This, frustratingly, had proved useless since the man never said a word, or even attempted to interact with her, except to give instructions upon her initial arrival: '*Stay here until you're summoned. You'll receive three meals a day and I won't tolerate any talking or screaming.*' That was all the man had said before tapping his gun threateningly, then leaving the room.

By the second day, and realizing that any form of further communication was never going to happen, she had instead turned her attention to the numerical code lock on her prison door. There wasn't a chance she would crack it, because she lacked both the skills and the tools to do so, so instead she had decided to remain vigilant to the waiter's comings and goings during mealtimes. Every time there was a knock at the door, she would instantly lie down on her bed and pretend to be asleep. Then, as he left, she would open her eyes just enough to watch her 'waiter' tapping on the door keypad.

After quite a number of meals, and almost getting caught staring at the keypad, she had managed to identify four of the five digits he pressed in order to release the door. Now, with her latest lunchtime meal, she had managed to catch a look at the final one.

Chloe slid quietly off the bed and pressed her ear to the door apprehensively. So long as her carer kept to his normal timetable, it would be another five hours before supper arrived and, with that in mind, she risked tapping in the five-digit code. To her relief the door unlocked.

She peeked out into the corridor and scoured its length for any sign of movement but there was none. So she crept out, closing the door quietly behind her. She had already thought about leaving it ajar in case the outer keypad code differed from the interior one and she needed to make a hasty retreat, but that consideration had been made days ago, before the intense feeling of desperation to escape had set in. This was now a one-way trip and she was not about to allow herself the opportunity to retreat back to her cell if fear got the better of her. She was getting out of this place right now and that was that.

Chloe made her way down the corridor and past the barred windows that let in welcome rays of light across the floor. Her cell had no windows and, except for that single visit to see Winters, she'd had only the flickering strip lights for illumination. Chloe briefly enjoyed feeling the warmth of the sun against her skin before she continued along the corridor, already knowing where she was heading. Oddly, she had not been blindfolded upon being taken that time to see Winters, and she found herself now retracing the way she had been led. The dark red-lit room had contained a telephone and a window without bars, and there she hoped to make a call and then make her exit, no matter what the drop. Better to face a sprained ankle and a slow getaway than await her fate uncertainly in that confined little cell.

She edged her way around the next corner and into a large circular walkway with extravagant cracked grey marble flooring. A number of small pillars lined the walls, supporting a selection of busts and, although she did not recognize most of the faces portrayed, there was a dark bronze one of Charles Darwin which she remembered passing the last time she had come this way.

Chloe headed past it and off down a corridor with a thick red carpet she recognized from before. As she came to the door at the end, and with a final look behind her, she clasped the shiny brass handle and eased it downwards noiselessly and then poked her head inside.

The familiar crimson bulb overhead bathed the entire room in red and, despite her fear of stumbling into Winters or one of his guards, the place was empty so far as she could see. Leaving the door slightly ajar to allow more of the outside light to penetrate the room, Chloe made her way further inside and over to the desk with the telephone. Despite the sliver of natural light shining through the doorway, it was still extremely difficult to see properly and, with one hand now resting on the receiver, she closed her eyes and counted slowly to five.

When she reopened them her eyes were beginning to acclimatise to the red gloom and so she picked up the receiver and began to dial the operator. It was only after a few seconds' silence that she realized the phone wasn't working. No dial tone, nothing. She was continuing to pat away at the switch hook frantically when the sight of something lying on the desk made her pause. A white – or red under the light – iPhone lay flat on the desk and she immediately scooped it up and began to tap into it. There was no lock on the mobile and within seconds she was successfully dialling, but any feelings of optimism were dashed once she heard the automated beeps of a disconnect.

Chloe glanced down at the screen and noted the signal bars were empty. 'Shit.' From what she had seen so far, the walls of this place were constructed of solid stone, which might explain this lack of reception.

She made her way over to the covered window and already had one hand on the heavy curtain, ready to pull it back, when she became aware of a soft whirring noise coming from the other side of the room. After a pause she slowly tiptoed towards what at first she assumed was a wall, shadowy in the red light but, upon reaching it, she realized it was a large velvet drape hanging from the ceiling as a room divider. With one hand she gently drew it back, cautiously at first and then all the way, as she peered to see what was behind it.

In the corner she could make out what looked like a large cylindrical barrel, resting on one side and supported by thick trestles. She moved nearer still and to one side, so as to prevent her shadow creating even further gloom, then touched the object. It felt cold but not like metal, rather plastic, and she directed the light from the iPhone towards it until she could now see it was a capsule made of white Perspex. At one end an assortment of tubes and electrical cables ran from it directly into the wall.

Chloe slid her hand along the capsule's smooth surface and up over the top, where she found a small square window cut into the surface. With the mobile still held out in front of her, she peered inside.

It was difficult to tell exactly what was contained within because there seemed to be layers of plastic sheeting, like shower curtains, concealing whatever it was. But she could just make out the shadowy outline of what might have been a head.

Chloe moved her face to within centimetres of the window and squinted inside, moving the mobile from side to side in an attempt to get a better look…

And that's when it happened.

Something slammed against the window, and with that the entire capsule began to shake violently. The impact made her jerk backwards against the wall and sent a metal tray crashing to the floor. The capsule was now shaking so hard that the supporting trestles began to sway.

As Chloe backed away from it, she could hear voices outside and further down the corridor. She ran to the window and tugged at the curtains, but they were firmly held in place by the railings above, and so she slipped behind them and began to fumble with the locking clasp as the daylight from outside stung her eyes.

Within moments the clasp finally gave way as the voices behind her got louder. She pushed open the window and looked downwards and, although her vision was dazzled by the natural light, she could tell that the patio floor was only a few metres below. With little else on her mind other than just getting out of the room, she hauled herself out and jumped, then rolled as she hit the ground, ending up crashing into a small hedge that brought her to a stop. Her vision had now adjusted and her eyes darted around as she took in her surroundings. It was a lawned garden surrounded by trees, and as the sound of voices emerged from the window overhead, she crouched down and hid herself in the bushes closest by.

The voices were muffled by a sound that must have been the capsule still rocking back and forth, and Chloe waited for what seemed like forever until she heard the window slam shut again.

There are times when the most obvious hiding place is the most easily overlooked; figuring that if the voices were aware she had just jumped out of the window they would surely be searching for someone making a run for it, Chloe decided to stay put for the moment, hidden in the bushes. She glanced down at the iPhone still in her hand and a wave of relief washed over her as she saw the reception bar was now full. She dialled the operator and could almost have cried when a woman answered.

'Good day, how can I help?'

'I need to be put through to the emergency services immediately,' Chloe gasped, keeping her voice low and cupping the receiver with her hand.

'Which service do you require?' the woman replied in a pleasant and professional way.

'Police...definitely the police.'

There was a pause followed by a series of clicks and then the same woman came back on the line. 'No, Dr Stanton, I don't think we'll be contacting them.'

This reply and the realization that came with it had Chloe dropping the phone just as behind her a pair of gloved hands grabbed her around the waist and began to pull backwards, uprooting a chunk of the hedge along with her.

'We've got her,' a voice called out above the crackling of a walkie-talkie as the foliage wrenched from the bush still smothered her face. 'Better get Winters.'

# Chapter 21

The sun was already disappearing beneath the ocean's horizon as the silver AgustaWestland AW109 helicopter swiftly made its way towards the awe-inspiring sight that was Le Mont-Saint-Michel abbey. Harker watched intently from the cockpit and was overcome by the sheer magnificence of it. Built upon a giant rocky outcrop of granite located half a kilometre offshore from the town of Mont-Saint-Michel itself, the ancient architectural wonder was as magical as anyone could wish for. Like a real-world Hogwarts from the Harry Potter books, the abbey would not have looked out of place gracing the pages of a fairy tale rather than as a bastion of the medieval Christian pilgrimage that it had become.

The Mont's layout reflected perfectly the feudal society that had created it, with the towering abbey having been built at the highest point of the small island, and with the great residences, shops and everything else needed to sustain the community around its base. A series of streets and walkways ran around the outer edges, allowing access to all areas of the Mont, all of them leading upwards to the towering abbey. Why anyone in their right mind would even consider building upon such an unforgiving site was not lost on Bishop Saint Aubert of Avranches, who had founded the commune in the first place. It had taken not one but three visions sent from the archangel St Michael himself before the man was finally convinced to build an oratory on top of this craggy granite slab poking out of the sea, and then convince followers to join him. Over the centuries the island had been raided and attacked many times by invading English armies but, given that the only access possible was during the few hours of low tide, it had proved resistant to any attacks and had become a military base for the French armies over time.

By the twentieth century the Mont had for a time become a prison, due to its isolated and secure location, but by the late eighties it was designated a World Heritage Site and the prison inmates had been replaced with tourists. With over three million people visiting each year, the stables and blacksmith's shops had been replaced with restaurants and a few small hotels. But despite the change in the visiting clientele, the abbey itself was still run by Benedictine monks, with four masses celebrated daily.

'Beautiful, isn't it?' Harker remarked as Carter poked his head into the cockpit and looked outside over the top of his glasses.

'Not bad, but you know what's even more beautiful?' Carter was looking decidedly twitchy. 'Being on the ground.'

Getting Carter onto the helicopter in the first place had taken some persuasion. Harker was puzzled by his friend's willingness to make the trip to Pisa, compared with his seeming horror at the idea of travelling in a helicopter.

'Planes can glide,' Carter had reasoned, 'but if a helicopter's engine goes, then that's it – you drop like a stone.'

His assessment was a fair one, but despite his protests the ex-don had been bundled into the Agusta with the help of Anthony, the Templar bodyguard Brulet had assigned to them. In his thirties, with jet-black hair and the frame of a lean athlete, Anthony had not offered his surname upon introduction and Harker had not felt any need to know it. So long as this man was good at his job, then that was enough for him.

'We'll be landing soon,' the pilot announced as they drew nearer to the brightly lit rock island, and it was Anthony who now pulled Carter back into his seat and then reached over to tap Harker on the shoulder.

'We'll be landing on the island itself,' Anthony explained, much to Harker's surprise. For, apart from a small car park used by the abbey's residents, there were no private vehicles allowed here, let alone a helicopter.

'Land where?' Harker demanded, scanning the tightly packed island rock where literally every centimetre of space had been built upon over the centuries.

Anthony pointed out a square patch of light just beneath the abbey itself, on the island's second level down. 'There's a small lawn over there we can use.'

'Will the authorities be OK with that?' Harker asked as the helicopter began to descend. 'It's a World Heritage Site, and didn't a major refurbishment take place here recently?'

His concern was noted and the Templar smiled. 'Who do you think helped pay for it? Don't worry, they'll be fine.'

The silver helicopter descended gracefully past the imposing stone walls of the abbey and hovered briefly above the turfed lawn before descending onto its surface with a gentle bump. The high wind from the rotors sent up a spray of dust and the engines were already winding down as Anthony swung open the side door and dropped onto the grass outside.

'Let's go, gentlemen,' the Templar urged politely and, needing no further encouragement, Carter exited hurriedly, followed by Harker, who instinctively ducked as the rotors continued to slow overhead.

'What is it with you people and dramatic entrances?' A voice with a thick French accent shouted the greeting, only just audible above the whine of the engine.

At one edge of the lawn, a man with short brown hair and wearing jeans and a pale-blue sleeveless shirt stepped out of the shadows and waved them over towards him. At first Harker thought he was smiling but, as he reached him, it became clear it was instead a look of irritation.

'We do have a car park, you know,' the man continued with a look of exasperation.

'Apologies, Michel, but we're rather constrained by time,' the Templar replied, shaking the man's hand. 'No more surprises, I promise.'

'Better not be. There's already going to be hell to pay for this little entrance of yours,' Michel growled, still struggling to be heard. 'Come on, follow me.'

With Michel leading, they headed away from the helicopter and up a long walkway leading up the next level to the abbey itself. It wasn't until the sound of the helicopter engine had died sufficiently that their guide began to talk again.

'Now we can finally hear each other, perhaps you would like to introduce me to our guests.'

'Alex Harker and his colleague David Carter,' Anthony declared, allowing them all to shake hands. 'And this gentleman is Michel Beaumont. He's with the Manche *département* who administer the Mont.'

'Yes, I know what La Manche is,' Harker replied, 'and it's a pleasure.'

'Likewise,' Michel offered, then abruptly turned his attention to Anthony. 'You know we normally ask that you give us a bit more of a heads-up than just a few hours.'

Anthony looked sheepish as he sought immediately to appease his counterpart. 'You're correct, of course, and usually, as you know, we would. But we have a rather pressing matter that requires us to gain access tonight.'

Michel appeared to think about it, more to make a point perhaps than to consider whether to refuse them, and after a few seconds gave a dry smile. 'Very well, come on.'

With Michel and Anthony in the lead, Harker followed a few paces behind alongside Carter, who was now looking ever more mystified with every step they took towards the abbey.

'Alex, I don't mean to be a bore but – what the hell are we doing here?' he whispered.

Carter had remained unusually quiet throughout most of the two-hour helicopter trip, and even during the refuelling stop in Lyon he had spent the time stretching his legs and preparing himself for the next part of the flight. Coupled with his inebriated state in the first place, the ex-don had not even asked why or to where they were taking this trip in the first place. But now he was sobering up and, with the long brisk walk to the Mont's summit it was clear that he was finally ready to know more.

'And weren't we on a boat or something earlier?'

Carter's apparent mental blackout had Harker chuckling. 'The man we met on the boat is a friend of mine,' he explained, not wanting to give too much away. 'He's a collector, of sorts.'

'A collector of what?'

'Historical artefacts,' Harker replied. 'And he may be able to help us with the Gigas pages.'

'Really. How so?'

There was no need to tell Carter all about the threatening phone call he had received from 'God', and so Harker kept it simple. The ex-don was already having a difficult time dealing with their earlier adventure, and the last thing he needed was to be given another reason to resume drinking again.

'Our good friend "God" gave me another call, and he now wants us to find the final page.'

'There's another page! Jesus, what's this one going to contain?' Carter shuddered as if unnerved at the thought. 'Not another raising the dead incantation, I hope.'

'I don't know, but amazingly it's preserved among my friend's rather extensive collection which he keeps here at the Mont.'

'That sounds like a coincidence too good to be true,' Carter gasped, starting to breathe heavily as the long trek up to the abbey began taking its toll.

'I know,' Harker muttered quietly. 'That's what's worrying me.'

It took five minutes to reach the Mont's highest level, and by the time they arrived Carter was red in the face. 'My constitution's not made for this kind of thing,' he puffed, and received a pat of encouragement from Harker.

'I think we're almost there,' Harker said as he watched Michel approach a steel-grated door built into the abbey wall. He unlocked it with a long metal key and headed inside, with Anthony on his heels.

'I bloody well hope so, or you're going to have another corpse on your hands.'

'Don't worry, this is it,' Harker reassured him.

The room itself was large but Harker found himself instantly disappointed at the shabby and dusty state of it. Extending in rows were wooden shelves spanning the room's entire length, each copiously loaded with boxed items and each individually identified with a serial number handwritten with a black marker pen. There were only a couple of rusting wall lights for illumination, and the smell of a decomposing rodent only added to the musty atmosphere.

'This is a bit of a shithole,' Carter declared flatly, then he reached to touch a box on the nearest shelf, whereupon the cardboard began to flake. 'You do realize just because you're storing ancient antiquities, it doesn't mean the facilities have to be ancient as well?'

His sarcasm was met with silence from Michel, who now closed the door behind them and made his way back to join Anthony next to the wall on the far side of the room.

'Contained here are some of the most important historical relics and objects ever retrieved. They have been collected for over a millennium and, besides,' Michel proclaimed defensively, 'they say you should never judge a book by its cover.'

'Not sure I even want to read that particular book, if I'm honest,' Carter continued before receiving a subtle dig in his ribs from Harker. 'Steady on, Alex, I'm just saying—'

'It looks fine to me,' Harker interrupted, now just wanting to find the final Codex page and get out of this dusty and rank-smelling room.

Michel pressed his hand against the wall next to him and a small square panel sank in and then slid downwards to reveal a shiny oblong pane of black glass about the size of a sheet of A4 paper. 'Give us some credit, would you?'

Michel next placed his palm against the glass, and a solid green light shone downwards, like that from a photocopier. This light then disappeared and a monotone female voice sounded from the panel. 'Fingerprints confirmed. ID accepted.'

With that confirmation half of the wall slid away to reveal a black steel walk-in lift with dimmed uplighters embedded in the floor, lightly illuminating its dark interior.

'Gentlemen.' Anthony gestured. 'Take your places, please.'

Harker wasn't sure if it was the surprising presence of the lift or just the pervasive stench of dead rat hanging in the air, but he suddenly felt giddy. *This is more like it*, he thought, and he took his place alongside Carter at the back of the lift before Michel and Anthony joined them. The doors then closed and they began to descend slowly.

Their short journey was made in silence, which only served to fuel Harker's feeling of anticipation, and he found it impossible to wipe away the large grin which his lips were forming.

He had heard titbits of information concerning the main Templar vault, but to be seconds from experiencing it had him more than a little excited. As the doors opened up again he found all the worries and concerns that had twisted his stomach in a knot were simply fading away.

'Welcome to the Mont vault, gentlemen,' Anthony announced as the Templar exited the lift and moved to one side, allowing Harker to get his first glimpse.

The huge warehouse-sized space had a fifty-metre lane running down its length, and as Harker made his way onto a grated steel platform with shiny chrome handrails running around the edges, he realized it was actually far bigger than that.

There were six lanes in total and, as he looked down from the raised platform, he could see that on either side of each lane were sturdy-looking shelving units, all holding a vast array of items. Even more interesting was that many of these items were encased in either glass or Perspex boxes which enhanced the protection of what must have been the centuries-old objects they contained.

'The temperature of this entire facility is strictly regulated, ensuring that moisture damage never becomes an issue,' Michel explained, pointing towards the rows of transparent cases. 'We also encase some of the more fragile items in hardened Perspex containers, and individual suction pumps create a vacuum to avoid any decay.'

'Now this is definitely not a shithole,' Carter said jovially as he joined Harker at the railings.

'Good to hear it,' Michel remarked, clearly pleased his unexpected guest was having to eat his words.

It was indeed an impressive set-up, but that was not what was on Harker's mind. 'How on earth did you do this? I mean, we're directly underneath the abbey, right?'

'Yes, about thirty metres down within the core of the rock itself,' Anthony explained.

'No, I mean, how the hell did you build this without anyone knowing?'

'Come. I'll tell you as we walk.' Anthony was already beginning to make his way down the steps which led from the platform down to the main floor.

Just then Michel called out after him. 'I'm going back up to the surface,' he explained as he stepped back into the lift 'We usually have a few days' notice to ensure we minimise the risk of anyone seeing us enter this place but, given your paltry two-hour heads-up, it's possible there are a few tourists wandering around who are staying overnight in the first-level hotels.' Michel tapped at the lift button and waited for the doors to close. 'Anthony, I will see you again when you're finished. *Au revoir.*'

'Thanks again, Michel,' Anthony managed to get in before the doors closed. Then he continued down the stairs, his two guests hard on his heels, and began to answer Harker's last question. 'Firstly, the entire rock that Mont-Saint-Michel sits on is composed of granite, so its natural hardness enabled such a large cavity to be excavated and yet still maintain its structural integrity. But it still needed a remarkable feat of engineering to make it happen.

'What truly made it possible, and what not many people know, is that this first-floor space was carved out sometime during the medieval period. The exact date is not known, but when the Mont became a military outpost during the Hundred Years' War, the French army excavated this large underground area. Some say it was intended for additional food storage in case the opposing English managed to lay sea siege. Others believe that it was meant to become a hideaway for troops if the Mont was ever overrun; the idea being that, once night-time approached, the concealed French troops could take the English by surprise and reclaim the rock.'

'What do you think?' asked Harker, fascinated by this piece of lost history.

'Honestly, I don't know,' Anthony replied as he continued to lead them along towards the furthest aisle, 'but what I can tell you for sure is that the Templars discovered it in the mid-eighteen hundreds, and then sought to increase its size. It was perfectly possible as it was then overseen by the Catholic Church and, although formally banished and disbanded by the Church, the Templars still had many ties with clergy throughout the world. Of course, the real renovation came when the Mont was later refurbished, during which time we secretly added another floor.'

'Wait,' Carter exclaimed, grasping Anthony by the shoulder and bringing him to a halt. 'What do you mean, the Templars?'

Anthony shot Harker a look of surprise at this, and not only did Carter notice but he was now eyeing Harker mistrustfully.

'Why do I feel like I'm the only one here who is not in the loop?' Carter complained, and the question was directed solely at Harker this time. 'So who exactly are these "friends" of yours, Alex?'

On their way to Brulet's yacht, Harker had given some serious consideration to bringing Carter up to speed regarding his association with the Templars but, given the ex-don's personal obsession with all things conspiratorial, he had decided against it. What's more, up until about three seconds ago, he'd really believed he was going to get the through this without Carter even getting a whiff of anything other than the smell of whisky on his own breath. However, Anthony's slip-up was likely to dash that hope to dust.

'Perhaps I should leave you two alone for a moment,' Anthony suggested gingerly, and he pointed over to the final aisle. 'I'll be over there when you're ready.'

As he went off, Harker prepared himself to drop a bombshell on Carter, and he knew his friend was going to love it. Possibly too much, but who knew? Maybe his excitement at the prospect of discovering that such a legendary group still existed, centuries in the making and steeped in the kind of history that he loved so much might have a majorly positive impact on him – it might even curb his drinking. At least until Chloe was safe. The only really troubling aspect was how Brulet might react. Harker had been instructed that it was his own decision as to which people he saw fit to tell about the Templars but, given the Grand Master's initial reaction to Carter, he wasn't sure his choice here would be welcomed.

'Do you still have your whisky flask on you?' Harker asked.

'Silly question – of course I do,' Carter replied, pulling the slim metal container from his back pocket, then holding it out in front of him. 'Need a tot, do you?'

Harker took the flask and, with a gentle shake, realized it was only about half full, maybe a couple of shots' worth. 'As a matter of fact, I do.'

He unscrewed the cap and took a measured swig, then passed it back to Carter. 'Now finish it off.'

Carter was taken aback by this order, but more than happy to comply, so he downed the liquid, screwed the cap back on and was about to put it back in his pocket when Harker wagged a finger at him.

'Now give it to me.'

Carter looked unhappy at the request as he continued to grip the steel drinking flask in his hand tightly, almost lovingly.

'David,' Harker said sternly, taking an intimidating step closer, 'if you want to know what this place is and who my friends really are, then the cost is no more drinking.'

'What, ever?' Carter spluttered, more than a little freaked out by the very concept.

'Until we find Chloe, however long that takes,' Harker insisted, still reaching out for the flask. 'If you're coming along with me, wherever it takes us, then we have to do it as a team and that means having you at your best.'

Whether it was the reminder of Chloe's predicament or the suggestion of being part of a team, Harker wasn't sure, but Carter's defiant glare began to soften and, with an involuntary gulp, he passed over the steel flask.

'Very well, Alex,' Carter conceded, and he cleared his throat and stood up straight like a man preparing himself for action. 'But if this is going to take us days and days, then I only ask that you allow me a small nip from time to time, or else I'm going to get sick.'

It was a sad truth to confess and Harker felt a pinch of sorrow for his friend, but he dismissed this emotion immediately. If Carter stopped drinking even for a short while, then his liver would surely benefit, which meant he could drink even more when he started up again. Of course, this was a nonsensical argument, but it did vanquish any feelings of guilt Harker had on the subject as he slipped the container into his inside jacket pocket with a nod of his head.

Carter assumed a look of fresh determination. 'Now why don't you tell me exactly who these people are?'

Harker braced himself because he knew Carter was likely to flip upon hearing the news. The man had long been obsessed with the idea of mysterious, secret societies, and now he was about to hear actual proof of their existence. Harker felt extremely proud to be among the ranks of the Order of the Knights Templar, but it was only recently that he had come to actually consider himself truly part of it all rather than an outsider who had just stumbled across them by chance. It was with this feeling of fully belonging that he now began to explain everything to Carter. In truth he had practised this speech many times in his head, and now finally he had a chance to deliver it.

'I am part of a brotherhood spanning a millennium of human history. Our mission is to protect the downtrodden of every race and creed from those evilly intentioned individuals who would seek to control humanity from the darkest of shadows.'

'The Freemasons?' Carter suggested. Then his eyes twitched excitedly as he guessed again. 'No, the Illuminati?'

Harker's expression went blank and his shoulders slumped. 'Look, do you want to hear this or not?'

Carter looked instantly apologetic. 'Sorry. Please continue.'

'OK, then, let's start again,' Harker grumbled irritably, and he resumed his stoic demeanour once more. 'I am part of a brotherhood that spans a millennium of human history...'

## *Chapter 22*

'So this vault, along with others, holds the Knights Templar's most prized artefacts,' Carter pressed, struggling to contain his excitement.

'Yes, but it's not just *a* vault but *the* vault,' Harker replied, succumbing to his friend's infectious enthusiasm. 'And, given that the last page of the Gigas is kept in here, it's exactly where we need to be.'

However, that they were so close to retrieving the final page was lost on Carter and he continued to, literally, drool over the idea that the Knights Templar still existed, and survived as such a potent organization. 'It's bloody incredible. I always knew in my heart that these kinds of mysterious societies existed in some form – they just had to – but that their influence is still so impressive...' Carter was licking his lips as he scanned the rows of Perspex boxes with delight. 'I wonder if I'll be able to take a proper look sometime.'

'Maybe,' Harker lied, not wanting to squash his friend's newly found zeal.

'The Knights Templar...it's unbelievable. Do you think they'll let me join?'

'Let's focus on the task at hand, shall we, David?' Harker received a disappointed look from Carter, who clearly took that to be a no. 'But consider yourself, as of this moment, a Templar associate.'

The offer was met with glee, and Carter mouthed the words proudly.

'Templar associate…it's got a nice ring to it, like someone who's in the middle of things but at the same time works stealthily from the outside, you know, to protect and serve the Knights Templar and vanquish the deviant… Do I get a badge or something?'

It was apparent to Harker that he might have over-egged his disclosure regarding the Order of the Templars and his role within it, so he thought it best he bring the thrilled ex-don back to earth. 'You're not a cop and so there's no badge. You're just working alongside, OK?'

Seeming undaunted by Harker's reality check, Carter folded his arms and snarled. 'Hey, I just sat through your self-serving and overly dramatic account without saying a word, so how about you offer me the same courtesy? This is unbelievably exciting for me.'

After rolling his eyes, Harker nodded. 'You're right, Detective. Now can we please proceed?'

'We can, but without the sarcasm.' Carter now began making his way towards the final aisle in search of Anthony. 'Let us retrieve the page that's been for so long amid the sands of time.'

'Oh God,' Harker groaned and then he followed. This was going to become really annoying, really fast.

Anthony was already uncoupling the vacuum pump from one of the Perspex boxes by the time they both joined him and, with a renewed sense of purpose, it was Carter who spoke first. 'So you're a Templar, Anthony? Well it's an absolute pleasure to be working with you, my friend.' He offered his hand. 'As we were never properly introduced, my name is David Carter and I am here to help.'

Anthony glanced over at Harker with a vacant expression, then he shook Carter's hand. 'I know who you are, Mr Carter. We already met on the helicopter.'

'Ah yes, but I was a bit under the weather on the way over,' Carter replied, obviously not willing to confess the real reason. 'But I can assure you that I am now running at a hundred per cent, and ready to serve.'

The man gave him a warm smile as Carter continued this attempt to confirm his usefulness. 'My first question is how, amongst all these items, did you know this was the one containing the Gigas page?'

'Now that's a good question,' Anthony replied before he raised up his Samsung smart phone. 'I have an app containing a full inventory of everything stored in here. Just tap in a search, and it shows you exactly where it is located.'

'Clever,' Harker remarked before pushing himself in front of Carter. 'Can we take a look, then?'

'Of course.'

Anthony diligently unlocked the four securing clasps around the box's lid and pulled at the side handle until, with a hiss as the vacuum seal was broken, the lid came off and he opened it fully and rested it back on its hinges.

'This is it.'

Harker reached inside and retrieved an item wrapped in chamois cloth, then gently unwrapped it to reveal a now familiar oversized page. Standing back, he unfolded it fully.

It was definitely a page from the Gigas, and the strange text and symbols it contained were identical, although this one was in far better condition.

'This is the one,' Harker confirmed.

Carter peered over his shoulder and offered his own thoughts. 'It's a match, all right. I just wish we could translate it.'

'We have tried to do so over the years,' Anthony assured them as he closed the container's lid and then cast his own eyes over the dark-coloured piece of vellum. 'But without any success,' he added. 'I doubt there's anyone living who can.'

It was an odd comment from Harker's point of view, given that the only people he knew who could read the text had ended up bringing back the dead to the land of the living. 'There are a few,' he began.

'How would you know that?' Anthony asked.

'Because we've seen them in action,' Carter interrupted in an unusually authoritative tone, now getting ever deeper into his role as 'associate'. 'And it caused the dead to rise.'

'What!' The very idea made Anthony flinch. 'Tristan didn't mention anything about resurrection.'

'He probably didn't want to alarm you, or perhaps he simply didn't believe me. It's hard to accept, but we did see it happen – and the one thing I am certain of is that it wasn't a resurrection.' Harker was about to explain further when Carter interrupted.

'No, it was the beginning of Judgement Day. But this is a twisted version of it.'

Anthony's expression suggested that he was either horrified at this claim or he thought they had both gone crazy. Either way it made for an uncomfortable moment, and one that Carter now made more confusing still.

'And the same people who performed that blasphemous ceremony wanted to torture me up my bottom with an electric cattle prod…but, luckily, Alex reached me before that could happen. Still,' Carter said, extending his neck well over the top of his shirt collar and trying to look bold, 'I would have taken one for the team… A bit like Ned Beatty in the film *Deliverance*…you know, where the rednecks deprive him of his anal virginity.'

'Anal virginity…' The very thought had Anthony wincing. 'I didn't even know there was such a thing.'

'Neither did I until they tried to take it from me.'

'Enough,' Harker growled. 'Suffice it to say we've been involved in some very strange goings-on during the last few days.'

'I'll say,' Anthony replied, looking at Carter with some unease as Harker folded up the page and slipped it into his pocket.

'I'm taking this page for the time being,' Harker said sternly. 'Tristan said I could have full access to it.'

There was no objection from Anthony and he merely nodded in agreement. 'Where do you need to go now, then?'

Until Harker received his next call from 'God' they were stuck in a holding pattern and, with an anxious glance at Carter, he decided the only thing to do was sit tight and wait for the psycho to get in contact. 'I really need to take a good look at this page, so is there somewhere we can hole up for an hour and get a drink? Maybe some coffee?' Harker was directing his gaze at Carter.

'Coffee sounds good,' Carter confirmed, without a hint of resentment.

'There's a restaurant and some coffee shops on the lower level,' Anthony informed them and, with a confirming nod from Harker, they made their way back towards the lift. 'So you really saw a corpse rise up from the dead?' Anthony asked, now opening up to the gruesome idea.

'I'm afraid so. And it was two of them…well, three if you count the man in Berlin.'

Anthony let out a deep sigh and he looked somewhat deflated. 'I've never heard of anything like it. It's so hard to believe… Do you know what it means?'

The question had Harker shaking his head. 'I wish I knew, but the Gigas pages seem to be at the heart of it.'

There was a sudden sense of aimlessness as to their next move, and it hung over them like a cloud as Anthony called the lift.

'On seconds thoughts, maybe we should head back to the mainland and find somewhere to hole up there, because it's likely to cause Michel a stomach ulcer if we stay at the Mont any longer,' Anthony said with a mischievous smile. 'He'll have got enough explaining to do already, and I don't want to give the poor man any more grief.'

The lift door slid open to reveal Michel himself standing inside with a bemused look on his face. 'Speak of the Devil.' Anthony frowned at the unexpected sight. 'Don't worry, Michel, we'll be out of your hair as soon as we get back to the helicopter.' He reached over and lightly patted the Manche official on the shoulder.

Michel didn't respond but his eyes fluttered oddly, then he slowly lurched forward and dropped like a stone, slamming down face first on the metal platform with a crack as his skull hit the floor.

It happened so fast that neither Harker nor Anthony could break his fall. As they began to turn him over, it was Harker who recoiled at the sight of the freshly spilt blood on his hands.

A bloody red patch stained one side of Michel's body just below his ribs and, as Anthony rolled him over onto his back for a better look, the barrel of an M4 Carbine poked out from inside the lift.

'I wouldn't waste your energy,' a voice declared and the barrel jerked towards Anthony, who was already reaching for the Beretta in his waist holster. 'Just don't be foolish. I have you cold.'

Vlad stepped cautiously out from the gloom within the lift and prodded his weapon at them in a threatening manner as two other men, wearing jeans, grey Kevlar vests and black balaclavas, exited from behind him, each with a silenced 9mm machine gun. One of these men retrieved Anthony's Beretta and pulled him roughly to his feet while the other shoved Harker and Carter back against the railing.

Satisfied his men had the upper hand, Vlad took a moment to gaze around the storage facility before lowering his gun and resting his elbows on the railing. 'So this is it?' he said, turning his attention to Anthony. 'This is where the Templars keep all their most precious trinkets?'

'Who are you?' Anthony snapped, before receiving a heavy jab in the back from the nearest gunman with the silencer of his 9mm.

'Be nice,' the armed man hissed in his ear as Vlad turned his attention to Harker.

'Our mutual friend here knows, don't you, Alex?'

Anthony now glared accusingly at Harker, as Vlad, with a decadent smile, turned his head towards Carter. 'And you and I still have a date with an electric cattle prod, don't we?'

Carter said nothing as Harker moved in front of him protectively. 'There's not going to be anything like that happening here,' he said firmly, and this defiance was met with a menacing look from Vlad.

'Oh no, I think we can come up with something far worse than that,' Vlad said before turning his attention back to survey the wide expanse of the storage facility. 'But, before we get to the fun part, let's get the business side of things wrapped up, shall we?'

Vlad now turned his attention to Anthony. 'So you're an honest to God Templar, are you? How interesting,' he said, eyeing the man with curiosity. 'You don't look anything special.'

'Tell your men to put down their weapons and you can find out for yourself,' Anthony growled boldly, and his offer was met with an amused grin from Vlad.

'Very tempting, but I just don't have the time, I'm afraid.'

The single burst of gunfire propelled Anthony forward as a bullet from the 9mm ripped through the right-hand side of his chest. He collapsed in a heap on the floor, where a pool of blood began to slowly spread out from his still twitching body.

'Now that guard dog is out of the way, we can focus on more important matters,' Vlad said with a smile.

Harker, his ears still ringing from the gunshot, yelled out furiously. 'The page isn't here,' he lied, feeling as if the thick piece of vellum in his pocket was visibly expanding in size.

'The Gigas page?' Vlad replied calmly and, nudging away Anthony's hand with the sole of his boot, he bent down and pulled the Templar's Samsung mobile from his pocket. 'It's not about the page,' Vlad continued before stepping over and extracting the thick piece of vellum from Harker's inside pocket, 'although I might as well take it.'

Harker fought the urge to snatch it back, and then watched as Vlad passed it over to the gunman standing beside Anthony's body. Vlad then proceeded to scroll though the Templar's mobile. It took him mere seconds to find what he wanted, then he passed over the mobile to the gunman behind him, who then made his way down to the main floor and began searching the aisles.

'Who the hell are you people?' Harker demanded, sick and tired of always being in the dark.

'Let's start with who *you* are.' Vlad flicked a gloved finger towards them. 'You, Alex Harker, are a professor at Cambridge University. And you, David Carter, are an ex-professor – a disgraced one, no less, who seems to have found a new calling at the bottom of an empty whisky bottle. That sound about right?'

'Apart from the "disgraced" bit,' Carter said, his feathers clearly ruffled by the insult.

'Call it what you will' – Vlad waved his hand uncaringly – 'but if I made the effort to discover who you two are, then I don't see why I should explain who I am if you haven't done likewise.' The arrogance in Vlad's tone was infuriating, but Harker remained silent as the man continued. 'Why you seem so interested in my business, however, is something that continues to elude me.'

'Let's not pussyfoot around, Vlad.' Harker was tired of playing this game. 'You know we're after the Gigas pages.'

'True, but that is not why *we* are here. This is about seizing an opportunity.' The condescension in his voice indicated that Vlad was unimpressed with Harker's grasp of the whole situation. 'The Gigas pages are indeed the key and, be under no illusions, the Day of Judgement is very real – as you witnessed for yourself back at Cervete cemetery. They once held the key to setting it all in motion but that irreversible moment has passed, and they are now as useless as the dead Templar behind me.'

'If that's the case, then what are you doing here?' Harker asked.

'The Templars have been known to us for longer than you know, and when the Dark Prince returns to consume this world, I will meet him with the reassurance that anyone who might stand against him has been destroyed. It is my gift to him and will serve to demonstrate my undying loyalty and devotion.'

'Oh my God,' Harker muttered, feeling as if the wind had been knocked out of him. He now finally realized what Vlad was talking about, and the unwitting role he himself had played in it. 'You want the Templar's *Illuminismo*!'

A deceitful smile crept across Vlad's lips as he gave a slow and unnerving nod. 'Within those pages are listed the names and details of every Templar, every hideout, and every business that those pathetically pious morons are linked to. They will be tracked down and destroyed until not a shred of the stain they have left on this earth exists, and all thanks to you, Alex. We would never have even considered attempting to waste our resources on such a task, but with your help it will be like taking candy from a baby. The utter destruction and dismantling of a sect that should have been consigned to the pages of history almost a thousand years ago.'

Vlad moved his head to within centimetres of Harker's face and his lips pursed grimly. 'When the judgement begins, and billions of people begin to see the world crumble around them, and their feeble minds struggle to comprehend the reality of truths that have been lost to history and replaced with science, it is of you that I will think of and the contribution you have made to making it happen.'

This last part was too much for Harker and he lashed out and grabbed Vlad by the neck, but before he could apply any real pressure, a firm blow to the back of his head from the butt of a 9mm machine gun sent him to his knees.

Carter was already helping Harker back up when the gunman searching the aisles down below called out enthusiastically. 'It's here, but there must be over twenty volumes.'

'Then bring me the most recent, we've no need for dead names,' Vlad shouted back, straightening his creased collar as Harker rubbed the back of his own head with a groan. 'The only question now is what to do with you two. Should I allow you to see our masterpiece unfold or kill you here and now and then watch you, when your time comes, rise up to be judged?' There was a sickeningly playful tone to Vlad's voice, and he took a few steps back and stared at Harker curiously. 'I wonder if your recent actions will have any effect on your fate. I must admit it would be amusing to see your bloated corpse and decaying brain try and rationalize your predicament.'

Vlad took a moment to consider it further, and then he gave a nod towards the gunman standing behind Carter. 'Yes, I think I would enjoy that very much indeed.'

Just as Harker heard the metallic click of the 9mm being readied against his back, he felt Carter grasp his wrist and looked over to find his friend looking decidedly confident. It seemed odd that, in these final moments, the ex-don should have lost his fear...but as Harker looked towards where Carter's eyes were focused, he understood why.

There was sudden movement behind Vlad and, as he stood readying himself for the no doubt gratifying execution about to take place, a bloody arm slid itself around his neck and wrenched him off balance, and then over the top of the railing, sending him downwards with a hard thud to the floor below.

Anthony gasped at the exertion the move had cost him, and he steadied himself again as blood dripped from the wound in his chest and his breathing strained due to the collapsed lung that kept him from standing fully upright. He managed one final desperate glance towards Harker as a single bullet struck the wounded Templar directly in the forehead and brought him crashing to the floor for the final time. In the same moment, Harker slammed his head backwards into the gunman's face and grabbed hold of the 9mm. The man's grip on the rifle was vice-like, and it was only because Carter swung his foot hard into the attacker's heel and sent him flipping backwards onto the platform floor that Harker managed to finally wrestle the weapon away from him.

'Go!' Harker yelled, barging Carter towards the open lift as bullets zipped past them from the second gunman, who had seen Vlad collapse onto the floor and kept firing as he ran towards them.

Carter reached the lift first and stumbled over Michel's body, which sent him ploughing face first through the doors As Harker dived after him, the bullets began to rain down on them, and he quickly reached up and slammed the button for level 1.

Nothing happened however and, with nowhere to provide cover, Harker did the only thing he could by raising the 9mm and firing indiscriminately. The kick from the machine gun was tremendous and he struggled to keep a grip on it as Carter continued lying flat with his face pressed against the floor of the lift. The quick offensive did its job and the gunman's return fire suddenly stopped. Whether he was reloading his clip or just taking cover it was impossible to say, but within seconds the doors were closing. As the lift began to rise, they could hear thudding sounds from below as further bullets hit the outer door panel below them.

'Bloody hell,' Harker yelled as the gunfire finally stopped and, holding the 9mm in one hand, he began to pat himself down with the other. Satisfied he had not been hit, he turned his attention to Carter, who was repeating the same ritual. 'Are you hit?'

'I don't think so.'

The man was panting heavily and sweating but he looked remarkably calm, given the circumstances, as he scrambled to his feet. 'Did you see what Anthony did? If it wasn't for him, we'd be dead.'

'I know but it's not over yet,' Harker replied, and he stood up with the 9mm pressed into his shoulder and aiming it at the other side of the lift. 'You hug that wall, and if there's anyone up top, I'm going to start shooting.'

Carter said nothing, and with a nod, he pressed himself against the side wall as tightly as he could.

The ascent only took fifteen seconds or so but it felt like several minutes. As Harker continued to aim the gun forward, the adrenalin in his bloodstream made his arm tremble. If there was anybody waiting outside when the door opened, for them it would be like shooting fish in a barrel and he knew it, but regardless he was going to take down as many of them as possible.

The lift stopped with a bump and the doors slid open and, even before Harker had time to tell if anyone was out there, he began shooting, his nerves getting the better of him. Bullets spewed out against the opposite wall, sending plumes of dust into the air. After half a dozen shots Harker eased off on the trigger and glanced nervously around the room beyond. It was empty, and without hesitation he rushed to the wooden door leading outside and opened it cautiously. He poked his head out, his neck muscles tensing as he prepared to get shot the moment he did so, but the outer walkway was also empty. He laid the 9mm on the floor and motioned for Carter to join him as he continued outside.

The night air was cool and they were already heading back the way they had come when Carter tugged at the back of his coat.

'Shouldn't we bring the gun?' he asked, looking perturbed at having dumped their only means of defence.

'It's a bit of a gamble, I know, but I'm not running around Mont-Saint-Michel with a machine gun,' Harker replied, picking up the pace along the narrow winding path. 'There are tourists staying overnight here and the last thing we need is to shoot someone by accident.'

It was a reasonable point, and even though Carter looked uneasy at the prospect, he didn't say a word and instead concentrated on navigating the stone steps leading them back to the Mont's second level.

'The helicopter can get us off this rock and we'll decide, once we're airborne, where to go next.'

'Sounds good,' Carter puffed, trying to match Harker's stride, which increased in speed with every step. 'Anywhere's better than here.'

They managed the journey in a couple of minutes, made easier now by the fact they were going downhill. Better still was the fact that they came across no tourists – and, even better, no psychopathic gunmen.

The last twenty metres proved the most nerve-racking, and as they approached the helicopter Harker was already swirling his hand in the air. Luckily the pilot saw his gesture, and by the time they were inside the rotors were already beginning to turn.

'Where's Anthony?' the man asked.

'I'm sorry but he didn't make it,' Harker replied briefly, glancing through the windscreen for any sign of Vlad and his henchmen.

'Didn't make it?'

'We got ambushed. They killed Anthony and they're going to kill us to if we don't get out of here right now.' Harker yelled the words, which were met with a look of confusion from the pilot. He had no idea if this aviator was a Templar too, or just one of the accompanying crew that came with Brulet's borrowed yacht, but the man immediately took action and within seconds the Agusta was lifting up into the air with speed.

Harker took his place in the cockpit passenger seat as behind him Carter buckled himself in too, and it was not until they were ten metres into the air that a degree of calm began to settle between them.

'I was instructed to bring you directly back to Mr Brulet,' the pilot explained as they started to pull away from Mont-Saint-Michel. 'We'll have to make a stop in Lyon again but—'

The pilot suddenly went silent as there was a loud popping sound, then he jerked in his seat and lurched forward against the control stick, causing the helicopter to veer sharply to the right. Harker was flung against the side window but managed to fight against the gravity pulling at his body, grab the pilot's shoulder and push him back into his seat. What he saw next sent butterflies swarming around his stomach. There was a circular bullet hole in the side window and a patch of blood on the pilot's chest, which increased in size as the wound bled profusely.

Harker didn't bother to look outside, because he already knew who had taken the shot, and instead he grabbed the control stick as the Agusta continued to descend. He had no idea how to fly a helicopter and he found himself screaming at the pilot when the controls refused to respond.

With their descent gathering speed, Harker was already pushing himself back into his seat and preparing for impact when the aircraft began to slow, and he looked over at the aviator, who was now grasping at the stick and desperately trying to take back control. The Agusta pitched forward and sped away from Mont-Saint-Michel towards the mainland, less than half a kilometre away, as the pilot fought against the extreme pain of his gunshot wound.

They could not have been more than twenty metres above the glinting, black waterline, but they were now flying straight and level as the pilot groaned through gritted teeth while struggling just to remain conscious.

Two hundred metres to go and the helicopter was on course. One hundred metres to go and they began to lose altitude, and with only fifty metres to go the pilot's eyes were beginning to flutter as his whole body started to shut down.

'Put us down here,' Harker shouted, and he did the only thing he could think of to keep the man going, which was to administer a hard slap across the pilot's face. It may have been an act of desperation and Harker could have sworn he heard Carter yell something like 'Are you insane?' but the pilot responded. With just metres to go, he brought the Agusta down onto a car park by the coastline, landing with an almighty crack, and he even managed to kill the rotors with a flick of a switch before finally succumbing to his wounds. The pilot's head sagged against his chest and, as the engine wound down, Harker pressed his forefinger against the man's neck but could feel nothing. He was gone.

Outside, a small crowd of passers-by were already beginning to gather and Harker pulled himself up from his seat to find Carter, white as a sheet, desperately clawing at his seat belt.

'That's why I don't travel in helicopters,' he cried angrily. After finally unclicking his belt, he reached for the door handle, threw it open and stumbled out onto the grey tarmac of the car park. 'What happened?' Carter then wheezed, unaware of the potshot the Agusta had taken in mid-flight.

'They shot the pilot,' Harker replied, wanting to kiss the ground after he too had exited the helicopter.

'How?'

'Presumably with a gun,' Harker suggested sarcastically, still trying to dispel the panic he was feeling. To pull off a shot like that, the person was either plain lucky or a highly trained marksman, and Harker was inclined to believe the latter as he remembered events back at the cemetery and the accuracy of the potshots as they made their escape. It had to be Vlad.

'Is he alive?' Carter asked, looking over at the slumped pilot and the bullet hole all too visible in the side window.

Harker just shook his head sadly, and then turned his attention to the lone sound of an approaching police siren somewhere off in the distance. 'We can't stay here,' he urged, pulling Carter by the arm. 'We have to go.'

There were no complaints from Carter and they both started walking towards the bright lights of the town, brushing past a small crowd of people who were far more interested at the sight of the motionless sagging body drooped forward in the helicopter's front seat than the two men slipping away from it and into the shadows.

With two men dead, the third Gigas page gone, and Vlad in possession of the Templars' most important and revealing document, things had gone from bad to extremely bloody terrible, and Harker knew it. The prospect of Chloe bearing the brunt of his failure, the entire Order of the Knights Templar potentially being wiped out, and not forgetting the unearthly idea of mankind facing Judgement Day with Satan at the helm was turning this day into a real doozy. He still found the reality of Judgement Day a difficult one to swallow but, with everything he had experienced so far, it was starting to feel ever more possible, no matter how unlikely.

'So what do we do now?' Carter asked in a shaky voice as they put ever more distance between themselves and the grounded helicopter, but Harker found himself without an answer. To him there was only one important question, and it sickened him to think about it. With the Gigas page now lost, it wasn't a matter of what they were going to do, but what 'God' would do.

## *Chapter 23*

'I have to say, Dr Stanton, you may be a proverbial pain in the arse, but I must commend you on your ingenuity,' Jacob Winters declared in a congratulatory tone. 'I would very much like to know how you managed to escape from your room.'

Chloe Stanton stood defiantly in front of Winters's desk, with Albert holding her firmly by one arm while a second suited man grasped the other. 'You mean my cell?'

Her reply appeared to offend the old man. 'We have no cells, Dr Stanton. You're my guest here.'

'Really? Because I thought guests were allowed to come and go as they pleased.'

'And you are: you came and you will leave. Of course, whether you leave alive or dead is another matter entirely,' Winters replied with a smug, wrinkled grin. 'So, and I won't ask again, how did you escape your room?'

Chloe squirmed against Albert's grip, more in frustration than anything else. Then with an annoyed grunt, she nodded. 'It was simple. I watched your food-delivery man tap in the code.'

'Pffh,' Winters snorted in disgust, and directed his attention towards Albert. 'Sloppy, Albert, very sloppy. Would you see to it that the man answers for such shoddiness immediately, please?'

Albert left Chloe in the hands of the other guard and made his way over to the door. The crimson light made his plain white shirt look as if it were drenched in blood.

'Oh, and I would like to hear the tunes if I may,' Winters called out after him. Albert nodded respectfully and left, leaving the door half open.

'Well, Dr Stanton…or should I call you Chloe?' Winters continued, clasping his feeble hands together.

'No, you should not,' came her answer, whereupon Winters continued to smile, clearly pleased by her agitation.

He lightly tapped his desktop. 'Well, Chloe, you've been a busy little thing, haven't you? Breaking into my office and nosing about amongst my things.'

Winters motioned towards the velvet drape that had since been pulled back in place, hiding the capsule behind it. 'You've observed my prize, then?'

'Yes, but I'm not sure what I saw,' she replied, genuinely not knowing exactly what it might have been.

'Well, then,' he said jovially, wheeling himself away from the desk to within reach of the drape. 'Allow me to show you' – the old man then pursed his lips together as if in a kissing motion – 'you pretty little thing.'

Chloe shrugged off the demeaning gesture as the suited man, still gripping her arm tightly, walked her over to the drape and pulled it back to reveal the shadowy outline of the capsule she had discovered earlier.

'I know it's difficult to see, Chloe, but my eyes are not good in natural light,' Winters explained, pointing up to the crimson bulb.

'A bit like Dracula, then,' she replied sarcastically, and the suited man gripped her arm tighter.

'Very good,' Winters replied, clearly somewhat irritated by the comparison. 'But let me dispel that myth. Would you turn on the lights, please?' He quickly retrieved a pair of jet-black Julbo sunglasses with protective sides and put them on before the suited man reached over and pressed a protruding wall switch to his left.

A series of wall lights now lit up around the capsule, and for the first time Chloe was able to get a good look at the object inside. The container was about two metres in length, constructed from thick white plastic, and apart from the various tubes linking it to the wall there were others connecting the sides to an assortment of tanks, including one labelled 'oxygen'. The pod sat on a white stone trestle which was bolted to its underside with thick steel screws, and next to it a glass tube respirator whirred away as a grey, plastic, ribbed pump rose and fell rhythmically.

'What is it?' Chloe asked, less taken aback this time around.

'Not what' – Winters leant over and lovingly rubbed his hand against the shiny surface of the pod – 'but who.'

There was a long silence as the old man continued to indulge his fascination with the concealed object, and finally Chloe realized that he was waiting for her to answer his last question.

'So *who* is it?'

'He has many names, but I prefer the Dark Lord,' Winters replied as he pulled his hand away and chuckled. 'It has a nice ring to it, don't you think? Ominous yet memorable.'

An uncomfortable chill ran through her body and she gulped at his preposterous suggestion. 'What?'

He was already nodding his head tremulously. 'I know, I know, it is difficult to get one's head around something so evil, so parasitic, so legendary being right here, snugly contained within this pure white pod. There have been many stories about this one' – Winters was chewing at his lips as he stared over towards Chloe, his black-lensed sunglasses glinting in the light – 'and they are all true, believe me.'

She found herself staring into the face of either a true believer or a complete madman and, given what they seemed to be talking about, both assumptions seemed apt. 'Mr Winters, are you trying to tell me that you have none other than the Devil stored in there?'

Winters once again smiled through cracked lips and he let out a hoarse laugh. 'You can call him whatever you wish, but be under no illusions that our sleeping resident here is everything you've ever been taught about or even dared to believe in your worst nightmares…and he belongs to me.'

The way Winters said the words made Chloe cringe, not because she believed that the actual Devil could be there inside the pod, but rather at the insanity of such a claim, and her disbelieving expression was immediately noticed by the old man.

'Dr Stanton, you work at Blackwater asylum for the criminally insane, do you not?'

'I do.'

'You are surrounded by some of the most evil men and woman to walk the surface of the earth in our lifetime, and you expect me to believe that you don't believe in pure evil?'

It was a question that Chloe had been asked by friends many times given her job as a psychiatrist for the criminally insane but it was the first time anyone had insinuated a link between their sick deeds and a supernatural entity acting as a puppet master. 'My patients have committed some of the worst acts imaginable, and they are mentally sick people. But they are just that…people, not some dark religious icon that has so long been held as a symbol of the very worst man has to offer. They are real and their acts are real, but the Devil is simply an idea, a warning…he's not real.'

'Oh, you are in for such a surprise, dear Chloe, you really are, because when this pod opens you will see that everything I have told you is the truth and nothing less.'

From the half-open doorway there now came the squealing of a man in utter agony and those piercing sounds drew a wide-eyed, excited look from Winters as he slumped back into his wheelchair.

'Ahh, good work, Albert, I have so been waiting to hear those tunes,' the old man muttered softly, and he raised one arthritic finger in the air and began to wave it back and forth, while Chloe winced at the pained cries echoing around the room. 'I do so love a good melody, don't you?'

## *Chapter 24*

'Can I get you gentlemen anything else?' asked the waiter, dipping both hands into the large front pockets of his black apron. 'We're closing early tonight.'

Harker sipped the last drops of his latte and shook his head. 'No thank you, we're fine.' After making it away from the ditched Agusta helicopter, they had flagged down a passing taxi and then travelled south to the small commune of Pontorson, before deciding on one of the restaurants in the area, called le Brazza. The small pizzeria had been busy and they finally found the furthest table from the door, in a corner, and had been there for the past forty-five minutes.

With the authorities undoubtedly looking for anyone connected to the dead pilot in the helicopter, Harker had thought of heading deeper into France but he had reconsidered. He had no idea how the authorities would be handling the situation and, not wanting to potentially get caught up in any police roadblocks, he had opted for the small town of Pontorson, just sixteen kilometres away from the Mont itself.

Harker had since called his Templar contact, John Shroder, multiple times but still heard nothing. Besides having Chloe's well-being on his mind, he was now preoccupied by the deaths of those two Templars – three if he included Michel Beaumont – and the stolen *Illuminismo*. Worse still was Vlad's threat to go after the Templar organization, and as of this moment he had no way to warn them. The past few hours seemed to have been nothing short of an unmitigated disaster, and Harker was feeling at his lowest ebb. Carter, however, was taking things remarkably well and, despite the attempt on both their lives, the ex-don maintained a stiff upper lip.

'Surely there has to be another way we can reach the Templars?' Carter asked for the umpteenth time. 'We can't allow those nutters to make good on their threats.'

'How many times do I have to say it, David?' Harker replied sharply, becoming increasingly wound up at hearing the same question over and over again. 'I only have a single number, and he's not answering it.'

Carter slumped back in his chair and took a sip of his coffee. 'Then what are we doing next?'

The question was fair, but with the third Codex page now in Vlad's hands, and with no way of getting in touch with the Templars, there was only one thing they could do. Harker let out a heavy sigh.

'What option is there? We wait for "God" to call.'

Carter sat there flicking at the rim of his cup in frustration as the last other patron headed outside, leaving them alone in the restaurant.

'Well,' Harker said, getting to his feet, 'I'm going to the toilet.'

'Yeah, four cups of coffee in a row will do that,' Carter replied, returning to his rim flicking as Harker made his way over to the other side of the empty restaurant and through the doorway marked *Hommes*. The toilet was empty and Harker stopped by the basin mirror to inspect his appearance. He looked tired as he rubbed at his eyes and then massaged his aching jaw muscles. Given the erratic nature of 'God's' communication, it was impossible to tell when the old man's next tiresome call would come or what the hell he would say. Should Harker lie and pretend the third page was still in his possession? But so far the bastard had managed to know exactly where and what he was doing at any given moment and Harker found himself struggling to figure out how. 'God' had known he was at Carter's house back in Berlin and, judging by that courier collecting the first page, he had been followed. This feat of stalking, though, didn't explain how the tiresome man had known he was with Brulet. Secondly, how was it that Vlad had been able to follow him to Mont-Saint-Michel? Carter? Not likely, but whatever was going on, the answer had to be somehow close at hand.

He turned on the cold tap, let some water pool in his hand and then applied it to his face. He was enjoying the refreshing sensation when behind him he heard the sound of the toilet door open and then swing shut. He looked up, shook the water from his eyes, and through blurred vision could make out the reflection in the mirror of a figure standing directly behind him.

Harker grabbed a paper towel from the dispenser to dry his eyes and the absorbent material was still doing its job when he felt something hard press against the base of his neck. His body went stiff and he let the towel drop into the sink as he now caught a clearer image of the person standing behind him. Harker turned around slowly and, although relieved to see who it was, the Browning automatic being levelled at him immediately dampened any enthusiasm.

John Shroder stood there with the gun in one hand and with the other raised his forefinger to his lips and shook his head to indicate silence. Harker obliged as the MI6 agent reached over and patted him down. Shroder then went straight for Harker's jacket pocket, retrieved the iPhone and, impressively, one-handed, removed its cover and popped out the battery. Satisfied the mobile was now dead, Shroder dropped it into his trouser pocket and placed the Browning automatic back in his shoulder holster.

'Hello, Alex,' Shroder began with a friendly smile. 'Getting yourself deep into trouble as always, I see.'

'Where the hell have you been? I've been calling you regularly for the past couple of days,' Harker almost yelled and then, pointing towards the gun concealed in Shroder's leather jacket, 'and what the hell was that all about?'

Shroder waved a placating hand in the air. 'I apologize, but it was necessary.'

'Why?'

'Because they were listening to you,' Shroder explained and tapped at the now inoperative mobile in his pocket. 'I know a place we can go,' he continued, reaching for the door handle 'Let's go get your friend and I'll explain everything to you, but not here…and not now.'

## Chapter 25

'I told you he couldn't be trusted!' William Havers shouted as Brulet took a seat at the writing desk. 'This is exactly the kind of problem I was talking about.'

'Calm yourself, William,' Brulet urged, watching the Templar pace back and forth. 'Let us focus on solutions, not causes.'

'Solutions!' Havers stopped pacing and he now looked even more furious, with his face visibly reddening. 'There aren't any solutions, only questions.'

Havers had every right to be upset, and Brulet knew it, but that Harker could be responsible was, to his mind, impossible.

'Take a seat, William,' Brulet demanded sternly, pointing to the armchair opposite him, 'I want to know everything.'

Havers stood defiantly where he was for a few moments and then, with a growl, he sat down. With arms folded he began to rock back and forth stiffly, like a volcano about to blow.

'Two of our operatives were alerted by the sound of gunfire at the Mont. They were there within twenty minutes and found both Anthony and Michel dead in the lower vault. They're still checking the inventory but so far the only thing unaccounted for is the *Illuminismo*.'

The mention of the deaths and the missing *Illuminismo* drew a look of profound shock from Brulet. 'And Alex?'

'The helicopter was found on the mainland, with the pilot shot dead, and of Harker and his fat friend there's no trace.'

'Surveillance footage at the vault?'

Havers was already shaking his head. 'Nothing. The cameras blacked out, so didn't record a thing. We're still trying to ascertain why.'

Brulet slouched back in his chair and removed his sunglasses, then dropped them on the desk. That three people were dead was a tragedy, and the *Illuminismo* being missing was extremely worrying, but to think, as Havers was insinuating, that Harker could be responsible was almost as troubling. 'Whatever has happened, I find it hard to believe that Alex had anything to do with it.'

'You're too trusting, Tristan,' Havers complained before standing up and waving his arms indignantly. 'Harker turns up out of the blue with some ridiculous story about the dead coming alive, and it just so happens that the Gigas page he needs is located in the same vault as the *Illuminismo*.'

Havers moved over to Brulet and knelt down in front of him with his arm resting on the desk. 'This was a set-up, plain and simple.'

Brulet gazed out of the *Excelsior*'s port-side window and across the dark rippling waves outside with a sense of foreboding. 'What possible reason could he have for wanting to hurt us? He's been a dedicated ally since his induction.'

Havers looked unconvinced and wore a deep look of mistrust as Brulet turned back to face him. 'The time it has taken for that man to entrench himself amongst the Templars is but a fraction it would take for most, and yet he's been given access to some of our most carefully safeguarded secrets.'

Brulet brushed off the suggestion and shook his head in disbelief. 'That same man helped us defeat the Magi, amongst other things, or have you already forgotten?'

Havers leant on the desktop with his arms outstretched to steady himself. 'Ask yourself this, Tristan. Who else but Harker saw your brother die, and in what circumstances? In fact, come to think of it, who led us to the Magi in the first place?'

'What are you talking about?' Brulet snarled, becoming angry.

'How do we know that Harker didn't lead your brother to his death...deliberately?'

The idea was repellent to Brulet, who immediately shot out of the seat. 'Enough, William. That is ridiculous.'

'Really?' Havers replied sarcastically. 'Don't you find it a bit strange that Alex Harker was the only person to get out alive?'

'Oh, please,' Brulet rasped. 'Dr Stanton made it out too.'

Unmoved by Brulet's reasoning, Havers manoeuvred closer to the Grand Master, while swaying from left to right like a shark approaching its prey. 'Maybe you're right, Tristan, but after today's events at the Mont can you really be totally sure of anything? First your brother...and now Harker disappears with the *Illuminismo*, which holds the identities of every Templar on the planet. Mere coincidence?'

Even though, in Brulet's mind at least, the accusation seemed ludicrous, he couldn't ignore the gravity of what Havers was suggesting and he remained silent as he considered the possibility. Could there be any truth to it? Even if there was the slightest chance Havers was right, he had to address it. With slumped shoulders and a grim expression, he gave a nod. 'Very well, William, it would be irresponsible of me not to explore the possibility, but for the record I don't believe it.'

Brulet looked disheartened by his own decision and he turned and made his way out of the room, pausing only at the open doorway. 'I don't want either of them hurt,' he ordered and now regained his composure. 'Just find them and bring them in. We'll then see what they know.'

As Brulet disappeared, Havers was already picking up the phone on the desk. He dialled a number and waited.

'We have a go on Harker. So find them both,' Havers instructed. Gritting his teeth, he added, 'Dead or alive.'

# *Chapter 26*

Heavy drizzle swept against the apartment window as John Shroder peered out between the blinds and surveyed the roadway outside. Except for a few parked cars, the only other thing he could see was a couple of tomcats snarling at each other in a high-pitched whine, which was the reason he had looked outside in the first place. Satisfied there was nothing more than a territorial spat between the local felines, he dropped the blind back in place and returned his attention to Harker and Carter, who sat eyeing him with a certain unease.

'Just a couple of squabbling cats,' Shroder explained, resuming the only other seat at the cheap plastic-topped kitchen table. 'Don't worry, this safe house is secure. So do you want to start or should I?'

The question was asked in a carefree and casual tone and Harker, despite Shroder's initially menacing appearance back at the restaurant, was glad to have the MI6 agent here with him. Carter on the other hand was still clearly unsure. Being naturally cautious, Shroder had so far refused to impart any information about who he was to the ex-don, though Harker had done all he could to allay Carter's fears. Being held at gunpoint and witnessing the murder of two people right in front of him had, naturally, left the man extremely mistrustful of any new faces, and he retained a tight-lipped silence. 'How did you find me?' Harker enquired.

'OK, I'll go first,' Shroder replied, placing Harker's iPhone in the middle of the table. 'I did receive all your messages, Alex, and I've been trying to reach you ever since, but every time I called, I got a message saying the phone wasn't in service.'

'That's impossible,' Harker replied. 'I never turned it off, even when charging it.'

Shroder smiled. 'I didn't think you would have, so after your second message I did a line check back at HQ and, much to my surprise, I found it was being blocked deliberately.'

The disclosure came as a shock to Harker. 'By who?'

'Who, indeed. But it isn't coming from any outside source, which means it's something on the phone itself.' Shroder reached over and tapped the mobile's display screen. 'Someone turned your phone into nothing less than a walkie-talkie.'

'What? How can that be? I've had it with me all the time...' The smiling face of Lucas now loomed in Harker's mind and he thought back to the moment when the man had taken the phone from him and entered his home address, shortly before killing himself. 'Shit,' he groaned. 'Lucas.'

'Ah, the fellow who committed suicide,' Shroder said. 'I attended the crime scene after you, and then had a rummage around his apartment.'

'How?' Harker asked, stunned now because he was the only one who had the address. And then it suddenly dawned on him: 'Doggie?'

Shroder was already nodding. 'I'll admit that Dean Lercher was a bit stubborn at first, but the threat of charging him with obstruction of justice soon had him singing like a choirboy. He's been trying to get hold of you as well, by the way.'

For the first time ever, Harker was actually glad that his old friend was apt to fold easily under pressure, but the real question in his mind concerned the mobile phone. 'But how did Lucas contrive to manipulate my phone, since he only had it in his hands for a few seconds?'

'Can't be sure without a closer look, but best guess is through a Bluetooth connection to a device he carried on him, which downloaded the necessary software without you even knowing it.' Shroder smiled drily. 'Not particularly difficult if you have the right tech.'

Everything was falling into place and Harker now understood how 'God' had managed to know everything he did and when he did it. 'Bastard was listening in on everything I said,' he muttered.

Shroder was now nodding, along with Carter, who – though enthralled by the conversation – was still eyeing the MI6 agent suspiciously.

'Whoever you've been talking to appears to have been listening in, whether you were using the phone or not, which is precisely why I pulled the batteries out.'

'How did you guess?' Harker asked, somewhat astonished by how much Shroder already appeared to know.

'I've seen this kind of software in action before, as it's quite common in the security services, but I can't be sure unless—'

Harker already knew where Shroder was going. 'Unless we switch it back on and give him a reason to call me.'

'Exactly,' Shroder replied. 'But, before we do that, perhaps you could fill me in on what exactly is going on, because at the moment things are not looking good for you, Alex.'

Harker couldn't be sure how much Shroder already knew, but with 'God' out of the loop for the moment, it was the perfect time to start filling in all the blanks.

'Hold on,' Carter interrupted, speaking for practically the first time since they left the restaurant. 'How do I know we can trust you?'

It was Harker who spoke up as he patted Carter on the arm. 'We can believe him, David. He's a friend of ours, and one of the few people I trust without reservation.'

Harker's statement of approval was met with a stern look from Shroder. 'That's true, Alex, but the real question is whether I can trust you.'

This rebuttal had Harker frowning and he felt a twinge of nerves ripple through his stomach. 'What's that meant to mean?'

Shroder leant forward and tapped his finger on the table top. 'You've been consorting with some pretty unsavoury characters, Alex. And you've also not been entirely forthcoming about what you're involved in, have you?'

'I know how this must look, John, but you have to believe me when I tell you that everything I've done has been done with the best intentions.'

'I'm not sure exactly what it is that you *have* done, but I did speak with Tristan Brulet less than thirty minutes ago, and whatever it is...it's not looking good for you.'

Harker was now getting increasingly nervous. 'What did he say?'

Shroder remained deadpan and an atmosphere of mistrust now descended upon the conversation. 'He told me that you came to him with some wild story about the dead rising again, and that you needed access to our vault at Mont-Saint-Michel.'

'That's true,' Carter interjected, then fell silent as Shroder shot him a look of disdain before the MI6 agent continued.

'A visit which ended in the deaths of some good men and with certain property missing.'

The unspoken allegations being made sent a shiver down Harker's spine and he shifted in his seat nervously. 'John, you don't believe I was responsible for that, do you?'

'If I thought you were responsible, Alex, then we would not be having this conversation,' Shroder replied with an air of menace. 'But as of this moment there are many others who believe you are.'

It was becoming clear now that the Templars blamed him for those disastrous events back at Mont-Saint-Michel and the very thought of it began to sap Harker's energy. 'And what does Tristan think?'

'He's not sure what to believe, but it is clear that you know far more than you've been telling us. So I am giving you this opportunity' – Shroder settled back in his chair and, whether deliberately or not, his jacket fell back to reveal the Browning automatic handgun nestling in its shoulder holster – 'to rectify that.'

'They have Chloe Stanton,' Harker blurted out, 'and the man I've been in contact with warned me that if I didn't do exactly what he asked, then they would kill her.'

Shroder looked unswayed by this admission. 'And what exactly did they want from you?'

'They wanted me to find three missing pages.'

'Ah yes,' Shroder said, 'from the Gigas Codex, Tristan told me about that. Including the one located in our vault.'

'Yes, but I had no idea they would follow me there, and that they were really after the *Illuminismo*.'

The very mention of the prized artefact had Shroder glancing over at Carter, and without a pause, Harker immediately set about allaying the agent's concerns over his disclosing such a thing.

'David here already knows about the Templars, and he was dragged into all this by the same person as I was.' The more he attempted to explain himself, the guiltier and more responsible he felt. As Shroder's lips tightened at what he was hearing, Harker decided to come clean about everything. 'What I'm about to tell you is going to sound crazy, absurd even, but it is the truth.'

Shroder settled back in to his seat and folded his arms. 'Try me.'

# *Chapter 27*

'Christ, Alex, the only thing missing from that story of yours is an ogre!' Shroder remarked sarcastically, leaning back further in his chair. 'Oh, wait a minute, I forgot, there's one still being held captive underneath the Vatican.'

Harker held his hands out in front of him as if pleading. His retelling of events had been going OK until he had mentioned the reanimated corpses – and the transformed 'demon' being held in the bowels of the Governorate building. To be fair, Shroder had been taking it all quite well, all things considered, even if he did occasionally look like he was about to blow a gasket. Fortunately the mention of Chloe's kidnapping had him taking the whole thing seriously. 'I know how it sounds incredible, but it's all true.' Harker turned to Carter, who had remained unusually silent throughout. 'David, tell him.'

'I can confirm it's all true,' Carter said wide-eyed, 'except for the demon part… I didn't see that. But the corpses rising, I saw them with my own eyes.'

Shroder stood up and stared at them both pensively. 'OK, let's get back to the question of this "God" character. Do you have any idea who this man actually is…any idea at all?'

Harker was already shaking his head. 'Absolutely none.'

'Well, it seems he knows a lot about you,' Shroder continued. 'And despite all these tasks he's forced upon you, he doesn't appear to want you to complete any of them.'

Given the speed that everything had been happening, Harker had not given it much thought, but this simple observation by Shroder now had him thinking more clearly. 'Go on.'

'At every turn, this man has thrown you right in the middle of things, and then he tells you to go to the vault. And who shows up there but Vlad, the very man you've been up against from the start.'

The notion had Harker feeling like a fool. It was obvious.

'You're saying that "God" is on the same side as Vlad?' Carter now asked, looking just as shocked.

'Well, all the evidence would suggest so, wouldn't it? How else would he know you were there at the vault, and then he didn't even seem bothered about the third page of the Codex – only the *Illuminismo*.' Shroder was sounding increasingly irate. 'You said so yourself, Alex.'

Harker's mind was now swirling with possibilities and, although he didn't know why, it was obvious that he had been played for a fool. 'But why bother dragging me into this whole thing when all I would do is cause unnecessary trouble? It doesn't make any sense.'

'It does if he's trying to drop you in the shit,' Shroder explained, before reaching over to the kitchen sideboard and picking up a grey steel iPad. 'You know those pictures you handed over to Tristan?'

Harker nodded and made his way over to join Shroder, who was busily tapping away at the touchscreen.

'He sent them to me and I was able to get a few positive IDs on them. Don't get too excited, because I only had a few hours, and I was tracking you down at the same time, but you need to take a look.'

They crowded around the small screen to see one of the pictures Harker had taken of the guests back at Spreepark.

'That' – Shroder pointed to one of the male guests – 'is Hans Vexer. You might recognize the name?'

'Vexer Pharmaceuticals,' Harker said, hazarding a guess.

'Yes, one of the largest medical companies in the world, and he is the sole heir.' Shroder next pointed to one of the women. 'And she is Marie Ledux, who is the last surviving member of the Ledux family. They are one of the richest families in the world, with fingers in everything from property to shipping lines.'

Shroder placed the tablet on the table and pulled out a small colour photograph from his jacket pocket. 'There's more. When I searched Lucas's flat I found something that you missed: a floor safe hidden underneath his bed.' Shroder dropped the picture on top of the iPad and pointed. 'Take a look.'

The image showed a close-up of an old man sitting in a wheelchair while talking to someone with his back to the camera. 'I asked the London office to do a facial check, and what I got back is disturbing to say the least.'

Harker didn't recognize the old man but he already guessed who the image was of, it had to be. '"God".'

'Can't be totally sure,' Shroder replied, as Carter now began to examine the photograph intently, 'but you did say that Lucas worked for him, and the voice was that of an old man.'

'Who is he?' Harker asked, and by the way Shroder was looking at him, he was dreading the answer.

'His name is Jacob Winters and up until recently no one had ever heard of him, but in a short space of time he has come to the attention of MI6 and our American counterparts. We suspect he's involved in a whole host of nasty trades, with drugs, gunrunning, human trafficking and cybertheft amongst them.'

Harker picked up the photo and stared down at it intently. 'He's an old man, so how come he only came onto your radar recently?'

The question had Shroder shaking his head. 'I have no idea, but he burst onto the criminal scene with a vengeance, and has already destroyed and taken over some of the largest criminal syndicates in a matter of months. I'm not just talking small gangs but serious, well-established Russian and Western organized crime families. The speed at which it has happened is nothing short of remarkable.'

Harker placed the photo back on the table, took his seat and held his head in his hands as Shroder continued with his unnerving analysis.

'Alex, no one knows who this man is, where he came from or how he was able to put together such a powerful organization without being noticed. It's unprecedented, and the intelligence services are struggling to catch up.'

Harker was now feeling queasy as all the fragments of this puzzle rattled around in his head, with no clear picture emerging in sight. Why would Winters drag him into something that was of his own creation only to cause himself problems? Was it all about gaining access to the Templars' *Illuminismo*? Was Vlad actually one of the old man's hired goons, therefore a member of this crime syndicate? What had Vlad said back at the vault? That acquiring the *Illuminismo* was an opportunity too good to pass up. As far as that psycho was concerned, it hadn't obviously been his main objective. And then there was the idea of Judgement Day, which was somehow connected to some of the wealthiest families on the planet.

'What does it all mean?' Carter now asked, the question directed at Shroder, as Harker began to emerge from his mental turmoil.

Shroder let out a deep sigh and sat down on one of the cheap kitchen chairs. 'In a nutshell it means you both have a lot of very powerful and dangerous people all extremely pissed off at you, including the Templars. And,' Shroder continued, now locking eyes with Harker, 'if you're even half right about this idea of Judgement Day, then it's not just you who's in deep shit, but everyone.'

Shroder's mention of the Templars had Harker sitting up straight in his chair. 'What are they going to do?' he asked, genuinely rattled by the notion of his own side coming after him.

'It's not what they're going to do but what they are doing right now,' Shroder replied with a look of despair. 'William

Havers, the man you met on Tristan's yacht, is the one you have to worry about. He's been put in charge of finding you and, from the signals he's sending, it's not going to be a pleasant outcome when he does.'

'What the hell does that mean?' Harker rasped.

'It means that he believes you either have the *Illuminismo* or know where it is, and he will do anything to get it back or else exact revenge on you for taking it in the first place.' Shroder suddenly looked uncomfortable. 'Even I was given orders to detain you when I found you.'

'Christ, John,' Harker said nervously.

Shroder raised his hand in a soothing manner. 'Don't worry, I'm not going to. I don't think you're responsible for this – not willingly anyway. But Havers does.'

Shroder's support did little to calm Harker's nerves, and he scooted his chair a bit closer to the MI6 agent. 'What about Tristan?'

'Our Grand Master is in a real bind over this one. I don't know if he told you but the Templar hierarchy is going through something of a rocky patch at the moment.'

'He did mention something,' Harker replied before Shroder continued with his analysis.

'Well, to ignore Havers's calls on this matter could be all that is needed to topple any faith in his leadership, which is already questioned by many.'

The idea that the entire Templar organization was currently on such shaky foundations was as worrying as anything else going on at that moment, but oddly it imbued Harker with a stronger sense of resolve rather than a feeling of hopelessness. 'Then we should focus on what we can do rather than worry about what we can't.'

Harker's upbeat attitude drew a smile from Shroder, who began to nod his head. 'Couldn't agree more,' he replied, then he reached into his jacket pocket and pulled out a white rectangular piece of card. 'That photograph wasn't all I found in

Lucas's floor safe.' He leant over and placed the item in front of Harker. 'It's a boarding card dated a few months back, for a one-way trip to the UK.'

'No surprise there,' Harker said in view of Lucas's suicide, and he picked it up and scrutinized it more closely. 'Departing from Corsica.'

'Yes, the birthplace of Napoleon Bonaparte, no less,' Shroder remarked with a wistful smile. 'I did some checking and found out the ticket was paid for with a credit card linked to an address in Bastia, which is on the north-east tip of the island.'

'You think that's where "God", I mean Winters, might be?' Carter asked, taking a look at the boarding card for himself.

Shroder shrugged his shoulders. 'Impossible to say, but it's as good a place to start as any.'

'It's the only place to start,' Harker decided, then turned his attention to his iPhone on the table, which was still powered off. 'But what to do about our "walkie-talkie"?'

'I've got an idea about that,' Shroder replied deviously, with one eyebrow raised, as he picked up the mobile and gave it a gentle shake. 'Tell me, gentlemen, how's your acting?'

# *Chapter 28*

'Enough is enough,' Carter bellowed, slapping his hand down hard on the kitchen table. 'How many more dead bodies is it going to take before you realize that we're out of our depth here? Or do you even care?'

Harker was instantly fuming at the suggestion and he moved to within centimetres of Carter's face and gritted his teeth. 'Don't you even lay that on me, you prick. I'm not responsible for that, and anyway, the only thing I do care about is getting Chloe back safely.'

Carter looked wholly repulsed by this response. 'Well, I do care about losing my life in this tangled web of yours that I never asked to get dragged into.'

'That's not my fault.'

'Yeah, well whose is it, then? Because if you hadn't come to me in the first place, then I would be settling down to a nightcap and a spot of TV.' Carter was practically screeching, his voice becoming noticeably strained. 'Truth be known, Alex, the only real mistake I ever made was getting to know you in the first place.'

Harker stared back with venom in his eyes as Carter's cheeks began to turn a rosy red.

'It's time you called the police to tell them everything, and let them sort it out.'

'No,' Harker shouted back, and he slapped the coffee mug off the kitchen table. It hurtled against the far wall, where it smashed into pieces.

'Fine, if you won't, then I will,' Carter seethed, and he was already dialling the emergency services on his Samsung when Harker's iPhone began to vibrate.

Both men froze and looked at each other apprehensively, before Harker reached over to pick it up, and then pressed the green answer button.

'Hello?'

The mobile's reception was terrible, but over its crackling came the familiar croaky voice of Jacob Winters. 'Where the hell have you been? I've been calling you for over half an hour,' he hissed.

'We had some trouble,' Harker replied, finding himself sounding riled.

'There's no surprise there. Getting into trouble seems to be your forte, Professor. How so?' The question was asked with little trace of concern but rather a gleeful curiosity.

'Vlad and his goons showed up at the vault and killed everyone. They must have been following us since we left Cervete cemetery.'

'What!' Winters yelled it so hard that he began to cough. 'Did you get the page?'

'No, they took it, and we barely escaped with our lives.'

Harker was tempted to mention the theft of the *Illuminismo* but he resisted, as Winters now flew into a rage.

'Can't you do anything right?' the old man screamed. 'Do you have any idea what you've just done?'

Harker was actually glad to hear the old monster so upset, but was it genuine? 'No, I don't, and that's the point. You've been as vague as anyone could be throughout. Isn't it about time you were upfront about a few things and told me who the hell you are and what's going on?'

Because of the heavy interference on the phone, Harker could not be sure, but he could have sworn he heard a light chuckle at the other end.

'I've already told you all you need to know, but I will be upfront about one thing,' Winters rasped. 'You have one chance and one chance only to redeem yourself. The remaining page. And if you get it for me, then you may consider our arrangement at an end. Do this and Dr Stanton will be returned to you as promised, but screw this up and you will never see her pretty face again. I will be in touch again regarding the precise location.'

There was a sincerity in the old man's tone and Harker seized upon it immediately. 'Not on this phone, you won't.'

'What does that mean?'

'My mobile got half destroyed during our escape from the vault,' Harker lied. 'That's why the reception is so bad. I'm amazed we've even managed to speak on it right now.'

At that moment the crackling became even louder and Winters had to shout just to be heard. 'Does the messaging still work?'

'Yes – but that's about it.'

'Then hold on to the phone and I will keep in contact via text messages,' Winters hollered as the crackling in the reception became almost unbearable. 'Do this last thing and both you and your girlfriend can go home and forget all this ever happened.'

*Forget?* That was a joke, Harker thought, as the line went dead. He looked over at Carter and raised a forefinger to his lips before placing the iPhone down on the table. With a nod from Carter, they made their way through the kitchen and into a small adjoining bedroom opposite, to find Shroder with his ear glued to the apartment's telephone receiver while holding his own mobile out in front of him.

'Did you manage to get a trace?' Harker whispered, but he was met with a frustrated grimace.

'The bastard's bouncing the signal off every relay imaginable but at least we know he's been listening in, and your little scene just proves it.'

–

Before turning Harker's iPhone back on, they had made the decision to test out Shroder's theory and engaged in an argument that concluded with Carter declaring he was going to call the police. The fact that Winters had called immediately and insisted that he wanted them to not replace the phone, despite it being almost wrecked, only confirmed what they suspected: that Winters had been listening in from the beginning. With a piece of black tape affixed over the camera, and Shroder's specialized phone app creating the heavy distortion, they could now be sure that although Winters would be able track them via the mobile's GPS, he could no longer hear or see what they were actually doing.

'Good job, David,' Harker said, whereupon Carter offered a polite stage bow with a wave of his hand.

'I am a thespian at heart, Alex,' he replied, clearly pleased with his own performance. 'So what's the next stage?'

Shroder hesitated before he raised his finger towards them and began to speak into the phone's receiver. 'Thanks for the trace, Bill, it was worth a shot. I'll be in touch.' He replaced the handset and stood up with his mobile still in hand, and aimed towards the kitchen. 'Firstly I install the software on Alex's iPhone which will stop the mics from working permanently, and then we have a decision to make. About who goes where. One of you needs to follow Winters's instructions to collect the final pages whilst the other heads to Lucas's billing address in Corsica.' Shroder was looking perturbed by the idea and made a clicking noise with his tongue. 'It could be a waste of time, but it could also lead us to Winters. There's no way to be sure, though, without going there.'

'How about you?' Carter asked him, looking less than enthusiastic at them having to split up. 'Where are you going?'

'There's a contact of mine with Interpol who's been tracking Jacob Winters ever since he first appeared on the criminal scene. I'm hoping he can provide something that we can use to locate him.'

'Can't you do that over the phone?' Harker asked, not particularly happy either at having to leave Shroder, having only just met up with him again.

'No.' Shroder shook his head firmly. 'I need to do this face-to-face. Winters is currently at the centre of an ongoing investigation involving multiple agencies, which means I have to tread carefully.'

'Christ, John, we've only just caught up with you.' Harker sounded a bit desperate, which he sought to rectify immediately. 'Will be fine, though.'

Shroder rested his hand on his shoulder. 'I know it's a shit deal, Alex, but if we're going to find this man, and with little time to spare, we need to explore any lead we get. Chloe's life as well as the Templars' survival may depend on it.'

That was clearly the right call, for Harker found himself grudgingly nodding in agreement, even though he still didn't like the idea of the three of them going solo.

'I'll track down the Codex pages,' Carter offered, much to the surprise of both the others. 'This Winters fellow will only be communicating by text, so he won't have any idea it's just me. And besides, if your Corsican lead can offer a clue to locating the men who kidnapped Chloe, then you need to get to it first.'

Considering his own previous encounters while retrieving Codex pages had been near-death experiences, this offer by Carter seemed nothing short of bloody heroic, and Harker was stunned. 'Are you sure about this, David? For all we know, Winters could be throwing you right into the grinder again.'

But Carter was already nodding his head thoughtfully at the prospect. 'Possibly, Alex, but if you do find something in Corsica, then you're the best one to follow it up. Besides' – Carter removed his glasses and began to clean the lenses with his shirt tail – 'I'm sure I can find ways to slow down my journey.'

'That's not a bad idea,' Shroder now interrupted as Carter popped the spectacles back onto the bridge of his nose. 'With the Templars now looking for you both as well, we could pretend to be playing it cautious. Wherever Winters sends you next, you tell him that air travel is out of the question because any place with a high security presence could potentially alert the Templars to your whereabouts, and therefore you'll need to take other, slower forms of travel.'

Carter looked pleased that his suggestion was being taken seriously. 'And cars break down, and trains and boats often get delayed.'

'Winters is not a very forgiving man,' Harker reminded him, playing devil's advocate.

'It's a gamble, yes, but we'll need all the time we can get,' Shroder replied.

'It is called stalling,' Carter stated confidently, and licking his lips enthusiastically at the challenge. 'Trust me, I'll give you as much time as is humanly possible without tipping the balance.'

Harker took a moment to think about it but the look of determination and assurance in Carter's eyes finally convinced him. 'OK, David, good man.'

All three of them shared a few seconds of calm as the encouraging feeling of gaining some control over the situation settled in the air.

'Right,' Shroder said, slipping into command mode, 'David will wait here for Winters's message regarding the location. Alex, you're going straight to Corsica to learn whatever you can. You can use the Templars' private jet I've already been using. In the meantime I'll meet up with my Interpol contact and discover as much about Winters as possible, and also anything else about these super-wealthy types you photographed in Spreepark. There's obviously a link between them all, and I need to find out what it is.'

So far, it sounded like a good plan, but there were still a few questions burning at the forefront of Harker's mind. 'Meanwhile, what about the Templars?'

Shroder looked unconcerned. 'I'll call Tristan and tell him I haven't found you yet, but have reports that you've returned to the UK… That should send Havers on a wild goose chase if we're lucky. And concerning the *Illuminismo*, well, I've got a feeling that Winters is definitely behind the theft, and so if we find him, we find that.'

'OK,' Harker agreed, 'and how should we contact each other?'

Shroder grabbed a black zip-bag from the bed and pulled out a couple of scratched-up-looking iPhones which he then passed over to Harker and Carter. 'We can use these, as they're both unlisted, but don't use them unless it's absolutely necessary. We can't be sure exactly what Winters's capabilities are, so let's play it safe and smart.'

With most everything settled, there was just one last thing that no one had mentioned thus far, and it was Harker who brought it up. 'And how about the small question of Judgement Day?'

Shroder looked unfazed as he pursed his lips. 'For the record, I believe what you say you witnessed, but don't ask me to jump on board with that whole supernatural shtick, Alex. There's nothing we can do about any of it right now and, from what you've told me, everything appears to revolve around Winters, so he's our priority. Finding him will lead us to Dr Stanton.'

The mention of Chloe brought everything back down to earth for Harker and he found himself in complete agreement. The only loose end was Vlad, but that madman now had everything he wanted, including the *Illuminismo*, so it was unlikely he would waste further time in chasing them. Or so he hoped. 'There are a lot of moving parts in this plan,' he said with a dry smile, and Shroder smiled along with him and placed a hand on Harker's shoulder.

'In my world there always are.'

# *Chapter 29*

Dr Gavin Wheatley trod carefully along the Governorate basement corridor as he approached the secured makeshift holding cell with the key already raised in front of him.

The past night had seen his patient, Bishop Alfonse Esposito, howling continuously and banging ceaselessly against the walls, but then for the past four hours there had been total silence. Since the 'thing's' arrival it had not been uncommon for an hour of eerie quiet before the screaming began once again, but never for quite this long.

Wheatley pressed an ear against the metal door to listen but all he heard was a light humming from one of the air-conditioning units positioned further along the corridor. He nevertheless kept his ear glued to it for over a minute, even closing his eyes in an effort to concentrate, but still nothing.

Wheatley pulled away from the door, then very slowly pressed the key into the lock. With his other hand he held the key's shaft firm as he slid it in further, wanting to make as little noise as possible. Then, centimetre by centimetre, he turned it until he heard a click.

The door slowly swung open under its own weight, the light outside illuminating a small portion of the room beyond through the grilled inner door, and he cautiously peered inside to scan its dark interior for the now massive and distorted shape of Bishop Alfonse Esposito. He couldn't see anything at first but, as his eyes became accustomed to the gloom, he eventually made out a large, huddled shape in one corner.

'Bishop Esposito,' he called out, still using the inmate's name even if he now resembled nothing of the man he once was.

No response.

'Bishop Esposito,' Wheatley called out again, this time louder, but still there was nothing, not even a groan. As he eyed the motionless, shadowy mass, he considered turning the lights on even though, since the bishop's transformation, he had kept the lights off continuously; to turn them on instantly generated the most violent of outbursts from the poor man but, given such a long period of silence, Wheatley could now see little other choice. He placed his finger on the light switch next to the doorway, then he moved back a step and prepared for the uproar he had come to expect. Wheatley flicked it on, the room lit up brightly as the mesh-covered strip lights above burst into life, and he found himself staring at the bishop's disfigured body as it lay in a heap in the corner. It was the first time in days he had been able to see properly the changes that had taken place in the man, and he winced as he took in their full extent.

Esposito's body had turned a blackened colour and the bony plates protruding from his shoulders had grown significantly. They appeared to now be attached to his spine as a single entity, with bulging back muscles that had caused tears in the skin. The face was hidden as the body hunched over in a kneeling position, facing the corner, with its thick bulky arms thrust behind to reveal open palms and sharp fingers. The digits looked claw-like, as if the individual finger bones had outgrown the enveloping skin and broken through at the tips, and they now lay against Esposito's thick swollen thighs, which terminated in little more than stumps where his feet had once been.

Wheatley reached down and picked up a billiards cue off the floor which he had used previously to prod the man in order to have him angrily rush the door, allowing him to examine the prisoner more closely. This was not how he would ever normally treat his patients of course, for he was a doctor not a sadistic baiter, but this was no ordinary patient and so far any attempts to actually converse with the bishop had proved futile.

Wheatley reached through the bars with the cue and gave a gentle prod to the man's buttocks. With no obvious reaction he followed this up with a far more forceful jab to Esposito's thigh – but still nothing. Undeterred, and needing to be sure, Wheatley raised the cue upwards with both hands and slammed the tip down hard against Esposito's lower back, which was as far as he could reach. Despite feeling as if he were striking it against concrete, the mass of deformed muscle and bone did not move a millimetre.

Wheatley drew the rod back towards him and placed it on the floor nearby, then did something that, during his whole career in medicine, he never for a moment had thought he might ever do. From his white lab coat pocket he pulled out a black 9mm Glock handgun and cocked its slide to chamber the first bullet. The guards outside had given him the gun at his request, even though they had no idea what it was intended for. Still, this seemed insane; he was a physician not a soldier, for God's sake, but this was his patient, ergo his responsibility, and it genuinely looked as if the physical changes Esposito was experiencing might have proved fatal.

Wheatley pushed his key into the lock of the inner door and turned it. Then, as the barred door opened, he slowly took his first step inside with the Glock held up in front of him.

-

The two armed guards stood at the locked entrance leading into the Governorate basement, chatting away casually as they always did. With little else to do except stand there, the two men continued their usual routine of swapping bad jokes and stories of conflict until the next change of shift. At age thirty-two, Richard Dice was already a seasoned veteran, having served one tour in Iraq and a further two in Afghanistan, but although his was an impressive résumé it did not compare to that of his counterpart. Fifty-year-old Kyle Evans had served in the first Gulf War before making it into the Navy Seals, where he had a distinguished, if not publicly reported, career serving in some of the worst hotspots the planet had to offer. Both men had since left the military and found work in the private sector, but without doubt this assignment had to be the most boring. Contracted directly by the Vatican to act as little more than doormen, the two of them had taken the job because it meant good pay for almost no work, but after days of doing nothing except letting in a few bishops and Dr Wheatley, their routine had become tedious. Whatever was going on down there was unknown to them, but so long as the pay was good, then fair enough.

'C'mon, that's a funny joke,' Dice moaned, giving his colleague a dirty look. 'Don't you get it?'

'I get it,' Evans replied, without even a hint of a smile. 'But you told me the same joke last week, and it wasn't even funny the first time.'

Dice went silent as he racked his brain trying to remember when but, amid the mountain of gags he had been delivering in recent days, he honestly couldn't recall the occasion. 'Then that's the last joke you get out of me, pal.'

'My days just keep getting better and better,' Evans replied, smiling. 'Now that's funny.'

A reply from Dice was cut short when the sound of tapping began on the other side of the security door. Evans immediately approached it and tapped in response.

'Dr Wheatley?' Evans called out, but there was no answer except for another couple of taps.

'Must be his break time,' Evans decided and, with a nod from Dice, he unlocked the door and began to open it slowly – when something on the other side hit it with such force that Evans was sent hurtling backwards across the room, slamming into the far wall.

Dice already had drawn his gun but a thick, muscular and discoloured arm flew out through the doorway and landed a blow across his face, sending him to the ground in a crumpled heap. As blood trickled into his eyes, he stared up to watch as something lumbered out from behind the security door.

The huge frame of the erstwhile Bishop Esposito plodded out into the centre of the room and glanced over at the unconscious Evans and then at Dice, who was reeling from the blow. With a screeching howl, Esposito took off at a run in the direction of the exit, as best his seriously deformed feet would allow.

Dice instinctively pulled himself upright and rushed to Evans's side. He pressed a couple of fingers against the man's throat and, satisfied he could feel a pulse, he about-turned and began sprinting after the howling sound in the distance.

Within seconds he reached the exit, having already wiped the blood from his eyes. As he burst out through the half-open door, gun at the ready, he spotted the bulky frame of Esposito lumbering down the steps leading to the courtyard. Dice aimed his gun and let off a single shot into Esposito's back, but it penetrated the solid muscle with a thud and did nothing to slow him down. Dice lowered his aim and shot three times at the creature's thighs, and this time he got a reaction. Esposito stopped in his tracks and then slowly turned around to face his attacker, who had now approached to within metres, and without pause lunged towards Dice, who managed to get off a couple more shots before the bishop's bulky frame had pinned him to the ground.

The stench of decomposition was nauseating and, as Esposito's long, scaly tongue slid down and slapped against Dice's cheek, the guard wrestled free his gun which had become trapped between them. He then jammed the barrel hard into what was left of the bishop's mouth and pulled the trigger, sending a thick spattering of blood down onto his own face. Then, with a deafening ringing in his ears, he shot twice more.

Esposito's tongue suddenly went limp and, as his single eye dulled, he let out one final deep, husky breath before collapsing right on top of Dice. After a few tries at going back and forth, Dice finally managed to roll the dead brute off to one side, then he slid out from underneath and scrambled backwards on his rear end. Still reeling from the shock of what had just occurred, he began wiping the thick clotted blood from his face and, unable to hold it in any longer, he vomited all over the stone slabs of the courtyard.

Vatican staff now began approaching him with looks of astonishment and circled the bloody scene as if not wanting to get too close to the disfigured, motionless corpse of what had once been Bishop Esposito.

The emergency services would not arrive for another five minutes, and it would be another twenty before the broken and battered body of Dr Wheatley was discovered deep within the bowels of the Governorate basement.

# *Chapter 30*

The refreshing Mediterranean air rolling in off the water energized Harker with every breath he sucked through the open window of the taxi, as it made its way through the winding streets of the small town of Bastia. Nestling between the shoreline and the base of a mountain, this rustic paradise was the kind of place in which a person would be happy to forgo the toils of work and everyday life in order simply to reside or to just exist. Being a minor shipping hub meant Bastia was the centre for trade and commerce in the north of Corsica, but the local economy thrived on leisure-ship travelling tourists, all eager to experience a slice of this picturesque region for themselves.

Unfortunately for Harker it was well past midnight and pitch dark by the time he arrived, so the only sights to enjoy were the street lamps and various house porch lights left on by the residents. Worse still, his taxi driver had been plagued by a chronic case of flatulence throughout the thirty-minute trip from Bastia airport, which was another reason for the passenger-side window being open.

Before leaving Shroder's safe house, he and Carter had shared a good-luck shot of the cheap whisky Shroder had on hand and, given the dangerous task the ex-don had elected himself for, it was the least Harker could offer. Just for his own peace of mind though, Harker had instructed Shroder to empty the rest of the bottle down the sink after he departed, leaving Carter subsequently unamused by his friend's lack of trust in him.

The taxi to Granville airport had taken about an hour from Mont-Saint-Michel and, as per the MI6 agent's promise, he had found a Cessna Citation X+ waiting for him on the tarmac. The pilot had barely said a word to him, no doubt under orders from Shroder, and within minutes they were in the air and heading south towards the island of Corsica. The flight had taken them a few hours, during which time Harker had slept. After waking up on their arrival at Bastia, he had still felt woozy, sluggish and tired. This, thankfully or not, had been swiftly rectified upon being confined in a car that smelt of high-grade methane courtesy of the taxi driver, and his eyes had been watery ever since, although he was now at least up and alert.

The taxi came to a slow halt at the entrance to a dusty driveway. Harker was out like a shot and, after gulping down a few breaths of fresh, untainted air, he approached the driver's window with caution and with his nose wrinkling.

'That will be forty-five euros,' the driver said. Harker gingerly lowered his head to hand over the notes.

'Thank you, monsieur,' the driver said, cracked off one final screeching fart, then apologized. 'Sorry, it's been a long day.'

'It's been a long ride!' Harker managed to reply as the driver, with an apologetic laugh, slowly turned the car around and headed back along the street, leaving Harker standing under a solitary street light as a plume of street dust enveloped him.

The address Shroder had given him was located in the Cordo district of Bastia, which was right at the base of the mountain and thus allowed a magnificent view over the town. Being only ninety kilometres from the eastern coast of Italy meant that on a clear day one could make out that country's shoreline. Of course, all he was getting now was the occasional flickering porch light and a low hum emanating from the electricity masts overhead. As Harker enjoyed the salty air nipping at his tongue, he made a promise to himself that he would visit here another time and properly enjoy the splendour now shrouded in darkness.

With an about-turn he began to make his way up a dusty driveway lined with blue-tinted ground lights that lit up towering eucalyptus trees on either side, allowing privacy for the owners he now hoped to meet. The drive was S-shaped, and as he cleared the final bend, what he saw made his jaw drop in awe. The building ahead of him was less of a house and more akin to a mini-castle, with two bastion towers augmented by thick stone corbels, which supported them, and a three metre stone wall that ran around it and offered complete privacy to the lower levels. The entrance was a stone arch, and above it the square merlons and embrasures only added to the fortified appearance.

Harker approached the sturdy wooden door, then paused underneath the dim porch light as he began to rehearse the fake identity he had already constructed for himself on the journey over.

'My name is Alphonse Dulac and I am from the French Department of Justice,' he recited in his mind. 'I am here at the request of my UK counterpart to help with a case. Why am I turning up here so late? Because it is of the utmost urgency. Why do I not have any ID? Because it was in my luggage which unfortunately was sent to Lisbon by mistake.'

Reassured he had his cover story straight, Harker reached over and pressed the round brass button, whereupon a deep chime rang out. After another few minutes, and a second ring, a light came on high up on the second floor, and Harker waited as the sound of footsteps began to echo closer from inside.

As they approached, a feeling of apprehension began to grip him and suddenly the concept of the character he had concocted for himself began to crumble.

*Alphonse Dulac! From the French Department of Justice!* What the hell had he been thinking? With every footstep he heard, he felt increasingly more stupid.

As the door was unlocked and swung open, Harker found his mind going completely blank. He began to fidget uncontrollably with his hands as an old lady wearing a white nightgown greeted him with a startled expression.

'*Oui?*'

'Hi, I'm a friend of your son's.'

The way he just blurted it out was near comical, and by the way the old lady was looking at him he expected the door to be just slammed in his face.

'My son? Who are you?'

'Sorry, I've just woken up after a long trip,' Harker explained, now making it far worse. 'My name is Alex Harker and, like I said, I'm a friend of your son's. Would it be possible to talk?' Of course, without knowing what Lucas's real name was, never mind if this woman even knew the man, he was forced to keep his explanation vague.

The old lady peered past him as if to check there were no other unexpected visitors and, once satisfied they were alone, she turned her attention back to him. 'You know Simone? But he's overseas, in the UK.'

*Bingo*, Harker thought as he took a step back so as not to impose on the woman's personal space, because she was still eyeing him with suspicion and, given the time of night, it was hardly surprising. 'That's why I'm here, because I'm afraid I have some rather bad news. May I come in?'

She was now looking worried and, after a few moments' thought, nodded and waved him in with a shaking hand. 'You better had.'

Harker gratefully made his way inside, entering a spacious hallway with expensive-looking oak panelling, gold-coloured horseshoe lamps running its entire length and lighting the interior warmly.

'Please follow me.' The old woman locked the door behind him, then headed for an open doorway on the opposite side of the hallway, with Harker close behind her.

The room they then entered was dark, and the old lady reached over to turn a small silver knob poking out from the wall. At first the overhead light was soft, but she swivelled the dimmer to its brightest, and Harker found himself standing in one of the grandest rooms he had seen in a long while. Unlike most Corsican homes, the furnishings had a distinctly Victorian feel to it. An exquisite three-piece gold-trimmed sofa set with walnut legs and red upholstery surrounded a round, gold-streaked, inlaid table with a glossy lacquered top. Dominating the room was a Gothic, blue-grey marble fireplace with intricate carvings of two lions' heads on either side and, above it, a lavish French Neo-Renaissance overmantel mirror hung from a mercury-black wall-plate.

The old woman motioned for Harker to take a seat, which he did. As she sat down carefully on the sofa opposite him, he scanned the various paintings hanging from the walls. They depicted individuals he did not recognize but it was clear that they were either a visual record of the family history, or maybe put there to make one think they were.

'Please, *monsieur*, tell me, is Simone all right?' she asked, looking dreadfully concerned. 'I have not heard from him in some weeks.'

By this point Harker was not totally sure they were talking about the same person, and he felt compelled to get that out of the way before proceeding.

'Forgive me, *madame*, but do you have a picture of Simone I might see?' This request was met with a look of disbelief, so he immediately continued, 'I just want to be sure I've found the right address.'

Without hesitation she slid open a drawer under the polished coffee table and retrieved a pile of photos, which she began flicking through. When she found what she was looking for, she placed the rest back in the drawer, then passed it over to Harker, who gently took and examined it. It was a head shot of a smiling fellow with long black hair and, even though he looked younger, it was definitely the man he knew as Lucas.

'That's Simone,' Harker declared confidently, and he passed the photo back to her. 'I'm sorry, but I had to be sure.'

She nodded and then clasped the photo to her chest. 'Is he OK?'

'I'm afraid your son is dead.'

Harker's tactless approach produced a look of sheer horror from the old woman and he immediately wanted to swallow back his words and try again with something a bit more compassionate. In truth he was as nervous as hell and the fact that he had torpedoed his own cover story from the start was making him edgy. 'I'm so sorry to be the one to have to tell you.'

She still looked horrified but said nothing and only clutched the photo tighter before placing it in her lap. Then, reaching over to an antique black telephone resting on the table next to her, she pressed the receiver to her ear.

Harker stayed silent, unsure what was happening, as the woman inserted her finger into the dialling disk and rotated it a single time and then waited. If she was calling the police, then he had a major problem, but a single number? No way.

'Carlu, you'd better come down. It's about Simone,' was all she said before hanging up. She then turned back to Harker who could already hear a shuffling of feet somewhere upstairs. 'Simone is my grandson, so you need to speak with his father.'

Harker could now hear heavy footsteps descending the stairs and he managed a smile towards the old lady before turning his attention to the open doorway. She herself seemed easy to deal with but he had no idea what to expect from the father. The good news was that whatever Lucas, or Simone, had been involved in, his family appeared to have no idea. But having to explain to them now that their son had died, and requesting to know everything about him without getting the police involved, could prove extremely difficult.

*I knew I should have come as Alphonse Dulac*, Harker cursed to himself just as a heavy-set six-foot man with short cropped black hair and wearing an embroidered red silk dressing gown appeared at the doorway.

'Who the hell are you?' Carlu demanded, already clenching his fists.

'My name is Alex Harker.' He jumped to his feet with his hand outstretched. 'I'm a friend of your son Simone.'

Carlu ignored the gesture and turned to the old lady. 'Mama, are you OK?'

She was now welling up with tears. 'It's Simone, he's dead.'

'Dead!' Carlu growled, his focus now solely on Harker. 'What the hell are you talking about? I spoke to him just a few days ago. He was fine.'

'I'm afraid not, sir,' Harker continued, maintaining the most calming tone he could manage given that the six-foot man was now bearing down on him aggressively. 'I'm afraid he was involved in a shooting back in the UK.'

Carlu looked unconvinced and pushed Harker back onto the sofa as Mama began to wail uncontrollably. 'Don't you move!' he instructed and made his way to the phone. 'I don't know who you are, but my son is not dead. The police would have contacted me.'

Carlu picked up the phone and began to dial. 'You turn up in the middle of the night with some bullshit story about my son,' he continued. 'You're lucky I don't take you outside and beat the shit out of you.'

'Please, sir, I am just a friend trying to make good on a promise I made to your son,' Harker pleaded, attempting to make Carlu at least curious as to why he was there and to distract him from the call he feared he might be making. But he was having none of it and began to speak into the telephone.

'Yes, I need the police urgently. I have an intruder in my house.'

Carlu was in the process of giving his address when a young woman in a white silk nightdress bounded through the doorway and then skidded to a halt on seeing Harker.

'Who are you?' she yelled and was immediately waved away by Carlu.

'He's crazy. Stay away from him,' Carlu ordered. 'He says your brother is dead.'

'Dead!' the girl exclaimed, wide-eyed, as her grandmother continued to sob.

'He's been shot,' Mama croaked, with tears pouring down her face. 'And no one told us.'

It was at about this point, as the young girl's eyes also began to fill with tears, that Harker decided that he was frankly crap at undercover work. He had only been in the house a few minutes and already had two women bawling over their dead grandson and brother, police on the way, and a father who looked set to beat the living daylights out of him. *Fine work, Alex*, he thought, as Carlu slammed down the receiver and assumed a protective position between Harker and the young woman.

'The police are on their way, so you can deal with them,' Carlu spat angrily, as his daughter peeked over his shoulder. 'Coming here in the middle of the night and upsetting my family with your lies… You don't even know my son.'

A curious thought now came to Harker and he straightened himself in his seat and eyed the father sternly. 'Did you know your son was interested in the Gigas Codex?'

The question lessened the anger in Carlu's face by a fraction, but whether this was due to curiosity or bemusement was impossible to tell. 'What?'

'I say interested, but in fact he was obsessed with it. Did you know that?'

'What are you talking about?' Carlu replied, then he took a step backwards as Mama's wailing began to diminish.

'It's just I notice you have a picture of it over there.' Harker was pointing to a glass-covered frame containing a photograph of the Gigas Codex which he had noticed moments earlier as Carlu had leant menacingly closer to him.

Carlu glanced towards the image. 'That is Simone's. He has much interest in such things. So what?'

'"So what" is that such interests have led, inadvertently or not, to a kidnapping and even a few deaths.'

When Harker first entered the house he had noticed a silver cross hanging next to one of the lamps in the hallway and, even as he spoke, he could see another one – brass this time

– hanging next to the mirror above the fireplace. Whoever Simone's family were, they were without a doubt religious; could it be that they knew or suspected Simone had been delving into the darker side of such things?

Carlu remained quiet and Harker took this as a sign that they did know the kind of man Simone was. To some extent at least.

'Your son, sir, has caused the deaths of more than just a few of my friends, and my real reason for being here is to find out why, and in doing so try to stop any further acts of violence from occurring.'

The whole room now went silent and Carlu's shoulders began to sag. After a few uncomfortable seconds of Harker looking back and forth between all three members of the family, the daughter tugged at her father's arm.

'You should tell him, Daddy,' she said softly and, with a slight nod, Carlu let out a sigh and rested one shoulder against the wall.

'My son is a troubled man. He was brought up to believe in everything that is pure and right, but always found himself distracted by other things.' He gestured to his daughter. 'Sofia was only sixteen when Simon tried to strangle her to death.'

'Carlu!' Mama yelled, obviously upset with her son's disclosure to an outsider, but he waved her aside dismissively and continued.

'We have covered this up for long enough, Mama. If Simone has been hurting people, as this man suggests, then it is time we accepted some responsibility by putting a stop to it.'

When Harker had first drawn attention to the framed picture of the Gigas Codex, it had been done out of desperation but, as Carlu began to explain further, he had by sheer luck, it seemed, stumbled upon everything he hoped to discover.

'Ever since he was a young boy, we knew that Simone was not altogether normal. He would regularly ignore his religious teachings and set about doing the exact opposite. As a result, he was a lonely child.' Carlu looked saddened at the thought as he gazed over at Harker. 'Corsica is a small place and its people are unique. They don't feel comfortable with strangers, and less so with any of their own people who seem strange to them. As such, Simone became something of a social outcast, but it wasn't until he tried to hurt his sister Sofia that we were forced to take action.'

Sofia placed her hand on her father's shoulder and squeezed it, whereupon he patted it with his own before continuing.

'We sent him away to a boarding school in Switzerland, but when he came back he was fully adult and worse than ever. He said he had met a group that had offered him everything he had ever sought, and then we learnt of his obsession with the Gigas Codex. It was a book I had never even heard of until that moment. He then left home and turned to travelling, where and who with I have no idea, but a few months ago he called to let me know he was in the UK and that he'd found all he was looking for. And that's the last time I heard about him until you turned up tonight.'

Carlu's account did not help Harker much, but he could tell how its simple retelling was clearly painful to the man and his family. 'It must have been extremely difficult for you, given that you are clearly a religious family.'

Carlu said nothing but just nodded his head, as did Sofia. And then, after a moment, he looked up with tears in his eyes. 'Tell me, Mr Harker, is my son really dead?'

'I'm afraid he is, sir. I'm so sorry.'

Carlu hung his head and Sofia wrapped her arms around him as Mama shakily rose from her seat and joined in the group hug. It was a heart-warming sight and Harker suddenly felt like he was intruding.

'I know it must come as a terrible shock,' he said, standing up. 'I'm sure you need some time alone. May I use your toilet?'

'Just off the hallway,' Mama explained, nodding back towards the front entrance.

'Thank you.' Harker slipped past the grieving family and out in to the hallway. If they had all calmed down by the time he returned, he considered asking if Simone had a room he could inspect, or if they knew anything at all that could help him track down Winters. Perhaps Simone could have met the old man, or someone connected to him, in Switzerland.

Harker poked his head through one of the open doorways leading off the hallway and reached for the light switch. Two overhead lights flickered into life, illuminating the room. Though of modest size, the toilet was just as lavish as the other rooms, its red wallpaper embossed with gold swirls, and the brass taps shiny. As Harker reached for his zip, something else caught his eye. On the walls there were framed photographs of various people, one of whom looked familiar. The black and white image showed a blond man in his thirties wearing a spiffy black-tie ensemble and holding a half-bent Dublin pipe in one hand, which he held towards the camera proudly. Harker couldn't place the face exactly but there was something familiar about it, so he leant in closer and scrutinized it. Finally, at a loss, he turned his attention to the next black and white photo which showed another man, dressed in hunting gear and topped off with a domed safari hat, kneeling next to a dead jaguar.

That face also looked familiar yet, after a few moments of further inspection, Harker was still at a loss. But it was the photograph next to it that sent Harker's heart soaring as he suddenly realized who he was looking at. The image was in colour and a close-up of a man raising a glass of champagne towards the camera in a toasting gesture, and the man's distinctively square jaw and beady eyes had him thinking back to Lucas's house and the photos of seven dead and terribly mutilated men that he had seen on the wall.

These were the same people.

'They all died screaming, you know?'

Harker spun around to see Carlu standing in the open doorway, his eyes wide and a manic grin on his face as he brandished an ivory-handled gutting knife in his left hand, the small hook glinting as he rotated it.

'They always do,' Carlu rasped, as Sofia and Mama now appeared behind him with equally unhinged expressions, 'and you will too.'

## *Chapter 31*

Since parting ways with John Shroder in France, things had not been going well for David Carter. By the time the message from Winters arrived, Shroder had already left on his fact-finding mission and although the directions had been simple – head to Athens airport and await further directions – Carter's chosen mode of travel had been deemed unacceptable by the old man. Carter had then sent a long-winded text message explaining how, due to the Templars now being after them, taking to the air would be reckless given the organization's ability to track all flights. They would therefore certainly get to him long before he had a chance to retrieve the final pages of the Gigas Codex.

With his usual finesse and charm, Winters had offered a brutal choice. 'Get yourself on the next flight out, or Dr Chloe Stanton dies here and now.'

With little room to negotiate, Carter had done exactly that and opted for a flight from Paris to Greece. And although this had taken a while, it had been nowhere near the length of time he had hoped to stall for. On his arrival, Winters had sent him further instructions about catching a train for the next leg of his trip. This had offered Carter hope of some leeway because, in his experience, trains never ran on time. Unfortunately for him, not only had the train arrived and then left promptly, but it turned out to be a direct line with no time-wasting stops on the way.

There was some good news to be had, though, amongst the menacing threats on Chloe's life.

One: the location of the pages was in a community of monasteries at a place called Meteora, which was a well-known tourist landmark, meaning there would be plenty of people around if any trouble should arise.

Two: Winters, by all accounts, had no idea Carter was travelling solo.

The latter consideration became the most important and, as Carter watched the Greek countryside slide past his window, he began to think further of Chloe. A woman he had never met, and had not even seen a picture of, yet here he was playing a dangerous game of cat and mouse across Europe, like in a James Bond-style spy adventure revolving at that moment around himself and his powers of deception.

*That's right, David*, Carter thought to himself, and he began feeling supremely confident and brave about his undertaking. *This one's for the ladies.*

It was about this time, as he checked out his own 'no-nonsense look' in the reflection from the window beside him, that he noticed a small man in a black suit standing at the far end of the carriage glancing towards him. At first he thought it was his own paranoia playing tricks, but as he stole another glance at the window's reflection, he noticed now that the man was most definitely eyeing him suspiciously.

Carter didn't flinch or look directly at the man, but instead remained calm and collected even as his heart began beating ever harder. He felt sure he did not recognize the individual, but then again, why would he? For if Winters had sent someone to keep an eye on him, then he certainly wouldn't be stupid enough to send someone familiar. Besides, given the number of people pursuing both Harker and himself, it could be anyone. The Templars or one of Vlad's men – take your pick.

Carter stood up and began to fiddle around beside his seat, his hands out of the man's sight, and he hoped this would signal a relaxed demeanour, like he wasn't in a rush. He then turned his attention to a sign with a toilet logo on it, pausing this time to indicate he was intending to use the toilet. He felt he may have overdone it because he stared at it for quite a few seconds with his forefinger pressed thoughtfully to his lips. This probably gave the impression that he was either a bit slow-witted or had a fascination with toilet signs.

After a few seconds more of pondering, he started making his way through to the next carriage. As the connecting door closed behind him, he sneaked a glance behind only to find the same man now making his way towards him. With a light step, Carter made his way straight to the next carriage doorway. As he crossed the threshold, he heard the door behind him opening. The fellow was obviously closing in on him, and he fought the urge to run because at that moment he didn't know if his pursuer knew that he'd realized someone was after him.

*Remarkable*, Carter reckoned. He had no idea a pursuit could be so complicated, and given that the train must have been going at ninety kilometres an hour and there were only two further carriages ahead, he was going to have to think of something quick. Much to his relief, he saw a group of three teenagers approaching the next connecting door, so he stepped up his pace and reached it before they could. He then opened it and bustled on past them, so the pursuer's view of him would be blocked, then he dived into the left-hand toilet cubicle and slid the 'Occupied' sign into place.

It would only be a matter of time before he was discovered, because there was only one carriage beyond, and once the man had checked it, he would undoubtedly backtrack to the last place anyone could hide...the toilet.

Carter scanned the grotty little stall for anything he could use as a weapon, but after finding only a half-used toilet roll, along with a dispenser well-stocked with paper towels, he began to panic. He turned his attention to the small, greyed-out window, opened only halfway, which would struggle to accommodate the girth of a pet chihuahua let alone a forty-something man with a capacious waistline.

Behind him came a knock at the door and Carter froze with his hands held out in front of him, like a panther waiting to strike…or perhaps someone about to surrender.

'Anyone in there?' asked a deep voice with a European accent, but Carter said nothing, remaining silent and motionless.

A few seconds passed and the knocking came again, only harder this time.

'I said, is anyone in there?'

Carter's jaw felt paralysed and, as the knocking began for a third time, he broke out of his trance. 'Yes, I'm having a few problems here. Do you mind?'

'Yes, I do mind.' The voice sounded more demanding with every syllable. 'You need to come out right now or there'll be trouble.'

Sweat was now beading across Carter's brow and he clenched his fist, tensed his biceps and reached over for the door lock. If this was it, then he wasn't going to go down easily, whoever it was. He took a deep breath, flicked back the lock and then slammed his full weight against the door, sending it flying open and into the man on the other side, who in turn slammed back against the far side of the corridor.

It was the same man in the suit that had been following him, and Carter grabbed him roughly by the shoulders and glared at him ominously. 'Who are you?' he shouted. 'What do you want?'

The fellow offered no resistance but, in one fluid movement, reached into his pocket, pulled something out and thrust it in front of him. Was it a gun? Was it a knife?

The glint of metal was all Carter could see and he was about to reach for it when he recognized the object and immediately loosened his grip on the stranger as the instrument was jabbed towards him.

It was a hole-punch.

'Ticket, sir,' the man explained, looking startled after Carter's aggressive exit from the cubicle. And it was at this moment the ex-don realized the fellow was not wearing a suit at all, but rather a black uniform with a tie.

'I'm sorry,' he offered apologetically, letting go of the man as he took a step backwards. 'I thought you were someone else.'

The ticket collector now looked angry and double-tapped the hole-punch threateningly. 'Who *did* you think I was, sir?'

'Oh, just an obsessive fan,' Carter replied, retrieving his ticket from a pocket. 'I'm a famous writer, you know, one can never be too careful.'

This explanation for his barging out of the toilet so aggressively was crap at best, but it appeared to soothe the collector's temper and he snipped a hole in Carter's ticket. 'Well, I am definitely not a fan, sir.'

'Of course not. I do apologize.'

With a grunt, the ticket collector headed back into the nearest carriage and Carter turned to the window and gazed at his own reflection, once again feeling supremely confident and now truly relishing the adventure. 'I hope Alex is enjoying all this as much as I am,' he muttered, and then began to make his way back to his seat.

# *Chapter 32*

'Welcome to my parlour,' Carlu proclaimed flamboyantly as he pushed Harker down the creaking wooden staircase with the tip of the gutting knife pressed firmly to his back. 'You should feel honoured at having the chance to see it.'

There were a lot of emotions Harker was experiencing at this moment, but being honoured was definitely not one of them. 'You didn't call the police at all, did you?'

'I'm afraid not,' Carlu replied, prodding Harker forward. 'There's really no need for them, you see.'

Following the sudden appearance of a knife in Carlu's hand, Harker had attempted to make a break for the front door, but after a short scuffle, of which he had been on the losing end, the larger man had dealt him a blow that had literally made his teeth rattle. After being momentarily stunned, any further plan to escape had come to a swift end when Mama had broken a large flower vase over his head. Following this, Carlu had finally pacified him by holding the knife to his throat, before leading him down into the basement. Both the vicious old crone and annoyingly attractive Sofia had been ordered to stay upstairs as Carlu proceeded to give Harker 'the tour', as he put it. The way the man said it had sent a chill through Harker's body, but as he was led into the area beneath the house he was consumed only with a feeling of dread. The 'parlour' looked like more of a dungeon than a storeroom for consumables and, as Harker surveyed the dank décor, his dread now turned into nothing short of terror.

Twenty metres or so in length and half as wide, the parlour floor was covered in shiny grey linoleum tiles, and in the corner there was a cage with rusting bars large enough to hold a crouching prisoner. On one side a series of steel tables linked to a washbasin were bolted onto the wall, and on another a large piece of blue tarpaulin hung from it to the floor, covering something that protruded out from underneath. Next to it was a worn hospital gurney, its cracked edges displaying the foam lining it was stuffed with; for Harker this would have been the most ominous thing in the room had he not noticed something above the steel tables opposite.

On the cracked plaster walls hung an assortment of what might have been described as gardening tools, but Harker could wager they had never been used by anyone with green fingers. A pair of shears, an axe and a saw were amongst the larger items above, with a selection of smaller knives, pliers and claw hammers filling up the bottom row.

'You're not a horticulturist by any chance, are you?' Harker quipped in a shaky voice, genuinely surprised with himself for being able to produce such a smart-ass remark given his current predicament.

'Ah, fear-induced humour, a strong quality. Keeps a man firm when faced with adversity,' Carlu responded with a venomous smile. He pushed Harker roughly towards the centre of the room, then pressed the gutting knife lightly against his own forefinger and spun it back and forth. 'Won't help you here, though.'

Harker was already eyeing the axe when Carlu began to tut. 'You wouldn't make it,' he growled, then reached over and, with one hand, grabbed a folding metal chair that leant against the back wall and threw it towards Harker so it landed at his feet. 'Sit.'

Harker stole another glance at the axe before thinking better of it. He picked up the chair, unfolded it, and sat down as Carlu waved the knife towards him.

'Good choice,' he said, moving closer. 'So you like my collection of trophies.'

'Trophies?' Harker glanced over at the rack of implements but Carlu was already shaking his head as he pointed upwards.

'The photographs.'

It was a bizarre way to describe them, and Harker winced. 'You mean the dead men, all killed ritually.'

Carlu looked surprised. 'You've been digging deeply, haven't you?'

'Deep enough. I found those same death pictures back at your son's apartment shortly after he killed himself.'

The grin on Carlu's face evaporated. 'I find that hard to believe, as Simone would not have been so sloppy.'

'What, to kill himself?'

'No, to leave any trace of his actions. I trained him better than that.'

'He left quite a few traces actually,' Harker replied as the image of what had been left of Lucas's head loomed in the forefront of his mind. 'So you know that he committed suicide?'

'Of course I do. I sent him to you in the first place.'

Harker felt like he was trapped between a web of plots that he was still struggling to understand and creating in him a very real sense of claustrophobia as his breaths became shallow. From Winters to Vlad, then his band of rich friends, and finally now to this bizarre family. They were obviously all connected, but how? With great difficulty he pushed aside the fact that his own life was in danger, and instead focused on assembling the pieces. 'I know about Winters, about Vlad, about the Gigas Codex…and I know about Judgement Day.'

Carlu remained silent and eyed him blankly, then he crouched on his haunches while still maintaining enough distance from Harker to make any sudden attempt to rush him impossible. 'The things I do have always been carried out with a healthy respect. When I take a life, I do it because I believe with every fibre of my being that I serve a higher purpose, and those needs are paramount.' Carlu twirled the knife he was holding back and forth gently with his wrist limp. 'But when the time comes, and our Saviour comes to judge their worthiness, it is impossible to say who will find redemption in his eyes and who will not. It is for this reason that I always allow them to know the reason for their sacrifice. For, if or when we meet again, who can say if an enemy will then be a friend as we sit together at the table.'

Harker's first inclination was that these were the ramblings of an extremely disturbed personality, but given everything he had now seen, it made a morbid kind of sense. 'So you yourself killed those seven men whose pictures I found?'

'Don't be an idiot,' Carlu hissed. He stood up straight, with the tip of his knife still pointing directly at Harker, and leant against one of the steel tables. 'Do I really look like I'm over two hundred years old? There was a group who came together centuries ago, let's call it a meeting of minds. They belonged to some of the wealthiest families in Europe, and they had just one single goal...immortality. They used their considerable resources to scour the known world, exploring and chasing every legend, every story that would further their goal. They even searched for the fountain of youth, but I am afraid I know little about that particular excursion, except it ended in abject failure. After years of toil they finally came upon a coven of witches, and it was here that they gained their first insight into stories about the Codex and its hidden knowledge passed down by Lucifer himself. In fact, the knowledge of everlasting life. The coven had at one time even held one of the sacred pages, but sadly it was stolen by a band of thieves that sought the knowledge for themselves.'

The story resonated with Harker and he immediately thought back to Brulet's account of the pages. They weren't thieves, rather they were Templars, but evidently Carlu didn't know that, or if he did he wasn't willing to admit it.

'The group then set about tracking down these pages and it was during this time that my own family entered into the fray.

My forefathers were endowed with the gift of great wealth, with just a single condition – a responsibility passed on to each generation.'

'A sacrifice,' Harker muttered, finally understanding the reason for the seven murders he had been made aware of back at Lucas's apartment.

'Exactly,' Carlu replied, now gazing at Harker longingly. 'A sacrifice made once a generation as a show of loyalty to him who will grant us a seat as his table. It is with this role that my family has been blessed, and we have carried it out for centuries, affording us wealth, luxury – and immortality when the time comes. And that time is now, for tonight the final ceremony will take place and I and my family will be present to see his rebirth, and with it everlasting life for those who are loyal to him.'

Carlu now slid off the table and made his way closer, and Harker, sensing that was as about much as the older man was going to reveal, racked his mind for any further questions that would prolong the conversation.

'So why would Simone commit suicide if you're so close to gaining immortality?'

'Once Judgement Day has been enacted, his dedication will ensure he is returned to us. His suicide is nothing more than the ultimate expression of dedication to our Lord, and don't be in any doubt he will be rewarded for it.'

'I've seen that reward on offer back at a cemetery in Cervete and, believe me, it's nothing you would want for your son,' Harker said bitterly, casting his mind back to the ghoulish zombies reborn from the Gigas pages.

'Those two priests were judged and found unworthy…hell, it was I who arranged their "accident" in the first place. They could not have expected anything less after devoting their life to such a false god as Jesus Christ. But we who are believers in him who is the truth can expect so much more.'

Carlu stopped a few paces away from Harker and tapped the knife against his own cheek thoughtfully. 'What are the chances that I and my generation would be the ones to reach this moment? My ancestors did it, although still with a true belief, for wealth and fortune. But to think that it is during my lifetime that the Day of Judgement will occur is almost unbelievable. It is almost enough to make one believe in reincarnation…or destiny.'

'So what has Jacob Winters got to do with all this?' Harker asked, fear for his life now giving way to curiosity.

'Mr Winters's bloodline stems from one of the founding fathers of the group, and without him we would still be searching for those missing Gigas pages. There were originally seven pages written by the hand of the Devil, but only three contained the knowledge that would allow the black Judgement Day to occur with him at the helm, instead of the false prophet Jesus Christ. Up until recently our search had only retrieved one, but Mr Winters, by the grace of Lucifer himself, discovered the other two.'

Harker was baffled by Carlu's response. 'Three?' The third had been locked away in the Templar's vault until only hours earlier and yet this whole business had been set in motion several days ago, as far as he knew. Add this to the fact that Vlad had not seemed at all concerned about the pages…and if that was the case, then what did he know that these Satanic followers obviously didn't? 'He found the other two?'

'Yes, months ago. How and where was not explained to me, but without them this final wonder about to come could not have been attained.'

'There's still something I don't understand. Why did Winters have Simone kill himself, and by doing so drag me into all this?'

The question had Carlu looking confused as he leant towards him with a frown on his forehead. 'You weren't dragged into anything,' he declared, much to Harker's surprise, 'but Mr Winters wanted one final token of loyalty from our family, and my son was more than happy to oblige. Indeed, he was honoured to be given the opportunity.'

The answer seemed surreal to Harker, but given the promise of immortality and considering the high esteem in which they held Winters after his discovery of the last pages, it made a twisted kind of sense. It also appeared that whatever Jacob Winters's game plan was regarding Harker, the old man was keeping it close to his chest, and Carlu now confirmed this.

'The truth is that only a few short hours ago I had a message from Mr Winters, requesting my help with a problem he has.'

'Oh yes,' Harker replied as the man moved even closer. 'What problem would that be?'

'You.' Carlu whispered it with a smile and began to move in closer still.

'You won't get away with this,' Harker growled, finally out of questions, but that did stop Carlu in his tracks, and he now backed away slowly towards the blue tarpaulin draped across the far other side of the room.

'Now that's funny,' Carlu said, and he gripped the corner of the plastic sheet and pulled it downwards to reveal something that had tears of fear welling in the corners of Harker's eyes. 'For it's exactly what he said.'

The bloody corpse hung from two meat hooks like a macabre hunter's trophy, with spikes entering beneath the man's shoulder blades and protruding through his chest just above the nipples. Both of the hands and feet were missing digits where they had been sliced off, and the torso was covered with deep, jagged cuts like those delivered by a saw. The blood-matted hair had dried and hardened into spikes deliberately styled to look like a crown of thorns and, even though the face had been battered to a mush, it was the man's groin area that really drew Harker's attention. The victim's genitals had been shredded, and now one lone testicle hung from a thin sliver of muscle dangling beneath him.

'What the fuck!' Harker gasped, totally transfixed by the gruesome sight. The amount of pain the poor fellow must have suffered was beyond anything Harker could even begin to imagine and, as Carlu now edged towards him in what could be described as a slithering motion, he stood frozen to the spot.

'My family's sworn duty is to arrange one sacrifice once every generation, which means only one of us ever gets the honour, but that hardly seems fair, does it?' Carlu hissed, moving still closer with the knife firmly held in one hand. 'So I have always allowed them to indulge in such things, which is only reasonable, I feel, and as for me…well, practice makes perfect, don't you think?' Carlu was now well within striking distance and his expression suddenly became glazed and misshapen, as if this were a different person Harker was now looking at. 'He lasted for seventeen days,' Carlu said as his breathing now became erratic, exhilarated at the thought. 'I wonder how long *you* will last?'

Without hesitation he slammed the gutting knife into the right side of Harker's chest, which produced a cracking sound. The knife was only embedded about three centimetres but it was enough to have Harker clasping it, as Carlu stood back and grinned. 'I think I heard a rib crack,' he said, rubbing his hands and, as Harker groaned, he turned his attention to the wall lined with rows of other cutting implements. 'Your lung will have been punctured, which is extremely painful, but don't worry as it's not life-threatening…not with my expertise. You won't die until I let you.' With arms raised he began to lovingly run his hands across the assortment of tools before him. 'There's more than one way to skin a cat.'

As Carlu continued to wallow in his own depravity, Harker was amazed to find he felt no pain at all, not even numbness. And, as he looked down and grasped hold of the knife sticking out of him, he understood the reason why. The knife had been driven not into his chest, but into Carter's metal drinking flask, which he had taken from him back at Mont-Saint-Michel. Harker stood up slowly on shaky legs and, as a surge of adrenalin took hold, launched himself forward in a single bound, slamming his shoulder hard into Carlu's back.

The impact sent the Corsican killer hurtling forward, slamming into the nearest steel table. His head flicked forward and collided with the wall with such force that a chunk of plaster broke off and fell onto the table top.

Carlu fell to his knees, quivering groggily as Harker ripped a small tree axe off the wall rack and, holding the heavy metal blade between his palms, he brought the thick wooden handle down against the stunned man's skull. The blow knocked him out cold, spread-eagled on the floor, whereupon Harker retreated and dropped the weapon. There was now a real feeling of pain in his chest, so he looked down at the gutting knife sticking out and realized that his attack on Carlu had actually pushed the blade deeper. He should have panicked at the realization but, considering what Carlu had planned for him, he instead felt nothing but relief. Harker placed both hands around the knife's handle and pulled it out with the same scraping sound that Carlu had mistaken for the cracking of his rib, as the metal flask underneath his jacket gave way.

Harker reached under his shirt and, although he could feel blood, he realized the damage inflicted was minimal and he guessed the tip of the knife had penetrated his flesh less than a centimetre. He gave a relieved sigh just as he heard the shuffling of feet from one of the rooms overhead. He immediately leapt towards the foot of the staircase and held the knife poised up against his chest, ready to strike.

A few seconds passed before the noises above him stopped, and now confident that his actions had not alerted the rest of the family, he quietly began to climb the steps. *Family, that was a joke*, Harker thought, pausing as one of the wooden planks creaked underneath his weight. *A family of bloody serial killers.*

This terrifying thought had him retreating back to Carlu's motionless body, where he slid the gutting knife into his own jacket pocket, then retrieved the small tree axe lying next to the man. Outside a few culinary efforts in the kitchen, his skills with a blade were next to zero, but surely anyone could use an axe.

Harker returned to the staircase and began once again making his way upwards, placing his feet carefully either side of the steps in an effort to avoid any creaking, and he succeeded in making it right up to the parlour entrance without so much as a squeak. With the axe grasped in his hand, Harker slowly turned the black metal knob, pushed the door open just a fraction, and peered out through the narrow gap.

The hallway beyond was empty, and even though he could see the front door from where he stood, making a dash for it was not an option. He had come here specifically to get answers, and so far all he had discovered was an unhinged family with a penchant for generational serial murder and a twisted belief in Satan.

Harker edged his way through the doorway and gingerly crept towards the sitting room he had been led into initially. The wooden flooring looked like it was just begging to make a noise and so, as he had done earlier with the parlour steps, he stayed as close as possible to the walls until he reached the room. There was no noise coming from the other side of the door and he quickly decided that leaping in brandishing an axe was not the best course of action. If Carlu's kin were in another part of the house, the noise he caused would immediately alert them to his location.

Harker pressed his cheek against the door frame and, after pausing to steady his breathing, slid around the edge of the door – only to come face to face with Mama.

Harker jerked back in shock and, as the old woman's eyes began to widen and her mouth opened, his instincts took over and in one swift move he punched the wooden axe handle into her face, sending Mama to the ground in a heap, clutching at her nose.

Ordinarily the thought of assaulting an old woman with an axe handle would have seemed to him appalling, but this was no ordinary situation and she was certainly no ordinary OAP.

'Don't move,' Harker growled as he saw Sofia leap up from the furthest sofa. She froze, staring at the axe in his hand rather than at him.

'Where's my father?' she finally yelled, seeming not to care about Mama, curled up in a ball and still nursing her bloody and most likely broken nose.

'He'll live,' Harker replied angrily, and he raised the axe above his head and directly over Mama, 'which is more than I can say for your grandmother if you don't do exactly as I tell you.'

Still dressed in her white nightie, Sofia scowled at him as she considered the situation and then gave a nod.

'Good.' Harker still held the axe high. 'I want two things and then I'm gone. Firstly I want a car…so get the keys now.'

Without a moment's pause she headed for one of the sideboards and opened the drawer so quickly that Harker instinctively took a step backwards.

'Easy,' Harker warned her, 'or the granny gets it.'

Sofia decided to comply, and very slowly pulled a key from inside the drawer and threw it over at Harker, who caught it with one hand while still holding the axe aloft in the other.

He glanced down at the Porsche tag. 'Nice,' he remarked, and pocketed it, then resumed his threatening stance as Mama sat up.

'You dirty thieving bastard,' she croaked, still clutching her nose. 'You'll die for this.'

'Well, you were going to kill me anyway, so zip it, Mama,' Harker replied, enjoying the feeling of being in control after coming so close to being dispatched and in such a terrible way. 'There's just one more thing I need to know. Where is the Judgement Day ritual taking place, and when?'

Both of them remained tight-lipped and Harker realized that the longer this business took, the sooner Sofia was going to realize that there was no way he would actually chop up Mama. He raised his foot and placed it against the old woman's chest, shoving her down onto her back. He then stood over her with the axe gripped tightly as if to show how serious he was. 'I'm not going to ask you again.'

Sofia's eyes darted back and forth between him and Mama, then after a few tense seconds her shoulders slumped and she slowly pulled a silver Cartier pen from the pocket of her nightgown and began scribbling something on the back of the photograph of Lucas that Mama had dropped on the table earlier. 'Here,' she said, before flicking the photograph towards Harker. 'At ten o'clock.'

Harker withdrew the axe handle and warily reached down to snatch it off the floor. He glanced at it briefly. 'Good,' he said, placing it in his pocket before taking a step away from Mama, though still keeping the axe semi-raised. 'Now get on the floor.'

'I am on the floor,' Mama hissed, rubbing at her chest.

'Not you, old timer...you.' Harker motioned towards Sofia, who dutifully lay down on her front. 'On your stomach, Mama,' he continued, and with a groan the old woman did as ordered.

He moved over to the telephone and ripped its cord out of the wall, then proceeded to tie Sofia's hands and legs together tightly and with surprisingly little resistance on her part. He then took the telephone over to Mama and, with nothing else available, bound her hands with the cord that linked the receiver to its base, before resting the instrument on her back. It would not take them long to loosen the knots, but it should give him ample time to reach the car and make a quick exit.

'Where's the Porsche?' he demanded, dropping the axe onto the nearest sofa.

'Round the side of the house,' Sofia replied, shooting him a nasty look. 'You won't make it.'

Harker dangled the Porsche keys in front of her eyes and smiled. 'I think I will.'

'Not to the car, you idiot. To the ritual. He's too powerful, and you don't stand a chance.'

Harker felt a twinge of anxiety twisting in his chest but he maintained a confident smile. 'You mean the Devil?' he suggested sarcastically.

Sofia shook her head and then let it drop onto the expensive white rug. 'You're in for a shock, Mr Harker, you really are. I only hope I'm there when it happens.'

'Well, then,' Harker replied, turning towards the door, 'I guess I'll see you in Hell.'

## *Chapter 33*

David Carter leant against the black metal, chest-high patio railing and gazed out across the lush green mountains of surrounding Meteora as the sun beat down upon him. As far as views went, it was one of the most naturally impressive he had ever seen, and the ex-don was thoroughly enjoying the feeling of crisp, clean air seeping into his lungs.

The train journey had gone smoothly despite a few angry glares from the ticket collector, who seemed to feel obliged to keep an eye on Carter for the rest of the journey. On arrival, he had caught a taxi to the small village of Kastraka, located at the base of the Meteora mountains, which housed six working monasteries including the second largest, Varlaam, which he was now looking down from. Constructed by monks during the fourteenth century, and built upon gigantic naturally formed pillars of rock soaring hundreds of metres into the sky, these retreats had been designed specifically to keep unwanted visitors from encroaching on the monastic hermits' way of life…or lack of, it to be more precise. In fact, until the modern age of tourism had dawned and steps had been carved into the rock face, the only way to reach them was by a single rope-and-net pulley system. As the legend went, the rope was never replaced until the previous one had snapped of its own accord, which was seen as God's will – which sounded peachy unless you were the one using it when it finally succumbed to wear and tear. More interesting still was the fact that the monks had initially taken refuge in caves once occupied by Ice Age man over twenty thousand years earlier, and maybe as much as fifty thousand. Of course, Carter known little about the subject until he picked up the free pamphlet on arrival, and following Winters's instructions that he should wait until contacted, he had now read it multiple times.

Only a few monks still occupied the monasteries today, due to the high level of tourism which offered the wrong type of ambience for hermits. But, as Carter looked down at the awesome scenery below, he could see why so many men had decided to settle here in years past. On one side a lush green valley weaved its way between two mountain ridges dense with foliage, and on the other side – and visible from where he was standing – lay the flat plains surrounding Kastraka village, with mountains looming in the distance.

For years, Carter's routine had involved spending time mainly indoors rather than outdoors, whether in classrooms, or in his house or car, but seeing such an awe-inspiring sight now awakened in him a sense that he had been missing out on so much – trapped inside a little bubble of going back and forth in his daily shuffle of existence. Of course that was exactly how a majority of the world spent their lives but, as he took in this sight, he made himself a promise to get out and about more often, and to make the most of it. His wife's death had caused him to retreat into himself and hide there gloomily but the last few days had woken him out of that place, that mindset, and he felt as if a slate had been wiped clean and he could finally allow himself a new start.

'Mr Harker?' someone called out behind him, and he turned to see a man with short, curly brown hair, who was wearing dark jeans and a plaid shirt rolled up at the sleeves. 'Professor Alex Harker?'

Carter moved to greet the man. 'Yes, and you are?' He shook the man's now extended hand.

'Alec Contos. I manage the tourism side of things. It's a real pleasure to meet you.'

'Likewise,' Carter replied, instinctively assessing the man's physical prowess, which seemed nothing to write home about.

Contos was only five foot tall with narrow shoulders and Carter felt confident he could defend himself, should the need arise.

'Please follow me. There is much for us to discuss.'

With a polite nod but a degree of apprehension, Carter followed him off the patio and into the tight assembly of buildings that made up Varlaam monastery. *What exactly was there to discuss? Why not just give me the pages?* he thought.

'When I received the call from your office, it came as a surprise but a most welcome one,' Contos explained with genuine enthusiasm in his voice, as he led Carter up some zigzagging stone steps and along the tight path running between the main places of worship.

'You're welcome,' Carter replied, though having no idea what the fellow was referring to.

'No, it is you who is most welcome, Professor,' Contos continued with a wide smile. On reaching a small wooden door, he opened it and waved Carter inside. 'Please, come in.'

Carter paused at the open doorway and peeked inside sheepishly but, seeing only an empty office with several seats and a desk, he happily ventured inside before Contos closed the door and sat down behind the desk. 'Can I get you a coffee or tea?' he offered, as Carter sat down on a grey plastic chair.

'No, I'm fine, thank you.' Carter took another look around the medium-sized room containing only furniture, filing cabinets, a coffee percolator on a side table, and a desktop PC.

'Very well, Professor, then let me say how excited I am by your offer. I can assure you that your film crew will be allowed access to every section of the Meteora monasteries.'

'That is good to know,' Carter replied, not missing a beat even though he still did not have the faintest idea what Contos was talking about.

'Will you be doing any filming today?'

'No, no, today is just to do a recce, scope the place out, as it were, before we start.'

'Very good,' Contos replied, with no sign of his enthusiasm waning as he rested his elbows on the table. 'I must tell you that your documentary on Meteora alone is going to be of great benefit to us, but when your office mentioned the donation to be made by Cambridge University, I was...well, stunned.'

'Not at all, Mr Contos. It seemed the least we could do, considering the access we are being given.' Carter found himself actually enjoying this role-playing and he had to stop himself from indulging in further amateur dramatics.

'Don't be so modest, Professor. Two hundred thousand pounds is, without doubt, one of the most generous donations we have ever received.' The mention of such a large sum of money left Carter looking shocked, and Contos's eyebrows suddenly contracted. 'The donation is still on offer?'

'Yes, of course. It's just... I thought it was three hundred thousand.'

This new amount mentioned had Contos beaming from ear to ear. 'Three hundred thousand! I just don't know what to say.'

'Neither do I,' Carter replied shakily, and he forced a smile, deciding that it was perhaps best now to move on to the real reason he was here, given that there was not a cat's chance in hell he was going to hand over that amount of money, even if he had it to spare...which he of course didn't. 'My office said you would have something for me. A package?'

The request had Contos's eyebrows lowering again, and he looked bemused. 'A package?'

'Yes, a package...maybe some pages, of the vellum variety.'

It was clear that Contos now had no idea what he was talking about and he shook his head. 'I'm sorry, but I don't know what you're talking about.'

'I think I do,' boomed a voice behind them, and Carter swivelled in his seat to see the cold eyes of Vlad staring at him from the half-open doorway. 'In fact I'm sure of it.'

Carter froze with an involuntary gulp as Vlad made his way inside, followed by two smartly dressed women in black suits and ties. He then approached the desk with one hand outstretched.

'I'm Mr Hodgkinson, part of a delegation from Cambridge University.'

Contos stood up and warmly shook Vlad's hand. 'It's a pleasure, Mr Hodgkinson. I was just telling Professor Harker how excited we are about the making of the documentary and your donation.'

Vlad towered over Carter, who now shrank back deep into his seat, looking extremely uncomfortable.

'Professor Harker, of course. Nice to see you again.'

Carter smiled nervously as the two women took up position on either side of his chair, with one firmly gripping his left shoulder.

'I was expecting your colleague to be with you, Professor.' Vlad licked his lips. 'What a shame… I mean for you.'

The uncomfortable silence that followed was now broken by Contos. 'Would anyone like some coffee or tea?'

Vlad continued to eye Carter menacingly for a few more moments, then he turned to face their host with an overfriendly smile. 'A coffee would be delightful, thank you.'

Contos turned around and began heading towards the coffee table, but only made it halfway before one of the women calmly strode forward, pulled something from her pocket and slipped it over the man's head and around his neck.

An unpleasant gurgling sound arose from Contos as she tightened her grip on the garrotte and he scrabbled frantically at his neck, where the wire was already slicing through, while his legs began to kick up in the air. The woman maintained her grip and, as his legs began to buckle, she pulled him downwards until the top of his spine was pressed against her crouching knee, so as to increase the pressure around the stricken man's neck.

Carter was now breathing heavily and beginning to sweat profusely. As Contos's convulsions began to subside and his body went limp, Vlad craned his neck towards him. 'I want to know where your friend is, "Professor"?'

Possible answers raced through Carter's mind as he felt the sour breath of Vlad on his cheek. 'I don't know…the Templars got him.'

Vlad stood back up and crossed his arms as the garrotte-wielding woman now abandoned Contos's corpse and resumed her position next to Carter, the wire noose still in her hand dripping droplets of blood onto the light-blue carpet beneath them.

'Mmm, if that's true, then it looks like we're going to have to take out our frustration on you instead,' Vlad declared, looking distinctly annoyed by the news. 'And that means you've got a date with an electric cattle prod, doesn't it, porky?'

# Chapter 34

A small group of young twenty-somethings stumbled excitedly past the all-night café at the end of an enjoyable and alcohol-fuelled night of fun, looking like they did not have a care in the world. Jostling with each other and cracking jokes, they barely registered the man sitting patiently at one of the outside tables with a look of sheer boredom, while tapping a single euro coin against its glass surface. John Shroder paused in his tapping to watch the group pass before resuming his boring coin play. He had been sitting here waiting for his Interpol contact for several hours, and although such a wait was to be expected due to the last-minute request for a meeting, he was becoming extremely restless.

After receiving a reply from his contact on the inside, he had left the apartment – and Carter, who was still waiting for his message from Winters – and caught a flight to Nuremberg in southern Germany, followed by a short taxi ride to the chosen meeting place at this café. During the preceding hours he had resisted any urge to call his two new partners, as agreed, but as the time rolled on he was finding it increasingly difficult to hold off from making a call. His main cause for concern was not Harker, because the man had been in enough scrapes to know how to look after himself; David Carter was another thing altogether. An unknown quantity with little experience in such matters, and because Carter had been assigned the most delicate and dangerous job of all three of them it was making the MI6 agent anxious. It was very likely he was walking straight into another of Winters's traps and it was this thought that was playing on Shroder's mind the most. Still, the man had guts to even accept his 'mission' – as the ex-don had kept calling it – but the idea of him walking unprepared into a trap was something that was now gnawing at Shroder's innards.

It was with this growing sense of foreboding that Shroder was preoccupied when a hand suddenly tapped him on the shoulder.

'John,' a voice said quietly, and Shroder looked back to see the one face he had been waiting for since his arrival here.

'Andrew,' Shroder replied, standing up to shake his contact's hand. 'Good to see you, and thanks for meeting me.'

Andrew Campus gave Shroder's shoulder a friendly squeeze and then sat down opposite him, letting out a deep sigh. 'Sorry for taking so long, but you caught me in the middle of something.'

'Not a problem, Andrew. I know you're busy... Nothing too hectic, I hope?'

'You know the life, John. When is it not?' Campus replied with a wry smile. 'There was a flag raised at Interpol, regarding a fugitive. A man had been arrested for being drunk and disorderly, and his wallet contained ID for the man we've been looking for, so off I went.'

'Was it a solid lead?'

'My friend, the only thing solid about it was the turd the drunk bastard had shat in his pants.'

'What?' Shroder replied, with a confused laugh.

'Turned out that the wino's day job is picking pockets, and by complete coincidence he'd lifted the fugitive's wallet earlier in the day and then proceeded to get blind drunk on the contents before being picked up by some local police working the night shift. What were the odds? I tell you, life is without doubt stranger than fiction.'

At forty-two, Andrew Campus was a seasoned Interpol veteran and one of the few to have worked within the organization for so long. Born and raised in the UK, initially serving in the London Met, this man with short brown hair and the physique of a military drill instructor had jumped at the chance to transfer to Interpol. It was not a conventional career path but Campus came from a police family which had served for generations, and their well-established contacts within law enforcement were something he had made the most of. He had wound up eventually in the narcotics and human-trafficking section of the organization, where he had excelled, and this was the very reason Shroder had contacted him.

'That's a shit outcome,' Shroder observed and added, grinning, 'literally.'

Campus laughed out loud and, in doing so, released some of the pent-up frustration of a futile night's work. 'I tell you, John, even when we do catch a big fish, another larger, meaner and more violent one takes its place. Makes me feel like I'm forever on a damn treadmill.'

'Actually, it's one of those big fish I'm currently interested in,' Shroder explained, wanting now to get to the point, given how many hours he had been waiting.

'Who?'

'Jacob Winters.'

The very name elicited a spark of enthusiasm in Campus's eyes, and the Interpol agent leant forward cautiously. 'I know him – or at least of him.'

'I need to know anything you have,' Shroder prompted, encouraged by this answer.

Campus mulled over the request, then without any hesitation in his voice, he folded his arms and sucked in a deep breath. 'He pops up here, then disappears there. In fact we've taken to calling him the mole.'

'Do you have anything other than a nickname?'

'He's a genuine man of mystery,' Campus declared, stroking his bottom lip. 'Appeared from nowhere some months back with a fully operational syndicate that has established links with most of the major crime families in Europe – including the Russians, and you know how ruthless they are. He's heavily into narcotics, mostly crack cocaine and heroin, as well as the usual bread and butter of organized crime: prostitution, gambling and extortion. The interesting thing is that, from what we can tell, he has no criminal history up until recently, and no previous indication of a budding organization either. Like I said, he just popped up, and astonishingly quickly took over rackets everywhere, and made them his own like in a bloody cooperate takeover.'

This was nothing that Shroder did not already know and he found himself edging towards acquiring information on the man rather than his deeds. 'When did he first appear?'

'You should know that better than me, John, as it was your office that was the first to clock him.'

'Really?' Shroder replied, genuinely surprised at the fact.

'Yes, some German national was offering arms – and not any old calibre, but nuclear. The seller got entrapped in a MI6 sting operation and gave up the Winters's name as being the supplier. Of course, that's just gossip, nothing official.'

'Always is,' Shroder said, now extremely curious. 'What happened to him?'

'He died in custody. I don't know the details but his arrest led to revealing Winters's links in the narcotics web and all the other lovely trades he's involved in. That's where I came in, and Interpol have been building a case against him ever since.'

'A case?' Shroder spluttered, almost choking on the words. 'Something as big as that is going to take years to put together.'

Campus said nothing at first and just raised his eyebrows, but as Shroder craned forward with an insistent expression, the Interpol agent began to nod. 'There is something else...something you may want to see.'

Without another word, he got out of his seat and began making his way across the road. Shroder dropped a couple of euros onto the coffee table and followed him with a renewed skip in his step.

They did not need to go far, just fifty metres away from the all night-café to a quaint-looking residential building with a red wooden door, whereupon Campus pulled out a Yale key from his pocket and let himself in.

'This is convenient,' Shroder remarked, surprised by the proximity of whatever Campus wanted to show him.

'Why do you think I asked you to meet me at that café?' Campus replied before ushering Shroder inside and then onwards into a small lounge located at the front of the house. 'I live here.'

The room was exactly what one would expect of a single working man. There were no paintings on the walls and just a three-seat black leather sofa with side tables supporting lamps on either side of it, while in the corner a new sixty-inch HD Panasonic flat-screen television on a bracket protruded from the wall.

'Love what you've done with the place,' Shroder commented sarcastically at the décor, or lack of it.

'Yeah, yeah,' Campus said dismissively with his eyelids drooping, 'the rest of the house is a lot nicer, believe me.'

'I'll take your word for it,' Shroder replied as Campus reached behind the sofa and pulled out a small cardboard box that had been taped shut. He placed it on the sofa and then pulled a narrow switchblade from his pocket, which he tossed over to Shroder.

'Go on.' He nodded. 'Open it and see for yourself.'

Shroder paused and shot him a wary look.

'You're getting skittish in your old age, John. Don't worry, it won't bite.'

With a shrug, Shroder cautiously made his way over to the brown box and flicked open the switchblade before picking up the container and gently shaking it.

'I warn you, it's not pretty,' Campus cautioned him.

Shroder glanced back and offered an unconcerned smile. 'Takes a lot to get under my skin,' he said, and began to cut away at the red tape covering the box's corners. 'Damn it, Andrew, how long have you known me?'

Shroder felt something hard being prodded into his lower back and instantly his whole body went stiff, before collapsing in a heap on the floor – as, above him, Campus brandished a blue plastic Taser in his left hand.

'Not long enough, it would seem, John.'

# Chapter 35

Harker winced as he rubbed against the square bandage underneath his shirt, which he had applied to himself from the first aid kit the pilot had provided him with upon entering the Cessna jet. His trip back to Bastia airport had proved mercifully uneventful, even if he had spent much of the short trip glancing nervously in the rear-view mirror for any signs of being chased. His paranoia had led to constant visions of the rabid serial-killing family closing in behind him and doing everything they could to run him off the road and thus silence him, as they had originally planned. With every new car headlight that had appeared in his mirror, he had pushed the stolen Porsche faster, and by the time he had reached the airport turn-off he was having to make a concerted effort to ease off on the accelerator. Getting pulled over by the police in a stolen car, along with the discovery of a minor knife wound to his chest, would have entailed more problems than he could handle.

Having a British EU passport had subsequently made access to his waiting jet a breeze and, with few other commercial flights on the tarmac that night, he had been in the air within minutes and heading to the address that Corsica's very own version of the Manson family had provided him with.

Harker resisted another urge to scratch at his wound and instead pulled out the piece of paper that Sofia had grudgingly given him back at their mansion. The address comprised map coordinates identifying a small island lying off the south-east coast of Greece and, as far as Harker could make out, it was in private ownership. That the same small island had been removed from Google Maps was to his mind already a reason to be concerned but, after some further quick Google research, the discovery that the small sea-girt rock had once been home to a leper colony only added to his feeling of unease. Despite the fact that it had been abandoned for over fifty years, this information only served to heighten the morbid and mysterious nature of the place that would soon be hosting the occult ceremony that Jacob Winters had orchestrated.

With everything Harker had already witnessed, the once fanciful notion of raising the dead seemed now all too real, but the idea that the Devil himself was about to make an appearance and initiate a new world order was something he was still not ready to countenance, even if the idea did have his stomach performing the bolero in anticipation.

Harker gazed out of the window into the dark night sky and pondered the realities he was being forced to confront. His earlier life in the priesthood had instilled in him the very tangible concepts of good versus evil but, despite believing in God, Harker had always viewed evil as something lying within the hearts of men and women, and not as some extraneous entity watching over us all.

He swiftly batted away these philosophical notions to one side because, although thought provoking, they were as of this moment completely redundant. This was primarily about Chloe, and how to get her back, and this was the only question that mattered.

Harker retrieved his iPhone and, for the third time since taking to the air, he dialled in John Shroder's contact number. As before, it went to voicemail, so he hung up and then tried Carter's number, but got the same response. He dumped the mobile onto the seat next to him and let out a frustrated sigh. Where the hell were they? This whole plan had been formulated to give him enough time to locate Winters, and now here he was with the man's whereabouts and unable to let anyone else know it. As he racked his brain for a way to resolve the issue, an idea sparked in his mind. If he could not reach them, then perhaps it was time to reach out to someone else. Harker grabbed his mobile and dialled in a number he knew so very well.

With each ring his feeling of desperation increased, and by the time the line connected Harker was ready to explode.

'Hello,' a weary voice answered.

'Doggie, it's Alex. I need help.'

'Alex, where on earth have you been?' Dean Lercher asked groggily. 'Do you have any idea what I've been through?'

'Yes,' Harker replied, glad to hear the dean's familiar if somewhat irate voice. 'I was worried about you too.'

'Bugger worried – that's not the half of it. I got interrogated by someone from the Security Service, for God's sake. A man in my position!'

The dean's reference to John Shroder had Harker smiling. 'It's fine, Doggie. He's a friend and was only trying to find me.'

'Fine!' Doggie yelled. 'He threatened me with a charge of conspiracy to murder.'

The dean sounded seriously pissed off but, given what Harker was about to say next, it was only going to get worse. 'I know and I'm sorry. However, it was a threat and nothing more. We have another more pressing problem at the moment.'

There was a pause, and when Doggie spoke again he sounded merely nervous and perhaps a tad concerned. 'Go on.'

'OK, you know the Templars?'

'Yes.'

'Well, I might have had a bit of a falling out with them.' This of course was a major understatement, but Doggie already sounded nervous enough without revealing to him that the entire Templar organization was now after Harker.

'OK.'

'I probably should have told you about this before, but it's been a ridiculously crazy few days and I doubt anything serious is going to happen. But you may be paid a visit by some of them looking for me.'

When Shroder had told Harker how he had sent William Havers on a wild goose chase to the UK, he had reasoned that the last person he would go after for information was Doggie. But he needed the dean to be feeling unsettled if this was going to work.

'Go on,' Doggie demanded in an uncharacteristically calm tone.

'OK, well, I need you to call this number and speak to one Tristan Brulet, who is the head of the Knights Templar, and tell him that I contacted you in need of your help. And you are now extremely worried about me, and don't know where else to turn.'

'Why don't you call him yourself?'

'Honestly, Doggie, I'm not sure he would believe anything I told him right at the moment, but coming from a concerned friend with no obvious involvement in ongoing events, he might be willing to listen.'

'How would I know his number?'

'Just tell him I gave it to you in case of an absolute emergency.'

'OK.'

Doggie was sounding far too calm and Harker couldn't help wondering why his friend was not howling at him for getting him so involved in such trouble. Perhaps events over the past few years had finally cured him of his cowardice. 'Are you sure you're all right, Doggie?'

Dean Thomas Lercher gripped the handset of his telephone tightly as he stared into the menacing gaze of the Templar William Havers with hands trembling. A number of bruises on his cheeks bore thin cuts where the man's punches had torn the skin, and a line of dried blood ran down from one nostril to his lips. 'I'm fine, Alex. It's just a lot to take in, that's all. Where are you anyway?'

'On a private jet, believe it or not, and heading for the same location I want you to pass on to Tristan Brulet.'

'Not a problem. Let me just write it down.'

'Don't bother. I'm going to text it over. I just hope the Templars can reach me in time.'

'Oh, I'm sure they will.'

'You're a good friend, Tom,' Harker replied as the connection began to fade. 'I owe you.'

Doggie stared down the barrel of the smoke-blue metal Colt 45 in Havers's hand and nodded, trembling. 'Yes, you do, Alex. Yes, you do.'

## Chapter 36

'What do you mean, they're jamming us?' Harker demanded, edging closer to the cockpit as a patch of turbulence hit the jet and forced him to grab hold of the pilot's seat.

'I mean everything's down: no radio, no tower, nothing,' the pilot explained, tapping at his mic button. 'I can't even get the worldwide emergency station.'

'Who would do that?'

'Someone who doesn't want visitors.'

Communication had gone down within eleven kilometres of the island, and the closer they got, the worse the static had become. With no idea where or if there even was a runway, the pilot was beginning to experience serious doubts.

'I can't see a landing strip, Mr Harker, and there is no way I am putting her down on a strip of grass. She's just not designed for it.'

Dawn had broken twenty minutes earlier but, with no map references, they were flying by visual sight only, meaning all they could do was wait to get close enough and take a good look at the area. Now within only kilometres of their destination, both Harker and the pilot were scanning the approaching landmass intently.

The island itself was small, maybe six kilometres by three, with high craggy cliffs surrounding its shoreline and thick green forest covering its entire surface between. Towards the far side, the terrain rose upwards to form a small mountain peak blocking any view of the other side, and it was this region that caught Harker's attention immediately.

'If there is a runway, it has to be on the other side of that mountain.' He pointed to the rocky outcrop. 'Can you bring us around?'

The pilot said nothing but with a nod began to turn towards it, then he made a sudden correction and pulled the jet back to a straight and level position. 'There,' he said, pointing down to the nearest edge of the island. 'It's a landing strip.'

Nestling amongst the trees was a modest tarmac runway with two hangars at one end of it, cut into the forest floor and difficult to see because of the surrounding high trees.

'Can you get us down there?' Harker asked, assessing its length.

'Should do,' the man replied, and he was adjusting their trajectory towards the quickly approaching shelf of land just as a voice crackled from the radio.

'Golf Charlie India Tango India, this is ground control. You have entered private airspace, please change your heading. Over.'

The pilot glanced over at Harker, who was now shaking his head fervently, and with barely a pause he cleared his throat and pressed down on the mic button. 'Negative, ground. We are experiencing engine failure and therefore request clearance for an emergency landing. Over.'

He eased back on the throttle and now lined up towards the runway as the aircraft began to descend. They were landing whether the go-ahead was given or not, but it wasn't until the jet's undercarriage was fully down that a reply came back.

'Understood, India. We have no emergency services here but you will be met upon landing. Please remain in the cabin until further notice. Over.'

The pilot shot Harker a grin and then tapped on his mic button again. 'Roger, understood. Over and out.'

'No one ever turns away a request for an emergency landing,' the pilot explained, as he began to lower the Cessna onto the tarmac. 'Although how they behave when they greet us is another matter altogether.'

Harker dropped into the co-pilot's seat just as the tyres hit the ground, and with a light bump the jet began to slow when its brakes were applied. He was already scouring the hangars at the far end for any signs of life. As the Cessna's reverse thrusters kicked in and they came to a full stop just a hundred metres from those two buildings, he was already out of his seat.

'They'll be here soon, so I have to get going. Will you be all right?'

The pilot gave a confident nod, then took off his headphones and undid his seat belt. 'The flight plan I filed indicates no passengers, in case they have access to it, and I'll play for as much time as possible. But when they realize there's nothing wrong with the engines, I could be sent on my way immediately.'

'I understand,' Harker replied, already making his way to the exit hatch. 'I'm heading for the other side of the mountain – it can't be more than a kilometre or so – but if meanwhile you have to go, then just go. I'll figure something out and...'

Harker unlocked the metal-handled door hatch and then paused to look back at the pilot, who was still staring in his direction. 'I never asked your name?'

'It's Frank,' the pilot replied, 'and in my position I never enquire why I'm being asked to fly to any location. I'm just the pilot, but I have to ask you, Mr Harker, what the hell are we doing here?'

Harker clicked the hatch and let the door fall slowly open before he checked outside for any approaching vehicles – of which there were none so far. 'It's Alex,' he replied, 'and that's exactly what I am hoping to find out.'

## *Chapter 37*

The soggy, humid atmosphere of the forest felt stifling as Harker pressed on, making his way around the mountain's base to the far rim of the island. Since leaving the airstrip he had cleared the three-kilometre hike in a little over twenty minutes, which was a bit of a miracle given the uneven terrain. The forest was far denser than it had looked from the air and his attire was proving totally unsuited to the venture at hand. It had taken him only fifty metres into the woodland before he had to discard his suit jacket, and with each new rip in his white Oxford shirt, due to sharp protruding branches, he now appeared every bit a Robinson Crusoe lookalike.

Apart from the swarms of flies and mosquitoes, and the unidentified snake that had lunged out at him minutes earlier after he'd almost stepped on it, the place was beautiful, in a lost-paradise kind of way. But everything was in mini form since the entire island could not be more than eighteen square kilometres in total, yet included all the features one would expect in a perfect tropical landscape. Brooks and streams extended out through the forest like life-giving arteries, and Harker had so far come across two clearings containing waterfalls, but with drops of only twenty metres or so. It was all very quiet and tranquil.

The four-hundred-and-fifty-foot 'mountain' Harker was now making his way around was like everything else, a mini natural wonder, and as he approached the clearing visible ahead he couldn't help but think it was all too perfect. Had this whole island been deliberately landscaped to someone's particular wishes? And if that man was not Jacob Winters, then

Harker was in the wrong place and, more importantly, in some serious shit, because it was the only lead he had.

With sweat pouring off him, he passed out of the trees and came to an abrupt halt as he found himself on a narrow rocky outcrop with a tight muddy path leading down a fifty-metre drop to the forest floor, and allowing him his first glimpse of the other flank of the mountain. Compared to the rest of the island, the area below him looked a virtual paradise, and Harker sank down on one knee not just to recover his breath but also so as not to be spotted from the hive of activity going on down below.

The lower part of the mountain had been stripped of trees, and a luxurious six-thousand-square-foot Spanish Churrigueresque-style mansion, on three separate floors, sprawled outwards from its base. In front of it extended a wide patio adjoining an Olympic-pool-sized pond with oversized lily pads floating on the surface and dark metal fountain spouts pouring fresh water into it constantly. Beyond this, and encompassing the estate, was an eighty-hectare garden composed of various lawns all protected by the surrounding forest. There were even two tennis courts and an outdoor swimming pool surrounded by Waikiki huts and a long open-air bar with stools, which only added to the luxurious appearance of what could only be a rich man's leisure retreat... Or so it would have been except for the twenty or so uniformed guards patrolling the front of the mansion, armed with black SIG Sauer MPX semi-automatic submachine guns with extended barrels.

Harker lowered himself to rest onto his stomach and continued to peer over the edge, as a feeling of desperation crept into him. That number of guards would make it bloody difficult to even get into the mansion, and he had originally planned to have at least Shroder at his side, who was far more skilled at this type of thing. Christ, he didn't even have a pair of binoculars.

Down below, a commotion on the patio near the entrance to the mansion now caught his attention, and he focused in on a group of guards dragging a woman along. At first he didn't recognize the captive, but when she wrestled an arm free from one of the men and then slapped him across the face, he knew instantly who it was.

Chloe Stanton landed a stinger of a slap before the guard grabbed the free arm and restrained her. Then she was pulled forcefully in through the mansion's main door, and out of view. The spectacle had Harker instinctively rearing up onto his hindquarters, but then he forced himself back onto his stomach even as one of nearest guards glanced up in his direction. The man must have been over one hundred metres away but had obviously noticed movement up by the trees. However, after a few moments of inquisitive peering, he turned back and resumed his patrol of the grounds.

*Shit!* Harker thought as he now realized how his white shirt would stand out against the greenery of the forest. He slowly edged back behind the trees and, in a momentary flash of genius, scooped up large handfuls of wet soil and began covering his shirt until most of the linen was stained a dark brown. Unfortunately this method of camouflage was not as clever as he thought, and within seconds he was being assaulted by hordes of excitable mosquitoes, which appeared to come from nowhere. Undeterred, and swatting constantly at the annoying insects, he headed back along the small plateau and began to carefully make his way down a thin, precarious mud path.

The descent was easier than it looked, and by the time he reached the bottom the mosquitoes had thankfully lost interest. Crouching down while moving as fast as he could, Harker slunk furtively over to the edge of the patio, then ducked down behind a waist-high hedgerow lining its perimeter. With his head lowered flat against his right shoulder, he slowly edged himself upwards and peered over the foliage with one eye.

The guard who had shown interest earlier was still moving away from him, and distant enough not to present a direct problem. But as Harker stared over at the mansion's entrance, he found himself facing two main holes in his intended plan. Firstly the white and pale terracotta colours of the house's walls would make his newly contrived camouflage shirt stand out like a sore thumb if he made a dash directly for the entrance. Secondly, and more troublingly, he didn't actually have a plan in the first place.

Throwing caution to the wind, he stayed put until the nearest guard was comfortably far away, then he nimbly jumped over the hedge and swiftly tiptoed towards the mansion's outer wall, where he then slid, with his back pressed against it, all the way to the entrance.

Harker gingerly stole a look inside and, finding the coast was clear, he entered through the open double doorway into the cool, air-conditioned hallway beyond. Now shivering because of the ice-cold air meeting the sweat and dampness of his soiled shirt, he made his way slowly further inside and along a corridor until he paused at the first door he encountered.

Hearing no sound of footsteps, he felt emboldened to go further, and was considering opening the door and heading inside when he heard a woman's voice somewhere deeper inside the building. Wide-eyed and alert, he continued until he reached another hallway intersected with corridors. He was about to take a gamble by heading right when he heard the same woman's voice again. It was coming from somewhere to the left and, as he got closer, he realized it belonged to Chloe.

With a renewed sense of motivation, Harker tracked the voice as it got louder and louder, until he was sure it was coming from an open doorway just a little further along to his left. He continued, still on tiptoe, but as he approached, Chloe's voice abruptly stopped, causing him to freeze in his tracks.

Harker held fast and steadied his breathing even as his muscles tensed in preparation to move quickly, should he need to, but still no sound came from the room. He cautiously took another step forward, bringing him to within centimetres of the door frame, then slowly he craned his head further and peeked inside.

Chloe Stanton was sitting behind a desk on a velvet covered armchair, with both arms at her sides and staring directly at the open doorway. As her eyes met Harker's there was no hint of surprise, no look of shock, but only a blank gaze as he leant in further and peered around the room. The décor was extravagant, with expensive-looking gold and black wallpaper, while on the ceiling a brass fan with four mahogany propellers spun slowly above a plush red nylon three-piece sofa with gilt trimming.

Satisfied that they were alone, Harker did the first thing that came to mind. He raised his hand and gave a friendly wave, but there was no response from Chloe, who continued to stare at him with emotionless eyes.

'Chloe,' Harker uttered in nothing more than a whisper. Then, as his greeting was ignored, he ventured further into the room towards her.

It was not until he got halfway inside that a movement caught his eye. He turned to see a man with rosy cheeks and a white handkerchief stuffed between his teeth and Harker suddenly felt as much relief to see the familiar face as he did despair to the state it was in.

Sitting crouched against the back wall, David Carter gazed back at him with one bloodshot eye, making no attempt to struggle against the silver duct tape wrapped around his wrists and ankles. He looked like someone had smacked him around a bit, but other than that there were no obvious signs of torture, which was at least something to be thankful for. Harker now turned his attention back to Chloe. 'What's going on?' he asked her as she continued to stare at him. But it was not from her that an answer was forthcoming.

'Finally you arrive,' a voice spoke from behind him.

Harker whirled around to see Vlad himself standing behind the door, grasping a large wooden-handled machete in one hand, with the blade glinting as he tapped it against his thigh.

'Now the whole family is together.'

'Please, don't hurt—' was all Chloe managed before Vlad raised the machete and pointed it towards her.

'Shut your mouth,' he spat, with a look of sheer murder in his eyes.

Harker was already preparing to rush the psychopath when two guards appeared at the door brandishing semi-automatic machine guns. Vlad walked forward with his weapon still raised, until the tip of the blade was pressed firmly against Harker's throat.

'You don't really think you made it here under your own steam, do you, Professor? We kindly let you in,' he mocked, 'but I assure you we will not be letting you out.'

# Chapter 38

'Wake up!' the voice demanded, as Shroder felt the firm slap of a palm across his face. 'No sleeping on the job.'

The painful sting of the unexpected blow across his cheek was quickly replaced by a hot swelling sensation and, for a moment, as his eyes flipped open, he was at a complete loss as to where he was. His wrists were firmly bound on either side of the wooden chair he sat on; it was in the middle of the same front room he had first entered – that much he remembered. His fractured memory returned to him quickly as he found himself staring into the unyielding eyes of Andrew Campus.

'Why did you have to go sticking your nose in, John?' Campus asked, looking genuinely perturbed as he sat down on the sofa opposite. 'I wouldn't have offered you any help at all if I had known you were looking into Winters.'

'Why?' Shroder rasped, his mouth dry.

Campus leant forward and jabbed his finger in Shroder's direction. 'You're the one in the interrogation chair, John. You'll answer *my* questions. So, what do you know about him?'

Shroder rolled his eyes before shaking his head. 'Not a lot, you idiot, or I wouldn't be asking you, would I?'

'Easy, John,' Campus replied, wagging his finger. 'You're the one who's currently in a bind.'

Shroder had known Campus for over fifteen years, and although he had been tasered and trussed up by his colleague he could not help but suspect that this was just routine work for the other man. But on whose instructions, he wondered. 'Are you working for another agency?'

Campus flashed an unamused smile. 'Don't make this messy, John, please. I just want to know: why your interest in Jacob Winters?'

An uncomfortable silence settled between them and then, pursing his lips, Shroder began to talk. 'OK, but first I want to know: what's in the box?'

Campus considered the request for a moment, then reached over and ripped off its top, holding the box in front of him as he tipped the contents, consisting of a three-pack of Sellotape and some other odds and ends, onto the floor.

'What's all that for?' Shroder asked, as one of the packs rolled towards him and came to a stop at his feet.

'No idea, it's not my house, just one I use,' Campus replied, throwing the empty box onto the floor. 'It was here when we came in, so I used it to catch you off guard. Now, once again, why the interest in Winters?'

There was now real impatience in Campus's voice but the short diversion over the box had given Shroder time to come up with a story. 'It's not just the criminal fraternity that Winters has been sticking his fingers into. He's been making some waves within the business community as well, and some of the company owners are extremely powerful and they are not happy. MI6 was asked to get a more complete picture of this "mole" of yours, which is where I come in. The task was merely dropped in my lap, and you were my first port of call.'

'Why me?'

'Simple, because my sources told me that you've collected more information on him than anyone else.'

He spoke the last few words with an honest shrug of his shoulders as Campus remained silent but continuing to stare sternly in his direction, encouraging Shroder to continue.

'Which is why it surprised me when you said that MI6 was the first to clock him because, unless I was kept in the dark, which is always possible, we know nothing about him, let alone the arms deal sting you spoke of.'

Campus continued to remain silent and then he tapped his finger against his forehead thoughtfully before getting to his feet and taking a step towards Shroder. 'You know what, John? I believe you.'

'Good,' Shroder replied. 'So are you going to return the favour and tell me what the hell is going on? Oh, and untying me would be a good start.'

Campus was already shaking his head before Shroder finished speaking. 'I'm afraid not. You see, you're right about MI6 not conducting the arms deal sting, because in actual fact it was me, and I was also the reason the man never told his story to anyone else but me.'

'What?'

'It wasn't so much a sting as a kidnapping operation performed by yours truly. A few months back, I got my first solid lead on Winters, which led in turn to the arms dealer.'

'Bullshit,' Shroder protested. 'There's no way an operation like that would be handed over to just one man.'

'Now that is true, but when I turned up at the address my source had given me, the dealer opened the door. He stood right there in front of me, so I decided to take him there and then. Fluke, really, but like with all opportunities, you never know when they are going to present themselves. But when they do, you cling on with everything you've got.'

With a heavy sigh, Campus moved over to stand next to the sofa and slouched against the wall. 'I followed procedure, pretty much,' he continued with a wink, 'and the man just started spilling his guts...told me everything he knew. After this unusual confession I was about to take him into custody when the phone rang, and I picked it up and was staggered when some old man introduced himself to me.'

'Winters,' Shroder guessed, and Campus slowly nodded.

'Yes...and he gave me a choice. I could either take the man in and go through the judicial process, or I could silence him for good and make a deal.'

'How much?' Shroder asked, knowing there are few deals other than those involving money that a man would give up everything for.

'A million pounds upfront, to be delivered to an account of my choosing within the hour, and one hundred and fifty thousand a year for the rest of my life. All I had to do was keep him informed of any nosing around by Interpol.'

The cavalier way in which Campus was talking had Shroder shaking his head in disappointment. He had known this man for longer than most, and in all that time never suspected that the fellow would jump ship and betray his oath so easily. Of course, he knew that Campus was prone to bending the rules, but that had always been to the benefit of the agency he served. 'Just like that?'

'Yes,' Campus replied without any hint of regret. 'Every time we make a conviction, every time we knock someone off their crooked pedestal, they are straight away replaced with someone else who's usually even far worse. All those years we spend building a case...the time, the effort, and in the end where does it get us? Nowhere, just right back to square one.'

'Andrew, we'll never succeed in eradicating crime,' Shroder replied, tensing against the ropes binding him to his chair. 'We can only keep it in check, maintain the balance as best we can.'

The logic in Shroder's argument had Campus waving dismissively. 'It's not enough any more. It's futile, and you know it.'

'Maybe, but at least we have others to watch our backs. How long do you think it's going to be before Winters sees you as a loose end? When will you reach a point where you aren't able to achieve what he wants, or you make a misstep? A man like that will get rid of you quicker than he does his enemies.'

Campus, looking unfazed by the prospect, sat down on the edge of the sofa and began to shake his head. 'That would be a distinct possibility had his contact not given up some even tastier morsels concerning Winters.'

'Like what?'

'He told me who Winters really is.'

'Who?'

Campus now began to smile shrewdly. 'You wouldn't believe me even if I told you, but suffice it to say that if it got out, the uproar would be like nothing that has occurred before. I told Winters I knew his true identity and that if he kept his word, then so would I. Of course, I used all precautions possible, so that if anything happens to me the word will still get out, but as of now I am fully protected.'

Campus's admission had Shroder laughing out loud. 'Are you really that dumb? That just puts an even bigger crosshair on your forehead!'

'If you knew who Winters really is, you would be agreeing with me.'

The force of Campus's conviction was unfathomable to Shroder because, whatever Winters's true identity, he was not a man to trifle with. 'Tell me, for the sake of whatever remains of our friendship, just tell me.'

'Not a chance, John. That's a secret I will take to my grave, simple as.'

A thought now rose in Shroder's mind and he found himself recalling Harker's rendition of events back at the safe house near Mont-Saint-Michel. 'This Winters fellow, his identity wouldn't have a mythological feel to it...would it?'

Campus said nothing and just stared at him blankly before stepping round the back of the sofa, where he reached down and retrieved a red metal canister. 'I'm afraid, John, that the only connection to a mythological character you're going to encounter here is Prometheus.'

Shroder fought the sensation of panic that ripped through him as Campus unscrewed the canister's lid and then began to splash petrol over his head.

'You're going to burn me alive!' he yelled, spluttering from the noxious fumes that had begun burning his eyes and throat.

'Sorry, John, but there can be no loose ends,' Campus replied, now sloshing the walls and sofa with the same oily fluid.

'You'll die in a house fire. Your ropes are already greased, so they should incinerate in the flames.'

Shroder was now struggling against his bonds and jerking in his chair like a maniac as Campus began to dribble a line of petrol towards the front door. 'Jesus, if I have to go, then just shoot me, don't burn me.'

Shroder had no desire to get shot, but at least it might offer an opportunity to escape because a gunshot would without question be heard by neighbours, meaning Campus would have to take him to another location, even if it was simply the basement.

'Sorry, John, but that would not look very accidental, would it?'

Campus put down the canister and pulled a pack of cigarettes from his coat pocket. After opening it he extracted one and then threw the pack itself underneath Shroder's chair. 'You fell asleep while smoking and set yourself on fire – at least that's what the authorities will determine.'

'I'm covered in petrol, you idiot,' Shroder raged, 'so I think they'd notice.'

Campus shook his head. 'It could certainly turn into a bit of a mystery, but without any leads, it could be considered death by misadventure, which would certainly not be the conclusion if I put a bullet in your head, now would it?'

'You're crazy,' Shroder howled as Campus began to search through his pockets for a light.

'No, John, you're the crazy one for ever going after Winters. Now where the hell did I put those matches?'

Campus disappeared from the room, leaving Shroder frantically rocking in his chair. His feet were bound to the chair legs and, with little other option and frankly crapping himself at the prospect of being burnt alive, he did the only thing he could do. Without a moment to lose, he rocked the chair backwards onto its hind legs and then rocked himself forward, the momentum propelling him upright until he was standing on the tips of his toes. Thankfully Campus had not paid as much attention to the slack of the rope as he should have and it allowed Shroder to remain standing although bent over and crouched due to the confines of the chair. Then in one fluid motion he flicked himself backwards in an arc off the balls of his feet like a person attempting a backwards high dive.

The chair landed on its two back legs with such force that the back of his seat cracked under the weight, followed by the joint connecting the legs. He collapsed on the floor and found the chair splintered enough for him to slip one rope-bound hand through the crack.

The rummaging sound of Campus searching for a match stopped immediately, and Shroder could hear the sound of quickening footsteps approaching as he stood up and pulled his other hand free. With the rest of the chair still strapped to his legs he managed a few pathetic bunny hops towards the doorway which he reached just as Campus appeared. With a final bounce he slammed his head into Campus's face with enough force to feel the cartilage of his former friend's nose crumple against his skull.

Campus let out an almighty shriek of pain as he collapsed to the floor with Shroder now on top of him throwing punch after punch after punch, and it was in this moment that any self-control deserted the MI6 agent. The sheer bloody fury he felt at being almost burnt alive extinguished any emotion in him but hatred, and he continued to land blows, again and again, until blood was dripping from his fists. Staring down at Campus's twitching body, he suddenly realized he had gone too far – way too far.

Both of Andrew Campus's cheekbones had completely caved in, and his nose was little more than a flattened mush of sinew and skin.

Shroder pulled away and untied the ropes, still around his legs, allowing what was left of the chair to fall to the ground, as Campus sucked in quivering breaths amidst a gurgling sound as blood was expelled from his facial wounds and trickled down his throat. In losing his temper, justified or not, he had come close to killing the man, and with a sliver of regret he pulled himself up and knelt down by the bloody body of his former friend.

'I'm going to call an ambulance,' Shroder gasped, panting for breath, 'but first I need you to tell me what I want to know. Who is Jacob Winters?'

Campus continued to gurgle horribly but managed a weak shake of his head.

'If I don't call an ambulance soon, Andrew, there's a real chance you're going to die. I'm now offering you more of a chance than you offered me.'

Campus's eyes flickered and the flap that was his nose lifted slightly as he let out another breath. With Shroder still hovering over him, he finally grunted with a shaky twitch of his head. His words were nothing more than a whisper, and so Shroder lowered his ear to the man's mouth, and strained to hear as Campus uttered just two words.

Shroder pulled away, his face full of shock and his eyes wide with disbelief. 'That can't be,' he said quietly, even as Campus gave an unsettling and painful chuckle. 'It's impossible...impossible.'

Campus managed a twisted smile, his left eye drooping due to the shattered eye socket. 'On my life...it's true,' he murmured softly. Then his eyes fluttered and he slipped into unconsciousness as Shroder sat back against the door frame in a state of shock.

'That can't be right,' he muttered repeatedly, until the full realization of what he had been told sank in.

He then found himself calling out a single name: 'Alex.'

# *Chapter 39*

Harker sank to his knees, then immediately sprang back upright as another punch slammed into his ribs.

'I said *move*,' a rasping voice yelled, but this time forgoing a further blow and instead grabbing Harker's collar and shoving him forward roughly. 'They're waiting.'

Within seconds of Vlad's ominous welcome, a sack had been pulled over his head and he was dragged away from Chloe and Carter to be locked up, handcuffed, in a darkened room somewhere deep within the mansion. With a rope securing the sack around his neck, he had been left on his own for hours except when on one occasion the door opened and someone had sloshed water over his head, shouting 'Tea time'.

Whether it was water or cold tea was irrelevant because the gross hospitality had merely left him wet and cold, with only a few drops penetrating through the sack to reach his lips. The cramped confines of what he had come to guess was a storage cupboard had become something of a torture in itself, and by the time he was pulled out again every muscle in his body was aching.

A succession of bright lights now infiltrated the fibres of the sack hood he was wearing and, as he was led forcefully up some stairs, Harker began to hear a low-level hum which grew in intensity the nearer he approached. It was impossible to judge if it was coming from a machine or something else, but as he reached the top of the stairs and the sack was pulled off, the sight that awaited him was unsettling at best. Squinting, Harker scanned his surroundings through blurry eyes.

The open-air semicircular amphitheatre before him had been carved into the side of the same mountain Harker had traversed in order to reach the mansion and, judging by the sight of the tennis courts in the distance, it was located on the opposite side of that palatial estate. Stone steps had been cut into the curving interior and, from where he stood now on the top level, Harker was able to get a bird's-eye view of the entire arena. Flaming torches had been positioned throughout and they flickered across the stone steps leading down to a stage hollowed into the mountain itself. But although the seating arrangement could have easily held a few thousand people, it contained fewer than twenty spread out randomly. Each individual wore the same robe Harker had noted back at Cervete cemetery and a black face mask adorned with an image that was impossible to distinguish clearly from his current position. The sight was dispiriting enough, but the low-level communal humming only increased the morbid atmosphere. At first Harker couldn't make out why the monotone sound was so loud, given the vast size of the amphitheatre, but a series of black rectangular speakers placed throughout soon provided the answer.

'Well, you made it,' a familiar voice spoke up, and Harker turned around to see Vlad standing before him with his arms crossed and staring at him with less than amused expression.

'Where are Chloe and David?' Harker demanded angrily, but Vlad simply ignored his question and motioned to the uniformed guard behind him. Without uttering a word, the man grasped Harker's shoulder and forced him roughly down the steps of the amphitheatre and onto the orchestra floor, as Vlad himself made his way up onto the stage.

The masked figures continued with their low-level humming as they watched Harker being led into the centre of the orchestra floor, and it was only now that he was able to get a clear look at the carved stone stage. Heavy red drapes hung from the concave ceiling to the floor, and in the middle stood a large white cylindrical pod, planted on a base like a monolith, with a darkened viewing window at the top which gave it the appearance of a single eye watching over surrounding events as they unfolded. The unusual object looked completely out of place on the ancient stage, but it was the movement at the platform's darkened edges that now caught Harker's attention. He began to struggle against his guard even as the man tightened his grip.

For, one on each side, Chloe Stanton and David Carter hung from large wooden crucifixes fixed into the floor, their wrists and ankles secured by ropes and cloth rags stuffed between their teeth, like horses chomping on a bit.

The look of fear glistening in their eyes had Harker slamming an elbow into his guard's chest as he attempted to rush forward, but a swift kick to the back of his leg brought him down onto his knees with a thud. His guard knelt down beside him and grabbed him by the throat, pressing firmly against his windpipe, and with his other hand he slowly pulled up the black face mask to reveal his identity.

Carlu, head of that Corsican family of serial killers, offered an excited grin as he tightened his grip on Harker's throat. 'I felt sure our paths would cross again.'

Harker felt his bottom lip quivering momentarily as a feeling of dread washed over him but, before he could attempt a response, Carlu forced his head in the direction of the two other attendees standing nearest, who raised their masks to reveal the smiling face of Sofia standing next to a vengeful-looking Mama, with a white butterfly stitch across her broken nose.

'The whole family is here to see you,' Carlu announced before raising his fist and delivering a solid punch across Harker's jaw, which sent him flying face down onto the ground. 'That's for Mama,' he rasped as he pulled Harker back onto his knees, before letting fly another powerful blow. 'That's for me,' Carlu continued, and then he uncurled his fist and landed a light slap on Harker's other cheek. 'And that's from Sofia, who for some reason has taken a liking to you.'

With blood dripping from his lips, Harker groggily gazed up at the two female family members, to be met with a friendly wave from Sofia as Mama looked on with hatred in her eyes.

'My little girl so does admire a spirited nature in her victims, and you, Alex, are a resilient one, aren't you?'

Harker's head was spinning, and he turned his attention away from Carlu's insane and inbred family towards Chloe. 'What are you going to do?' he asked, the words slurred due to the throbbing in his jaw.

'You'll see soon enough,' Carlu replied with a firm slap across the top of Harker's head, 'and you'll have a front-row seat.'

Up on the stage, Vlad motioned towards the hanging red drapes and, at a click of his fingers, they pulled apart to reveal an old man sitting in a wheelchair. A black-suited attendant gently rolled him forward, then brought him to a stop right next to the upright pod. Backlights began to brighten the stage, illuminating the old man dimly.

Jacob Winters reached over and pressed his palm against the surface of the white cylinder and then stroked it lovingly, and for the first time Harker was able to see clearly the man who had dragged him into this whole affair.

Winters was clearly recognizable from the photo that Shroder had produced earlier, and although this was the first time Harker had laid eyes on 'God', there was something recognizable about the old man. What it was Harker couldn't put his finger on, but as Winters now shot him a glance and smiled, there was an eerie familiarity to him that Harker just could not shake.

Vlad made his way over and, from his pocket, retrieved two clip-on microphones, one of which he attached to Winters's lapel and the other to his own. Winters now pressed the tips of his fingers together respectfully and began to address his waiting audience, who finally ceased their incessant and frankly creepy humming.

'Welcome, brothers and sisters, on this most hallowed of evenings, and allow me to commend the wisdom and strength you have shown in all coming here. I sit before you now as merely a representative of the hardship, the toil, the sacrifice that every one of you – and your ancestors before you – has undergone in order that our vision of the truth may be brought to fruition. As I look at you, I see the dedication you have all given to a truth that has long been lost to the corrupt religious lies spread throughout the era of humanity.'

Winters tapped the cylinder beside him lightly and began nodding his head thoughtfully. 'But we here know better. For we see the world, and our place in it, with a clarity that those charlatans filled with centuries of self-righteous dogma can neither see nor hope to understand. Our power lies in the truth of the one true king that we seek to restore to his rightful place in this world, he who will in turn grant us the gift of eternal life and the chance to serve at his side, as humanity is relegated to its rightful place.'

Throughout the arena, the shadowy figures remained silent, with the flickering light of the torches creating the only movement.

Winters stretched out his hands towards them. 'You have bestowed upon me great trust and belief in guiding you all towards a destiny that is and always has been yours by right, and you have witnessed with your own eyes the power of the Gigas Codex and its ability to deliver you from the disease that not only unites but plagues us all.' Winters reached under his lap blanket and produced a single folded page of the Codex which he held up in front of him like a sacrificial offering. 'Death...but no more. For by the master's own hand he has given us not only this miracle of everlasting life, but the ability for us to restore his very being to its rightful place, with you at his side. You will become his generals, his champions and the very foundation on which the world will be rebuilt in his image and yours.'

Once again Winters placed his open palm against the side of the pod and stroked it. 'For, with the guiding words of the Codex, he is now again amongst us and tonight he will walk the earth once more, and with that you will be reborn as gods.'

The pod began to tremble and throughout the amphitheatre the onlookers began to murmur excitedly. Winters passed the Codex page over to Vlad who, with a dutiful nod, unfolded the oversized piece of vellum.

'This night we will all be judged and, in doing so, begin our journey towards enlightenment and a seat at the true Lord's table,' Winters continued, with a beckoning gesture. 'Come and make your offering to the saviour and prepare for the new wonders that await you.'

Without hesitation all the cloaked spectators removed their face masks and, in an orderly fashion, made their way down the amphitheatre steps towards the stage. It was difficult to see all the faces clearly but Harker immediately recognized a woman he had seen back in the cellar at Spreepark. There were a couple of others who looked familiar too, and there was no doubt in his mind that these were the same group he had seen at each of the rituals, including some of the wealthy heirs Shroder had shown him pictures of back at his safe house.

Carlu now motioned for one of the guards to take his place at Harker's side and, with one final satisfied smile, he joined the swelling group of participants along with Sofia and Mama, who looked equally pleased with themselves.

The sight of these black-robed men and women organizing themselves into a line in front of the stage was an eye-catching scene in itself, but Harker found himself entranced by the upright pod that continued to shake. Could this be real? Did the Codex have some supernatural power able to bring back the Devil himself?

An unpleasant shiver ran down Harker's spine as the guard pressed down on his shoulder, keeping him firmly on his knees. His mind began to ache with the possibility: was he really about to meet an entity that, in some form or another, had preoccupied the minds of human beings with terror and foreboding since the dawn of time? Was a dark malevolent presence seeking to corrupt and control all life about to be made real, right here and now, presently contained within the confines of that cylindrical white pod perched less than twenty metres away from where he knelt? No matter how Harker's mind rationalized the absurdity of such an event, he nevertheless felt a very real nervous twitching in the pit of his stomach.

With an unsteady hand, Winters pressed a small, flat circular button located halfway up the pod, and a green light began to pulsate further up, just below the still darkened viewing window. The sound of mechanical locks uncoupling could be heard, and with a pressurized creak, the front half of the object slowly swung back on it hinges releasing a strange puff of mist as it did so.

Harker leant forward and peered into the dark interior of the pod with trepidation. The uplighting to the rear of the stage only managed to make it more difficult to get a clear picture, but as he narrowed his eyes into a squint, he could finally discern something behind the white plastic sheet hiding the pod's contents. It was no more than a shadowy outline, but even at this distance, Harker could tell it was of human form at least.

'Come closer.' Winters gestured to the line of robed figures before him, even as Vlad pressed his finger against the Codex page in preparation to recite the text. 'Now meet your master and let your body absorb these words. Words written by the Dark Lord's own divine hand, and the very scripts you have been seeking for generations, which will now imbue you with the gift that only he can bestow.'

The line of the faithful obediently took a step forward, and differing expressions of wonder now transformed them as they gazed upon the silhouette of their fallen master, who continued to stir.

'Now make your offerings and then enjoy his protection for all eternity,' Winters instructed. 'Demonstrate your loyalty with the ultimate expression of your love and belief in the destiny you have created for yourselves.'

Without hesitation and with military-drilled precision, the line of believers pulled back their hoods and in unison slid their hands beneath their robes to retrieve thin steel daggers with light-brown wooden handles. Even though Harker could see a few of their hands shaking, clearly apprehensive at what they were about to embark on, they all nevertheless raised the blades to their throats just as Vlad began to read aloud from the Codex in that unintelligible language even Harker could not understand. One by one, starting from right to left, each participant drew his or her dagger sharply across their necks, slitting their throats from ear to ear. The grisly ritual moved on down the line as blood began to squirt onto the floor.

Harker watched in disgust as it pumped from their throats and descended all around them with a sickening pattering noise. As the last in line made his demonstration of loyalty, the first in line had already crumpled to the ground.

The nauseating sound of gurgling filled the amphitheatre as many clasped at their throats, blood pouring through their fingers and down onto their robes, dampening them with expanding dark stains. Some fell to their knees with fists clenched as they fought off their self-induced panic, while others simply collapsed in convulsions as their muscles tensed up sporadically in a twitching frenzy of death while life drained from their bodies. Tongues protruded rigidly in spasm and eyes rolled in either pain or the shock of committing such a final act of self-mutilation. But now all began to lie still, even though severed arteries continued to pump out the sticky red fluid all around them.

All except for two.

Carlu stood above his motionless mother and daughter with the dagger still in his hand and eyes locked on the single other person still standing upright amongst the fallen. The middle-aged woman had tears rolling down her cheeks as she looked up at Winters and began to shake her head.

'I can't,' she choked as her body trembled. 'Please forgive me but I can't do this… I was wrong. You can keep the money but I have to leave.'

This mention of money instinctively pricked up Harker's ears but the revolting sight of the bodies still had him feeling woozy, so he put all his effort into not vomiting as the woman continued.

'You can have everything I own but please just let me go.'

Up on the stage Vlad had meanwhile paused his recital, and Winters lowered his head in disappointment as she dropped her knife to the ground. But he then looked up again and nodded. 'Very well, you shall forfeit everything you own, but this day will come back to haunt you when you are eventually judged. And there is no escaping that… For everyone will be judged.'

Her expression was haunted as she dropped her head in shame. In fact she was so absorbed with her own disgrace that the approaching dagger never caught her attention. That is until it was jammed into the back of her skull and a hand grabbed hold of her forehead to provide leverage as the blade was dug deep into the back of her head.

Carlu twisted the dagger clockwise, producing a scraping sound as the metal ground against the woman's cranium. Then he pulled it out and she sank to the ground like a lead balloon.

'Thank you, Carlu,' said Winters, as Vlad now to begin reciting from the Codex text once more. 'Your loyalty knows no bounds, brother, and you will be rewarded more than anyone.'

The Corsican killer looked elated by this acknowledgement and, without speaking, he looked over at Vlad and closed his eyes. Then his head swayed as if he could actually feel the precious words of the Codex passing into him. He finally raised the same bloody dagger to his neck and drew it firmly across his throat, from ear to ear, before collapsing to the floor where, after a few moments of shaking, he too went still.

The amphitheatre was in total silence and Harker managed to pull himself away from the macabre sight and turn his attention to Chloe. With nose flaring and eyes wide open, she looked more disgusted than terrified. Carter, on the other hand, had his eyes limply shut, either because he'd fainted or didn't want to face the gruesome mass suicide that had just occurred before him.

A sudden rustling sound brought Harker's attention back to the stage and to the shadowy figure inside the pod, who was beginning to move about more and more as every second passed.

'Bring him to me,' Winters demanded in a croaky voice, pointing towards Harker, as Vlad stopped reciting the Codex text and refolded the vellum page.

The guard yanked Harker to his feet and he was forced to hop-step over the line of fallen bodies, his nose wrinkling at the coppery stench of warm blood. But it wasn't the number of dead bodies strewn out beneath him that now commanded his attention. It was the distinctive tone of voice. Winters's voice, which had a high-pitched quality to it when he shouted. One that seemed very familiar, but even so, Harker couldn't place it.

Any further curiosity was extinguished as he was led up onto the stage and to within just metres of the open pod, whose occupant was becoming increasingly agitated, but either unable or unwilling to pull aside the protective plastic cover shrouding the interior.

'Welcome, Professor Alex Harker,' Winters began, with a keenness in that husky voice. 'I cannot tell you how pleased I am to have you here at this very moment. In fact I am immeasurably satisfied.'

The old man appeared overjoyed and Harker took a moment to glance back down at the line of bloody corpses on the floor. 'Well, at least someone is.'

'Oh, please, they are the most satisfied of all. The chance to offer yourself to Lucifer himself is not something to be passed up.'

Harker turned his attention back to the open pod and the shapeless figure now emitting a deep growling sound from beneath the plastic cover. 'I don't know what that thing is, but I highly doubt it's the Devil.'

Winters looked offended at Harker's scepticism and he shook his head. 'Oh, ye of little faith… I assure you that standing just metres from you right now is Satan himself, made flesh and under my control.'

There were a lot of things Harker wanted to do at that moment but playing games was not one of them. He glanced over at Chloe and then at Carter, who now had his eyes open and was looking as defiant as was possible for someone gagged and tied to a crucifix. 'So you're "God", then?'

'I go by many names but you are welcome to call me Mr Winters.'

Harker ignored this pathetic response and instead dived into the basic question that had been on his mind since first being recruited to play in Winters's bizarre games. 'Just who the hell are you and what is this all about? You kidnap my friends and force me into whatever this charade is…why?'

'I know you must feel extremely confused, Professor.' Vlad had now joined in the conversation. 'But don't worry, because I assure you everything will be explained before the night is out.'

'Really?' Harker queried, not knowing what to believe.

'Of course,' Vlad assured him, and he reached over to slap the back of his hand against Harker's chest. 'You may not realize it yet but you are the reason all this is happening. From the search for the Codex pages to the kidnapping of your girlfriend.' Vlad let out a booming laugh. 'Christ, it's even because of you that all these people sacrificed themselves.'

The statement was perplexing and, as Harker looked on in confusion, Winters raised a finger in Chloe's direction.

'As for your friends here, they are safe and sound. They may be a little the worse for wear, but undamaged, as I promised you.'

Carter uttered a groan beneath the linen gag stuffed in his mouth and, although he was clearly in pain, his eyes continued to radiate defiance. Chloe, on the other hand, was beginning to look immensely fearful, and Harker took the opportunity to call over to her. 'You all right?' he asked, and an unexpected tingling of relief swept through him simply in conducting this one-sided communication.

'I'm afraid Dr Stanton and I have come to an agreement,' Winters rasped. 'She has promised not to speak until I say so, and in exchange I promised not to cut out her tongue.' The old man shot Chloe a wink. 'Still, I decided to do her a favour and gag her anyway, because I doubted she would be able to keep her side of the bargain. She's quite the chatterbox, Alex, but you already know that, don't you, lover boy?'

Harker and Chloe gazed intently at one another, with only their stares to offer comfort, as Winters now settled snugly into his chair.

'I must congratulate you, Alex, on your sterling performance over the past few days,' he continued, with a sarcastic smile and a slow clap of his hands. 'You have gone above and beyond what I expected of you, and the fact that you made it all the way to this island, and to me, is a feat in itself, given the contempt you are now held in by your former friends.'

There were so many questions Harker wanted to blurt out, but he said nothing because it was clear that Winters wanted – no, needed – to explain it for himself, and was now taking great pleasure in doing so.

'Your Templar friends, once your allies, want you dead. Your name is now high on Interpol's most-wanted list after you absconded from Mont-Saint-Michel, leaving a dead helicopter pilot in your wake, amongst others. And meanwhile the person you love most in the world is here by my side and in my clutches.' Winters looked over and raised his eyebrows up and down slowly. 'I have no doubt we can find a good use for her, once our business here is concluded.'

The salacious insinuation already had Harker springing forward before the sound of something metallic clicked into place and a thin blade pressed up against his throat, stopping him in his tracks. He glanced to his side to find Vlad with his arm raised towards him and the almost foot-long blade protruding from under his sleeve and now held tightly against Harker's windpipe.

'What!' Harker gasped as he recognized the unique piece of weaponry, and a cold sweat began to form on his brow along with an increasing feeling of dread. The arm-sword was a spring-activated blade strapped to a person's forearm, which shot out above the top of one's hand and thus was used as an extension of the arm. It was deadly if you knew how to wield it, and there was only one group of people who still used it.

'You're Templars!' he gasped.

Winters laughed so loud that he began to cough, till he drew a white handkerchief from his pocket and mopped up the thin line of drool seeping from one corner of his mouth. 'Hold on, I want to enjoy this,' he croaked, wiping the last remaining drops. 'Alex Harker, the confusion and fear you must be feeling right at this moment is extremely heart-warming and satisfying to me, and I don't mind saying so.' He placed the soiled handkerchief back in his pocket, closed his eyes and raised his face to the concave ceiling up above. 'How wonderful it is to have you here before me, with your life in tatters, your friends wanting to kill you and everyone else wishing they had never known you – as I am sure Mr Carter here would agree.'

Carter uttered a muffled groan as Winters continued to revel in his achievement.

'This is exactly how I imagined it, with you sporting that dumb, lost look and knowing that everything you are and possess now belongs to me. Ladies and gentlemen, I give you Professor Alex Harker, a man with no future and now at his lowest ebb. Truly a sight for sore eyes, for mine at any rate, thanks…to you. Tell me, Alex, before we get going, would you like to meet the Devil in person?'

Harker said nothing, because it really didn't matter. Winters was obviously going to do whatever he wanted, and offering a reply would just mean receiving more of the man's inane and insulting banter.

'Of course you would,' Winters continued, wheeling himself backwards as one of the guards made his way to the pod and gripped the strip of plastic covering. 'Everyone loves meeting celebrities – and they don't get more famous than this one, do they?'

That familiar tone in Winters's voice was back, but as hard as he tried, Harker could still not place it. As the guard unzipped the covering, he focused his attention on what lay behind it.

With it now completely unzipped, the guard slowly pulled the covering back to reveal the face of a man squinting into the light. He was naked except for a pair of plain white linen boxer shorts, and his arms and legs were held in place by thick rubber restraints attached to the interior of the capsule. His pale white body glistened with sweat and a feeding tube inserted down his throat was held in place by thick tape across one cheek. The man's torso was covered in multiple thick scars resulting from a whole host of wounds and, as the guard pulled away the tape and gently tugged at the mouth nozzle, a foot of tubing slid out from his throat, causing the prisoner to cough wildly.

Long white strands of damp hair hung from his scalp and Harker already knew who he was looking at even before the eyelids fluttered open. The realization had Harker slumping back against Vlad's chest and, as he gazed into those unique pupils, his mind became fuzzy and blank even as the impossible was made real. 'But you're dead!'

Sebastian Brulet, previously Grand Master of the Knights Templar, stared back through those distinctive star-crossed pupils of his and managed a weak smile before collapsing against his restraints. He hung there for a few moments before the guard released him and then laid him out on the floor face down, as Harker, his mind now racing, turned to look at Winters, who had a gigantic grin plastered across his face.

'Now do you know who I am?' Winters asked as he curled a finger towards him. 'Come closer, Alex,' he continued and, at a wave of his hand, Vlad drew his arm-sword away from Harker's neck and pushed him closer.

'Closer,' Winters said, as Harker was thrust down until he was merely centimetres from the old man's face. 'Tell me, my friend, do recognize anyone?'

Harker stared down into Winters's cold dark eyes and, although there was something familiar, he still could not grasp it. It was like one of those TV pranks where a celebrity dons a face mask and pretends to be someone else. You cannot for a moment recognize them, but when you look directly into their eyes, there is something familiar you just can't place, and so it now was for Harker. He spent the next few seconds scanning Winters's pupils, and was about to shake his head when something clicked. He wasn't sure what it was, maybe a flickering of the eyelid or the colouring of the irises, but in a single instant, and as his synapses sparked and made the connection, he suddenly knew.

Harker jolted backwards and into the waiting arms of Vlad, who once again slipped the arm-sword blade under his chin and held him fast as Winters began to smile and raised his arm and extended a crooked index finger out in front of him.

'I see you.'

With his mind buzzing, Harker glanced over at Chloe, who had a knowing look on her face and clearly knew already what he had just discovered. Suddenly so much of what had happened during the past few days began to fall into place and to make sense.

But that was impossible, it could not be. Yet here he was, in some form, and as Harker tried to get his head around it, the initials of Jacob Winters's name lit up in his head brightly and he suddenly felt sick to his stomach. 'J.W.,' he murmured, struggling to reconcile the fact that Brulet was still alive after being thought dead for over six months, but this...this was beyond crazy.

John Wilcox, one-time pope of the Catholic Church and also head chieftain of the Magi, glared up at Harker with a grimace, then he clamped his brown teeth together firmly. 'You didn't really think you would get away from me that easily, did you?'

# *Chapter 40*

'It's impossible. I saw you die,' Harker protested, struggling against Vlad's arm-sword which had once again been swiftly pressed against his throat. 'I saw it with my own eyes.'

'Yes, you did,' Wilcox replied with apparent disdain at the mention of his demise, 'but I am not the only one you have seen resurrected recently, am I?'

With thoughts of the two decomposing priests he had encountered, Harker shook his head soberly. 'No, but they looked a lot better than you do.'

His sarcastic quip was met with pressure from Vlad's blade, but Wilcox looked neither bothered nor angry.

'Being brought back to life is not without its consequences, sadly, but given the miraculous nature of such a thing, it is a price worth paying. Please, Vlad, take off his cuffs. I don't think Alex is going to make any fuss. Not unless he wants his friends here killed on the spot.'

Vlad fiddled with the cuffs and, after releasing him, threw them over to one side of the stage and stepped back from Harker, who began rubbing his wrists and stretching his aching shoulders.

'By "miraculous", you mean your judgement by...the Devil.' Harker struggled to say the word and was met with a blank stare from Wilcox.

'Please, Alex, you didn't really think that cock-and-bull story had any basis in reality, did you?'

'With everything I've seen so far, I'm not sure what to believe.'

'Well, how delightful,' Wilcox replied. 'What one will believe, when out of the loop, as it were, never ceases to amaze me, so allow me the pleasure of enlightening your feeble little mind.'

Now that Harker knew it really was John Wilcox underneath all that dead skin and wrinkles, he could see that, although his appearance had been terribly altered, the man's narcissistic character had not changed one bit. He was just as much a self-serving, megalomaniac pain in the arse as he had always been.

'Now I want to tell you a story and I want to enjoy it, even if the first part is something I would be happy to forget.' Wilcox's tongue made a clicking sound and he let out a wheezy sigh. 'Let us start at the beginning or, to be accurate, the end...of my life.' The leader of the Magi shuffled in his chair and, once comfortable, he raised his hands like a conductor about to begin a performance. 'When your albino freak of a friend, Sebastien Brulet, dishonourably stabbed me in the throat with my own blade.' Wilcox glared down at Brulet's sprawled out, motionless body. Noticing that Harker was already taking a step towards his old friend, Vlad moved in between them and waved a finger menacingly.

'Don't worry, he's fine,' Wilcox scoffed. 'Believe me, he's been through worse, but I will get to that. Now where was I... Ah yes, my unfortunate death. My memory is a little bit fuzzy after that, but I do remember the highly unpleasant sensation of choking on my own blood, before everything went black.'

For the first time Harker detected a sliver of humanity in Wilcox as his eyes dulled in contemplation of that event, and he almost felt sorry for him. Almost.

'At the time I didn't think about what might come next,' Wilcox continued, now regaining his composure. 'I was far too busy dying, but what I can tell you is that I remember nothing more until I saw a distant white light, which came closer and closer, and then – wham! – I was staring into the face of Vlad here, with my wounds all healed but my body decrepit.'

Wilcox seemed to drift off into a daze, as though the simple recalling of such a terrible personal experience was consuming him. So it was Vlad who now dutifully spoke up.

'You and your Templar zealots thought they had destroyed all of the Magi, right there and then in the destruction of our base at Macuira National Park. But, as always, your greatest weakness is your optimism. Not all the houses of the Magi were present that day. There was another, the most powerful one. My own house. *La casa degli assassini.*'

'The house of assassins,' Harker murmured through taut lips. Brulet had once mentioned them as among the most fearless and dangerous of all those who composed the Magi and, as he stared in to Vlad's soulless black eyes, he believed it.

'Yes. As the first line of the Magi defence, we were the last to arrive at Macuira, and only once everyone else had arrived safely. Unfortunately, by the time we did arrive by helicopters, the whole mountain had been brought down, and all those heroic troops gathered from all nations were nothing but a blip on the horizon.'

Vlad paused a moment to look over at Wilcox, who was staring into his lap with a glazed expression. 'That's when we retrieved the body of our Lord, took as many others as we could carry, and stole away into the sunset.'

Vlad was clearly hamming the story up, and in doing so revealed that both he and Wilcox shared a certain tendency for the dramatic, but to Harker it still seemed like a highly unlikely scenario. 'How could you have managed that? The whole mountain collapsed in on itself. Everyone was crushed, and during the clean-up there were very few bodies intact to even recover.'

Vlad raised his hand and gave Harker a good slap across the back of the head. 'You idiot, do you honestly think the Magi would go through all that time and effort of building a subterranean city without putting in suitable exits? The whole place had a number of escape routes in place and, although many died when the whole thing went down, some of them made it out.'

Vlad leant closer to Harker, with his arm-sword still extended and hanging at his side. 'You yourself and Dr Stanton managed to escape, didn't you?'

With all the destruction the Magi's HAARP weather project had caused to their base, Harker had not even considered that anyone might have survived and, given there were emergency services and the Venezuelan military on site within the hour, it seemed unlikely. But clearly not impossible, and Wilcox was proof of that. 'OK, then how about Sebastian? The last time I saw him he was engaged in a fight to the death with one of your henchmen, McCray, and the whole place was collapsing around him.'

The mention of Brulet woke Wilcox from his daze and he leapt back into the conversation. 'Yes, Sebastien Brulet, he is one tough bastard, I will give him that. He killed Captain McCray and then, while fleeing to find another way out, he came upon some of my subordinates dragging my lifeless body towards an exit route. He was one of the last to make it out as the mountain crumbled inwards. He even helped carry my body, as he tells it.'

Harker looked down at the man mentioned, still lying on his front and barely moving, and it stung him to think that while he and Chloe had been helicoptered to safety, Brulet had been fighting desperately for his life.

'That bastard took down three of my men before we managed to subdue him, and later on he even managed to escape during our stopover in the UK.' Vlad administered a sudden hard kick to Brulet's thigh, which was greeted by nothing more than a moan. 'But he was never completely out of our sight. Do you know he made a dash to join two of his friends and their baby boy in some hick country village – thinking it a good place to lie low I suppose – but we tracked him there and had him transferred back to this island in no time.'

This mention of a family living in a country village had Harker worried, and he had to suppress a rising sense of panic. Had Brulet's first instinct been to check on the safety of the Christ child, and his adopted parents, before all else? Not wanting to draw any attention to them, Harker had made very few visits, but if something had happened there, he would have been among the first to know. 'What did you do to them?'

'You mean the family?' Vlad replied, curious as to why Harker should care. 'Nothing, as there was no need to invite any unwanted attention, and besides we had bigger problems at the time. Why, do they mean something?'

Harker immediately shook his head. 'No, it just sounds strange, given he was trying to escape you.'

Vlad thought about it and then, with a smile, he cocked his head. 'Maybe we will pay them a visit after all. I don't like leaving any loose ends.'

'Yes, yes,' Wilcox now said dismissively, 'but he has already paid the price and, of course, he has so much more punishment to come.'

Harker had never seen Brulet half-naked before but the scar tissue that disfigured the Grand Master's body did not look well healed. Whatever Wilcox had been inflicting on Brulet, it was unquestionably an ongoing process.

'What have you done to him?' Harker demanded, this being the first time he was able to address the sad state of his friend.

'Nothing that he did not richly deserve.' Wilcox's smile disappeared and his crusty lips curled up in disgust. 'I told you how the Devil resided in this capsule, and I did not lie. For Sebastien Brulet was and is my personal devil, Satan incarnate, and he is paying the price – call it penance, retribution or simple bloody revenge.' Wilcox scowled at Harker with such intense loathing that one of his eyes began to twitch. 'Your friend Mr Brulet has been demoted from the position of Templar Grand Master to my plaything, and how we have played. I keep him drugged and unconscious most of the time, but when I feel like it, we wake him up occasionally and have some fun. Cutting, electro-therapy, anything that's painful really. We even had a spell of waterboarding, but he dealt with that far too well, I'm afraid, so we went back to the previous techniques. Don't worry, apart from that he is kept in tip-top medical shape. I can't have my favourite entertainment toy ruined. His screams of pain do so warm my heart.'

Harker gazed down at Brulet's still body with a great sadness in his heart. Six solid months of torture! He could not even begin to imagine it.

'Anyway, enough of that, Alex, for you and your friends will experience for yourselves all his woes soon enough,' Wilcox continued with a chuckle. 'So, there I was, surrounded by the remnants of my precious Magi, my plans in ruin, our networks almost obliterated – contacts, companies and funds seized by either the authorities or the good old Templars, I still don't know which. We were so desperate at the time that we had to enter the world of crime just to keep ourselves going. I can't take the credit for that myself because Vlad had most of the contacts there, but we actually made a lot of money. You would not believe how easy it is to take over crime syndicates if you have properly trained men, no one knowing who you are, and get in and out as quickly as possible. Long-term crime may last for the organization, but rarely for the individual.'

Vlad smiled grimly. 'My house was never averse to a spot of crime here and there. In fact it's what we were trained to do...as well as kill on behalf of the Magi, of course.'

The last admission had Wilcox smiling proudly at his men's ingenuity, but he now gestured for silence. 'Either way, after the debacle of Macuira National Park, we appeared finished, with barely the manpower or resources to chase any real ambition. And I myself was trapped in this ragged and useless body you see before you.' His hands began to clench with anger, but then they relaxed and he placed them on his lap and gently stroked the tartan blanket laid across his lap. 'But I was alive still and not without purpose, because you see, Alex, there was one thing you never did understand and neither did the Templars, and it is that we never put all our eggs in one basket. We had one final card to play, one more trick up our sleeve, and it has proven in such a short time to be the most potent of all… Belief.'

Harker was now frowning because, as he had discovered time and time again, getting a straight answer out of Wilcox was near impossible. The man was like some medieval storyteller who went from village to village, spinning a tale and drawing it out in the hope of getting a meal in payment. A raconteur of the very worst kind…an annoying one.

'Belief has the power to make men do things they never would have dreamt of, good and bad alike, but the most useful part is that it can be manipulated and moulded to another's will.'

He raised his hand and limply pointed it in the direction of the line of fallen bodies lying collapsed on top of one another. 'Hundreds of years ago when science was still in its infancy and the world still offered the lure of exploration and fresh knowledge, these families were brought together by a single common purpose… Money. They bestowed upon themselves the name of *the enlightened ones*, bloody corny, if you ask me, but then power and money weren't and never will be a substitute for taste. Many in this "club" were born from such groups as freemasons, merchants and bankers, all of them bonded together by wealth. The archaic practices of paganism and the dark arts were still seen by them as valid tools in a world that, although modernizing rapidly, still held many unknowns. In their minds the concept of Shangri-La and the fountain of youth were very real possibilities and, over time, this combined with a shunning of the usual dogmatic catholic practices of the time and instead veered towards the darker side of human nature. Elements of Satanism and witchcraft became incorporated and, over the generations, intertwined with their beliefs so that they considered themselves special above all others. They embraced many ideas that were deemed an offense to practices of the norm, and in doing so they came to believe that they truly were in name and by nature *the enlightened ones.* They were the holders of truth while everyone else was plain wrong. They were *special.* Was it simply human vanity or just their increasing wealth that reinforced this belief that they were all-knowing, and above everyone else? It is debatable, indeed, but in truth it was mixture of the two. It is curious yet understandable that people who are born into wealth and positions of power sometimes believe that their very existence is somehow a divine right, theirs a destiny that mere mortals can never hope to attain.'

Winters sucked up a pool of saliva from inside his mouth and spat it in the direction of the bodies. 'Idiots, the lot of them, but useful nonetheless. The Magi crossed paths with this *enlightened* group many times over the centuries, and friendships were forged, trust gained, because people of such huge financial resources should never be overlooked, and you never know what the future will bring. To be fair, they never held any real interest for the Magi…that is until six months ago, when our own family was brought to ruin.'

Wilcox shot Harker a dirty look and then, with his hands clasped, he began to smile. 'I became extremely interested in them after that. You see, the *enlightened ones*' original mandate to discover a cure for death was over the years added to by successive generations. Its original members had pooled their resources and scoured the world for anything that might aid them in this endeavour. There are tales of the expeditions they financed to search for the fountain of youth amongst other quests, interesting stories of exploration and courage, but ultimately proving useless. That is until they heard of the Codex Gigas and the mystery pertaining to the missing pages – pages that many believed were written by the Devil himself, and contained knowledge of how to achieve everlasting life. And so the obsession began. Funded by the group, paid agents tracked and searched for any information as to the pages' scattered locations. And, as generations passed and another piece of the jigsaw was found, it was delegated to the next generation to continue the search. I like to think of it as a sort of Chinese whispers that, although beginning with a rational idea, then becomes distorted over time and culminates in something far different from what was originally articulated. It's a shame really, because I doubt that their forefathers' – Wilcox motioned towards the robed corpses – 'would even have recognized the pathetic bunch of sycophantic Satan-lovers their great-grandchildren had become. Rich heirs and heiresses saddled and indoctrinated with a belief that the Dark Lord would rise up again and make them immortal, simply because they or their bloodlines were special above all others. They were easily manipulated, though, and that's what I liked about them.'

The laborious history lesson that Wilcox was delivering, although a fascinating insight into how dogma could corrupt over time, was beginning to prove frustrating to Harker and he let out an agitated sigh. 'John, with respect, what has this got to do with any of the supernatural tragedies I've witnessed?'

'Shut up and show some respect, Alex,' Wilcox scowled, 'and you can call me Jacob or Mr Winters from now on. John Wilcox is no more, and only I remain.'

'John, Jacob...Barry! Whatever. What the hell has this got to do with me and my friends?'

Without direction from Wilcox, Vlad stepped over and landed a solid punch to Harker's ribs. 'Listen and learn, you idiot. Don't make me cut you.'

Harker's pained groan had Wilcox smiling and, without any further berating, and clearly satisfied the blow had done its job, he continued with his account. 'When I told you back at Macuira National Park that I was happy to live out my life underground so as to ensure my children saw the new world we had created, you didn't really believe me, did you? Do you honestly think we would go to all the trouble, time and effort of creating and perfecting HAARP, a weather machine with the ability to reshape the world, with me at its head, without my being able to experience and enjoy it for myself?'

Wilcox began to laugh but he soon succumbed to a bout of coughing, and as the old man struggled to gain control of his lungs, Harker looked on in fascination. Fascination not because it completely made sense that Wilcox was so self-serving, but rather that Harker had never questioned it in the first place. John Wilcox was a narcissistic psychopath with zero empathy, and the idea of him giving his life for a greater cause just didn't make sense. It was bloody obvious.

'You idiot,' Wilcox rasped as he regained his composure. 'The whole point was so I could be there, so that I would be the one to harness the shackles of what was left of humanity and guide it towards the world it should now become... My world.'

Vlad suddenly began to look irritated but, on seeing Harker notice his change of expression, the man quickly returned to his previous impassive look as Wilcox explained further.

'You actually believed that it was our ability to clone Christ which motivated us to set into motion our plan, didn't you? Would it surprise you to learn that procedure was one of the first things we perfected, followed by the technology of HAARP? For we would not have even contemplated beginning on such a path without first developing the most important cog of all.'

Wilcox waved a hand and Vlad reached into his pocket and produced a thin tube containing a milky-looking substance, which he proudly held up before Harker.

'Life,' Winters declared pompously as Vlad placed the vial into his waiting hands. 'Regeneration, to be more accurate. A biological substance that not only repairs but regenerates the tissues, the organs at the cellular level.'

Harker stood dumbfounded and just stared at the white liquid as Wilcox shook it in delight.

'I once told you, Alex, how we spent tens of billions on cloning development, but only a fraction of it went to that particular project. The vast bulk of it went to this.'

'How...? I mean the reality of such a thing must be decades away, if not longer,' Harker uttered in disbelief, now entertaining the idea that this was yet another smoke-and-mirrors trick that the Magi so loved to pull.

'Ahead of its time, yes, but impossible, no. Don't misunderstand me, for the technology and research that went into this was triple, even quadruple, the annual GDP of some countries, but I can assure you it is as genuine a compound as anything you or I are made up of.'

Wilcox passed the small vial back to Vlad and then, by his own effort, wheeled himself closer to Harker. 'I am and always have been a believer in the impossible being made possible and, although I freely admit the research and development behind this stuff is staggering, it must be placed in context. Decades ago, the Magi formed a plan to infiltrate as many pharmaceutical and medical research and development institutions as possible. All over the world we targeted companies with an interest in the biological nature of things, and we have since financed and used our resources to overcome any political and judicial issues along the way, but we never sought to control them. As shareholders we have made huge profits from these ventures, but the political branch of the Magi has been extremely successful in getting our own men onto the boards of these companies. Once this was achieved, we set up our own research and development company...off the books of course, and based in countries with little or no interest in anything else but cash. And then we siphoned off whatever data we needed. We had the time, the research data, the professionals and a lot of money all focused towards a single goal – the one you see in that vial. We also had something that put us decades and decades beyond any other legitimate company or pharmaceutical institution on the planet. Namely a resource without which we could never have managed such a feat.'

Harker groaned because he knew where this was leading even as Wilcox explained further. 'Do you know how the Nazis were able to make such gigantic leaps forward in medicines, drugs and anything else they cared to research? Human testing.

They had at their disposal thousands of people – millions had they wanted them – on whom to test anything they wished. There were no test trials undertaken on lower-form animals, or moral standards committees to tell them what they could and could not do. No, they just did it, and whether it took a hundred patients or a thousand, it didn't matter. They could do whatever it took to achieve their scientific goals and they did so. It's one of the reasons their work was so sought after by the Allies at the end of World War II. Their advances were literally decades ahead.'

Wilcox wore a grizzled look of severity as he nodded his head slowly. 'We aimed towards one single goal without any of the constraints the outside world would normally impose on such a scientific venture, and because of that we succeeded in achieving the impossible.'

Harker was still marvelling over the possibilities of this designed compound– as well as sickened at the methods of attaining it – because what the Magi had created was nothing short of a miracle…*the* miracle. In all of human history there has been a single dream that has been pursued, wished and prayed for at one time or another by every soul to ever grace the planet's surface – the one of everlasting life – and now this little vial held the hopes and dreams of billions. And it was in the hands of a total psychopath with empathy for just one person and one person only… Himself.

'Do you know the motto of the SAS, Alex?' Wilcox continued.

Harker was transfixed by the small vial still being held in Vlad's hand but he managed a nod. 'Who dares, wins.'

'Exactly, he who dares, wins. And the Magi dared and the Magi won, but unfortunately the research in its current form only allows for a certain amount of regeneration. Take that compound within twenty-four hours and there is a good chance the body will heal perfectly, but when you allow for decomposition, then the results are…well, mixed. I myself did not receive the treatment for over thirty-six hours and as you can see its effects were…limited.'

Harker's nerves were tingling as he began to understand, in part, all the things he had witnessed over the past few days. 'So the priests back at the cemetery were too far gone to make a full recovery, then?'

'Not at all. Their appearance was just as we intended.'

'And the cardinal locked in the basement of the Vatican?'

'Ah, now that was more of an atonement. It had no other purpose really.'

'Atonement,' Harker gasped, still confused.

'That man almost cost me the papacy back when I was seeking to be elected as pontiff. Jumped-up little shit never trusted me, and therefore tried everything he could to stop me. It only seemed fitting that he was changed into the very thing that must have horrified him to the core: a demon, a servant of the Devil. And with a tinkering of our compound, it worked extremely well. I only wish he could have known it was me who arranged it, but we cannot have it all, can we?'

Everything Harker was hearing made little or no sense as yet apart from that crazy plan for revenge, which was classic Wilcox, but why would anyone spend billions of dollars and precious remaining resources on a simple revenge scheme? 'So you're saying that all this time and effort was just a way of getting back at somebody? Christ, Wilcox, why not just have the man killed? And the others…? And why even bother dragging me into all this?'

Harker's questions elicited an annoyed grunt from Vlad, who was now staring angrily at Wilcox.

'God, Alex, you sound just like Vlad here. Why cause complications? Why take the chance?' Wilcox snarled and once more turned his attention to the bloodied corpses. 'They were but a means to an end. You and those pious Templar idiots brought the Magi to its knees. It pains me to say that but it is true. When I reawoke in this husk of a body, we as an organization had nothing. The money was confiscated, and with it our power, influence and any chance that we would survive. Can you imagine the Magi going from strength to strength for over two thousand years only to be obliterated in little more than the blink of an eye? Preposterous. I could never let that happen, so what was there to do? Well, you work with what you have and, aside from this island as the Magi's final place of refuge, a smattering of connections and Vlad's band of assassins, which have proved crucial by the way, we only had this – our regeneration treatment. But how to use it?'

Wilcox raised his eyebrows and another devious smile crept across his face as he motioned to the dead bodies one final time. 'That is where *they* came in, a chance to prey upon their idiotic notions of Satanic worship and the Devil's dark gift of everlasting life. I knew of their obsession with the lost Codex pages, and their group had even managed to obtain one of them – which, I might add, was neither useful nor written by the Devil. Isn't that so, Vlad?'

'It was useless and written by the same piddling Benedictine monk who wrote the damn thing in the first place,' Vlad explained with a sarcastic snort. 'Something about the inner workings of their monastery, but the group believed it contained some hidden message, which of course it didn't.'

'You had some fun acquiring that one, didn't you?' Wilcox said enthusiastically as Vlad gave a smirk. 'You managed to convince him to burn out his eyes with a hot poker, and all in the name of Satan and the need for a show of faith. Brilliant. He's a very persuasive soul when he wants to be. The other pages, we forged. That text you heard Vlad reading was made up.' He again glanced over at Vlad. 'He can barely speak English, let alone the words from some ancient undecipherable text. But they believed it, and so all we had to do was convince them that their belief in the Codex, and everything that came with it, was genuine.'

'The sacrifice at Spreepark,' Harker spoke up, as the ritual he had witnessed at the abandoned amusement park now made sense.

'Yes, although I will admit I had not expected you to cause such trouble when I sent you there.' Wilcox gave a solemn nod towards Vlad. 'You were right about that one, for which I apologize. Still, we were able to snatch the resurrected man from outside the morgue, and those dead clods over there were in awe at his rebirth.' He now gave a chuckle. 'I even managed to spin them a line that you were after the pages because of your own desire to be immortal, which explanation they bought hook line and sinker. Now the priests in the cemetery involved nothing personal, but I needed our friends to believe that, although the Codex could bring them back from the dead, it would only bring back those deemed worthy, and so their bodies were left to decompose for a while before we administered the regenerative treatment. It needs some hours to take effect, which was more than enough time to get them buried before the show began. When you turned up, it only cemented the group's concern that others were after the gift that they considered was by destiny rightfully theirs. It's always the same when making a pitch – sell the sizzle and not the sausage. When a buyer sees others are interested, it only serves to encourage them further, and your antics made them even more determined than before.'

Harker rubbed at his temples, feeling sickened by the heartless way Wilcox treated everyone else as a mere resource, and was completely uncaring about the degradation and pain he caused. 'OK, John, I get it. This has been one long con job, but why?'

'Because, my slow-witted friend, something of the magnitude of what we were offering would be a valuable thing to some. Some might even give everything they owned to gain such a prize...the prize of fulfilling the hopes and dreams of their ancestors. And those dead idiots there signed away half of their net worth earlier today in exchange for what they most seek...everlasting life.'

'They don't look very alive to me,' Harker remarked.

'Don't knock it, Alex. They went to their deaths believing they would wake up to a new world and serving the master they all loved so much. That's not a bad way to go, really.'

'And how about that woman who changed her mind?' Harker replied, referring to the one Carlu had cut down after she expressed second thoughts.

'Well, you can't please everyone, can you? Besides, nineteen out of twenty isn't bad in my book.'

To Harker, Wilcox had proved himself again and again to be a psychopath of the highest order, therefore he should not have been surprised at the callous tone on display, but he could only be astounded at the complete lack of a soul in the man, or even the merest ounce of decency. 'So this was all about a simple robbery?' Harker exclaimed, shaking his head at such a mundane motive. He had never felt fully convinced that the Devil was going to put in an appearance, but between bodies rising from their graves and cardinals turning into demonic monsters, he had been tugged back and forth in his mind about what was possible and what was not.

'A simple robbery!' Wilcox looked disgusted at the description. 'Because of you, the Magi have been left flat broke and with nothing. If you know another way to make half a trillion pounds in assets and shares, then by all means speak up.' Wilcox looked affronted, and he began to breathe as heavily as his weak lungs would allow. 'The money we have acquired will allow the Magi to regain their power. We will become a force to be reckoned with once more, but this time, with your help, we will do it unimpeded. Vlad, would you fetch it out please?'

The other man disappeared behind the red drapes and returned, a few moments later, carrying a thick leather book which he placed in Wilcox's lap. The weight of it elicited a wince of pain but he maintained a satisfied smile as he opened it and began to read.

'Here is inscribed the name of every Templar which we will now liquidate, and we have you to thank for that. You see, I told you, Vlad, that getting Alex involved was a good idea. We never could have acquired this without him.'

As Vlad made a conciliatory bow, Wilcox began tapping his finger against the page. 'I've only had enough time to flick through these Templar curios since there are so many volumes, but did you realize the name Harker comes up quite a lot?'

Tristan Brulet had once mentioned how he had been mentioned in the *Illuminismo*, and at the time he had taken some pride in that, but now it sounded more like a damning indictment of his failure to protect everything the Templars held dear. More like a death note than a footnote. 'Yes, I do know.'

'Really?' Wilcox continued. Licking his lips, he looked up with a searching expression. 'I didn't know your name was Liam.'

'Liam?'

'Yes, Liam Harker. He appears a lot in the more recent records.'

Harker looked dumbfounded, and Wilcox was clearly delighted to be making the revelation. 'Your father?'

Harker was momentarily at a loss for words and the insinuation had him feeling light-headed. 'My father was indeed Liam Harker, yes. But he wasn't a Templar.'

'Well, that's not how this book tells it,' Wilcox replied, and he licked his finger and turned the page. 'Your father appears to have played quite a role.'

Harker's mind was buzzing. His father had worked for most of his life in a chicken factory, for Christ's sake, and had lost his life in an IRA bombing back in Belfast. His father, a Templar?

'Brulet never told you that, did he?' Wilcox laughed maniacally and slapped his palm down on the open page of the *Illuminismo*. 'Oh, this is too much. What a delicious betrayal of trust.'

Harker's shoulders sagged and he stood there in stunned silence as Wilcox looked down at Brulet's limp body and pointed his finger at him. 'You lying little devil, Sebastian.

Perhaps we have more in common than I could ever have believed.'

Vlad now joined in the laughter and their condescending mirth incensed Harker as his shock quickly turned to anger. Was that why Brulet had always appeared so giving and open with him regarding the Templars? And why he had been allowed access to so many secrets that it would have taken decades for most to learn? Was he actually a Templar by birth?

'I knew there must be a reason I always hated you so much,' Wilcox continued, his frail body still quivering in delight at having unearthed such a personal truth. 'It's genetic, in the genes, so we were enemies from the start, and we didn't even know it...priceless. I wonder who killed him, then? It wasn't the Magi, but if it had been, well, what a turn-up for the books that would have been!'

Harker's head was brimming with questions, but for all he knew, this was just a psychological game that Wilcox wanted to torture him with, so with great difficulty he pushed it to the back of his mind. In all the madness of Wilcox's master plan to essentially mug a bunch of rich people, Harker focused now on the only question that had been eating at him since his arrival here. As Wilcox flicked through the pages of the Templars' highly treasured *Illuminismo*, he sought to address that. 'You still haven't answered my question, John. Why drag me and my friends into all this?'

'I understand, Alex, that this must be a big shock to you, and I am happy to move on for the time being. We have all the time in the world still to discuss your family issues.' He continued scanning through the book, page by page, then he stopped, looked up and his eyes turned steely and cold. 'Simple, Alex, it's because I hate you more than any other person I have ever met, and so I wanted you to suffer like I myself have suffered. You are now hated by all those you care about. The police are after you, which would be a worry enough, but must seem trivial given that you have apparently betrayed your Templar allies, who will track you down – and I suspect would have killed you had you not made it to this island. Imagine that: death at the hands of your own family! Your girlfriend and, of course, Mr Carter will suffer greatly at the hands of my men before they die, and at the end they will wish they had never met you. You, like your good friend Mr Brulet here, will suffer unimaginable pain and degradation till eventually you beg me to have you killed. I will additionally have that old fart Dean Thomas Lercher murdered in some terrible way that has not even occurred to me yet.' Wilcox hissed at him through brown clenched teeth. 'By the time it's all over you will wish you had never been born and, within the annals of Magi history, your name will become synonymous with the pain that is inflicted upon those who would cross us.'

The words sapped Harker of his strength and his body wilted. Vlad raised his arm-sword and rested the tip up against Harker's throat. 'We're going to get to know each other very well during the coming weeks and months,' Vlad said with a snarl. 'And I must say that I am very curious to see how long it will take to break you.'

He began to nudge the blade harder, until Harker felt the tip break the skin, then the pressure was released. Vlad suddenly pulled back and stared over Harker's shoulder, scanning the amphitheatre as his face became ashen. 'What is that?'

In the distance what looked like a star flickered in the night sky, and it was quickly joined by others which spread out in a line high up in the air. Each of the lights started to wobble from left to right and, with every second that passed, they grew in size as they drew closer. A low-level humming could now be heard, getting ever louder as the lights grew brighter, then a single beam of shone directly onto the stage, where Harker raised his hand to protect his eyes from the intense glare.

Vlad snatched the Motorola walkie-talkie from his belt clip and began shouting into it as a tremendous downwash of air blew dust from the amphitheatre floor up onto the stage, which left Wilcox wrapping his arms around his face protectively.

'All units, breach detected, converge on the amphitheatre now.'

The noise was now deafening and reached a climax as two Sikorsky UH-60 Black Hawk stealth helicopters hovered overhead. The doors slid open and black nylon tethers dropped to the ground, like dangling vines, as a voice crackled out from above.

'John Wilcox,' the voice boomed and, through the slits between his fingers pressed against his eyes, Harker caught the sight of Tristan Brulet leaning out of one helicopter with a handset pressed to his mouth. 'It ends here.'

# *Chapter 41*

The sound of sporadic gunfire rattled around the amphitheatre as Harker slammed his shoulder into Vlad's sternum, sending them both tumbling backwards onto the stage's floor with a hefty thud. Behind them, scores of uniformed men in full black assault gear slid down the helicopter tethers and formed a circle around the landing area as, over at the ground exits, a tide of the Magi's island guards began to pour inside. It was organized chaos, and except for the arriving force's plain black face masks, it was near impossible to tell one side from the other.

Harker pulled himself to his feet and rushed at Vlad, slamming his full weight against the man's shoulder, but it barely made an impression and he was thrown backwards, with the wind knocked out of him. He rolled onto his front then rose up on all fours, waiting for the momentary paralysis in his lungs to pass, as Vlad now lurched forward and kicked him in the ribs and flipped him onto his back. Out of the corner of his eye, Harker could see Wilcox being rushed by one of the guards to the rear of the stage, who then propelled him behind the heavy red drapes with such force that the old man was nearly toppled from his chair.

The dark tint of unconsciousness began to cloud Harker's vision as finally his lungs began to work properly again, giving him a massive head rush. He nevertheless sprang up into a sitting position and sucked in a deep breath, his ribs aching, just in time to receive a punch across the cheek which sent him back onto the floor.

Vlad grasped him tightly around the throat and began to press down with his full weight. 'If it's over for me, then it's over for you too,' he spat, manoeuvring his knees on top of Harker's arms to prevent him from fighting back. 'I should never have allowed our Lord to involve you in our affairs, but I will at least have the opportunity now to rectify that mistake.'

The flashes of gunfire down on the amphitheatre floor began to intensify and, although Harker could see yet more soldiers dropping from the stealth helicopter, none of them had noticed him – because if they had, surely someone would have shot the man attempting to strangle him. The Magi home team was obviously putting up one hell of a fight, drawing all the newcomers' attention, and as Harker watched the helicopter glide away, only to be replaced by a new one which began to drop off more soldiers, he realized he was going to die no matter how many troops arrived. There was no way now they would reach him in time, and he began to feel himself slipping away.

For the second time in just as many minutes, Harker's vision began to fade as unconsciousness beckoned him. But with his last remaining strength he twisted his head towards Chloe, still hanging from a crucifix and staring back at him. She nodded to him, then looked over at something else, then right back at him. As Harker's whole body began to tingle while Vlad constricted his throat with yet more force, he gazed up at the killer and then, as his eyes began to glaze, he caught the blurry image of something close, something white. Then an arm swished down and connected with Vlad's head, and his grip loosened and he fell to the floor beside him.

The release of pressure on his throat caused Harker to momentarily black out as blood rushed back into his brain. When his vision returned, he could discern only the shapes of two glistening crosses.

Sebastien Brulet knelt over Harker with a relieved smile and let drop the thick *Illuminismo* volume from his hands, before he grabbed the hunting knife from Vlad's belt sheath and plunged it deep into the back of the killer's neck. 'Choke on that, you sick bastard,' he managed to utter over the buzzing rotors, as the helicopter dropped off the last of the troops. He stared down at Harker and his eyes widened. 'Alex?'

With that the Grand Master collapsed on top of Harker, who, still choking after his attempted strangulation, grabbed onto the man and stopped him from rolling onto the ground. 'Nice to see you too,' Harker yelled over all the commotion, and he glanced over at the amphitheatre floor, where he saw Tristan Brulet staring towards him with his mouth hanging open. Surrounded by masked soldiers, he was oblivious to the bullets zipping past him. As his protection unit continued firing back at the considerable number of Magi guards who had now taken up position on the steps surrounding the arena, the younger Brulet pulled himself up onto the stage and dashed over towards the pair of them.

'Oh my God,' he huffed, as some of his soldiers followed him before crowding around the three of them protectively. 'You're alive.'

Sebastian made no response, and his eyes twitched as his brother pulled him upwards and, in a commanding tone, shouted to the nearest soldier. 'Get him to safety, now!'

The soldier nodded and, with help from three others, made a shield around him and carried him off one side of the stage and out of sight as, deeper in the amphitheatre, the battle raged on.

'You're not going to kill me, are you?' Harker asked, having to raise his voice over the all the noise.

'I never was going to kill you,' Brulet replied. 'How the hell did Sebastian get here?'

With everything going on around them and Wilcox making a run for it, Harker had little time to explain anything now. 'I'll tell you everything – but we don't have time now. I need you to protect my friends.' He pointed over to Chloe and Carter and, without hesitation, Brulet issued orders to one of his men, who in turn began organizing the remaining five members of Tristan Brulet's protection unit. Splitting into two squadrons of three, they split and approached the two crosses. In no time Carter was cut down, followed quickly by Chloe, but as they were dragged off the stage and away to safety elsewhere on the island she struggled against the three men in a bid to get back and join Harker.

He gestured emphatically for her to get out of there, and reluctantly she stopped resisting her escort and, with a final look of concern, she disappeared around one side of the stage.

'Thank you,' Harker shouted while rubbing his sore neck. 'Now I'm going after Wilcox.' He motioned towards the rear of the stage.

'OK,' Brulet replied without need of encouragement, and then pulled a Beretta from a concealed holster and placed it into Harker's open palm. 'Do you know how to use this?' he asked, and Harker nodded. 'Good,' Brulet said and extended one hand so his arm-sword clicked into place. 'Then let's bring this matter to a close, shall we?'

Leaving the ongoing conflict in the amphitheatre behind them, and with Harker in the lead, they pushed past the red drapes to find nothing but a stone wall. The only way forward appeared to be a flight of steps heading downwards, like the entrance to a wine cellar.

'Let's take this slowly,' Brulet cautioned and, with a nod from Harker, they began to descend.

Overhead light fixtures lit the way, and as they went deeper, the air grew stale. At the bottom they were confronted by a thick metal door that had been left wide open.

'Not very secure leaving it open,' Brulet remarked, tapping the metal surface with his sword.

'Forget the door, Tristan. I want to know how Wilcox got himself down all these stairs in a wheelchair so quickly.'

The two men exchanged mystified glances and then, with Brulet taking the lead, they headed through the open doorway.

The room they entered was one of the most unwelcoming and uncomfortable sights imaginable. It looked like a prison, as a series of cells were spread out in a grid formation, with pathways running in between them so as to surround each cell on all sides. Stranger still, the cells had no bars but were instead made up of thick Perspex boxes, around eight foot by eight, with a single letterbox-sized opening covered by a grille with a padlock on it. The Perspex was frosted, meaning it was impossible to see inside, and these cube-shaped cells stretched as far as the eye could see.

'What on earth?' Brulet muttered, approaching the nearest cube and then walking all around it. 'No door... Someone doesn't want anyone looking in.'

'No,' Harker corrected, 'someone doesn't want anyone looking out.'

At one side of the room a monitor flared up and Harker moved over to check it out. The touch screen displayed a graphic image of forty square boxes, and with an encouraging nod from Brulet, he tapped the first in line, labelled H1. The frosted glass of the cube nearest to them suddenly became clear, revealing an empty interior.

'Whatever was once in there is long gone,' Brulet observed, taking Harker's place and tapping each box icon in turn as, one by one, the cubes in front of him began to clear. By the time the last cell had been triggered they had a clear view all the way to the other side of the room and towards an open doorway leading off into another part of the facility.

'It's like someone's own personal zoo,' Brulet suggested, 'minus the animals and with little or no care for their well-being.'

'It's not a zoo, but a lab,' Harker stated, and he returned his attention to the touch screen and to the three icons that had appeared next to each of the boxes. These consisted of a water droplet, a lightning symbol and, finally, a fire sign. He pushed at the droplet icon and water began to spray down inside the nearest box. 'A warning?' Harker queried, then he pressed the lightning icon, whereupon the crackling of an electric current began to emanate from inside the cube. 'A punishment?'

By this point Harker already knew what the last button would do but he pressed it anyway and the entire interior of the cube was consumed by a hot fireball which, although it looked hot enough to melt steel, did not blacken the Perspex walls one bit. 'Game over.'

'God almighty,' Tristan gasped out loud as Harker directed his attention to the 'H' labelled inside each box.

'Human 1, Human 2 and so on,' Harker explained in disgust. 'Wilcox said they did human testing, and he wasn't lying.'

Neither of them spoke a word as the gravity of it sank in, then Harker headed along the nearest path in the direction of the doorway on the other side of the room.

Brulet followed close behind. 'Test on humans, for what?'

'You know I told you about those two priests coming back to life?'

'Yes.'

'Well it seems the Magi have been synthesizing a compound that regenerates dead tissue and that's how they were able to achieve it,' Harker revealed as they reached the open doorway. 'So I would guess that the lab rats used in those experiments were kept here.'

There was little time for Brulet to respond for, as they reached the doorway, they suddenly saw the very man they had been looking for.

At the end of a long dark corridor, Wilcox sat in his wheelchair in front of a control panel covered in buttons and monitors. With a light-hearted wave he called out to them. 'It seems I have nowhere left to run, doesn't it?'

Both Harker and Brulet paused to survey the corridor as best they could, and once satisfied it was built out of solid rock, they ventured along it. It was probably a foolish thing to do because Harker knew full well that Wilcox would never in a million years give up in the face of his most reviled foes. But he was done caring by now and they would just have to deal with anything as and when it happened. Tristan Brulet had been right when he had shouted out from the helicopter 'It ends here', because he was damn right, either way.

'Well, we know how you managed to get down all those steps.' Harker motioned to the red-faced wheelchair assistant who was standing in a corner, still catching his breath.

The young man did not appear to have any kind of weapon, but nevertheless Brulet raised his arm-sword towards him and silently shook his head in warning.

'Oh, don't mind Albert here. He is but a lowly servant to my needs.' Wilcox raised both arms upwards. 'Welcome to my church.'

'More like a slaughterhouse,' Harker replied venomously, and Wilcox gave a shake of his head and tutted loudly.

'You couldn't be further from the truth, Alex. This is a modern form of Genesis, but a Garden of Eden for anyone with sufficient vision. Just see for yourself.'

Wilcox pressed one of the many buttons on his control panel and, through a viewing window, a large excavated cave was illuminated by overhead lightning. For Harker the sight before him was just another damming indictment of Wilcox's moral depravity and he couldn't help but feel an urge to shoot the old man in the back there and then. Close to a hundred rectangular boxes were stacked high upon thick metal girders, like storage containers waiting to be shipped out from a supply dock. Their fronts had been cut away and replaced with sealed Perspex windows, so that the interior of each was always visible. But it was not the boxes themselves that were the cause for concern but the sorry-looking individuals housed inside them. Each 'hutch' contained an uncomfortable-looking metal bed with a single pillow, and water and food tubes ran into a single trough secured to the wall. Separate air pipe nozzles were connected at the front of each hutch and, from what Harker could judge, they were all independent of each other.

'Each living space is hermetically sealed and self-contained,' Wilcox informed them proudly, 'which ensures accurate and viable testing for every experiment conducted.'

The patients were a mixture of men and women of different ages, and they shielded their eyes from the sudden light with most not even bothering to stand up or even pay attention to the small group of men now studying them through the viewing window opposite. The only consolation, and there was precious little, was that Harker could see no children amongst them.

'We used to go down the human-trafficking route, but we will soon breed our own. I feel it's so much more humane that way. Otherwise it's like taking zoo animals from the wild…it's just not humane, is it?'

'You sick piece of sh—'

'Careful,' Wilcox warned, holding his finger above a red button with a fire symbol on it, 'or I will not hesitate to torch everyone inside there.'

At that moment Harker could have sworn blindly, reasoned for humanity's sake and finally resorted to pleading, but he knew it would not have made the slightest difference. 'What do you want, Wilcox?'

'Not a lot really,' he replied in a cavalier manner. 'I just want you and the cross-eyed wonder here to die horribly.'

With his free hand he pressed another of the buttons, whereupon halogen bulbs flared up revealing two frosted rectangular cells, bigger than the others, and running the entire length and either side of the corridor they had just walked down. 'This whole facility is an engineering marvel, you know. It's fully equipped with the mechanism to move each of the containers down there into any cube we wish, which means the patients are completely isolated from the moment they arrive to when their usefulness comes to an end.'

'Don't like to get your hands dirty, John?' Brulet suggested, wincing in disgust at the set-up.

'Not at all,' Wilcox replied, as he pressed another button so that the sides of the two corridor cells now became clear. 'Would you want to handle these things?'

Inside each container a hulking beast spun around and began to eye their audience with aggressive curiosity. As Wilcox chuckled to himself, Brulet looked mortified but Harker hardly flinched. He had seen these creatures before, deep in the basement of the Governorate in Vatican City.

'Consider these beasts the prototypes for that cardinal wretch,' Wilcox said smugly, 'except this time you're both going to enjoy a little one-on-one time with them. What do you say...you game for it?'

At that moment the whole room began to shake as an explosion went off outside, undoubtedly part of the battle raging in the amphitheatre above.

'Even if we die, the Magi are finished,' Brulet stated categorically, still pointing his arm-sword in the direction of Wilcox's wheelchair attendant, whom he addressed as Mr Reed. 'The Templars must outnumber your men three to one, so it's over whatever happens.'

Wilcox looked unperturbed by this prospect. 'On that we can both agree, but there is one other thing you don't know.'

'Like what?' Harker said with a scowl.

'Like, that just down there is a corridor leading to a small helicopter pad,' Wilcox explained, pointing to the only other door in the room. 'And after you make your ultimate sacrifice, I will use it to take off to pastures new.' He pointed to a rectangular steel box at the feet of Mr Reed. 'In that case is all the regeneration compound I will ever need, and a disc containing the fruits of our work on this project.' Wilcox began to laugh like a man without any cares. 'With a half a trillion pounds at my disposal, I'm sure I can live comfortably for the rest of my life and restart on the research to cure my withering body, wouldn't you say? As for you two morons, you only have to offer yourself up to these fine specimens and then, with me gone, your men will be able to free those poor, desperate test subjects... What do you say? Sound like a fair deal?'

Harker glanced over at Brulet and then towards the nearest 'demon', who was licking his forked tongue against the glass, leaving a slimy trail down its surface.

Sensing some resistance, Wilcox continued pushing for an agreement. 'Come on, Alex, you always wanted to be a hero and...well, now's your chance. Just think, you two could go down in Templar history as the men who saved a hundred wretched souls from being burnt alive. I can think of worse epitaphs.'

Both men stared at each other for a second and then, with a weary nod, Harker turned back to Wilcox, looking like a beaten man. 'OK, John, you win,' he said, as Brulet lowered the sword to his waist. 'I'll go first.'

'Good,' Wilcox said. 'It's the right thing to do, for honourable men like yourselves.'

Harker nodded solemnly, then he turned to Brulet and reached over slowly to hug the man tightly.

'Very touching, it really is,' Wilcox commented sarcastically. 'I might even shed a tear.'

Brulet wrapped his arms around Harker and then began to lower his arm-sword further. But the moment it was level, and with lightning speed, he thrust forward and sliced into Wilcox's forearm with the tip of its blade. At the same time Harker grabbed the old man's chair and flung him away from the work desk, as Brulet now retracted the bloody tip, turned it on Mr Reed and drove it right through his chest.

The younger man began to shake as Brulet pinned him to the wall. With one final gurgling breath, he became motionless and, as the sword was withdrawn, he crumpled to the floor.

Wilcox was screaming as he nursed his injured arm, and Brulet grabbed him by both shoulders and spun him around on his wheels so he was facing him. 'I told you it ends now, and I am a man of my word.'

Without any hindrance from Harker, Brulet wheeled the old man all the way down to the far end of the corridor before stopping at the sliding door leading into one side of the left-hand transparent cell. He then glanced over at Harker, who was already at the monitor and searching for the right button. The door controls were simple. It was like a turnstile: slide it open, person enters, slide it shut and you are inside the cube.

Harker pressed the appropriate button and the door slid open. Even as he did so, the hulking beast, dripping what could only be described as slime, began to get noticeably excited. It was evidently not the first time this creature had been given someone to play with.

Brulet shoved the wheelchair into the turnstile as Wilcox began to beg for his life. 'Please don't do this…it's not your way… I beg you. We can make a deal.'

But his pleas fell upon deaf ears. For as Harker stared at Wilcox, who was crying like a baby, he did not feel a thing. After all the pain and hurt this man had caused to so many men, women and children, it was difficult to feel one iota of empathy for an individual who would destroy every human being on the planet if he had the chance. I mean, would you really consider killing the Devil himself murder?

'I once said to you, John, something that still holds true today,' Harker declared as he pressed the door button, then made his way back up to Brulet while the turnstile began to rotate slowly. 'I've met some evil bastards in my time but you…you're special.'

Harker and Brulet continued heading out of the corridor even as Wilcox's screams turned into shrieks, and the sounds of a body being slammed against the cell's walls reverberated past them. 'We'll make sure all's clear outside, then we'll come back and liberate everyone on this island. Give them back the life they deserve.'

'Agreed,' Harker said emphatically, and they continued towards the exit as meanwhile the screams of John Wilcox began to subside. 'And half a trillion pounds should go a long way to buying them some comfort.'

## *Chapter 42*

The sounds of laughter and restaurant music filled the air as Harker made his way up the narrow stone street in Mont-Saint-Michel. A light snowfall had blanketed the small island commune hours earlier, and with it the narrow walkways leading up to the Benedictine abbey towering above. The Mont was an already a magical-looking place, and this white dusting of powdered ice only added to its mystique, even if Harker felt uneasy due to his earlier and rather unpleasant encounters on this rock. Up ahead of him the glassed-paned wooden door of a small restaurant, Le Mouton Blanc, opened suddenly, and an attractive woman stepped out wearing a halter-neck, knee-length pewter evening dress, and waved.

'Where have you been?' Chloe Stanton asked in a hushed tone as she closed the door behind her and made her way down towards him as fast as her high heels would allow.

It was freezing, and even in his blue Armani single-breasted suit and tie, Harker was feeling the chill, yet Chloe barely batted an eyelid.

'You said you'd be right behind me, and that was almost half an hour ago.'

Harker drew her towards him and wrapped the left side of his suit jacket around her as best he could. 'Just went for a short walk,' he replied. 'This place is quite beautiful when you don't have people chasing after you with assault rifles.'

Chloe stroked his chest and offered her most supportive smile as she began to feel the effects of the frosty air. She quickly slipped her arm around his waist and tugged him gently in the direction of the restaurant. 'You were so very brave,' she said with a hint of sarcasm.

'I was, actually.'

'Yes, you were, and you're my hero,' Chloe replied sweetly, before she gave him a loving kiss on the lips. 'Now can we go inside, please, before your bride-to-be dies of exposure?'

Two months had passed since Wilcox's demise at the hand of his own creation, and in all that time Harker had not heard once from either of the Brulet brothers. Even David Carter had dropped off the map after being whisked away by helicopter during the island battle, and apart from a letter Harker had received stating that he was alive and well with a promise that he would be in contact very soon, he had heard nothing since.

By the time Harker and Tristan Brulet had returned topside from Wilcox's twisted idea of a laboratory the fight was all but over and the last few remaining Magi guards, realizing that the battle was lost, had turned the guns on themselves in a group suicide. Another waste of human life, as Harker saw it, dressed up as a code of honour, albeit a twisted one.

After the gunfire fell silent the Templar soldiers had immediately, on the orders of Tristan Brulet, been sent to release those hundred poor lab rats being held below ground. It had taken some time to break into the sealed human zoo but eventually the captives were set free and boarded onto a fleet of private jets that had begun landing at the runway strip, at Brulet's command.

This whole evacuation had taken some twelve hours in total, with jets constantly coming and going, and it was during this time that the body of Harker's pilot, Frank, had been found. The poor man had been strung up in one of the runway hangars, tortured and then summarily shot. With little or no information to disclose except that Harker had been dropped off on the island, the only hope was that his torture had been quick. Brulet had promised to take care of what family the man had, but apart from that there was little that could be done, and Harker still carried with him a real sense of guilt about the whole thing. If it hadn't been for him, then Frank would still be alive, but then without Frank a lot more people could have died.

The remaining Templar soldiers had secured every corner of the island in search of information, and much had been found pertaining to the Magi and their activities. The island itself had been owned privately since the nineteen-thirties, and from the discovered records it emerged the laboratory had been initially built in the late forties and updated through the decades that followed. This island had unquestionably served as the main site of research and development when perfecting the cloning process that would go on to create the Christ child, as well as other things. The disks that were recovered contained thousands upon thousands of gigabytes of data covering over sixty years of experimentation, and only time would reveal what other atrocious experiments the Magi had pursued.

There were some positives, though, with the finding of data relating to the regeneration compound: doses of the compound itself and finally details of bank accounts in Switzerland and the Cayman Islands containing almost half a trillion pounds. The money had been unimportant as far as Harker had been concerned, but he had been more than pleased when he saw a news report concerning the anonymous deposit of over four hundred billion dollars spread across charities around the world. The figure was so large that the UK and US tax agencies began to demand an overhaul of the laws pertaining to tax-exempt charitable status, and the arguments now raged on all sides. As to the fate of the remaining money Harker had no idea about, but he had faith in the Templars to do the right thing, although paying off his own mortgage seemed to him a good place to start.

Tristan Brulet had stayed on the island until the last released patient had been evacuated before leaving via helicopter to see to his brother and begin his recuperation. Over the hours, they had both set the record straight, and by the end there was no animosity on the part of the Templars, especially since the *Illuminismo* had now been taken back into their protective care. Wilcox's kidnapping of Chloe and Harker's forced servitude to the madman had been accepted by Tristan Brulet as extenuating circumstances and, given that his brother had now been returned to him, he was more than gracious when it came to closing the book on the whole tawdry affair. He had also disclosed that between William Havers's interrogation of Dean Lercher, which revealed Harker's intended destination to be Wilcox's island, and with Shroder's discovery of Jacob Winters's true identity, the Templars had been able to assemble the rescue party which had arrived on cue.

The Grand Master had been far less willing, though, to disclose or even discuss anything pertaining to Wilcox's claim of Harker's father being involved with the Templars, but the fact that he insisted only his brother should talk on the subject gave some credence to the Magi's assertion. The idea that his family was of Templar blood produced in Harker as much anger as it did confusion, and he had wrestled considerably with the notion over the past few months. Anger because his father had not brought him into the organisation as was the right of all Templar members and confusion for the very same reason. Why? Coupling that with the lack of communication from the Templars since leaving the island, and even Shroder's unwillingness to return his messages, the ensuing months for Harker had been filled with a sense of tremendous loss and disappointment.

Things had not been made much better after a somewhat fractious reunion with Doggie shortly after arriving back in the UK. The dean had been furious because of his 'shoddy treatment', as he put it, at the hands of John Shroder. But what had really pissed him off was his violent interrogation with the Templar, William Havers, which had left him bruised and with a small scar on his cheek. Doggie had rattled on about this unpleasant incident but, as the weeks passed, he began to show a degree of pride in his tiny scar. So much so that he had invented a story for his friends and peers involving an attempted mugging that he had valiantly fought off, leaving him with this battle wound as a memento.

As for Chloe, after being cut down from her own personal cross amid the firefight, she had refused to be bundled onto the waiting helicopter with Carter, and insisted furiously – as only Chloe could – that she was not leaving until she saw Harker face-to-face. In fact by the time he reached her over an hour later, she was still in a heated discussion concerning his whereabouts.

Their reunion was the best part of that entire nightmarish few days Wilcox had planned for them, and perhaps with the adrenalin rush of the surrounding events, he had asked her to marry him on the spot. Of course, like any rational man, he had regretted that in the coming weeks, but the anxiety over such a commitment had soon passed and, as he looked down at her now, patting his chest impatiently, he knew it had been the right decision.

'You ready to do this or what? Chloe asked, as another shiver rippled through her. 'They're all here, including a few unexpected faces.' With his curiosity now brimming, Harker, with Chloe clasped still underneath his jacket, guided them both over to Le Mouton Blanc and went inside.

The warm air inside the restaurant felt pleasantly smothering, and as he took in the sight of the crowd of people all enjoying themselves, he immediately felt at ease. The place was a buzz of activity with couples joking, laughing, hugging and generally enjoying themselves. He instantly recognized Tristan Brulet and William Havers over in the corner, who only tipped their imaginary hats towards him, but it was the sight of the round-faced man smiling in his direction, wearing a dapper silver double-breasted suit, that had him grinning from ear to ear.

David Carter strode over directly with a cool suavity in his step and inflicted a tight bear hug that had Harker gasping. 'Alex, you beautiful bastard,' the ex-don proclaimed as he released his grip and then gestured towards Chloe. 'I was just telling your beautiful wife-to-be that she looks a damn sight more composed than when we last met.'

'Yes, David, but not hanging from a cross while surrounded by armed gunmen tends to have that effect,' she replied, affectionately touching his forearm as Harker now grabbed the other man by his shoulders.

'Where have you been?'

'You got my letter, didn't you?'

'Yes, but it didn't say much, David.'

Carter was now looking duly apologetic. 'Sorry, Alex, but it has been something of hectic time. However, suffice to say I am alive and extremely motivated, but as to the reason, I promised someone else I would let them…enlighten you.'

Carter's reticence was intriguing, but the fact that the man looked so well was enough to assuage any curiosity Harker had – for the moment.

'Wait a minute.' Carter turned his attention to someone behind him and called out, 'John, he's here.'

Harker peered past Carter's portly frame to see John Shroder making his way over, wearing a knowing smile.

'You got the invitation, I see?' Shroder grasped Harker's hand and gave it a firm shake.

'It arrived last week, John, but apart from mentioning your name, it only had a place and a time.'

'As it should have, Alex. We Templars are a secretive bunch and you, better than anyone, should know that.'

Before Harker could reply, Carter slipped his arms between them both. 'Quite an adventure we've been on, gentlemen, or should I now say "special agent compadres"?'

The sly look in Carter's eyes had Harker laughing, whereas Shroder merely shook his head in embarrassment.

'"Gentlemen" will be fine, David, and let's not get ahead of ourselves, shall we?' the MI6 agent said with a snort.

'Of course, of course, but I still say we put together a bloody fine plan and executed it like pros, wouldn't you say?' Carter countered excitedly. 'I have a few tales to tell you, Alex, including a rather embarrassing moment on a train when I mistook a conductor for a—'

'Hold on a second, David,' Harker interrupted, and he pulled Shroder to one side as Carter began to beckon over a waitress holding a tray of champagne in narrow crystal flute glasses. 'Where the hell have you been? I must have left forty messages for you.'

'Sorry, Alex, but everything's been up in the air until recently, what with Sebastian coming back from the dead and the Templar infighting, which I am glad to say has come to an end.'

Harker's initial elation was quickly turning to one of feeling ostracized. 'Not up in the air for David, though, or for you.'

Shroder's body sagged and he placed an arm around Harker's shoulders. 'Don't be angry. I know you must feel out of the loop, but I promise you everything will be explained.'

'Yeah, by who?'

'By me,' a voice interrupted, and Harker turned to see the one person he had wanted to see most since walking through the restaurant door.

Sebastien Brulet stood before him, wearing a charcoal-grey Savile Row pinstripe suit and black steel-rimmed aviator sunglasses, as Carter, Chloe and Shroder quietly moved aside. As the two men stared at each other, the whole restaurant became hushed. Brulet stared at Harker with a blank expression for a few moments, then a great big smile formed on his face.

'Alex Harker...my friend and saviour.'

The room erupted into rapturous applause and Brulet gently embraced his friend and gave him a warm, heartfelt hug. 'We do get ourselves into some scrapes, don't we, Alex?' he whispered.

'As always, that's an understatement, Sebastian,' Harker whispered back. As the applause receded, the two men pulled apart, now grinning at each other.

'I know you must have plenty of questions,' Brulet continued as Carter began to pass around the champagne flutes. 'Let's take a little walk, shall we?'

Before Harker could agree, a hand patted him on the shoulder from behind, and he looked back to see someone who made his jaw literally drop open in surprise.

Dean Thomas Lercher stood there proudly with a glass of champagne in one hand and a monocle held languidly in the other. He was dressed head to toe in black-tie splendour. 'How do I look?'

Harker almost burst out laughing, but he restrained himself as Chloe slipped her hand around the dean's arm.

'I think he looks rather distinguished,' she remarked with a subtle wink.

'Doggie…I mean Thomas, what are you doing here?'

'I thought that after all the years of being such a help to you and the Templars, it was only right that Dean Lercher be recognized,' Brulet intervened, offering a gracious bow to the bow-tied dean. 'He's thoroughly proven his ability to hold a secret, and as such I would like to appoint him an associate…if you agree?'

Harker did not need further convincing, for Doggie had proven himself time and time again, and all he had ever wanted was to be part of the whole Templar cloak-and-dagger thing, as he viewed it. 'Absolutely. I can't think of anyone more worthy.'

Harker was handed a champagne flute and, as the small group of six prepared to raise a toast, he leant over discreetly towards Doggie. 'You look like you're going to meet the Queen!'

'The invitation said "smart dress", and it's not like I know what the secretive and highly wealthy wear, do I?'

'Why didn't you tell me?'

'Because the invite strictly instructed not to – a surprise and all that.'

'Fair enough,' Harker replied, as they now raised their glasses, 'but do yourself a favour...ditch the monocle.'

'Ladies and gentlemen,' Brulet began, 'a toast to family, wherever we may find them.'

The six of them clicked glasses and, after a healthy first sip, the banter began. Brulet soon put down his own glass and leant towards Harker. 'Let's take that walk, shall we?'

Harker handed his half-full glass to Chloe, who gave him an overdramatic kiss, and then he began to follow Brulet out of the restaurant, pausing only as he passed Carter on the way. There was something that, no matter how inconsequential, had been niggling him for months. 'What became of that electric cattle prod Vlad threatened you with?' he whispered.

'Officially nothing, because it was just an idle threat,' Carter whispered in reply, then he pulled a grim face, 'but unofficially I had to use an inflatable doughnut to sit on for weeks afterwards... The Preparation H has helped though.'

Harker made a pained grimace. 'We'll talk later,' he said, then joined Brulet, who was waiting for him in the narrow street outside.

Side by side the two men began to make their way through the winding, snow-covered streets up towards the main abbey on the summit of the island.

'I owe you a great debt, Alex – you saved my life.'

Harker shook his head. 'No, Sebastian, I must thank *you*. Chloe and I would never have made it out of Macuira National Park if not for you.'

'I almost didn't make it out either,' Brulet reflected with sadness in his voice. 'I cannot tell you how terrible it was to go from feeling overjoyed at having made my escape only to proceed from the frying pan into the fire...Wilcox's fire.'

'I can't even begin to imagine what that must have been like for you.'

'It's really difficult to describe being heavily drugged then woken up and tortured, then drugged and awoken and tortured, over and over again. There were moments when I would have given anything to be allowed to just die. That man Wilcox had an anger and an instinct for revenge inside him that knew no bounds. It's been two months since then, and I still find myself waking up suddenly in the middle of the night, drenched in sweat and screaming in sheer bloody terror.'

'I'm so sorry, Sebastian.'

'Don't be, my friend. I am still alive and Wilcox is finished and although I will carry the mental scars for a long time to come, it does get better with each passing day.'

They continued in silence now, navigating the streets and steps until they reached the abbey. Brulet came to a halt outside the same wooden door Harker had entered when being taken to the Templar vault, during his last and highly eventful visit. Brulet placed a key in the lock and then headed inside and on to the fingerprint ID, where he placed his hand on the glass scanner.

'We're going to the vault?' Harker enquired as the lift arrived and its doors opened.

'Yes, there's something I want to show you.'

The trip down did not take long, and by the time the doors opened and they stepped out, Harker was ready to ask a question that he wanted – no, *needed* – to be answered.

'Sebastian…was my father a Templar?'

Brulet ignored the query, making his way down onto the vault floor. 'Since the Templars were first formed, we have stored every manuscript and artefact, every item that has ever come into our possession. Our storage vaults have changed location over the centuries, but nothing has ever been let go. In fact everything we ever collected has been carefully restored and lovingly protected. When I got back from serving as Wilcox's torture toy and I learnt of the *Illuminismo*'s theft, I began to wonder why.'

Harker wasn't sure exactly what Brulet meant, but he took a guess. 'Why they stole it, you mean?'

'No.' Brulet raised his hands towards the thousands of items cramming the vault's numerous shelves. 'Why do we keep all this? We don't really use it and, to be honest, I only ever come down here if I want to either update or refer to the *Illuminismo*.' He now pointed along the nearest aisle and to the stack of *Illuminismo* volumes neatly placed there, having been returned to their rightful places. 'Seems like a waste, doesn't it?'

Brulet began running a finger across the shelf nearest. 'This vault holds mysteries from human history dating back two millennia and further, and yet here its contents sit year in year out, doing absolutely nothing. It seems their only real purpose is to be targeted by thieves, a prize for someone like John Wilcox, wouldn't you agree?'

Harker made his way to Brulet's side and gazed across the rows of priceless antiquities. 'I'm an archaeologist, Sebastian, so you know I do.'

'Good, because I want to create a new division within the Templar organization, and I want you to head it up.'

'Doing what?'

'Doing what you always do best…chasing the truth.'

Harker felt immediately in awe at the idea. The Templars had always seemed extremely protective and cagey whenever he had asked to even take a peek inside one of their vaults, and now here was its Grand Master offering him the keys to the kingdom. 'What exactly would you have me do?'

Brulet turned around to give him a firm slap on his back. 'This collection predates the birth of Christ, and it doesn't just contain religious items. It holds every conceivable piece of lost history imaginable. From the mysticism of the Druids and the witch covens of the Dark Ages to the enduring legends of monsters and sorcery, it's all here. Don't get me wrong. I doubt that you will come across anything supernatural like the Codex pages purporting to be imbued with the power of the Devil made real, etc. etc.' Brulet gave a fake yawn. 'But if there is something to be discovered, this is where you'll find it.'

Harker now felt a further ripple of excitement throughout his body and, witnessing his reaction, Brulet continued to explain his proposal. 'Your friend David Carter has proved himself to be an avid historian, and highly knowledgeable on many subjects. You should know he has been a guest – a willing one, I might add – of the Templars since you were last together. And after getting to know him, I feel he could be of real benefit to you in this endeavour…'

Brulet paused as Harker raised his eyebrows. David was knowledgeable, there was no doubting that, but hardly a man suited for the field.

'I mean, of course, as a curator of this and all the other vaults we possess, which is why I want to make him an official member of the Templar Order.'

Harker was taken aback by the suggestion, because he himself was only an associate. 'But I'm not even a Templar, only an associate like Doggie…now.'

Brulet looked serious as he placed his hands in front of him and, for the first time since Harker had met him, the man actually looked…nervous.

'You asked me earlier whether your father was a Templar, and I can tell you now he was.'

Harker had been speculating for months about the truth Wilcox had laid on him, and had considered all the possibilities, but having Brulet say it out loud now was shocking.

'Please allow me to explain.' Brulet raised his hand in a calming manner. 'I need you to know that it was your father's expressed wish that you should not know – for your own safety. I knew your father personally, and I gave him that promise on my honour. But that seems to be a moot point since John Wilcox let the cat out of the bag, doesn't it?'

Harker could have felt mad at having been kept in the dark, but he didn't, and instead felt an insatiable curiosity and a need to know the truth. 'Is that why you allowed me access to the Templars' world so readily?'

'Yes,' Brulet replied. 'And it is also the reason I have always sought to protect you with everything at my disposal.'

These revelations had Harker's mind swimming with questions and he rubbed at his eyes as Brulet continued.

'You asked me how you could do the job if you are only an associate, Alex… An honourable reaction, but in fact I asked you because you already are a Templar…by blood. Your father was a brave man and he played an instrumental role within the Knights Templar.'

'What did he do?'

Brulet thought about it for a moment, then made his way down to the *Illuminismo*. He dug out the volume he sought, then brought it back and placed it in Harker's hands. 'Perhaps you should see it explained in your father's own words.'

Harker flipped open the precious book and began to scan through its pages. 'Which parts pertain to my father?' he asked eventually as Brulet headed back to the main lift and pressed the call button.

'The whole thing.'

Harker stared at him dumbfounded, because there must have been over a hundred pages in this volume. He turned to look over at Brulet, who had now moved inside the lift.

'You should have some privacy. You only need to read the first couple of pages or so to realize what he did for the Templars, and you can read the rest any other time. Now, when you're done, just press the buzzer and come rejoin the party. It's being held in your honour, by the way, so don't be too long.' Brulet lowered his sunglasses to reveal his unique cross-shaped pupils, and he then winked. 'Welcome home, Alex.'

The lift doors closed and Harker was left alone in the vault with nothing but the calming hum of the temperature-control unit for company. He looked down again and opened the book at the first page and, with an apprehensive smile and a tear forming in his eyes due to nothing else but sheer excitement, he drew a deep breath and did what he had been asked to do. He began to read.

# *Acknowledgements*

A special thanks as always to my editor, Peter Lavery, thank you.

And as always Alison.

## *The Harker Chronicles*

*Relics*
*The 4th Secret*
*The Last Judgement*
*The Dark Temple*
*The Shadow Conspiracy*

**'A thrilling, highly imaginative and action-packed fantasy with family at its heart.'**

Louie Stowell, author of *Loki: A Bad God's Guide to Being Good*

**'A fresh, wild, gripping adventure, full of shadowy magic and awesome creatures. I want my own umbra!'**

Kieran Larwood, author of *The Legend of Podkin One-Ear*

**'I really enjoyed this thrilling story, with its feelings of Pokémon, *Fireborn* and Final Fantasy.'**

L. D. Lapinski, author of *The Strangeworlds Travel Agency*

**'I absolutely loved it. A richly imagined world, with brilliant characters. I can't wait to read the next instalment.'**

Tọlá Okogwu, author of *Onyeka and the Academy of the Sun*

**'A deliciously dark and magical world that video game fanatics will devour.'**

Aisha Bushby, author of *A Flash of Fireflies*

**'Has everything I love: cinematic world-building, pulse-pounding action scenes and characters so vivid I miss them already.'**

A. F *nicorn Thief*

**FABER** has published children's books since 1929. T. S. Eliot's *Old Possum's Book of Practical Cats* and Ted Hughes' *The Iron Man* were amongst the first. Our catalogue at the time said that 'it is by reading such books that children learn the difference between the shoddy and the genuine'. We still believe in the power of reading to transform children's lives. All our books are chosen with the express intention of growing a love of reading, a thirst for knowledge and to cultivate empathy. We pride ourselves on responsible editing. Last but not least, we believe in kind and inclusive books in which all children feel represented and important.